STARGAZING

Jen Wang

STARGAZING

Color by
Lark Pien

First Second
New York

Thanks to Calista Brill, Rachel Stark, and Andrew Arnold at First Second for whipping this book into editorial and production shape, Lark Pien for taking on the ridiculous task of coloring a book in three months and doing it with grace and gusto, Judy Hansen for being my career champion, and Jake Mumm for all the homemade dinners, scooping of cat litter, and general advice and support during a whirlwind creation.

First Second

Published by First Second
First Second is an imprint of Roaring Brook Press,
a division of Holtzbrinck Publishing Holdings Limited Partnership
120 Broadway, New York, NY 10271

Don't miss your next favorite book from First Second!
For the latest updates go to firstsecondnewsletter.com and sign up for our enewsletter.

Library of Congress Control Number: 2018944915

Paperback ISBN: 978-1-250-18388-0
Hardcover ISBN: 978-1-250-18387-3

Our books may be purchased in bulk for promotional, educational, or business use.
Please contact your local bookseller or the Macmillan Corporate and Premium Sales Department
at (800) 221-7945 ext. 5442 or by email at MacmillanSpecialMarkets@macmillan.com.

First edition, 2019
Edited by Calista Brill and Rachel Stark
Book design by Chris Dickey
Color by Lark Pien
Song lyrics on pages 37, 39, 77, 109–111, 210–213 by Hellen Jo

Penciled with mechanical #2 pencil, inked with Uni Jetstream ballpoint pen,
and colored digitally in Photoshop.

Printed in China by Toppan Leefung Printing Ltd., Dongguan City, Guangdong Province

Paperback: 10 9 8 7 6 5 4 3
Hardcover: 10 9 8 7 6 5 4 3

For Mama, Baba,
Lynn, and Dr. Smith

CHAPTER ONE

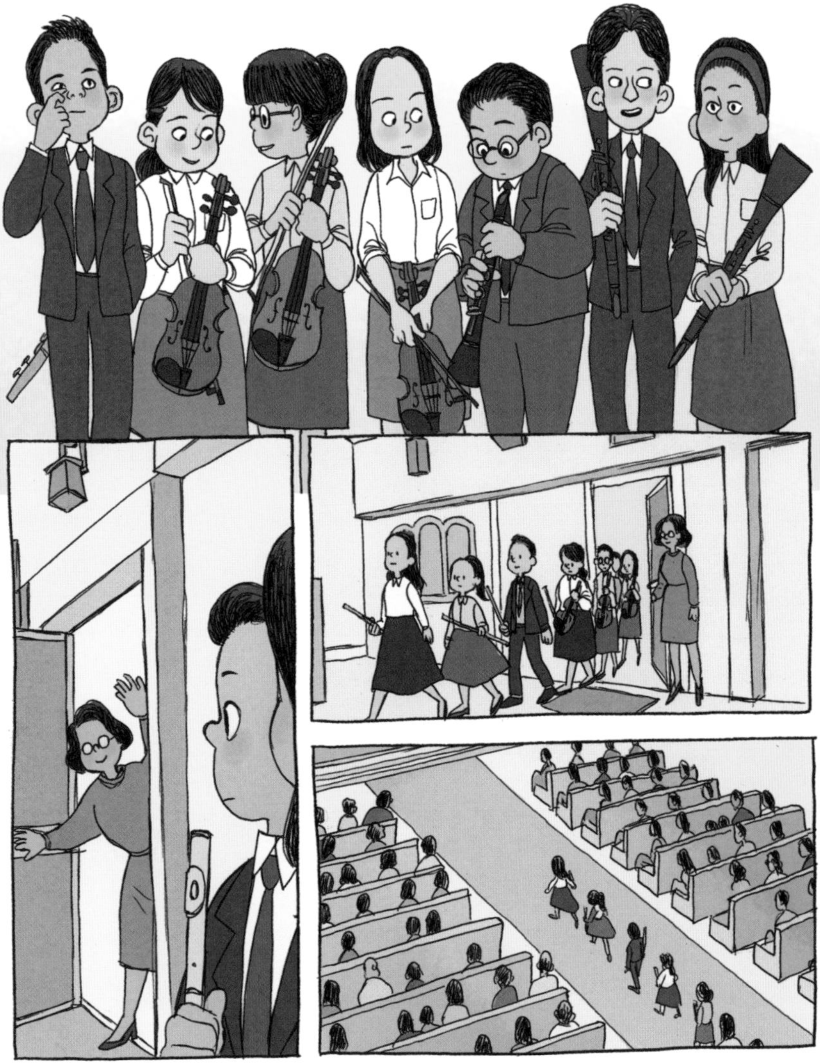

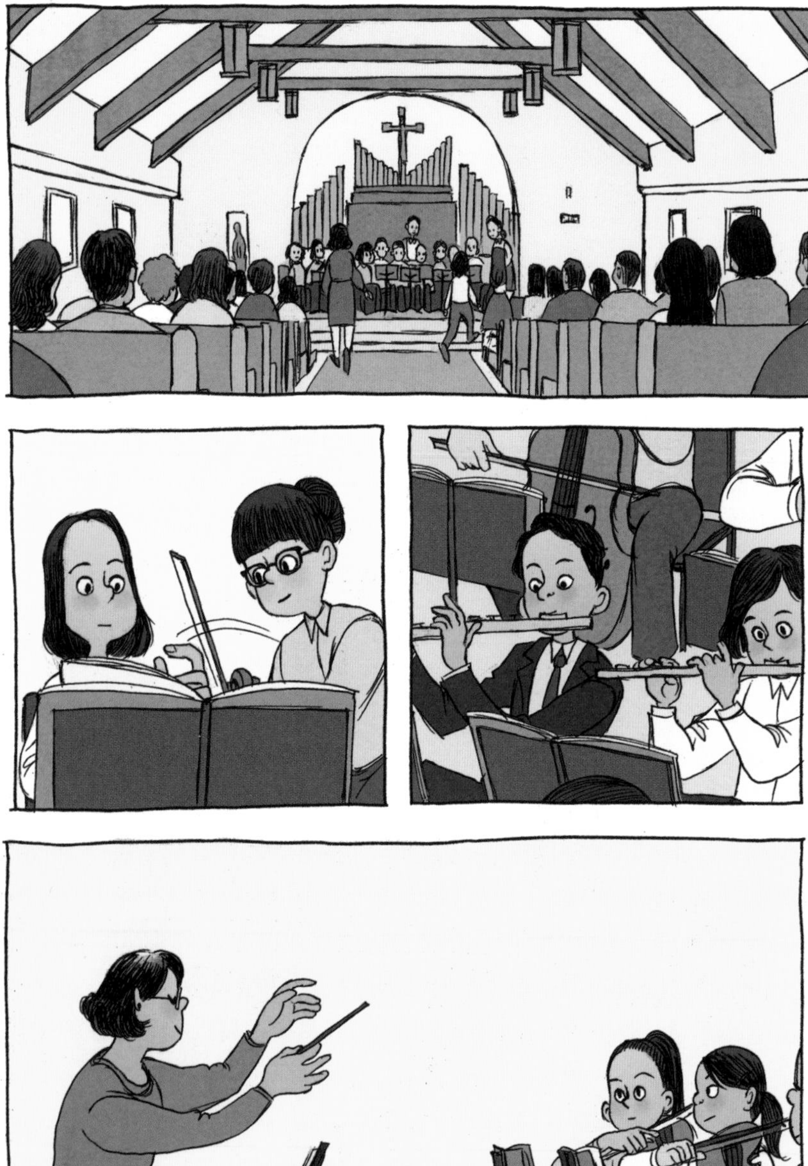

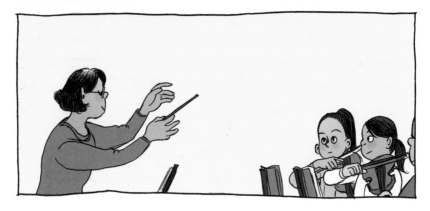

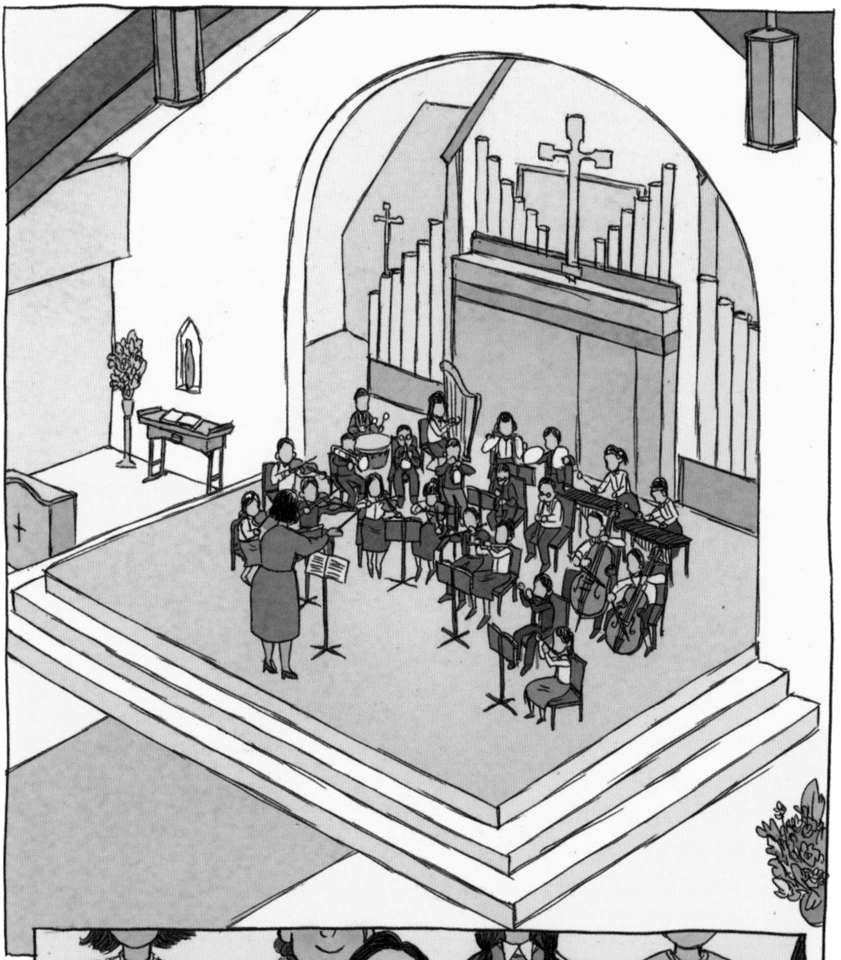

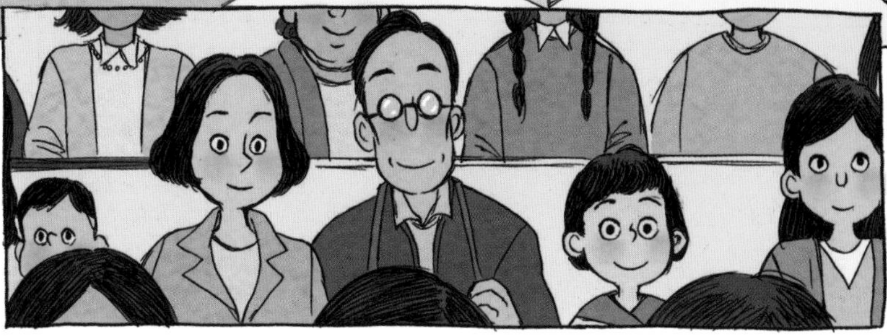

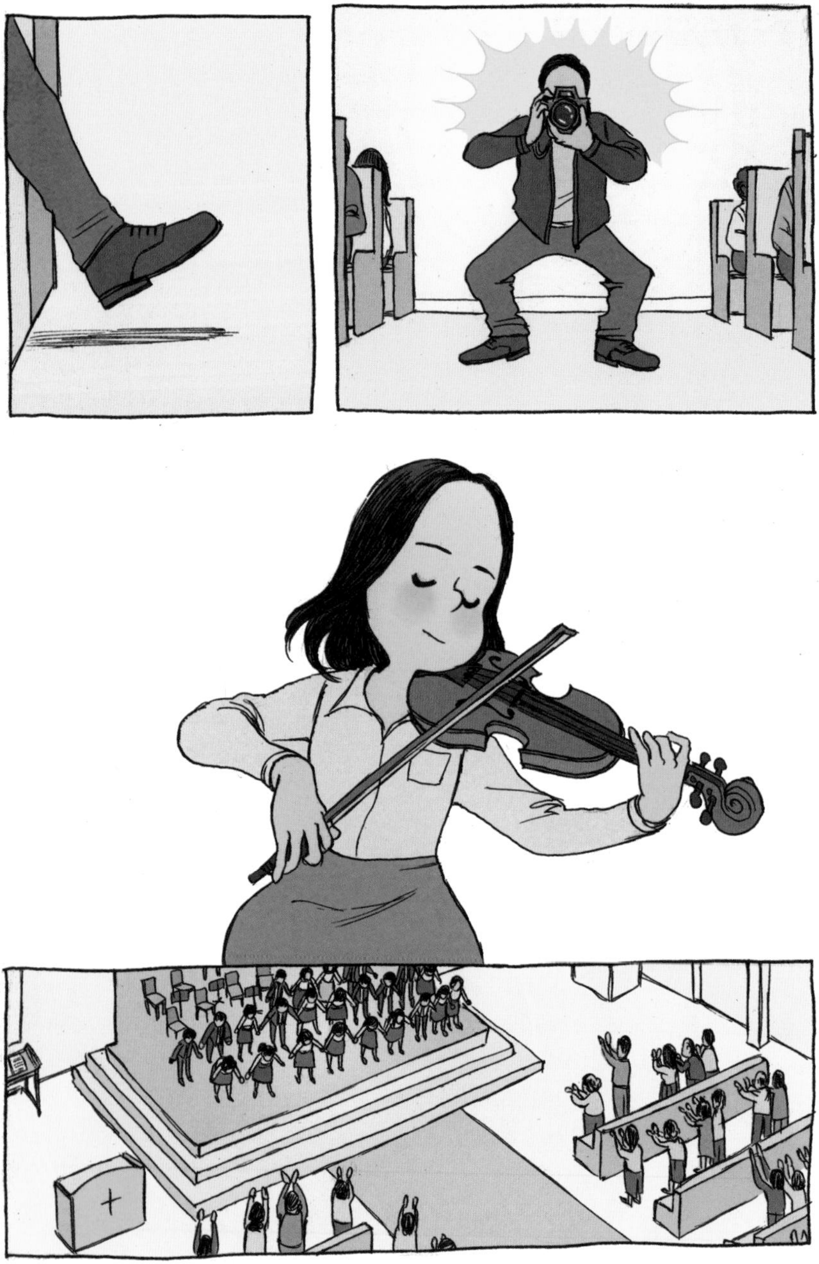

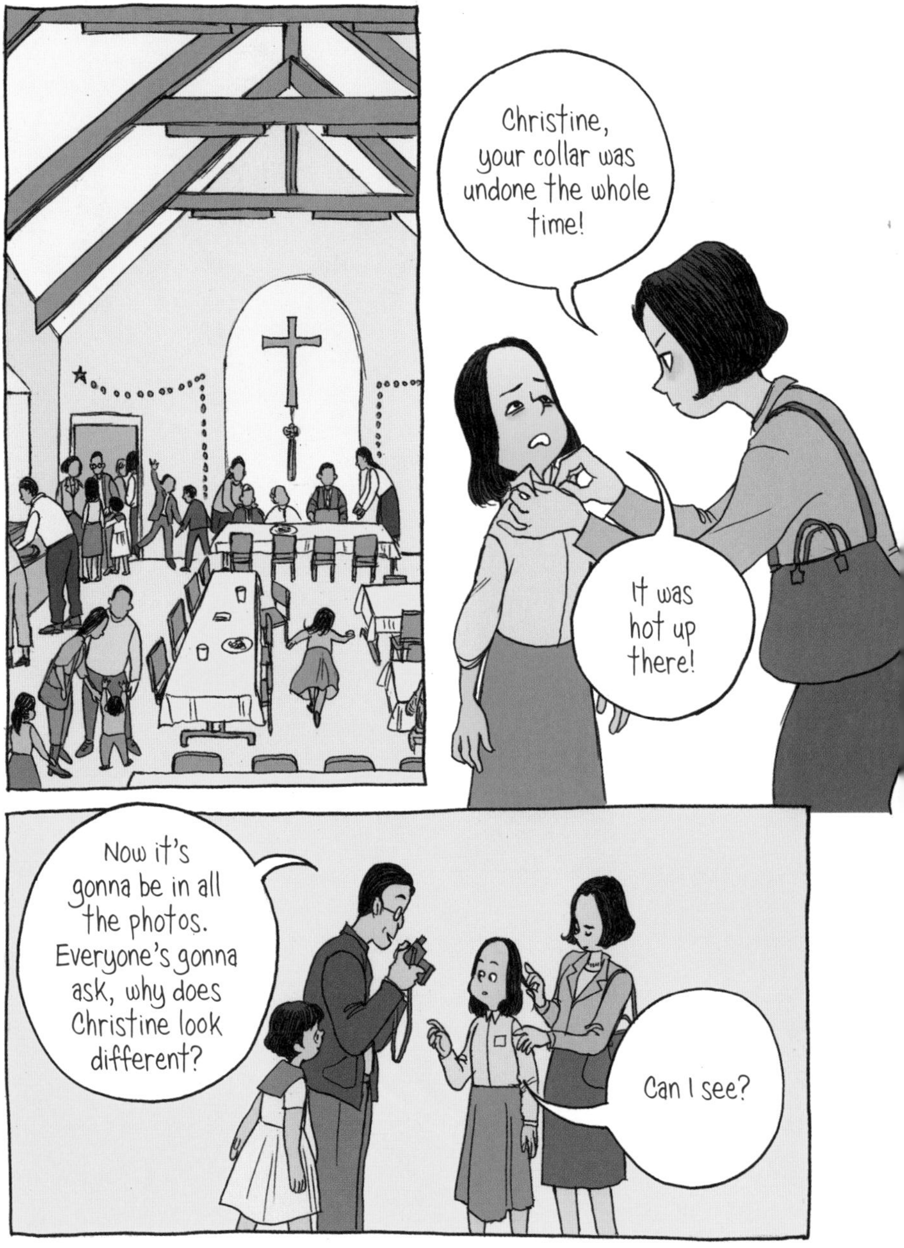
Christine, your collar was undone the whole time!
It was hot up there!
Now it's gonna be in all the photos. Everyone's gonna ask, why does Christine look different?
Can I see?

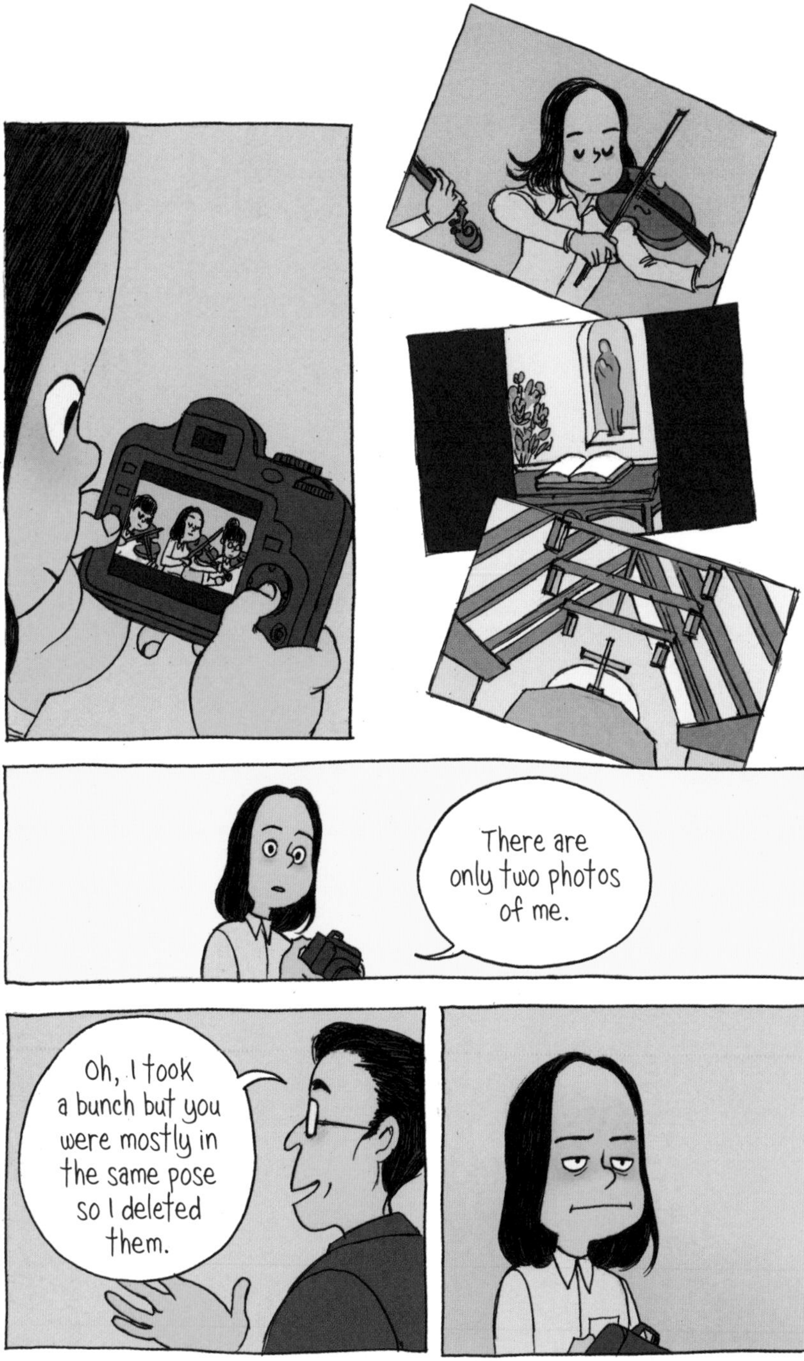
There are only two photos of me.
Oh, I took a bunch but you were mostly in the same pose so I deleted them.

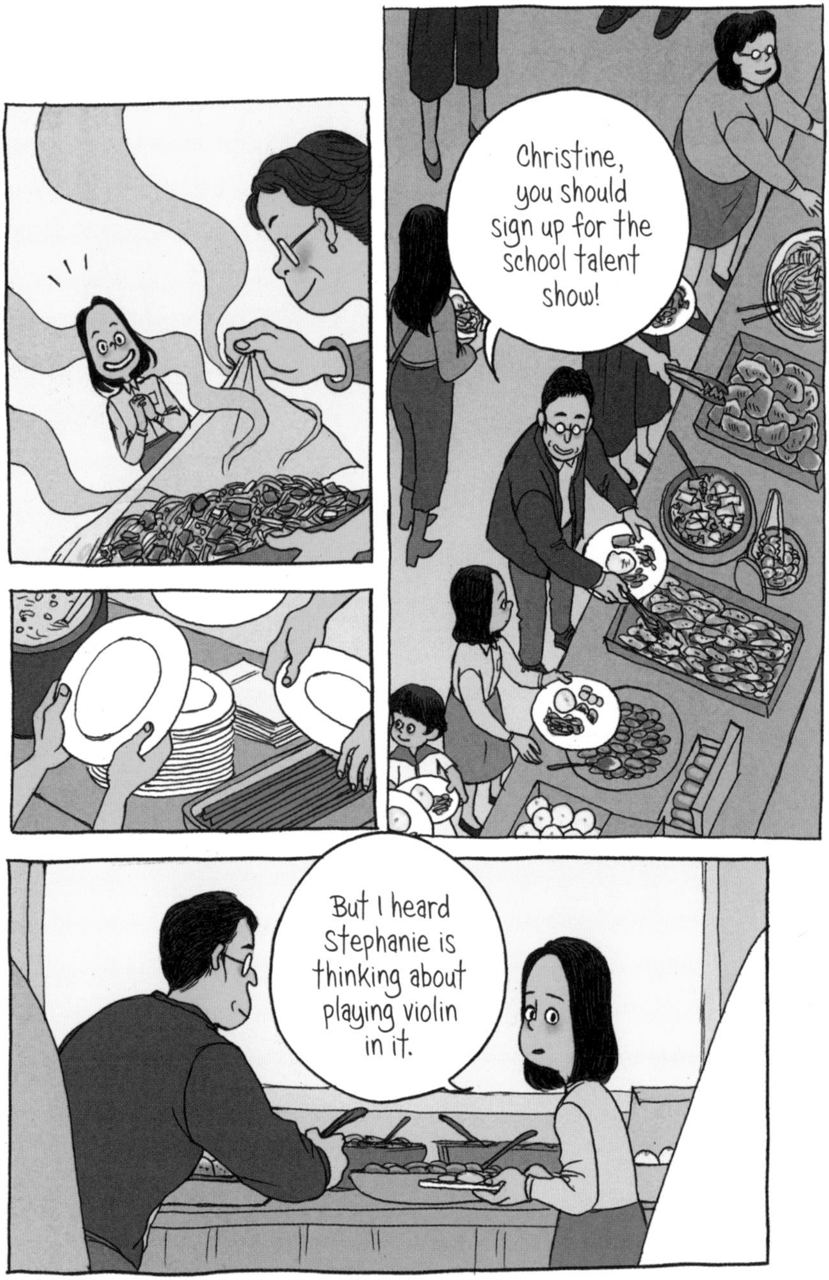
Christine, you should sign up for the school talent show!
But I heard Stephanie is thinking about playing violin in it.

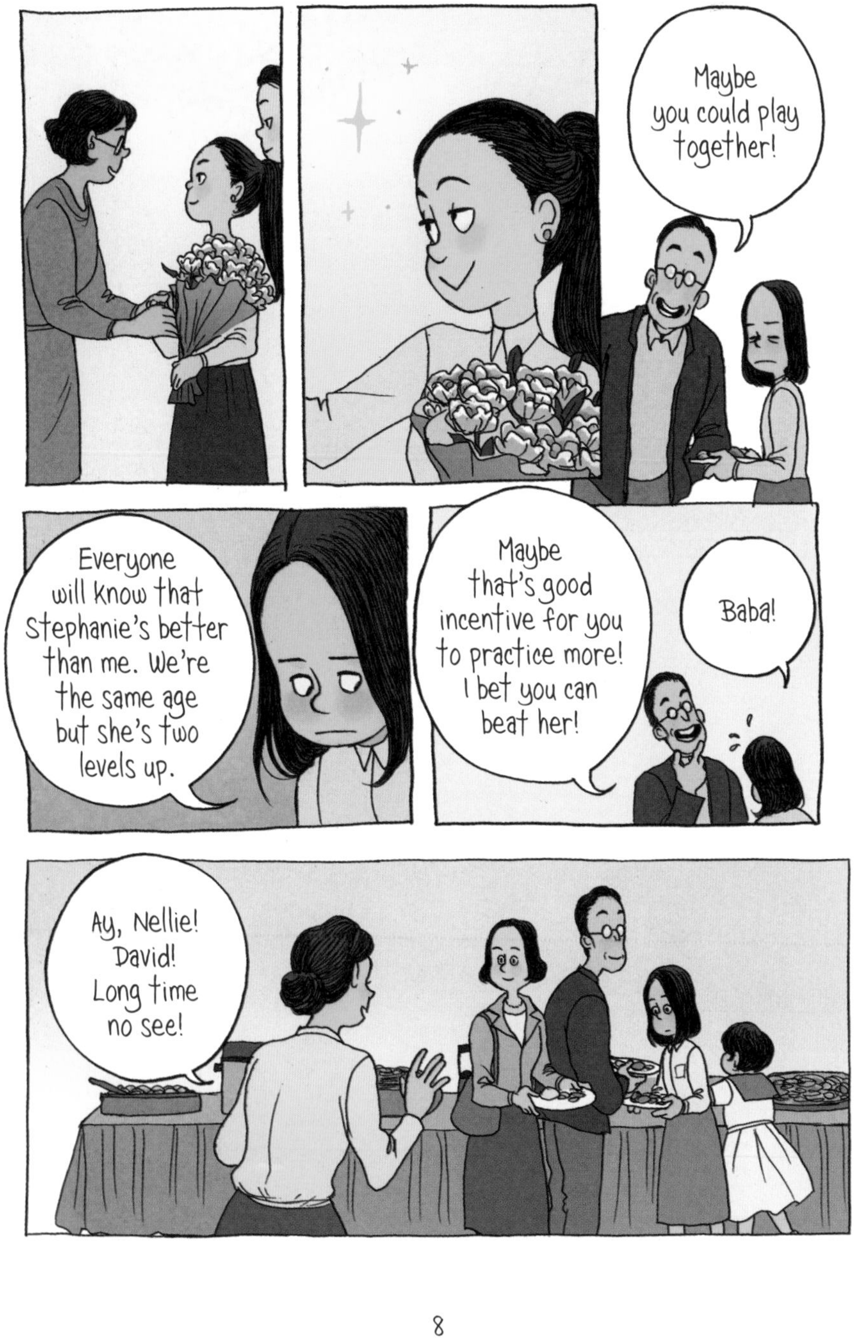
Maybe you could play together!
Everyone will know that Stephanie's better than me. We're the same age but she's two levels up.
Maybe that's good incentive for you to practice more! I bet you can beat her!
Baba!
Ay, Nellie! David! Long time no see!

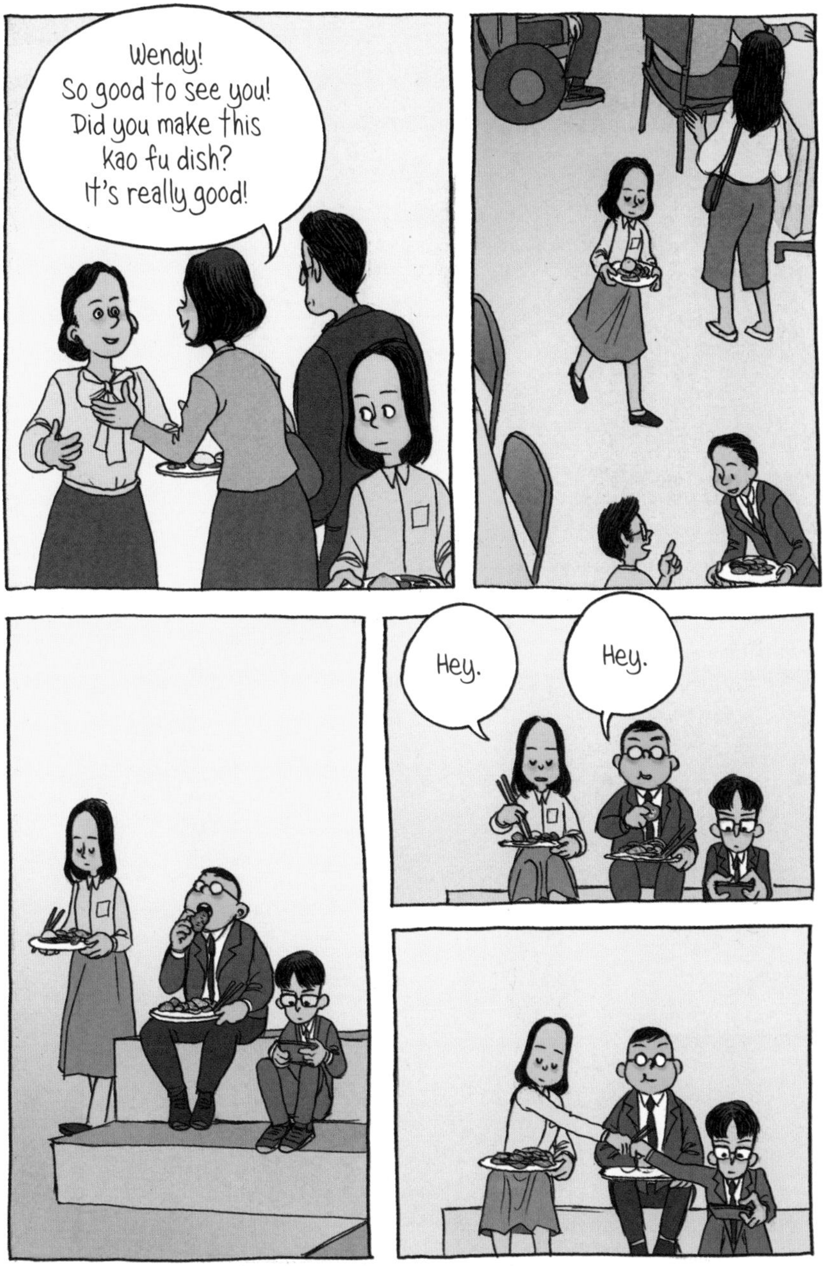

Wendy! So good to see you! Did you make this kao fu dish? It's really good!
Hey.
Hey.

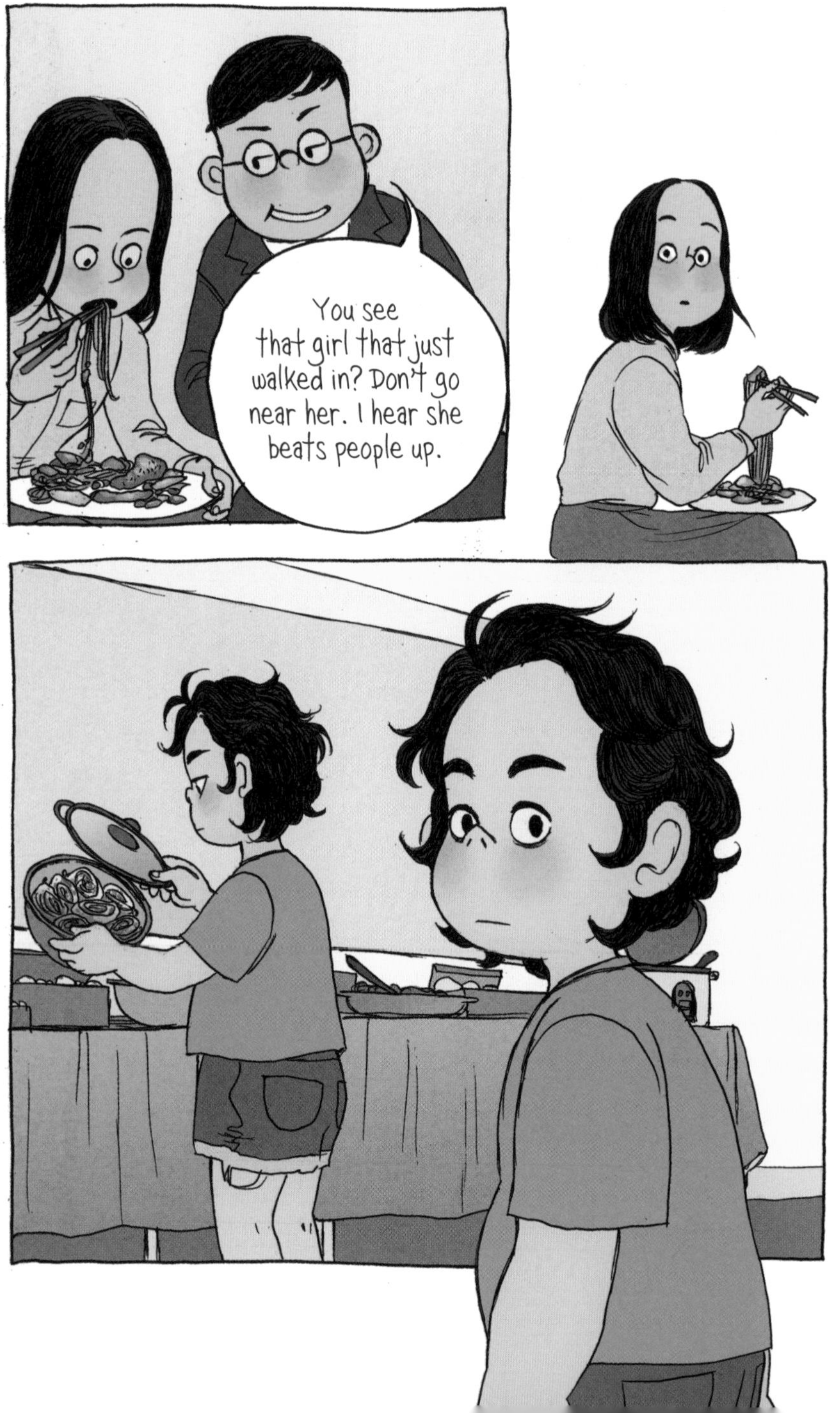
You see that girl that just walked in? Don't go near her. I hear she beats people up.

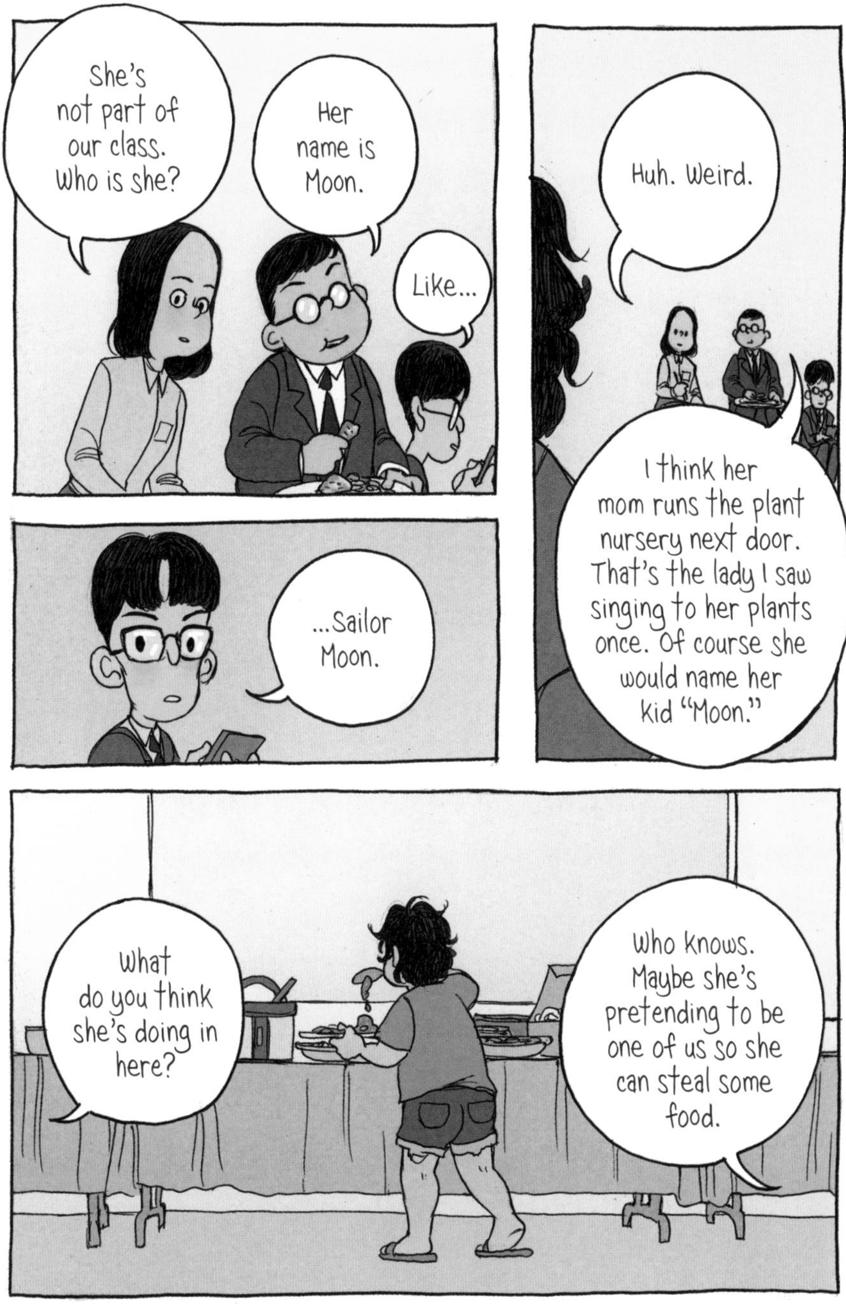
She's not part of our class. Who is she?
Her name is Moon.
Like...
Huh. Weird.
...Sailor Moon.
I think her mom runs the plant nursery next door. That's the lady I saw singing to her plants once. Of course she would name her kid "Moon."
What do you think she's doing in here?
Who knows. Maybe she's pretending to be one of us so she can steal some food.

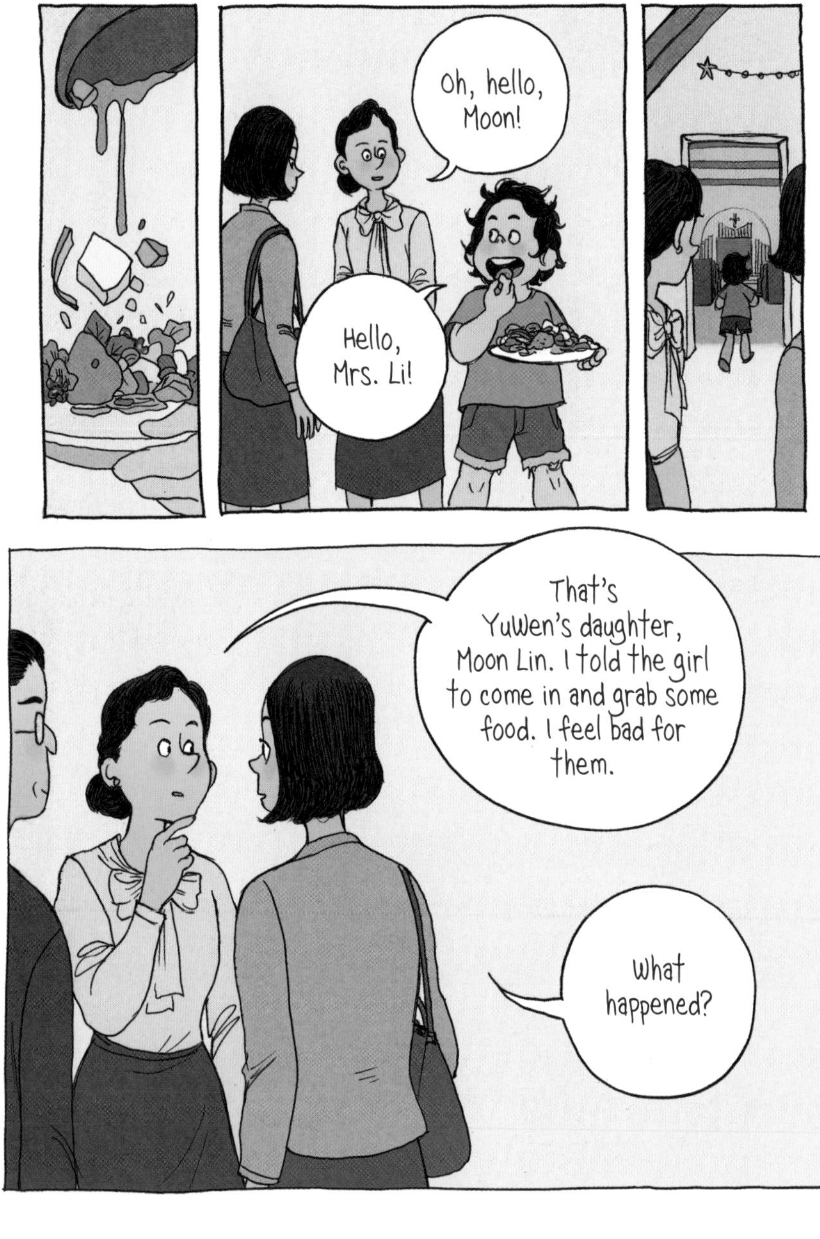
Oh, hello, Moon!
Hello, Mrs. Li!
That's YuWen's daughter, Moon Lin. I told the girl to come in and grab some food. I feel bad for them.
What happened?

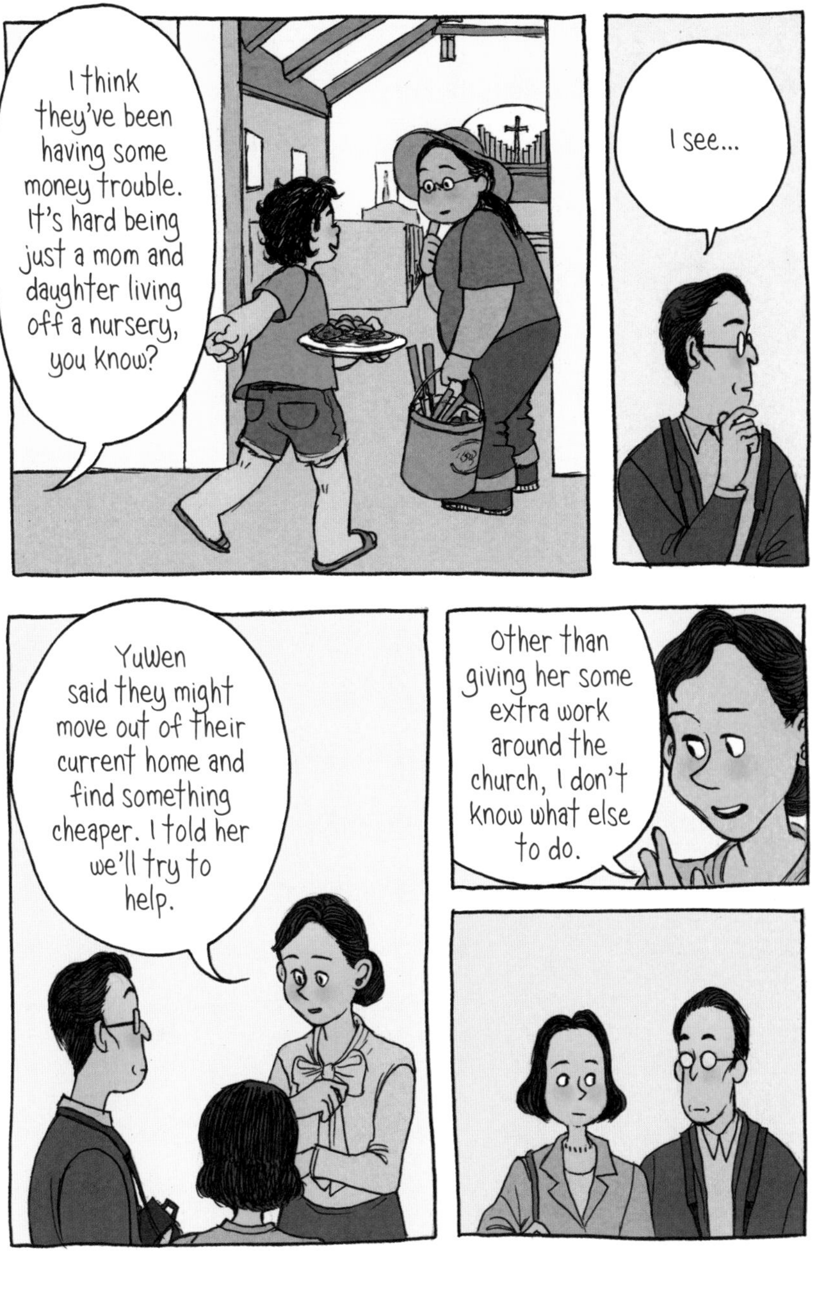
I think they've been having some money trouble. It's hard being just a mom and daughter living off a nursery, you know?
I see...
YuWen said they might move out of their current home and find something cheaper. I told her we'll try to help.
Other than giving her some extra work around the church, I don't know what else to do.

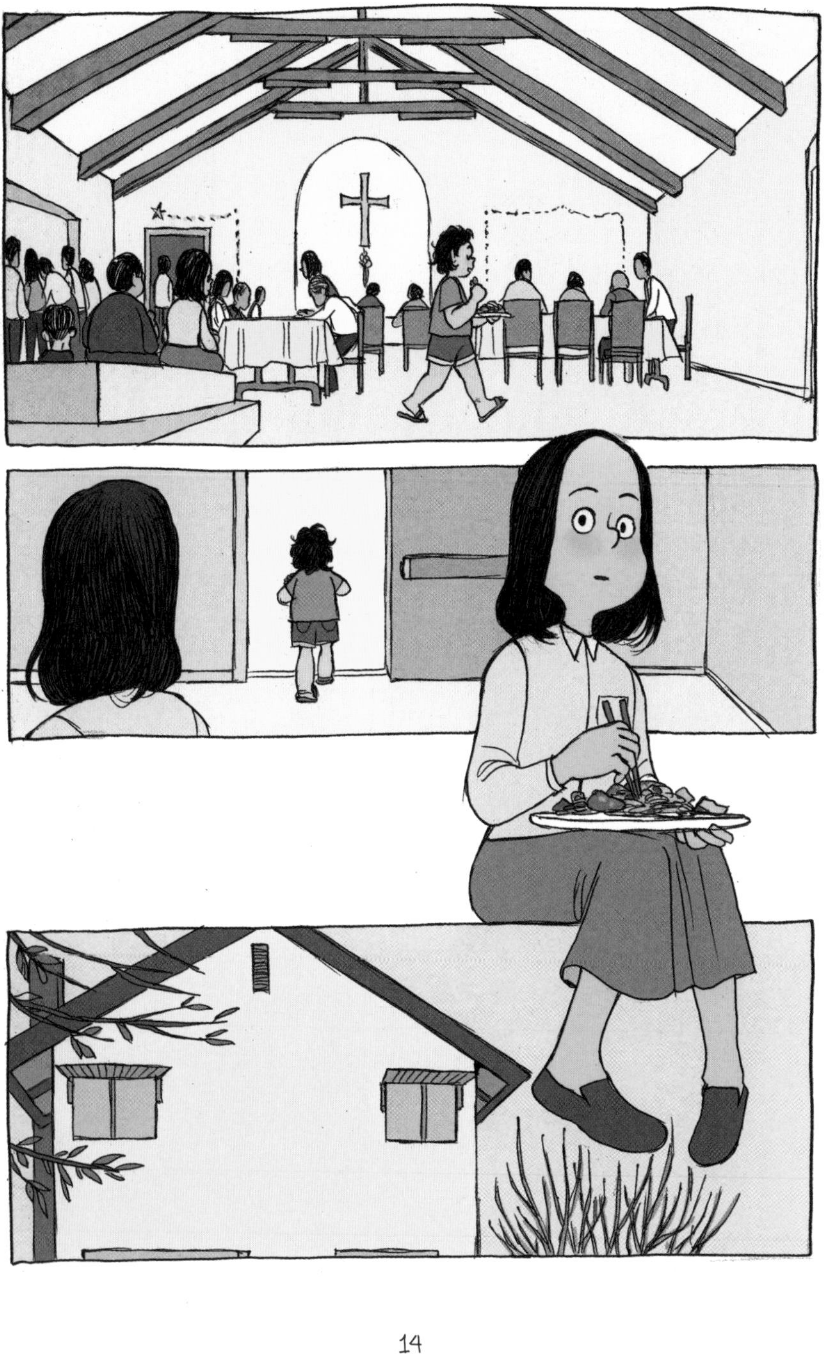

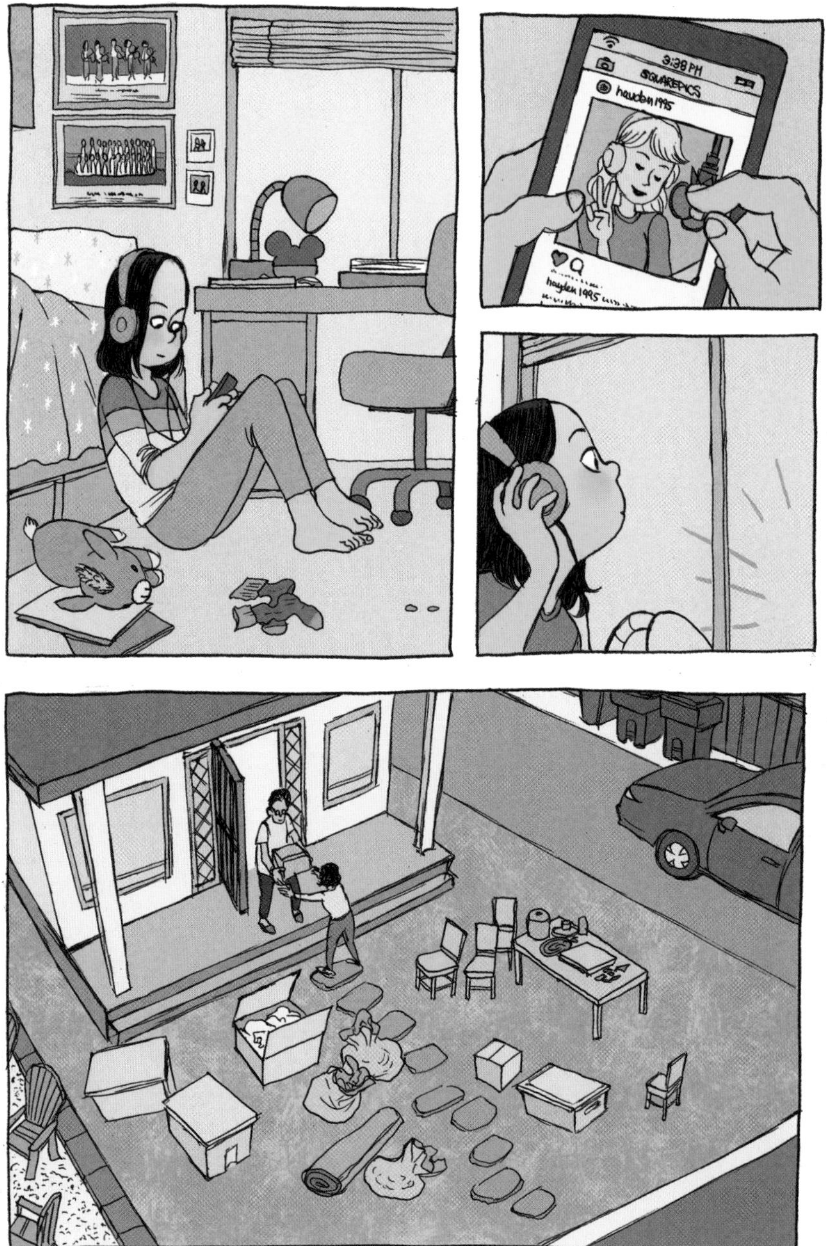
3:38 PM
SQUAREPICS
hayden1995
hayden1995

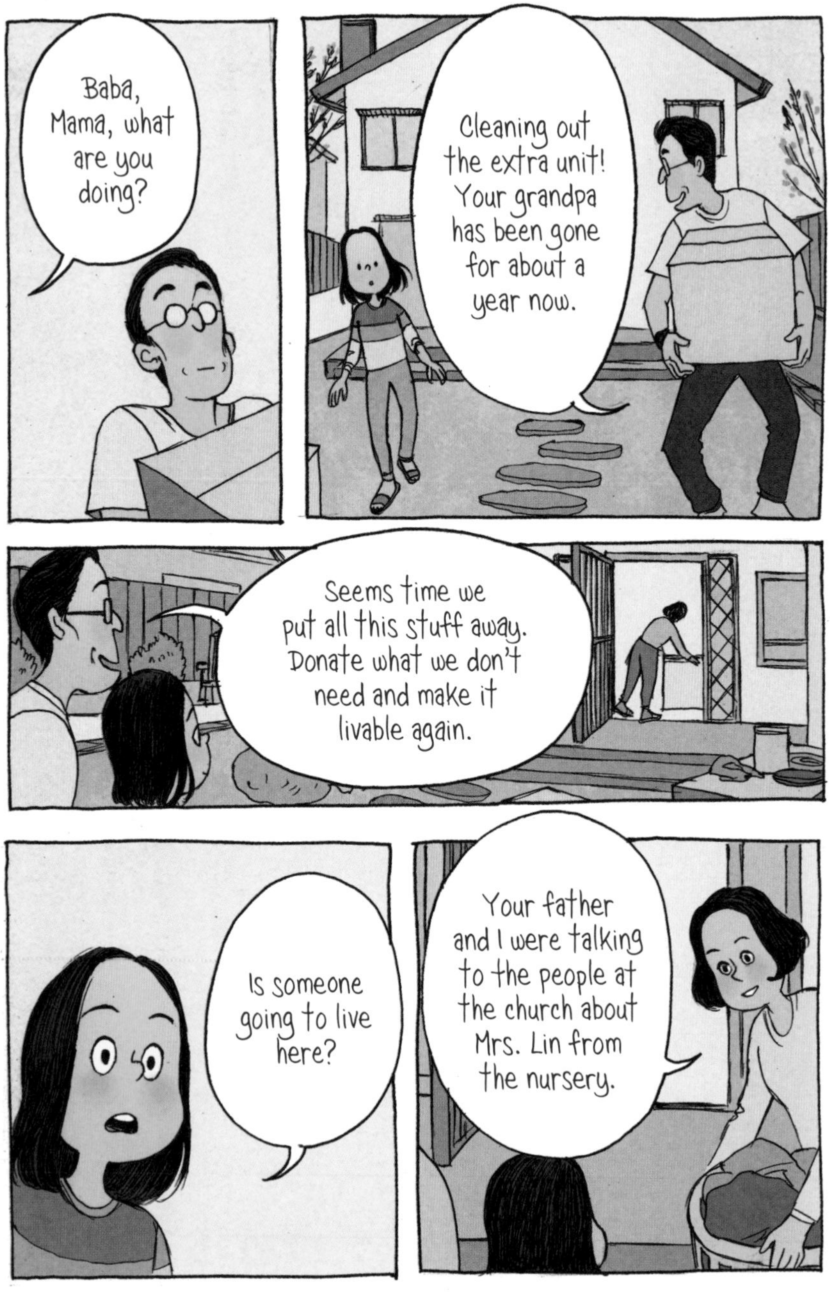
Baba, Mama, what are you doing?
Cleaning out the extra unit! Your grandpa has been gone for about a year now.
Seems time we put all this stuff away. Donate what we don't need and make it livable again.
Is someone going to live here?
Your father and I were talking to the people at the church about Mrs. Lin from the nursery.

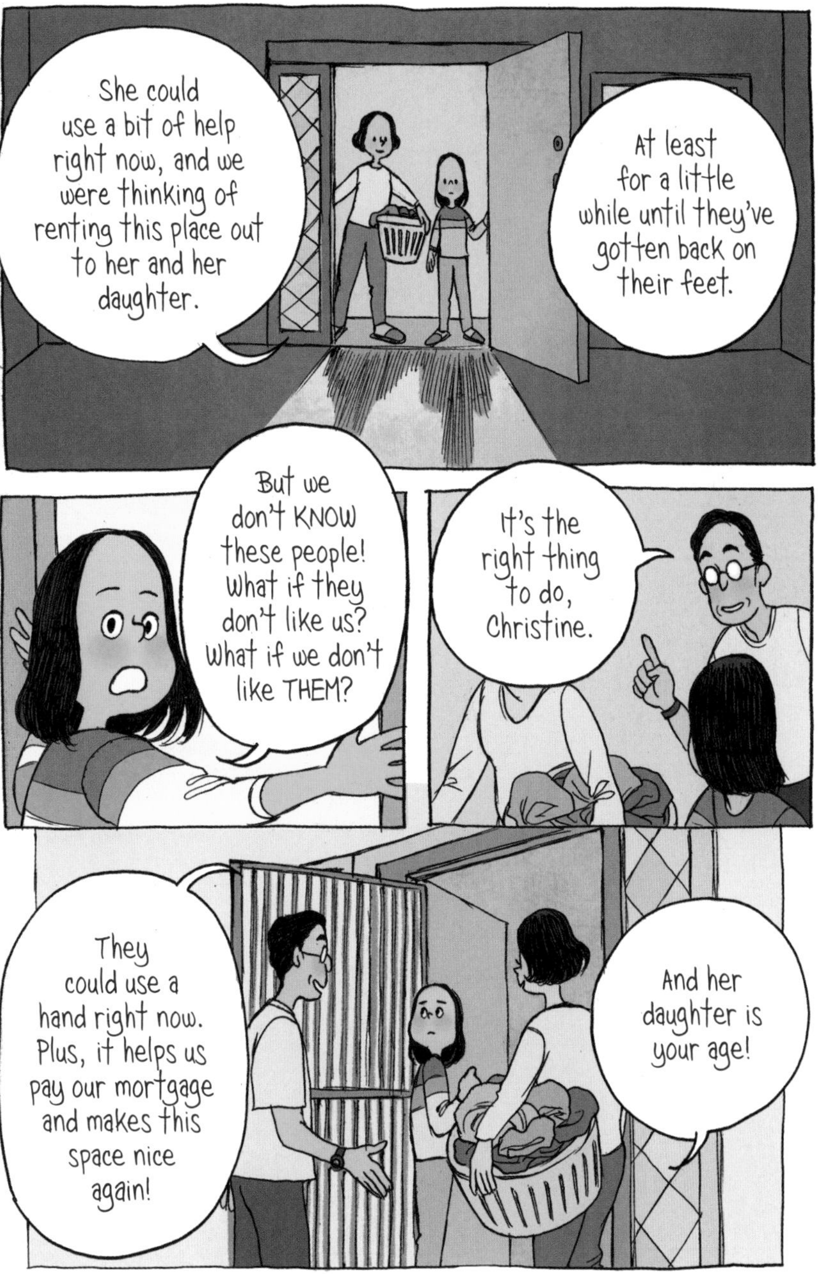
She could use a bit of help right now, and we were thinking of renting this place out to her and her daughter.
At least for a little while until they've gotten back on their feet.
But we don't KNOW these people! What if they don't like us? What if we don't like THEM?
It's the right thing to do, Christine.
They could use a hand right now. Plus, it helps us pay our mortgage and makes this space nice again!
And her daughter is your age!

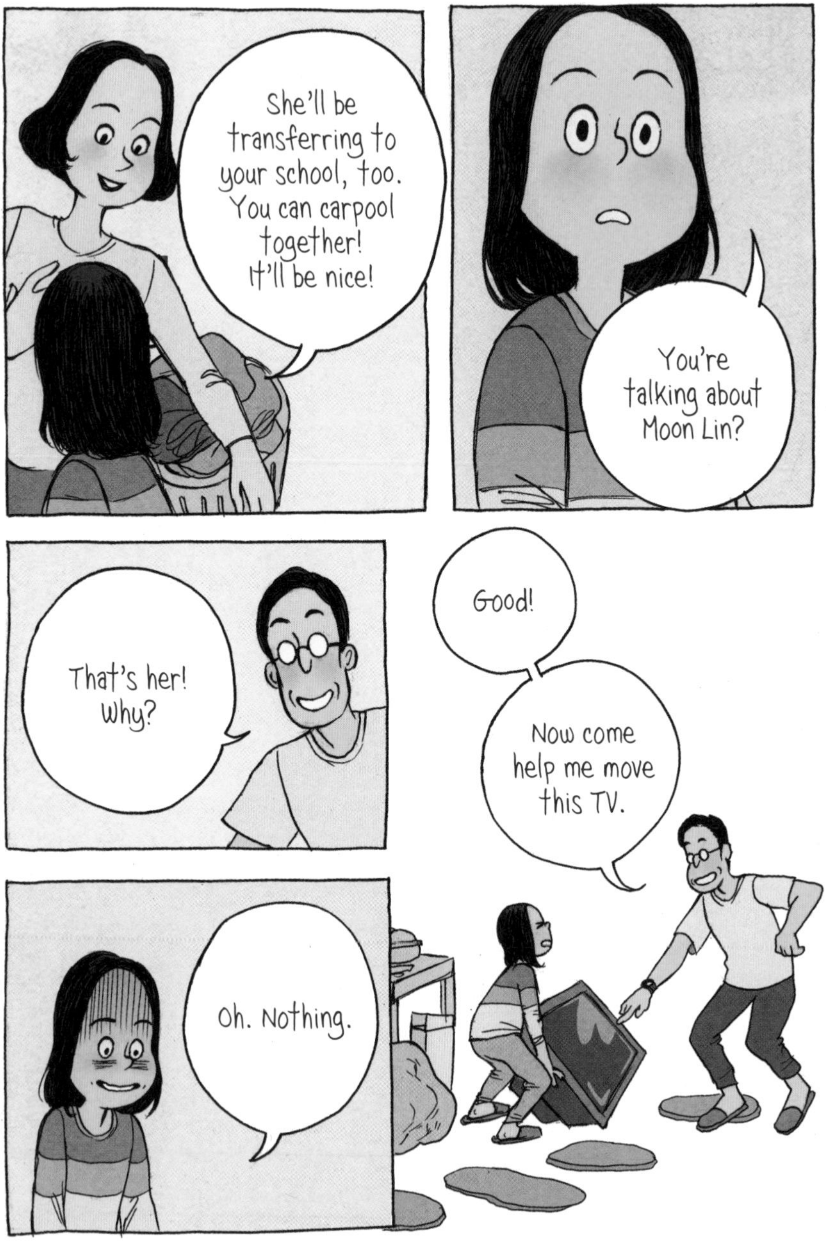
She'll be transferring to your school, too. You can carpool together! It'll be nice!
You're talking about Moon Lin?
That's her! Why?
Good!
Now come help me move this TV.
Oh. Nothing.

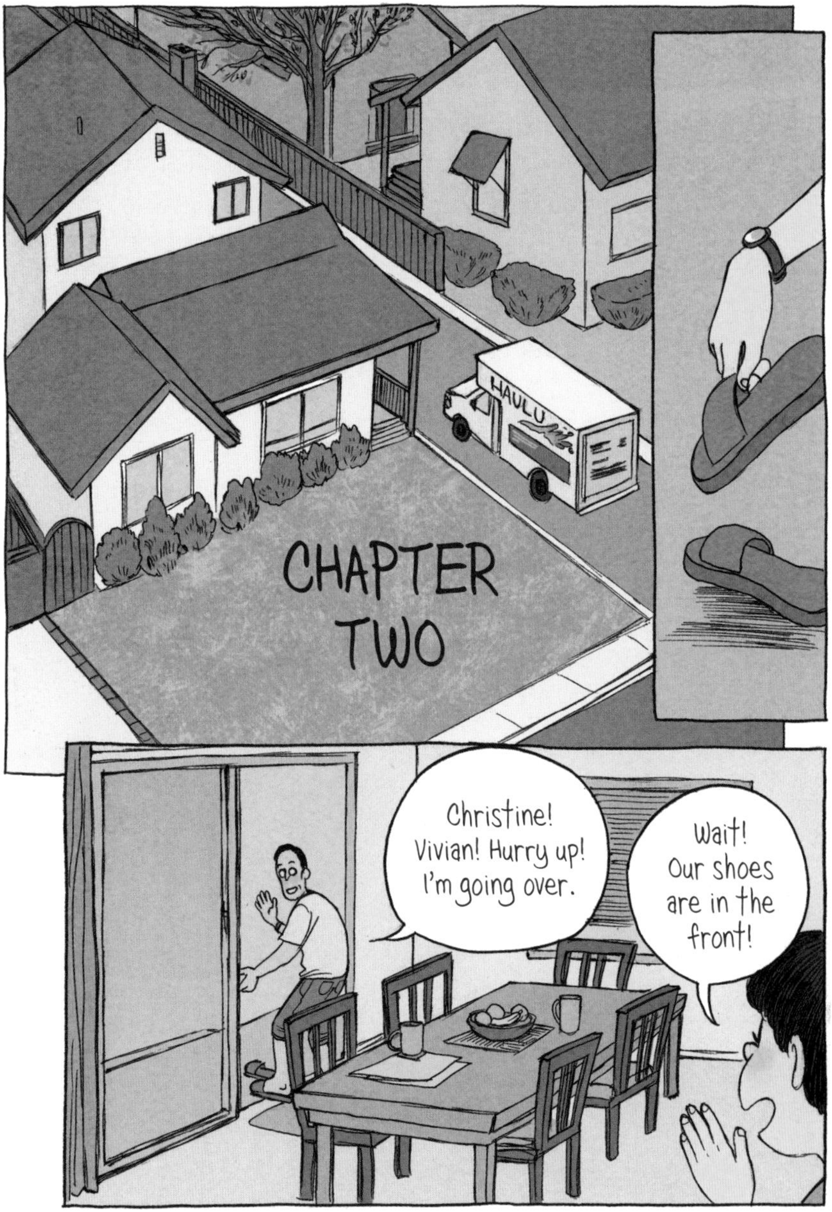
CHAPTER TWO
HAULU
Christine! Vivian! Hurry up! I'm going over.
Wait! Our shoes are in the front!

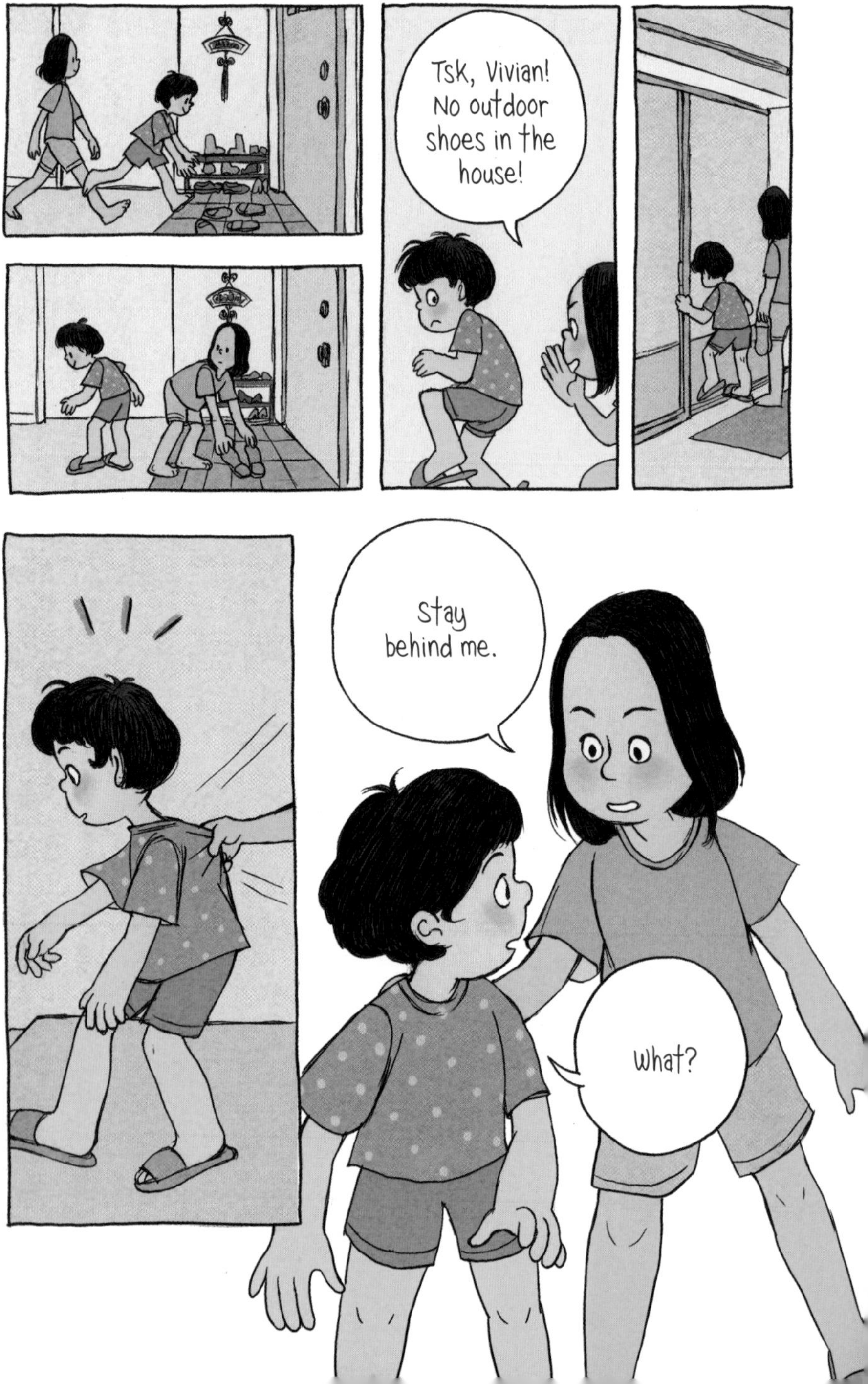
Tsk, Vivian! No outdoor shoes in the house!
Stay behind me.
What?

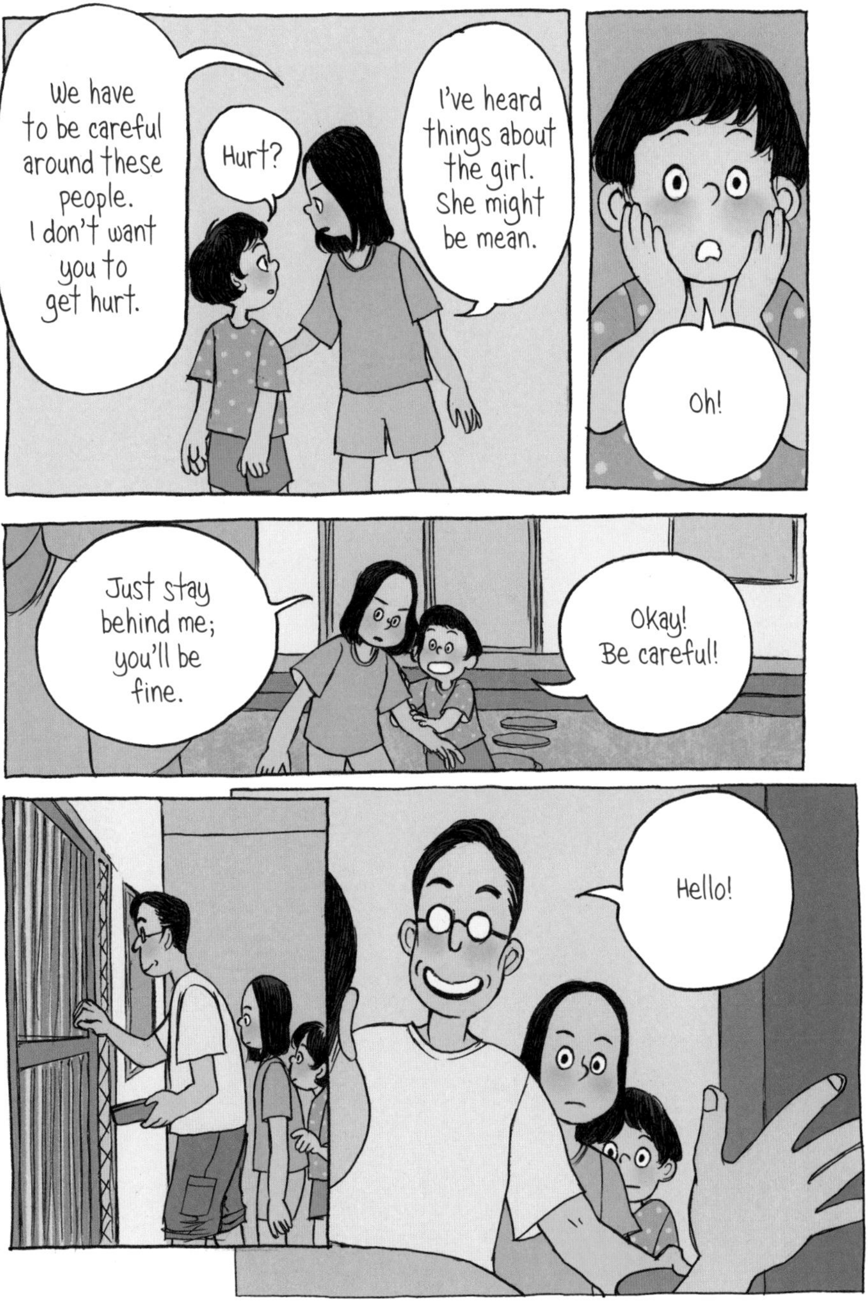
We have to be careful around these people. I don't want you to get hurt.
Hurt?
I've heard things about the girl. She might be mean.
Oh!
Just stay behind me; you'll be fine.
Okay! Be careful!
Hello!

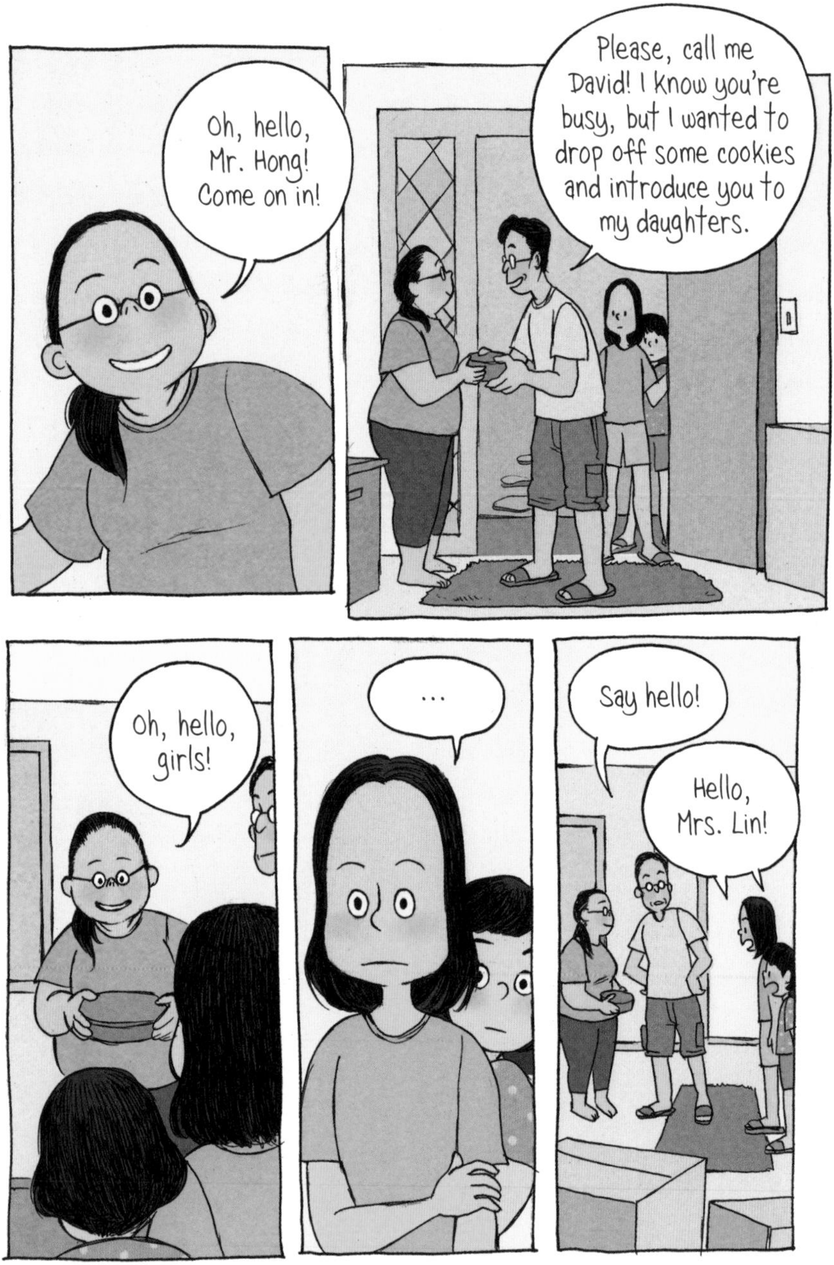
Oh, hello, Mr. Hong! Come on in!
Please, call me David! I know you're busy, but I wanted to drop off some cookies and introduce you to my daughters.
Oh, hello, girls!
...
Say hello!
Hello, Mrs. Lin!

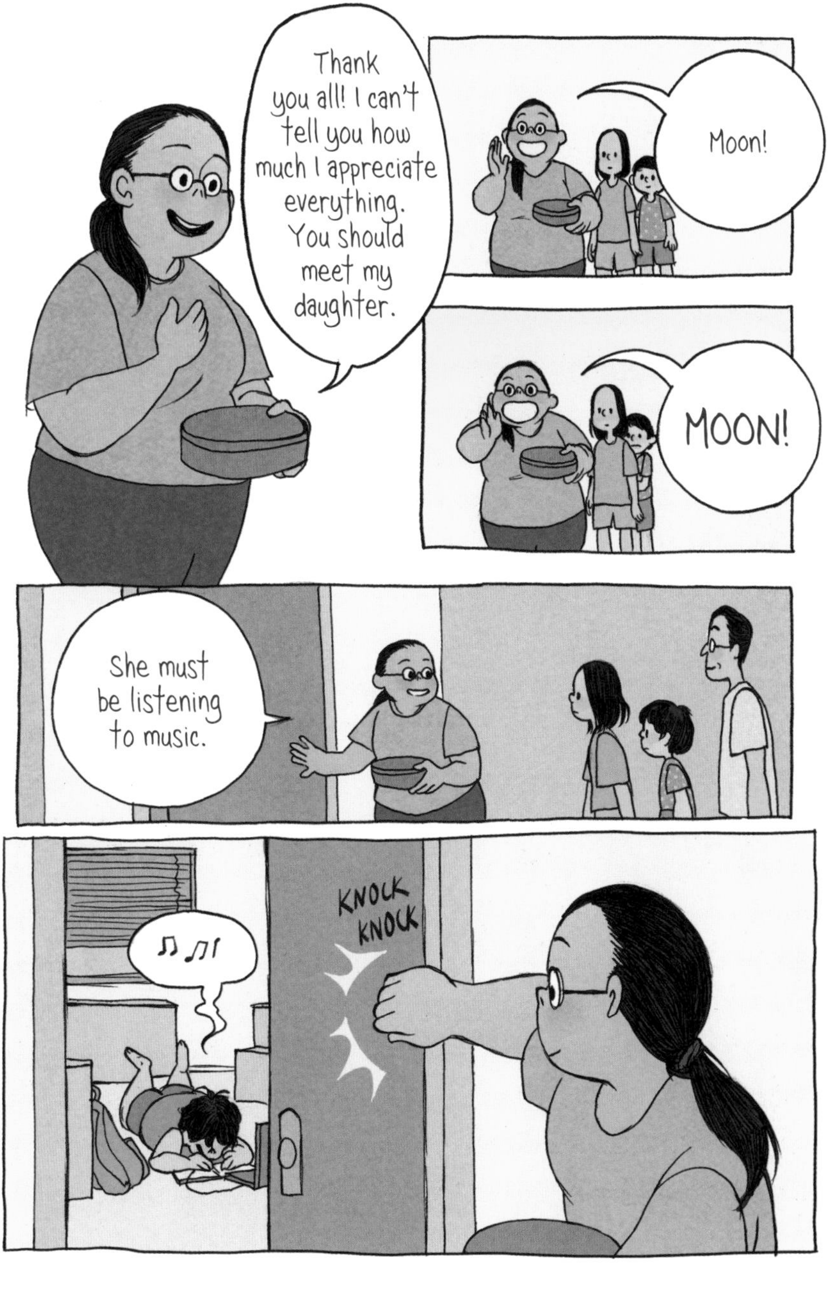

Thank you all! I can't tell you how much I appreciate everything. You should meet my daughter.
Moon!
MOON!
She must be listening to music.
KNOCK KNOCK

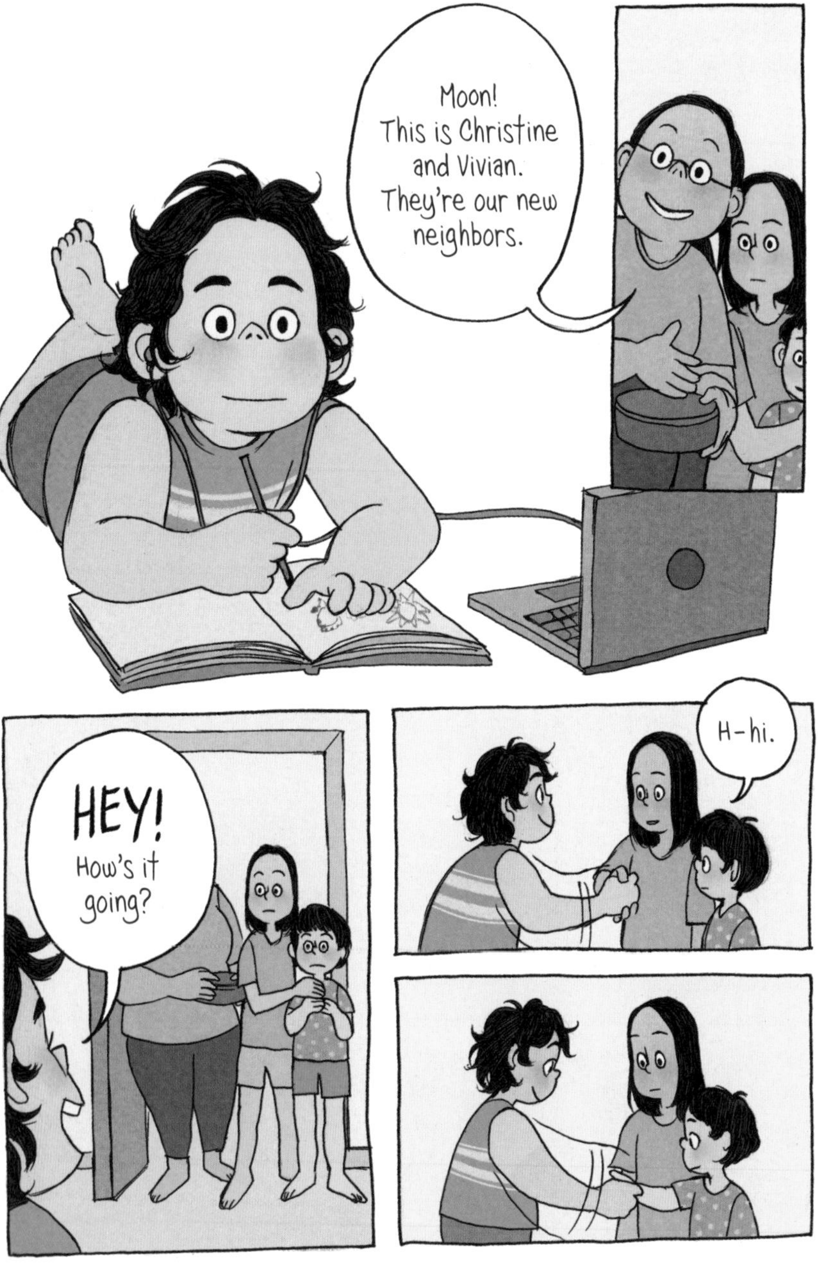
Moon!
This is Christine and Vivian. They're our new neighbors.
HEY! How's it going?
H-hi.

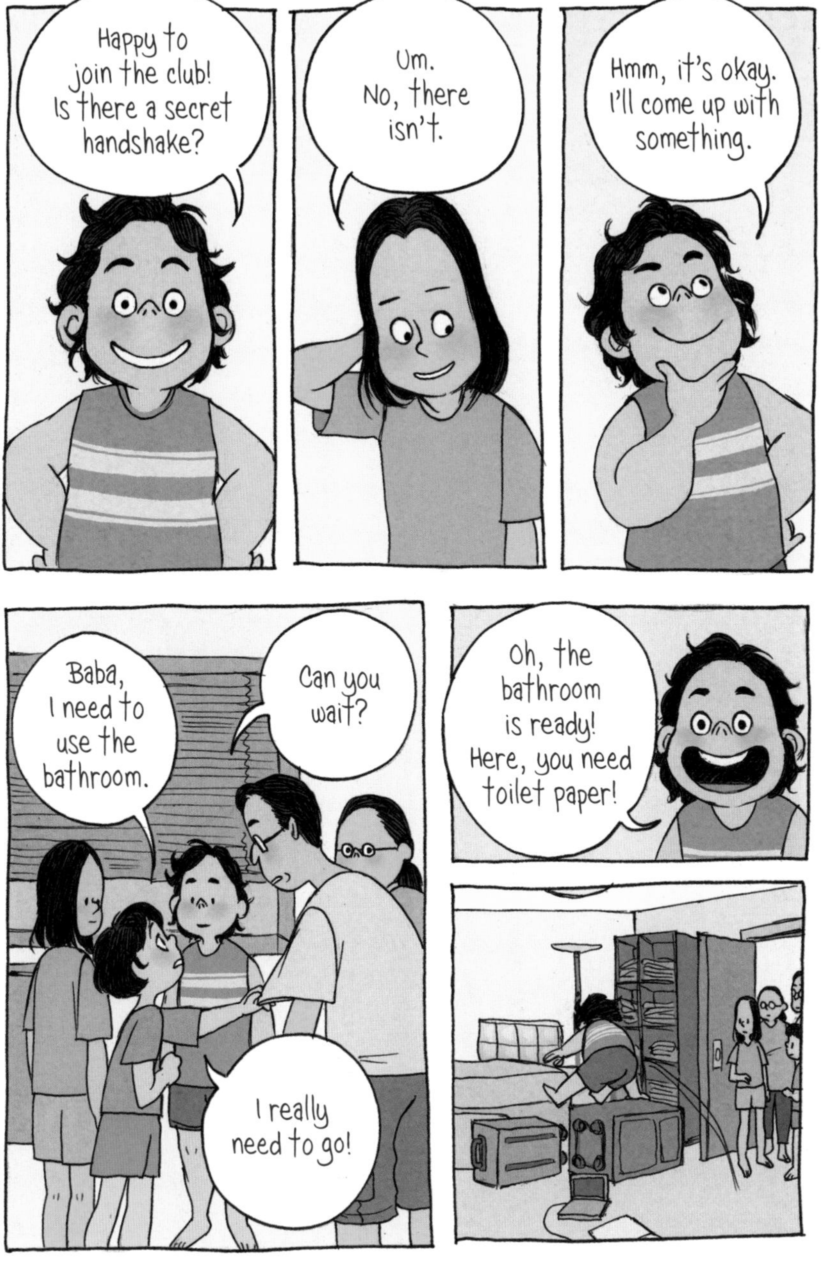
Happy to join the club! Is there a secret handshake?
Um. No, there isn't.
Hmm, it's okay. I'll come up with something.
Baba, I need to use the bathroom.
Can you wait?
I really need to go!
Oh, the bathroom is ready! Here, you need toilet paper!

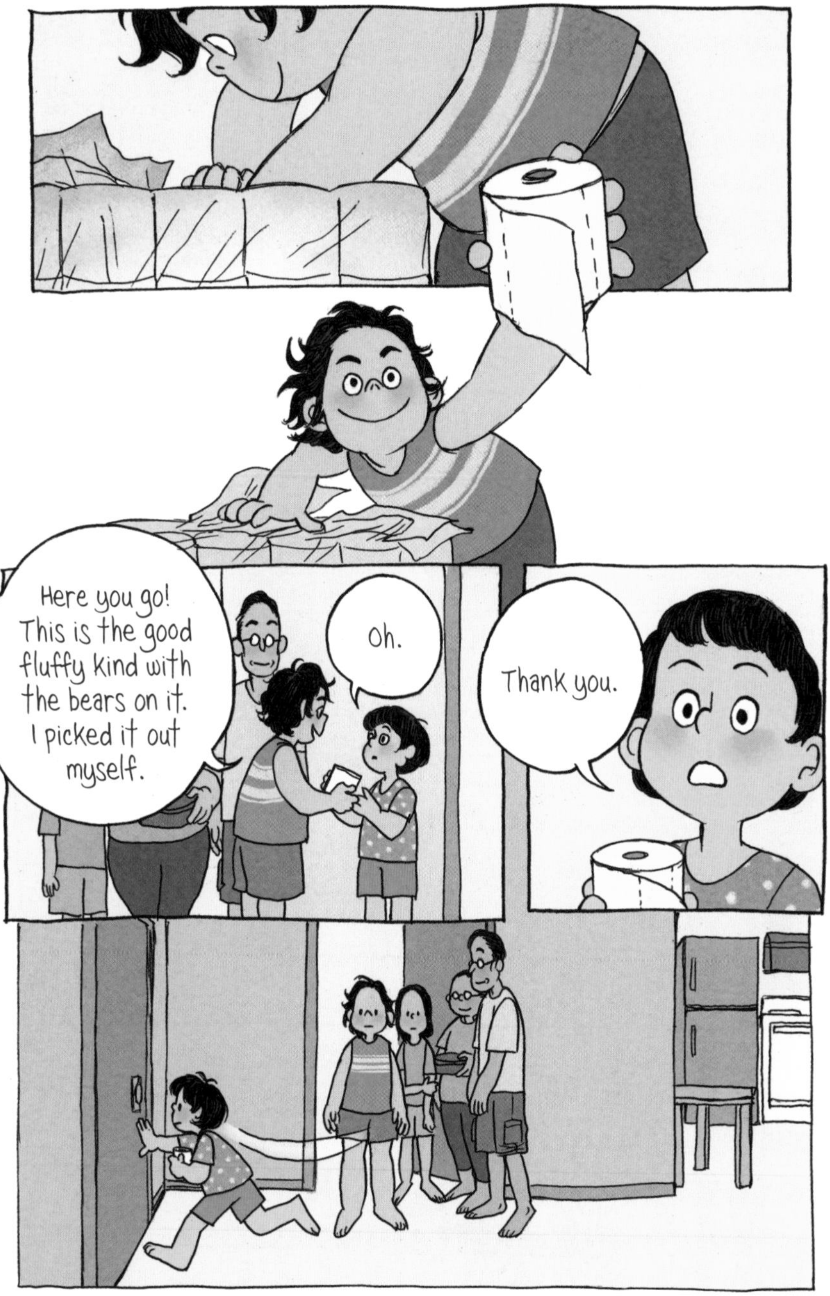

Here you go! This is the good fluffy kind with the bears on it. I picked it out myself.
Oh.
Thank you.

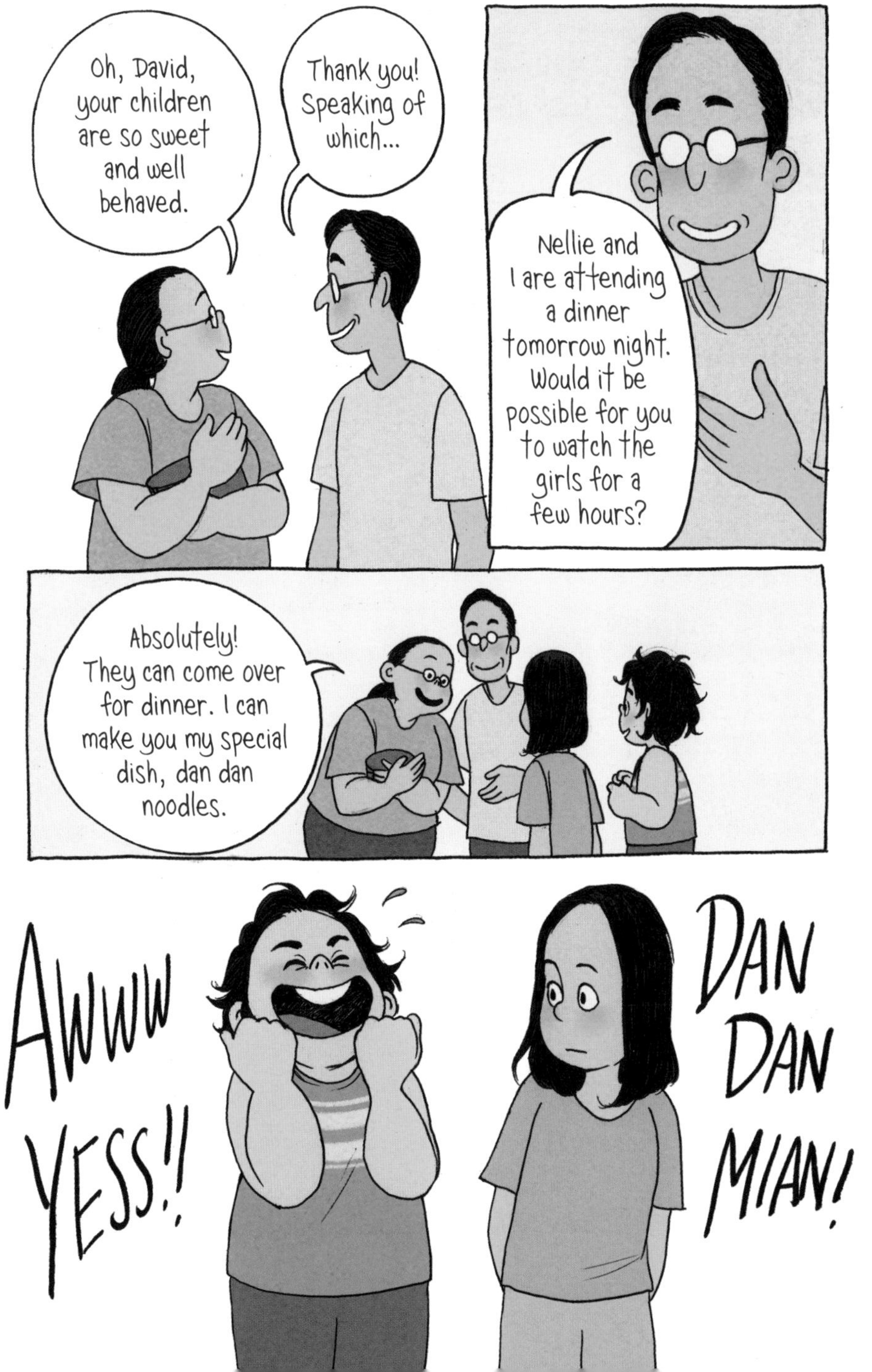
Oh, David, your children are so sweet and well behaved.
Thank you! Speaking of which...
Nellie and I are attending a dinner tomorrow night. Would it be possible for you to watch the girls for a few hours?
Absolutely! They can come over for dinner. I can make you my special dish, dan dan noodles.
AWWW YESS!!
DAN DAN MIAN!

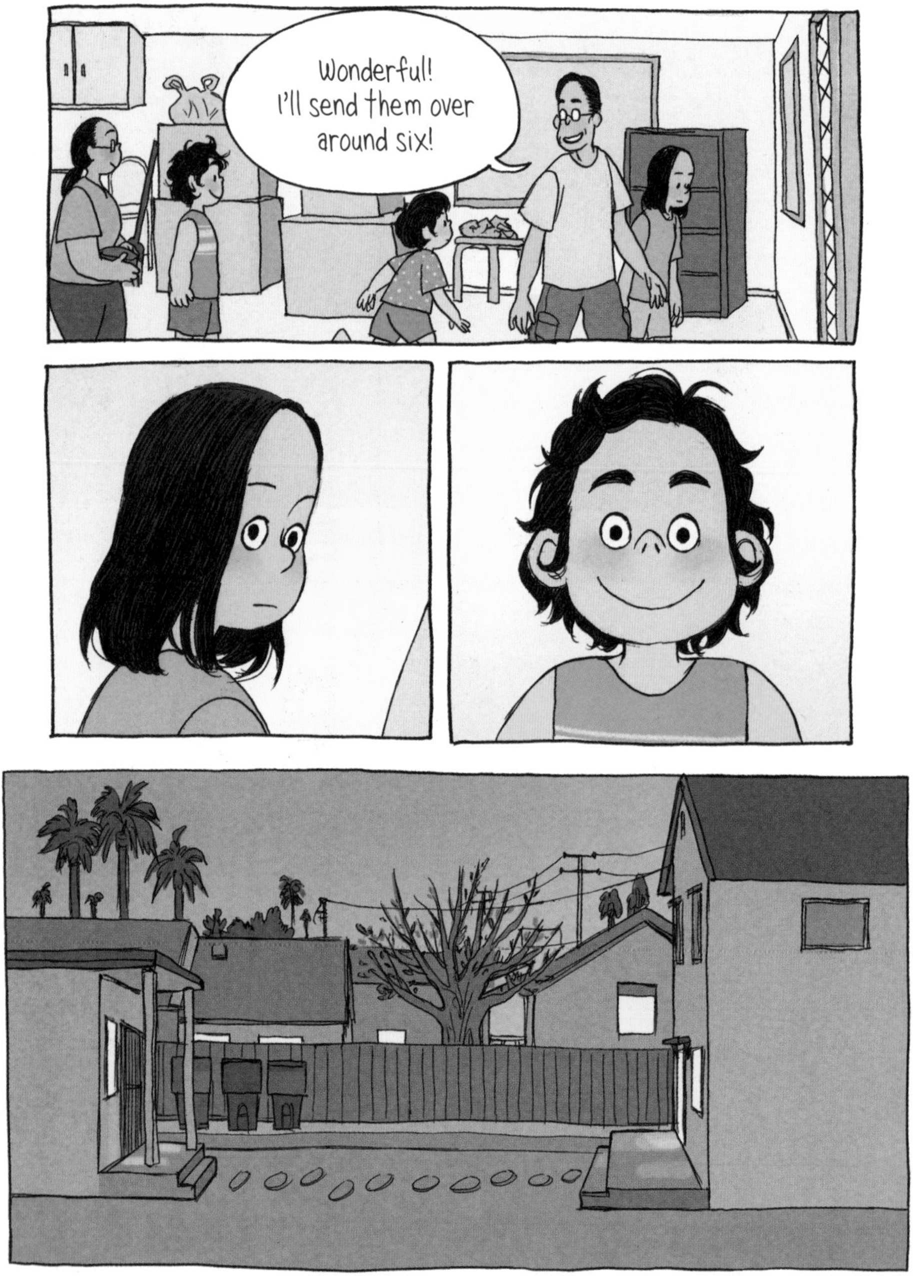
Wonderful! I'll send them over around six!

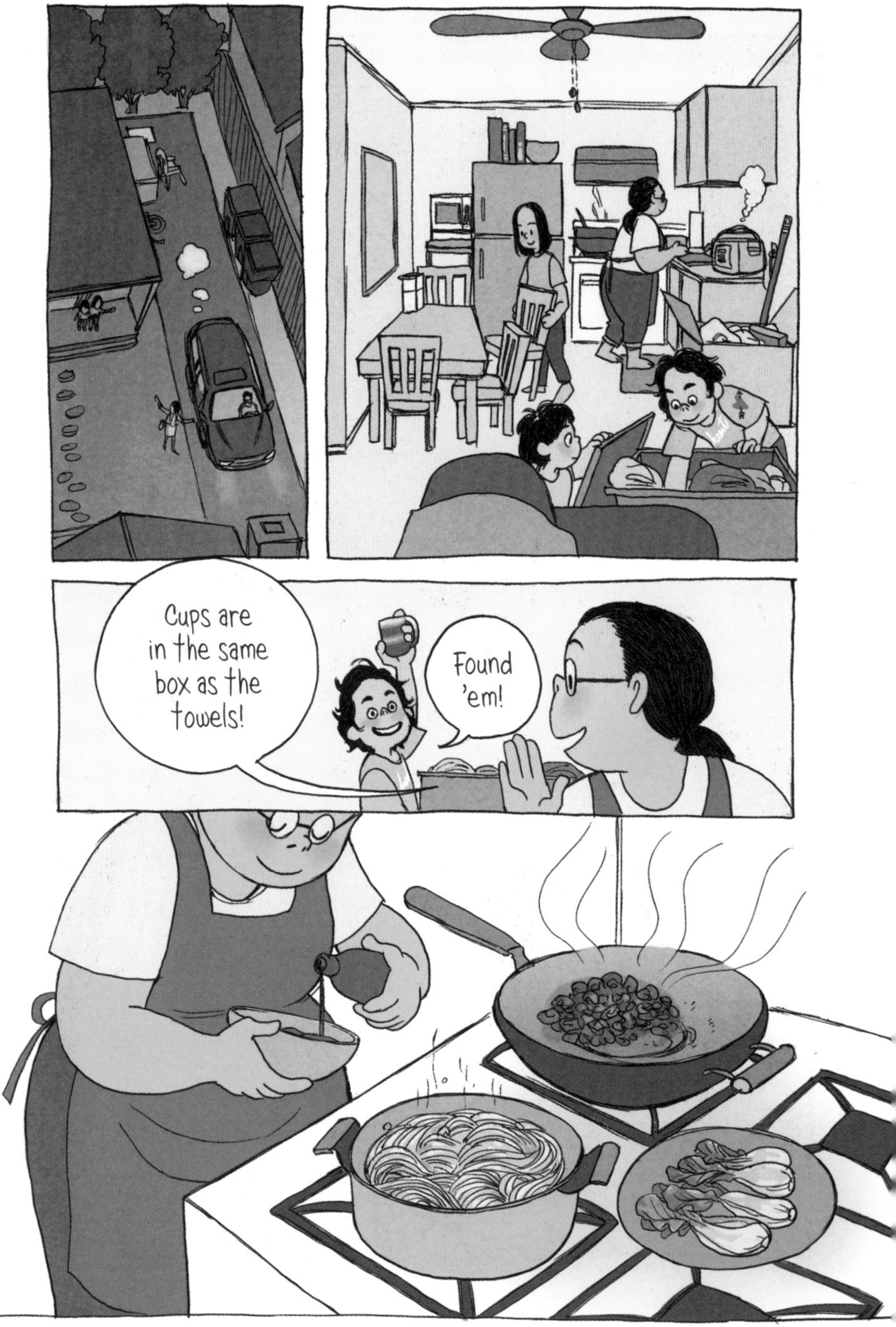
Cups are in the same box as the towels!
Found 'em!

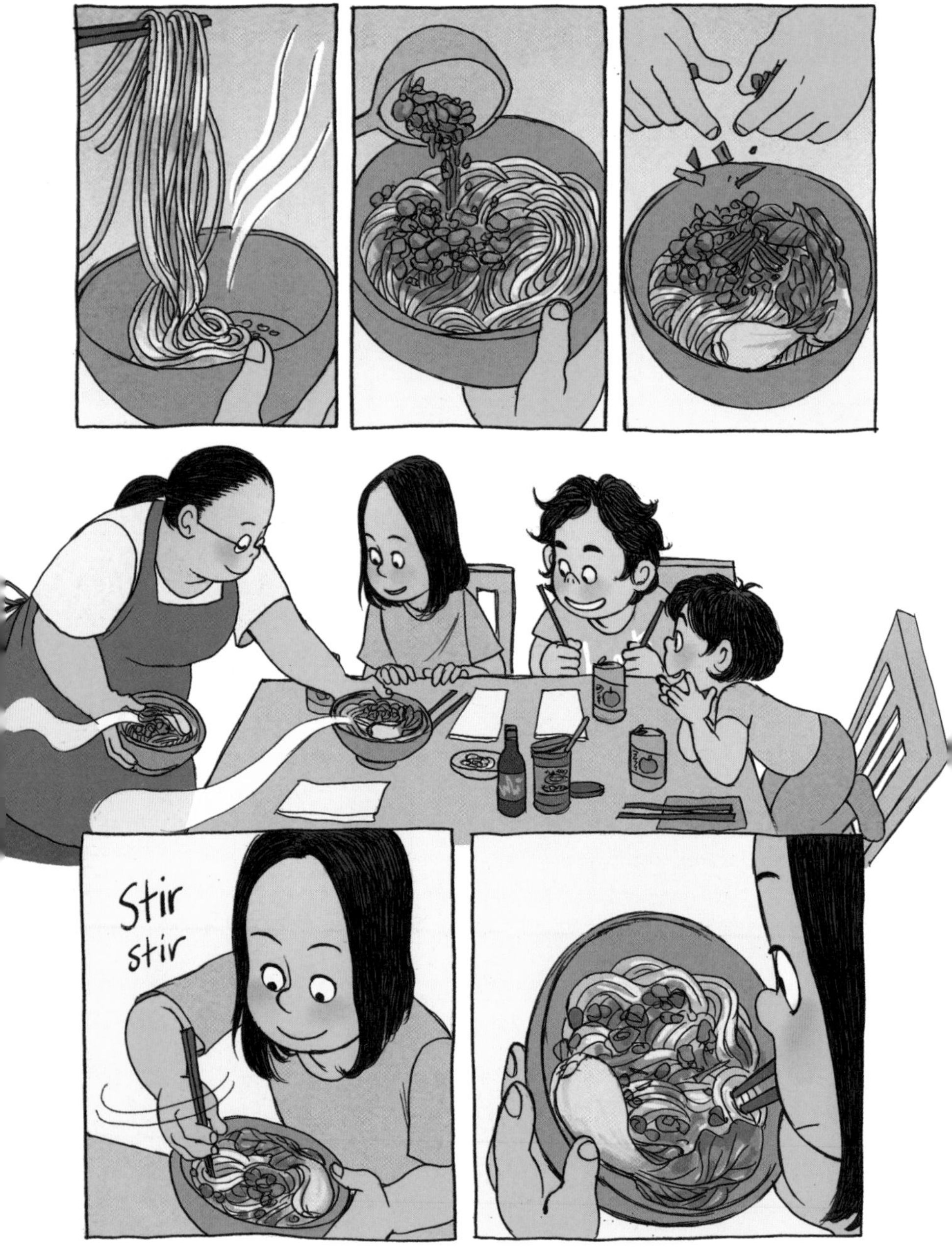
Stir
stir

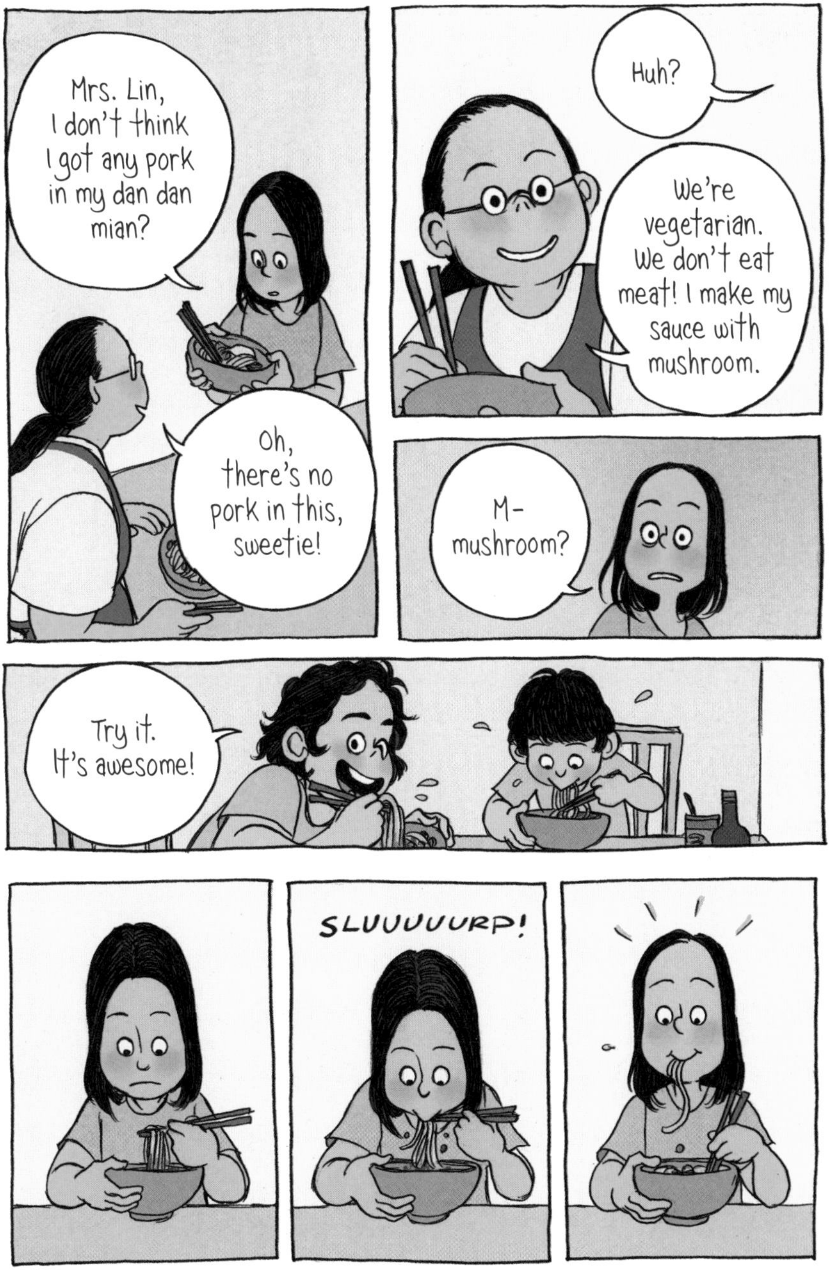
Mrs. Lin, I don't think I got any pork in my dan dan mian?
Oh, there's no pork in this, sweetie!
Huh?
We're vegetarian. We don't eat meat! I make my sauce with mushroom.
M-mushroom?
Try it. It's awesome!
SLUUUUURP!

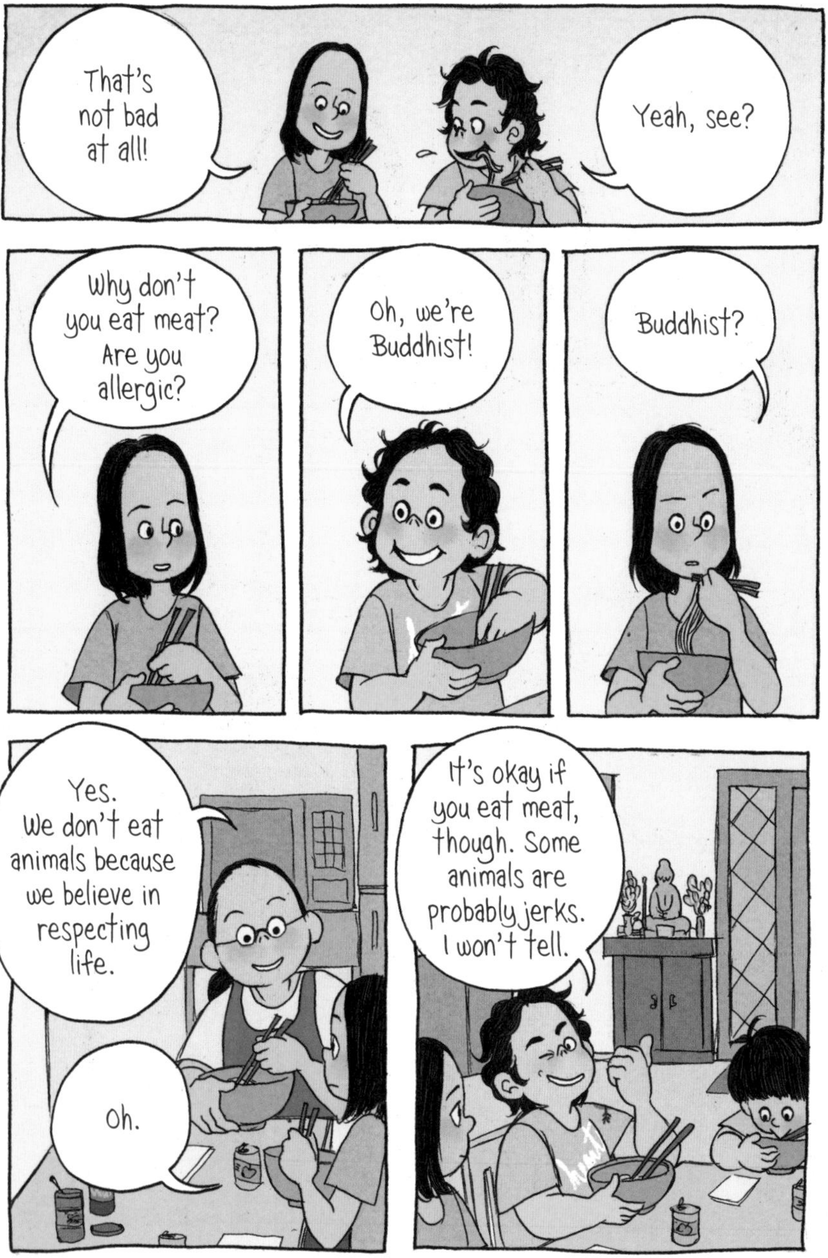
That's not bad at all!
Yeah, see?
Why don't you eat meat? Are you allergic?
Oh, we're Buddhist!
Buddhist?
Yes. We don't eat animals because we believe in respecting life.
Oh.
It's okay if you eat meat, though. Some animals are probably jerks. I won't tell.

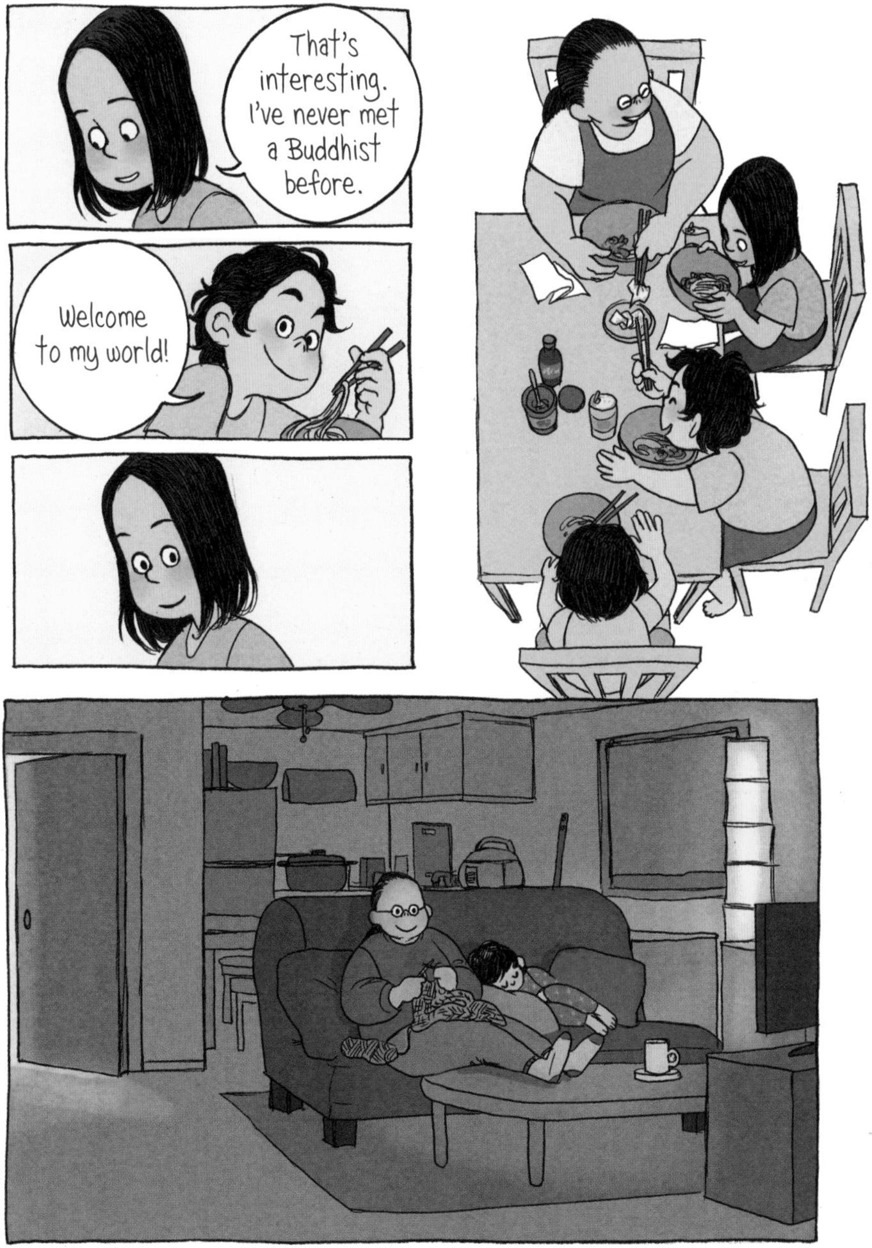
That's interesting. I've never met a Buddhist before.
Welcome to my world!

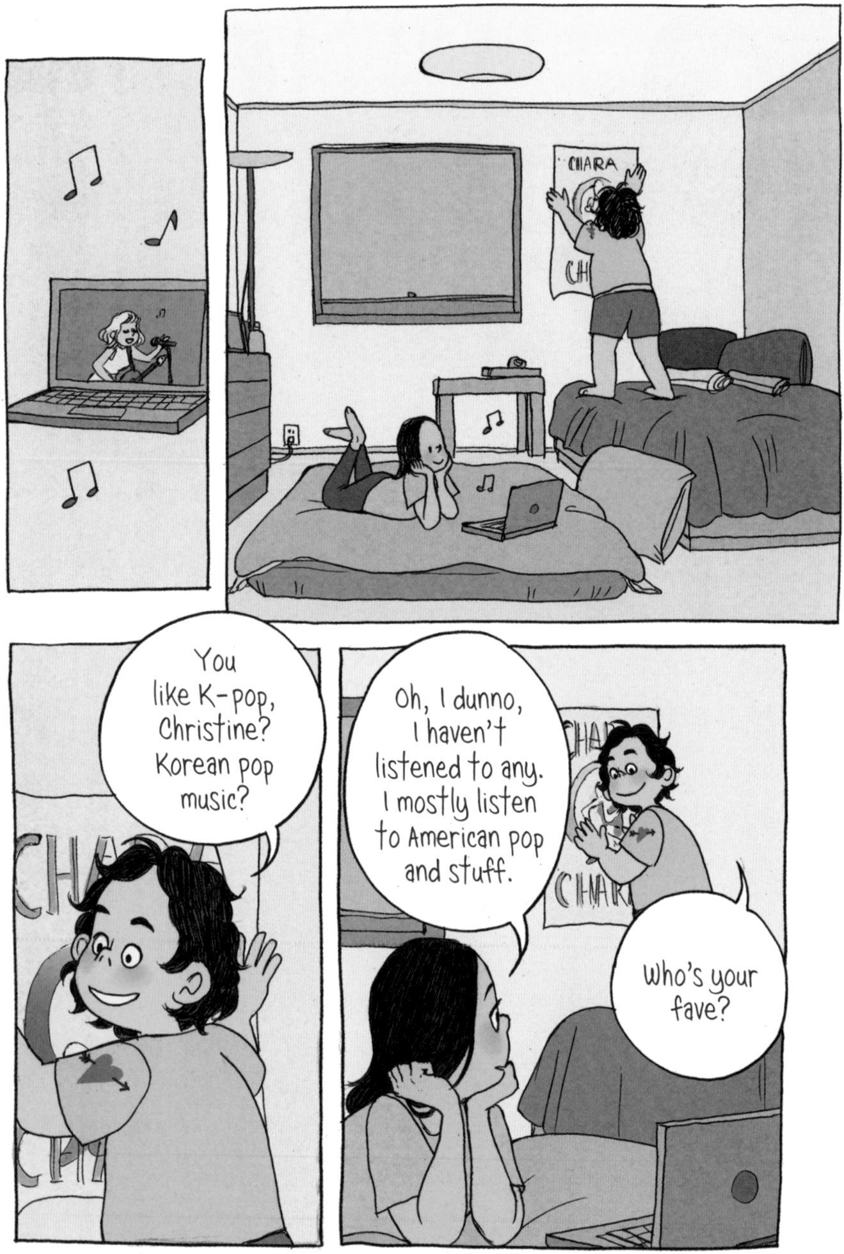
CHARA
You like K-pop, Christine? Korean pop music?
Oh, I dunno, I haven't listened to any. I mostly listen to American pop and stuff.
Who's your fave?

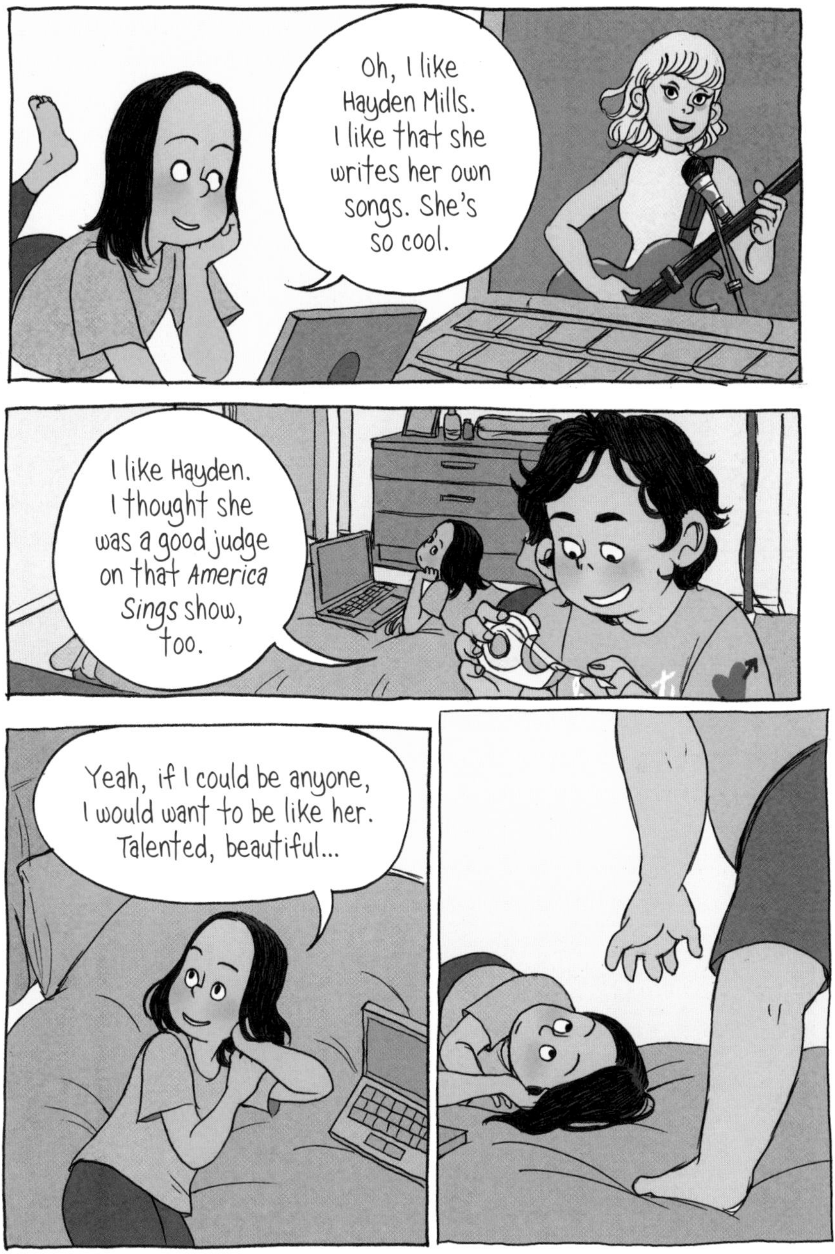
Oh, I like Hayden Mills. I like that she writes her own songs. She's so cool.
I like Hayden. I thought she was a good judge on that *America Sings* show, too.
Yeah, if I could be anyone, I would want to be like her. Talented, beautiful...

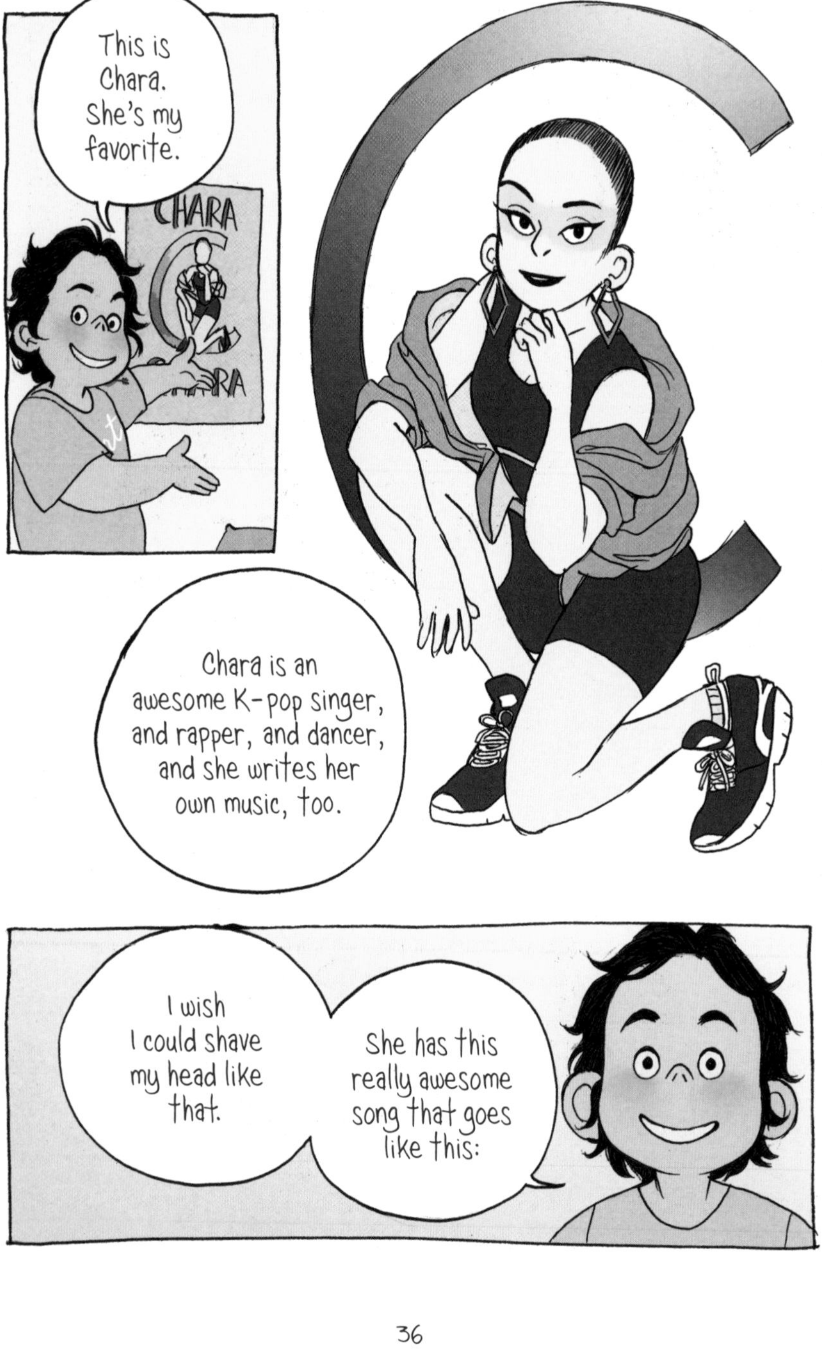
This is Chara. She's my favorite.
CHARA
Chara is an awesome K-pop singer, and rapper, and dancer, and she writes her own music, too.
I wish I could shave my head like that.
She has this really awesome song that goes like this:

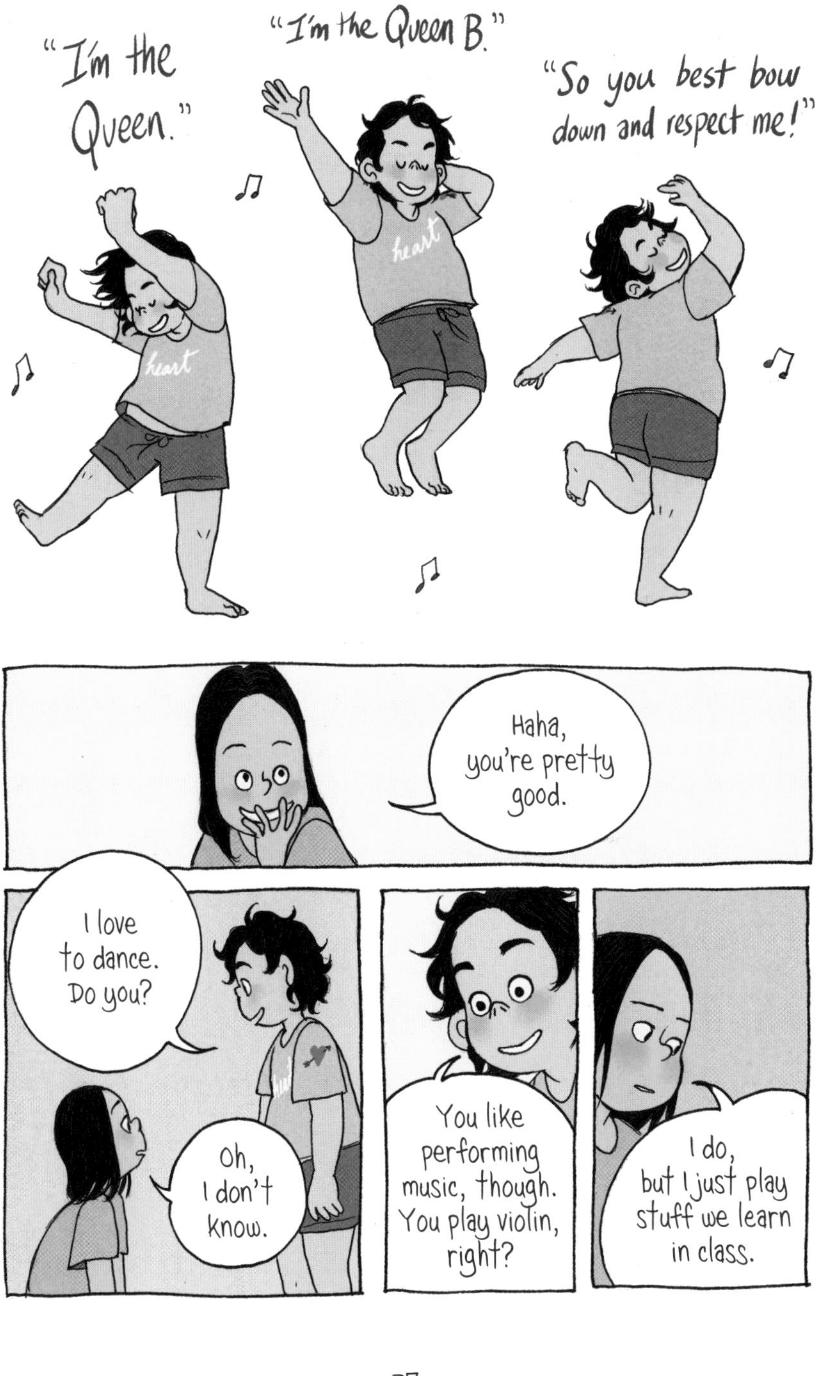
"I'm the Queen."
"I'm the Queen B."
"So you best bow down and respect me!"
Haha, you're pretty good.
I love to dance. Do you?
Oh, I don't know.
You like performing music, though. You play violin, right?
I do, but I just play stuff we learn in class.

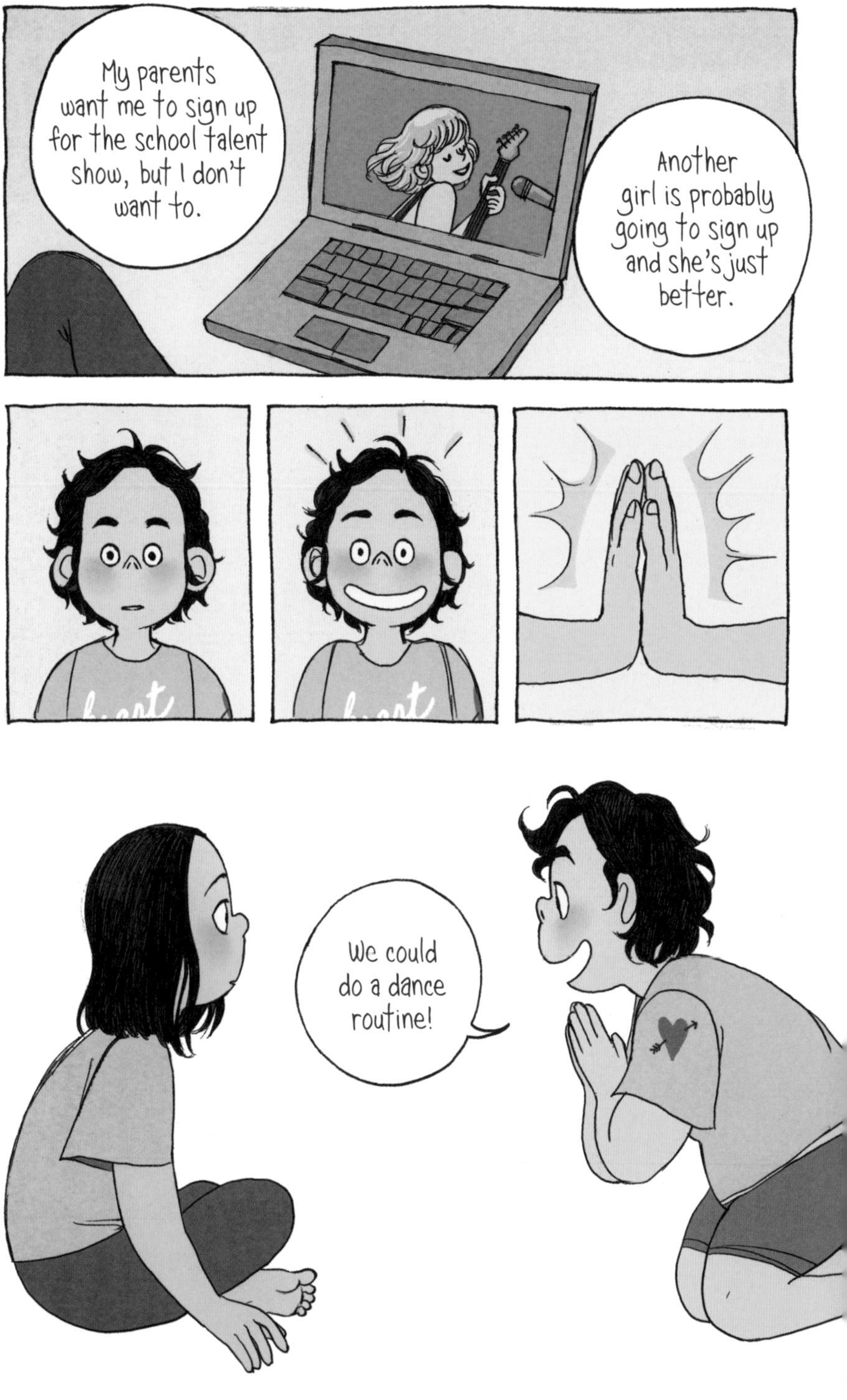
My parents want me to sign up for the school talent show, but I don't want to.
Another girl is probably going to sign up and she's just better.
We could do a dance routine!

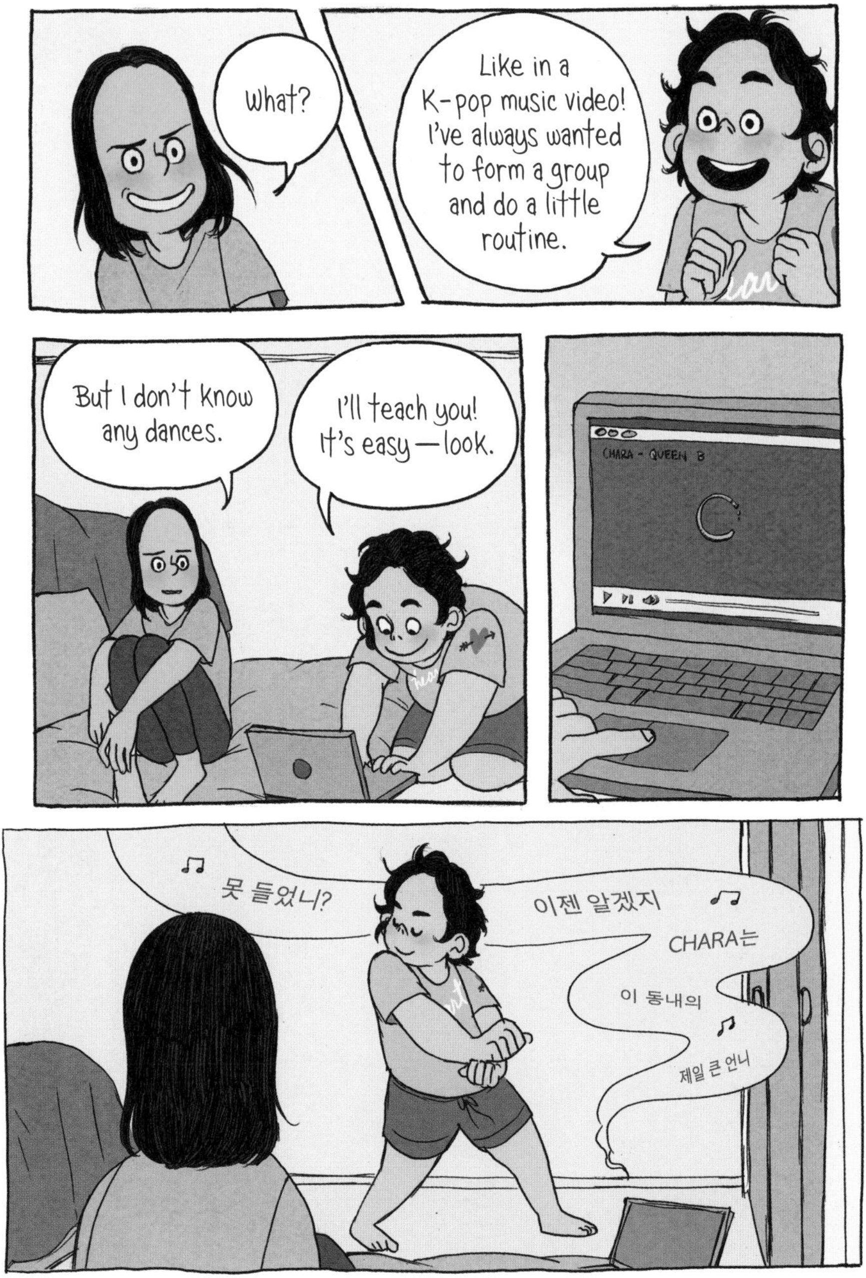
What?
Like in a K-pop music video! I've always wanted to form a group and do a little routine.
But I don't know any dances.
I'll teach you! It's easy—look.
CHARA - QUEEN B
못 들었니?
이젠 알겠지
CHARA는
이 동네의
제일 큰 언니

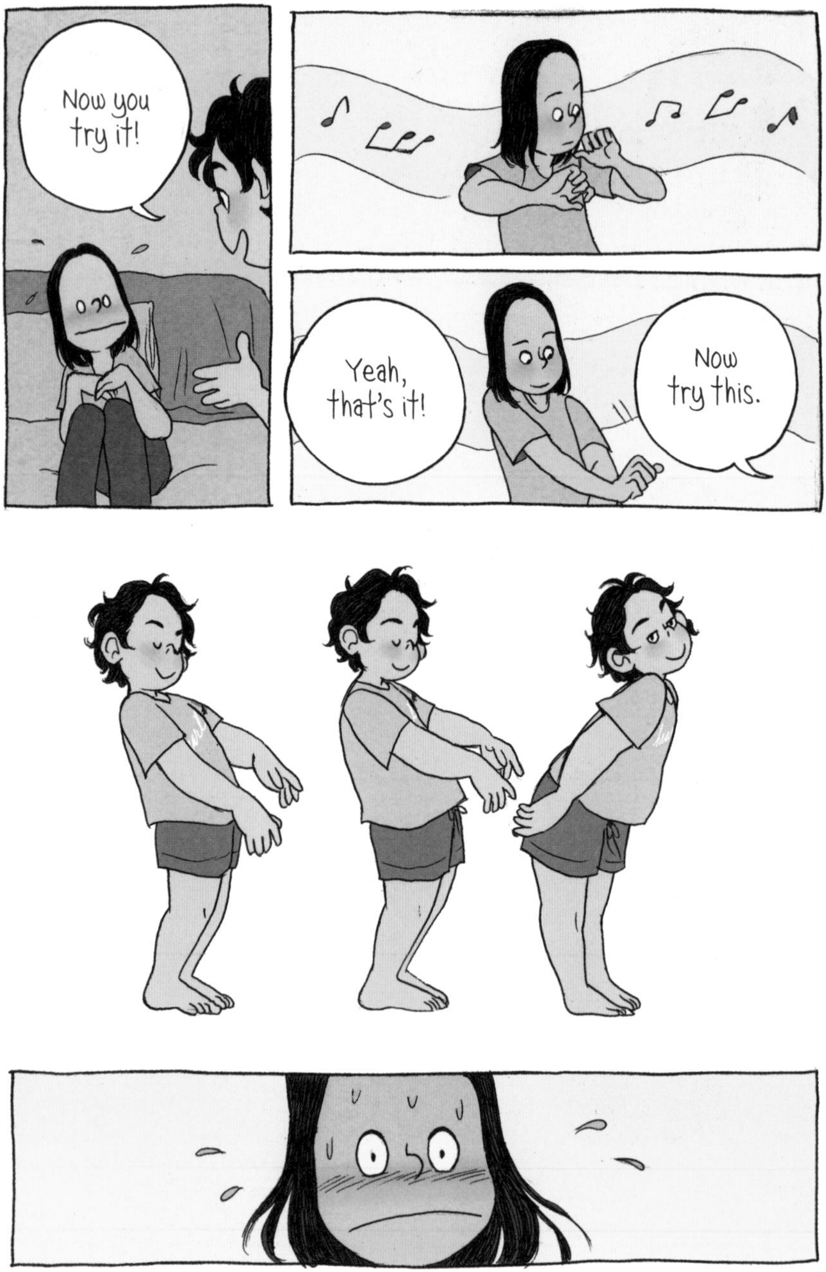
Now you try it!
Yeah, that's it!
Now try this.

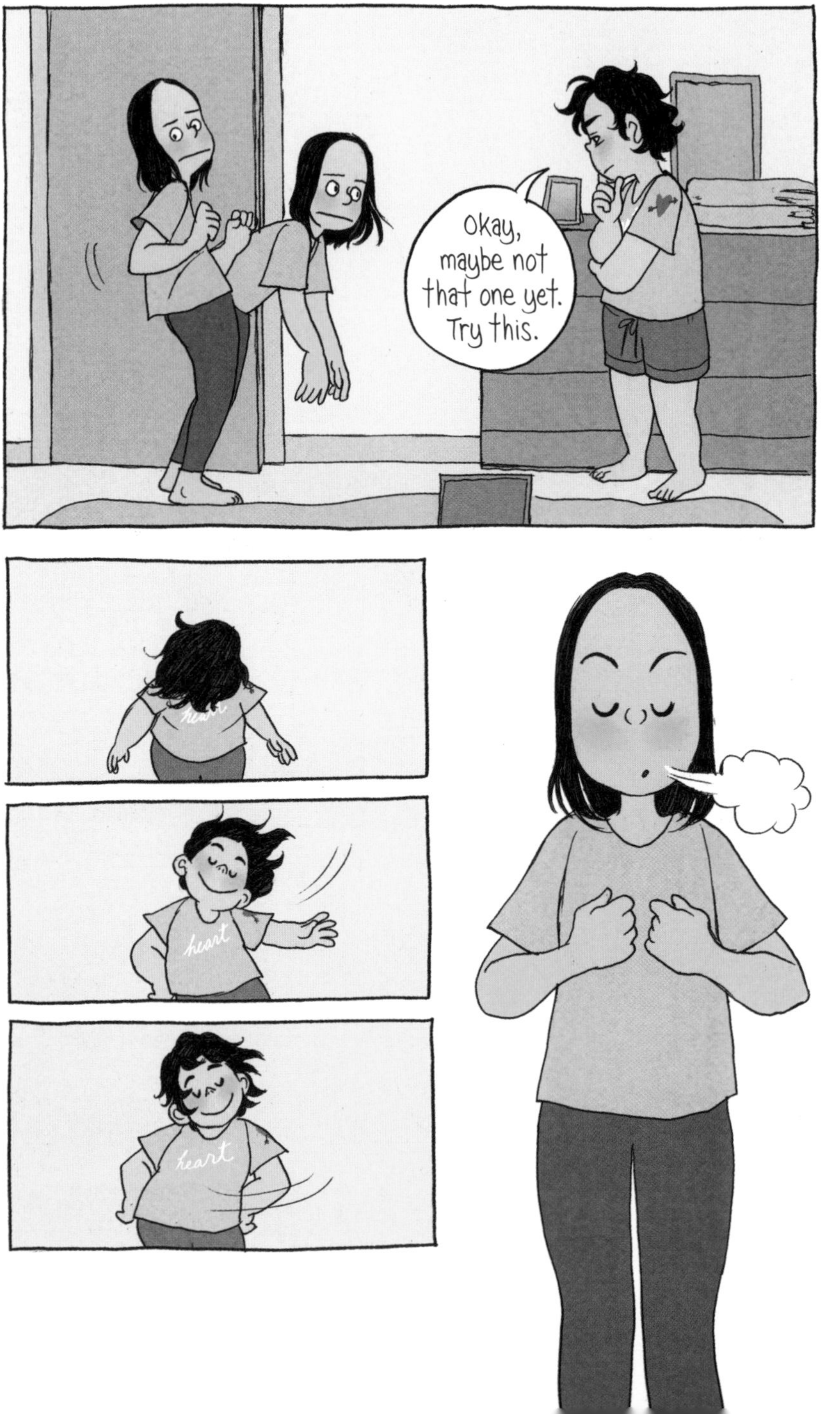
Okay, maybe not that one yet. Try this.

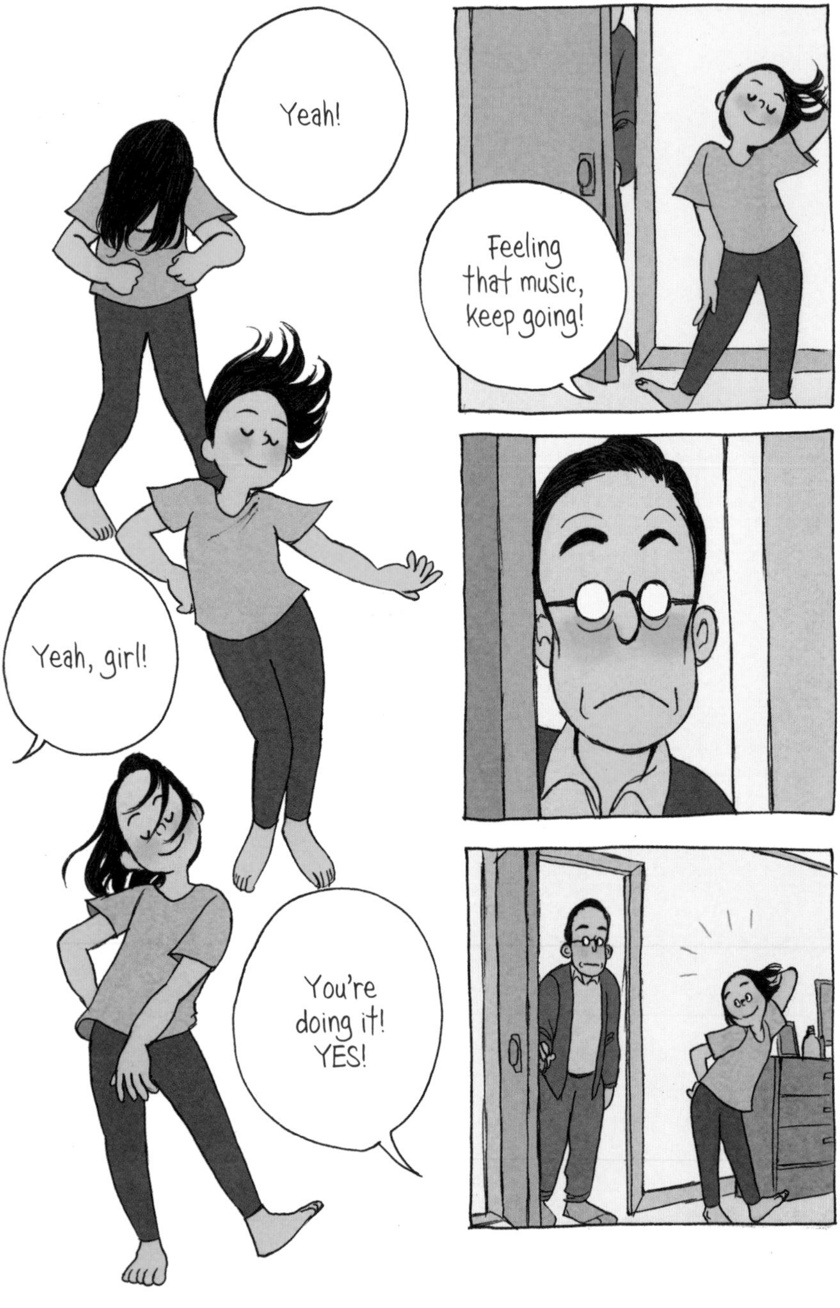
Yeah!
Feeling that music, keep going!
Yeah, girl!
You're doing it! YES!

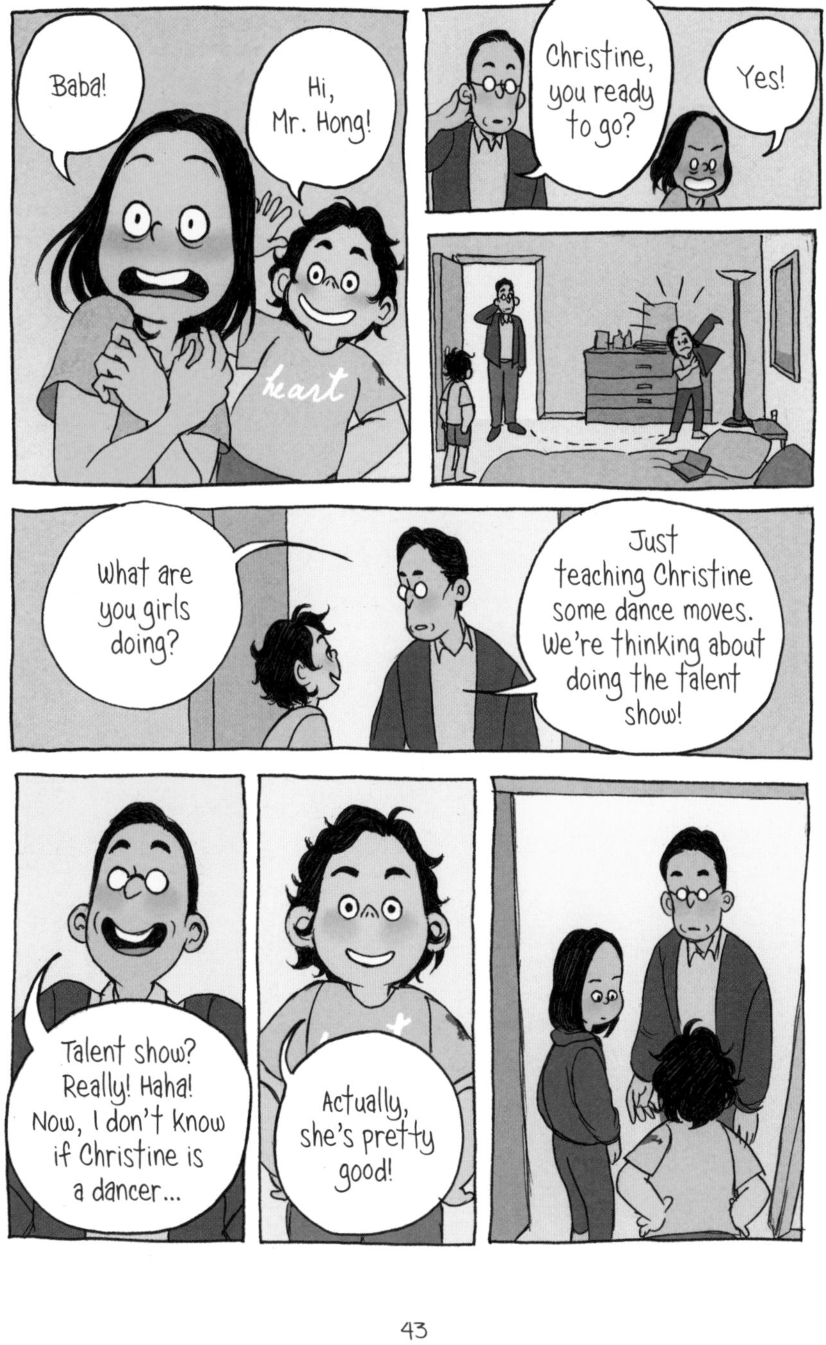
Baba!
Hi, Mr. Hong!
heart
Christine, you ready to go?
Yes!
What are you girls doing?
Just teaching Christine some dance moves. We're thinking about doing the talent show!
Talent show? Really! Haha! Now, I don't know if Christine is a dancer...
Actually, she's pretty good!

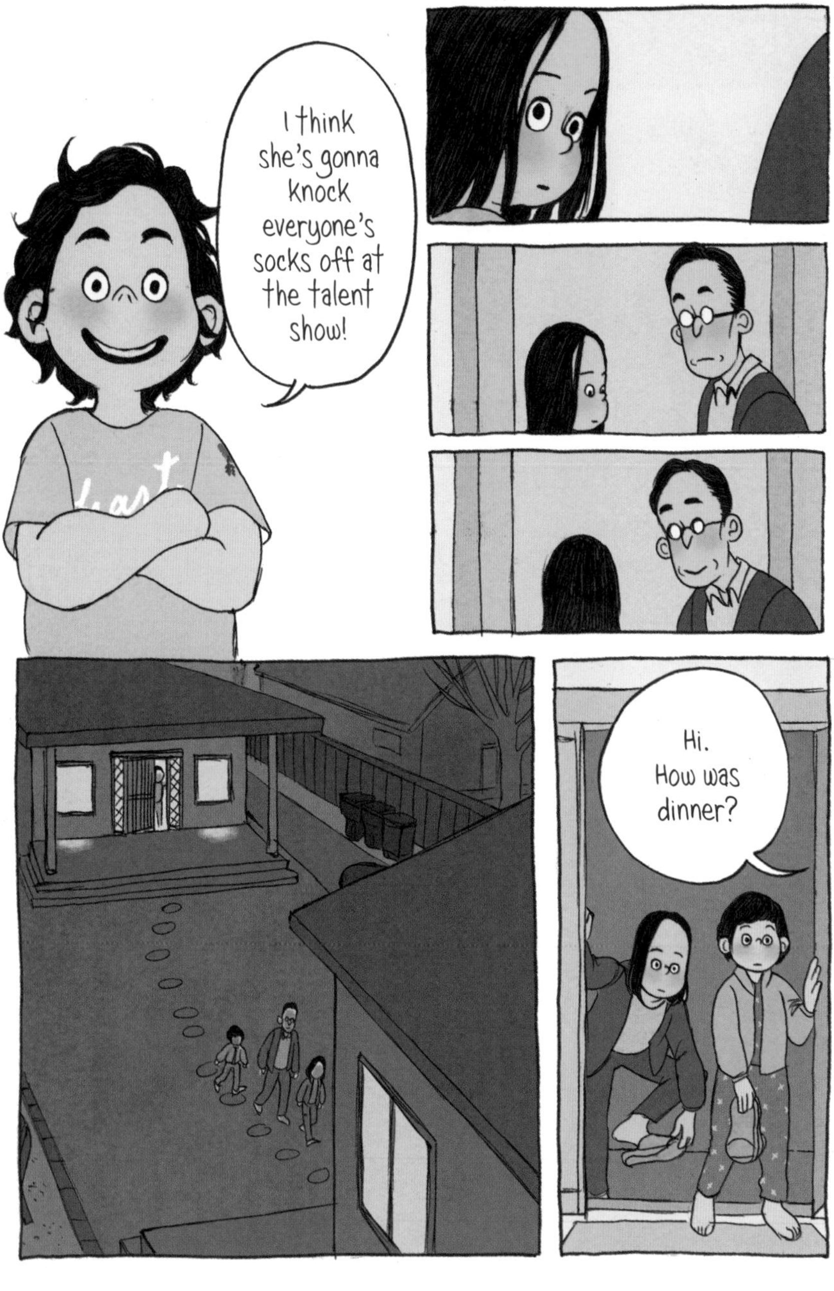
I think she's gonna knock everyone's socks off at the talent show!
Hi. How was dinner?

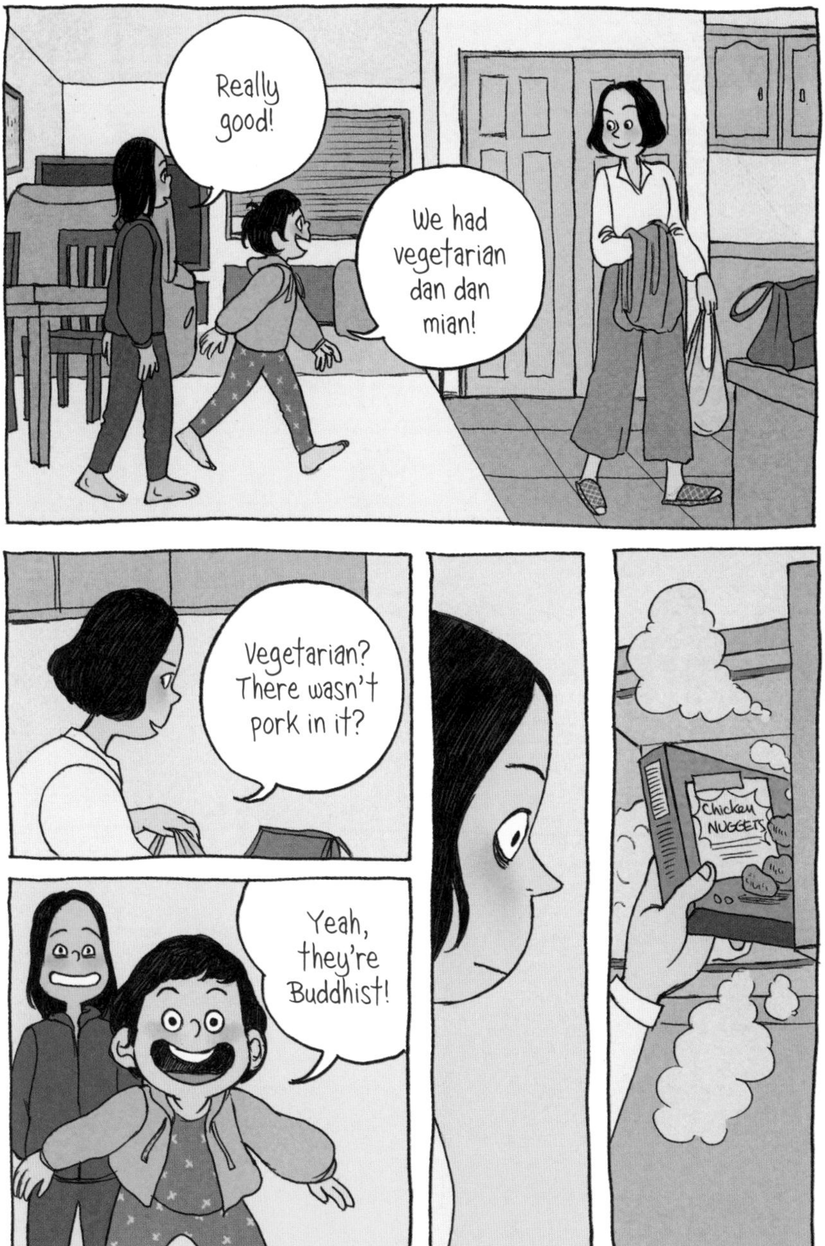
Really good!
We had vegetarian dan dan mian!
Vegetarian? There wasn't pork in it?
Yeah, they're Buddhist!
Chicken NUGGETS

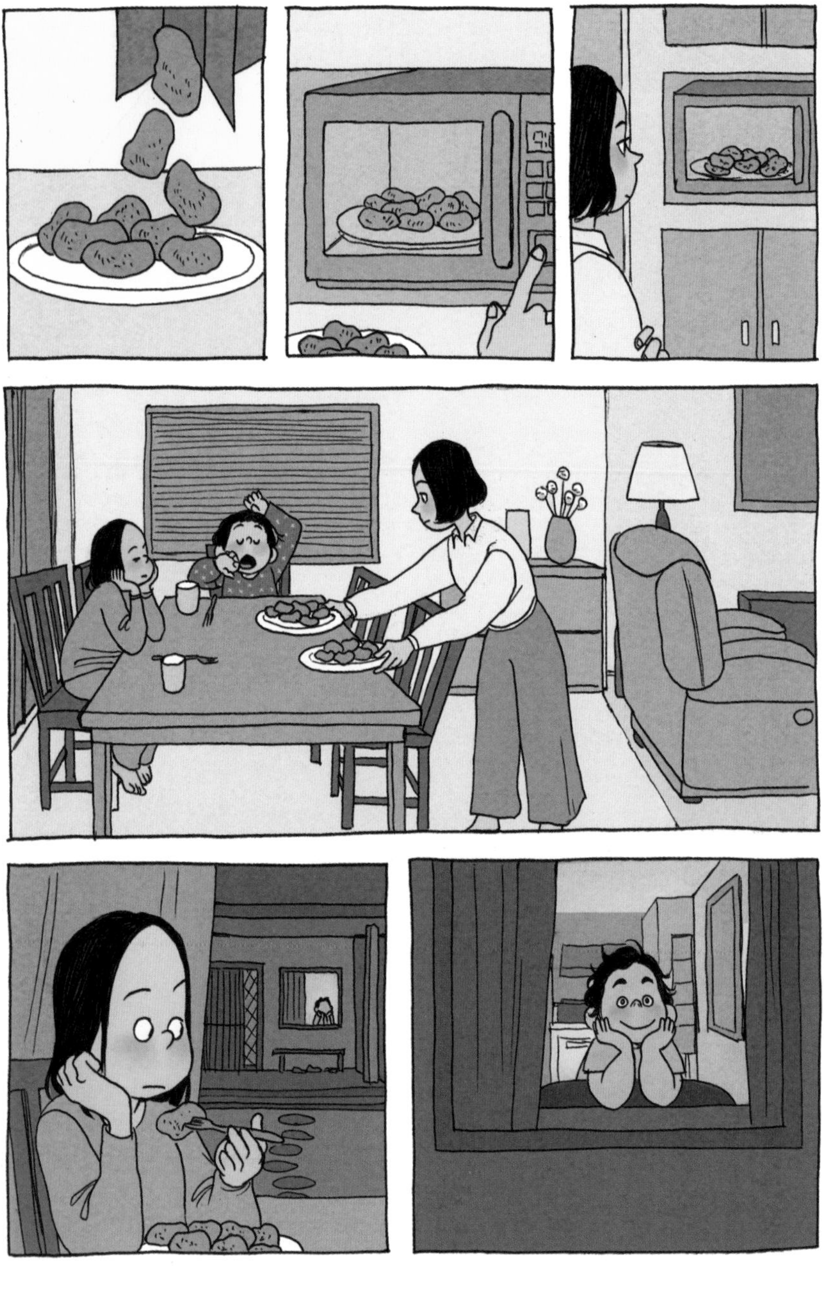

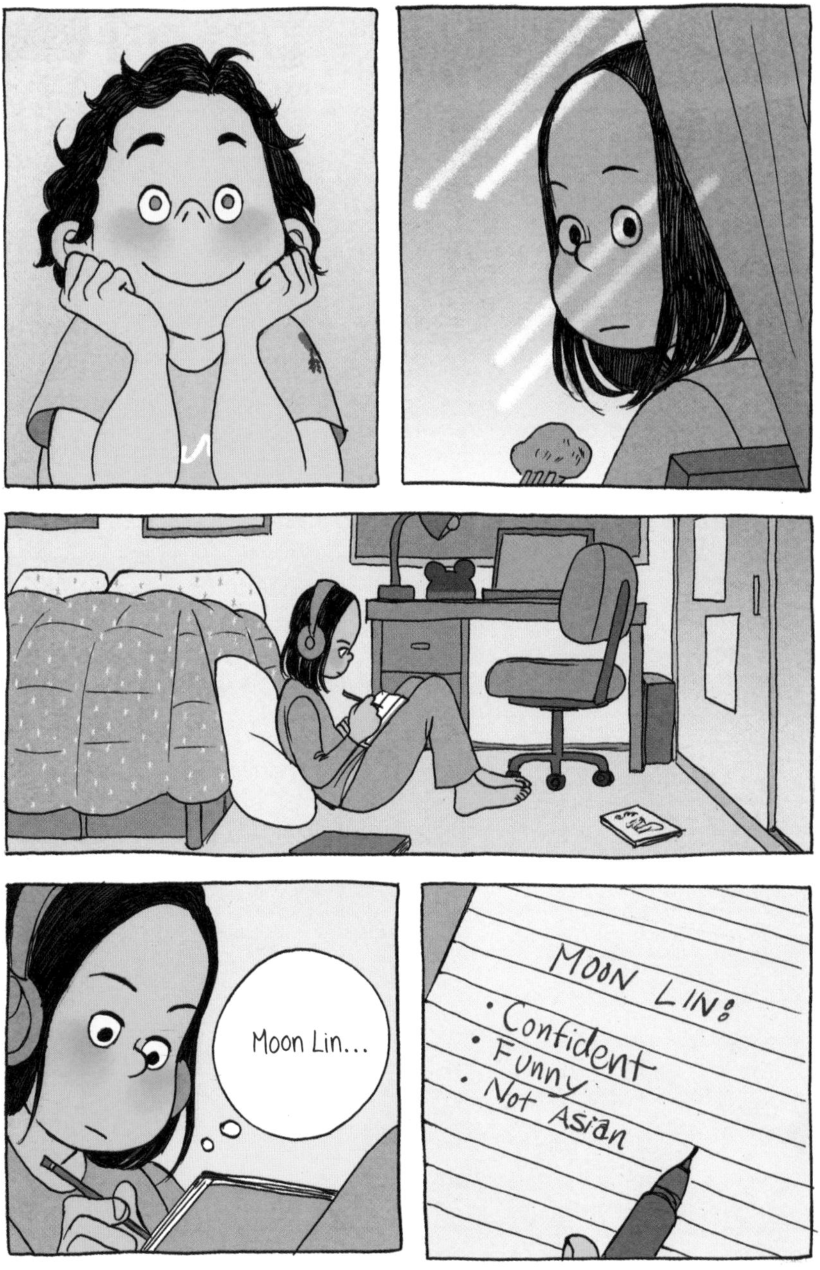
Moon Lin...
MOON LIN:
• Confident
• Funny
• Not Asian

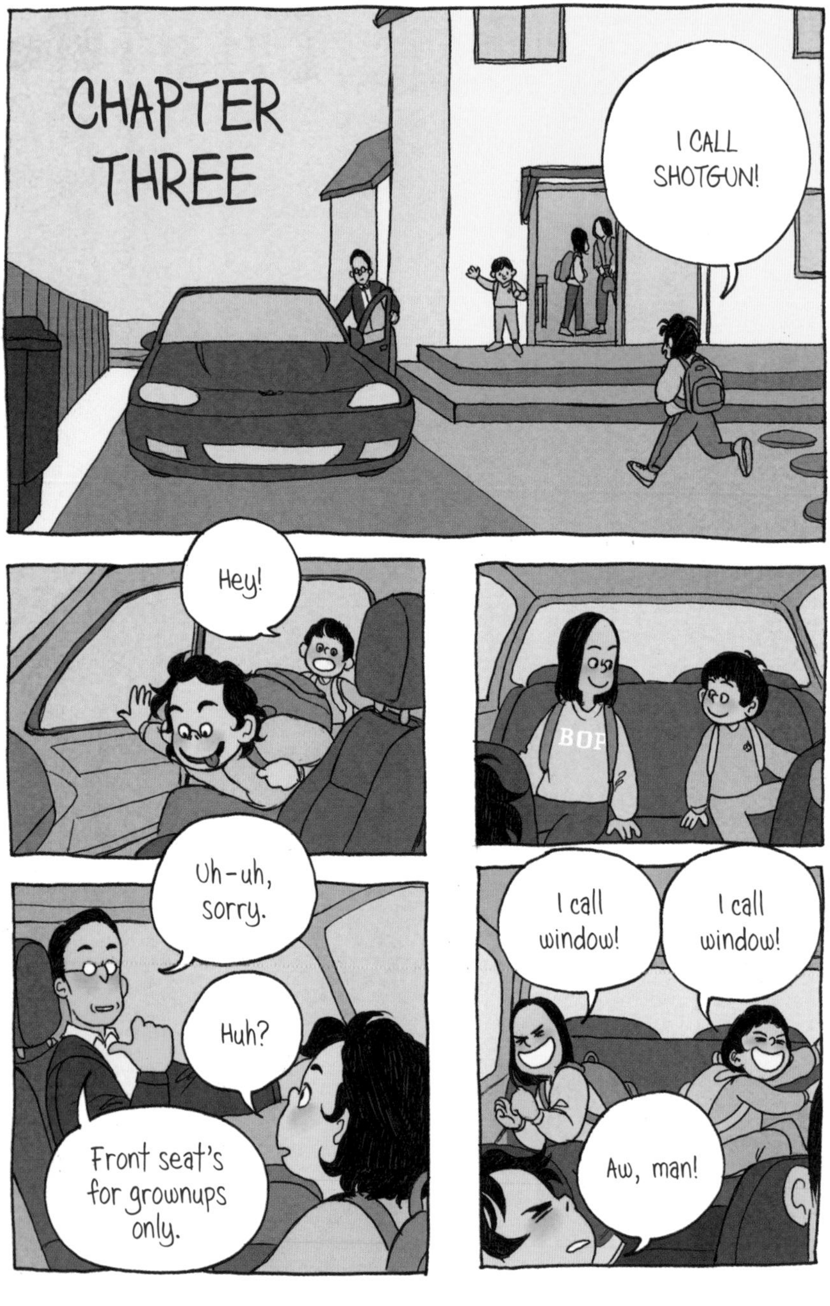
CHAPTER THREE
I CALL SHOTGUN!
Hey!
BOP
Uh-uh, sorry.
Huh?
Front seat's for grownups only.
I call window!
I call window!
Aw, man!

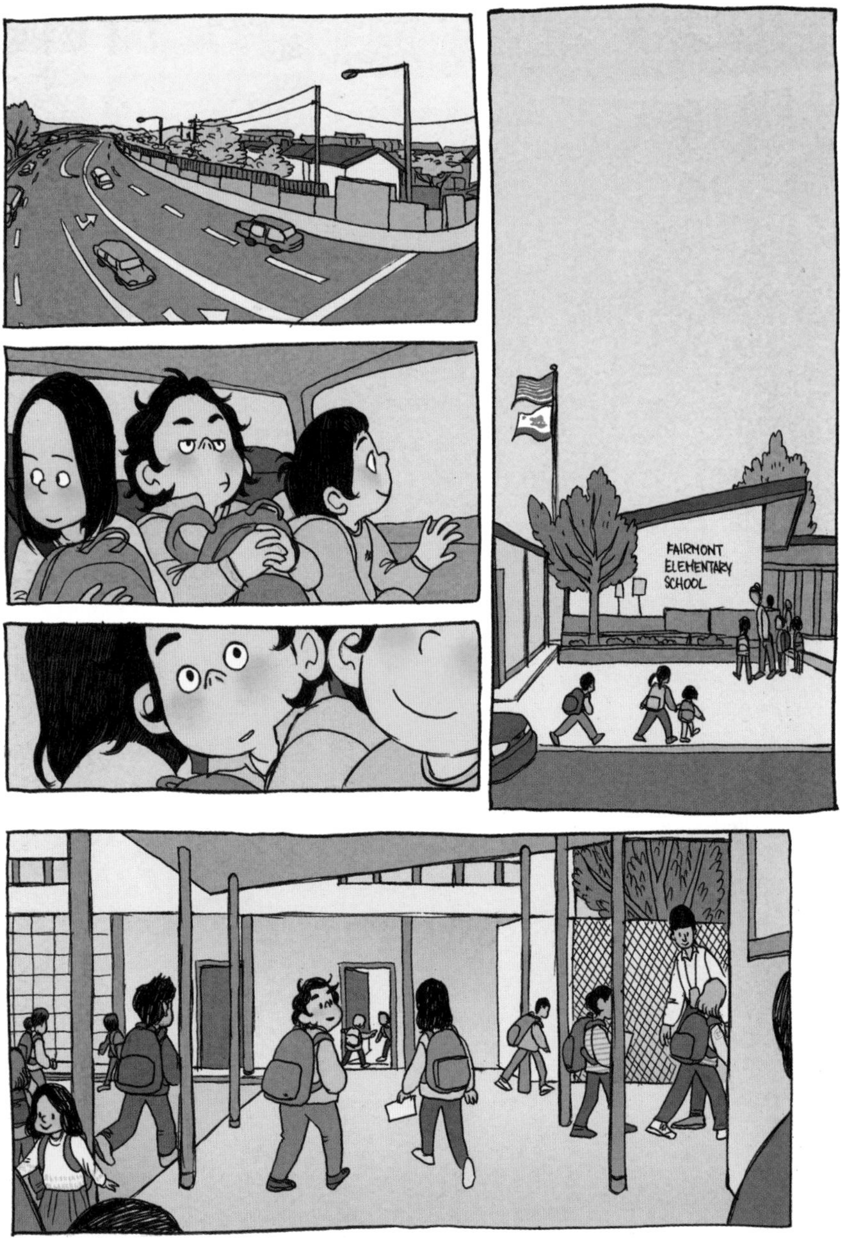
FAIRMONT
ELEMENTARY
SCHOOL

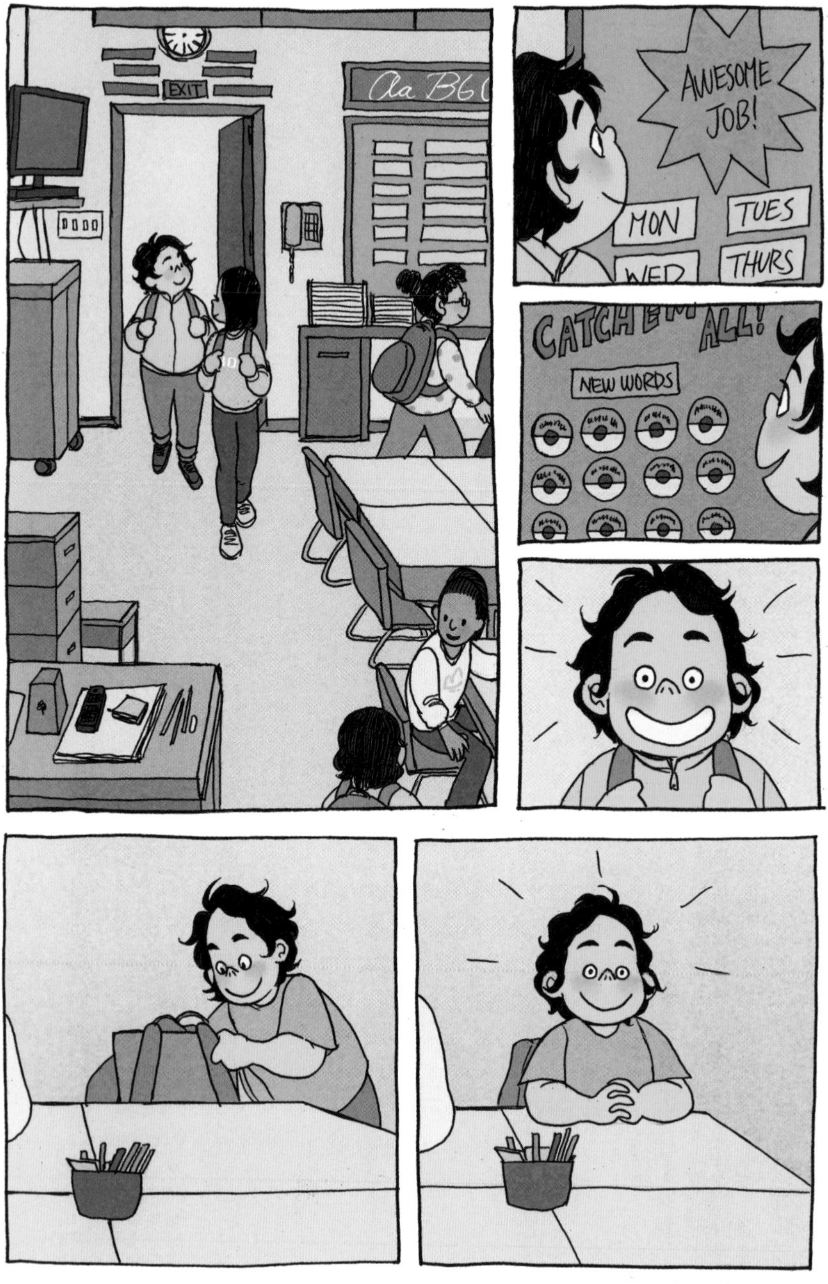
EXIT
Aa Bb C
AWESOME JOB!
MON
TUES
WED
THURS
CATCH 'EM ALL!
NEW WORDS

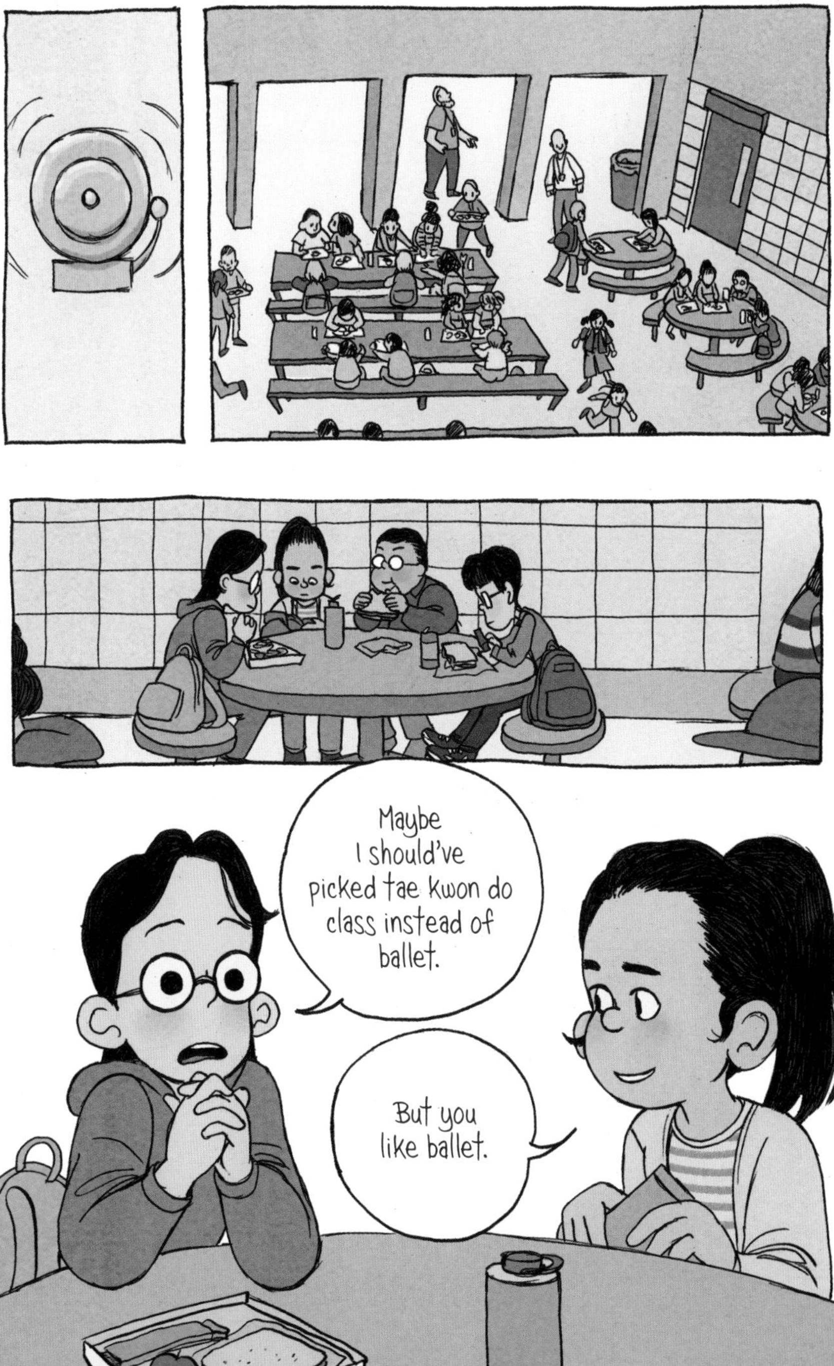
Maybe I should've picked tae kwon do class instead of ballet.
But you like ballet.

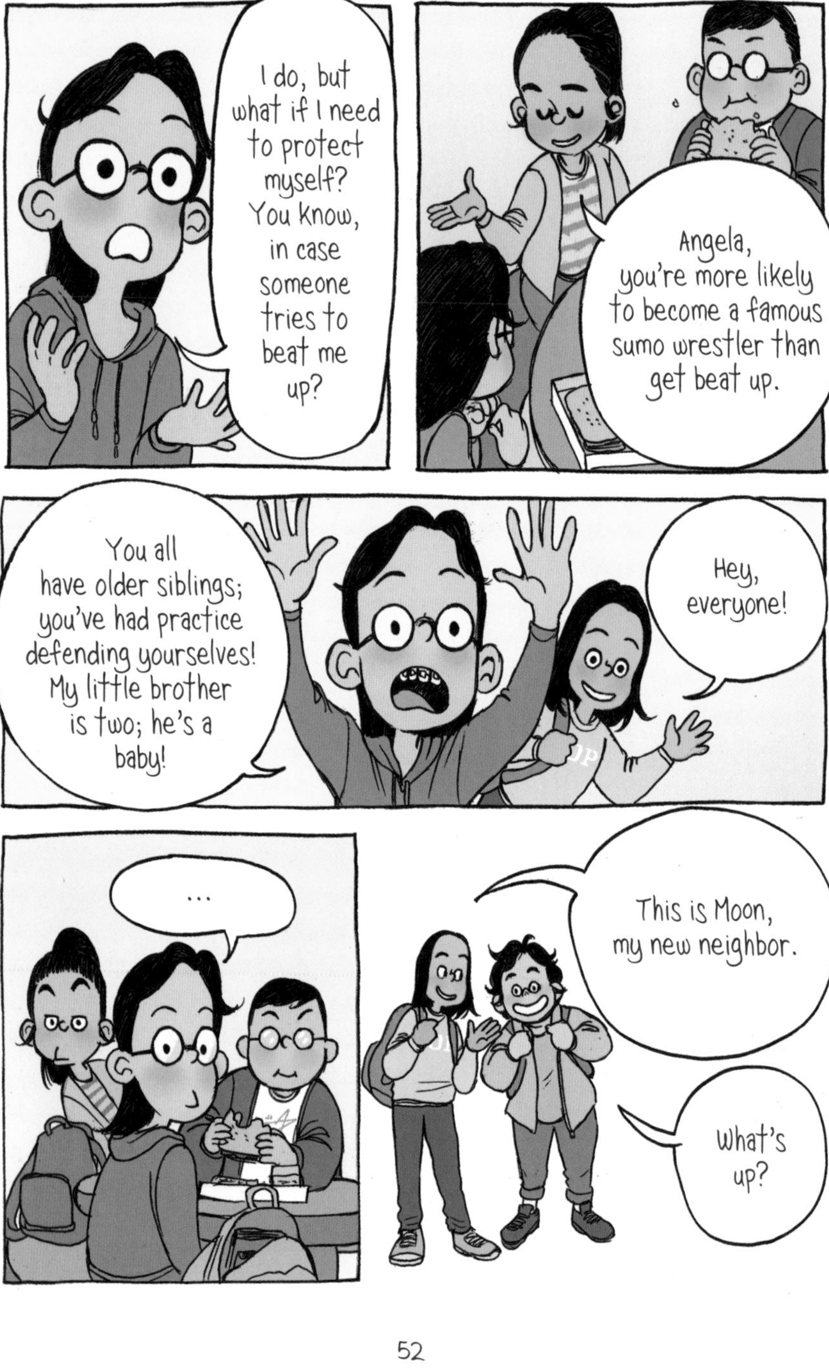
I do, but what if I need to protect myself? You know, in case someone tries to beat me up?
Angela, you're more likely to become a famous sumo wrestler than get beat up.
You all have older siblings; you've had practice defending yourselves! My little brother is two; he's a baby!
Hey, everyone!
...
This is Moon, my new neighbor.
What's up?

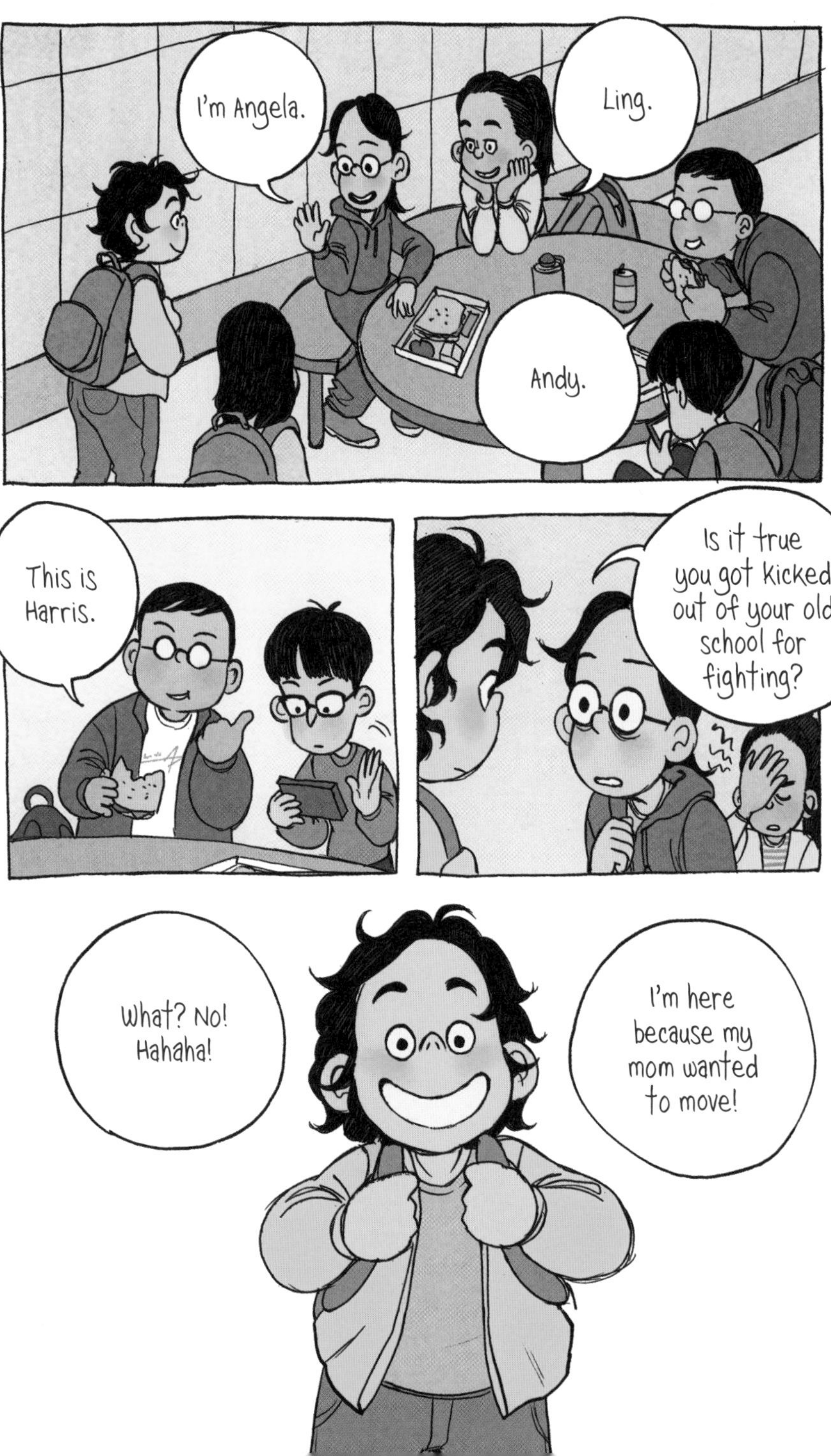
I'm Angela.
Ling.
Andy.
This is Harris.
Is it true you got kicked out of your old school for fighting?
What? No! Hahaha!
I'm here because my mom wanted to move!

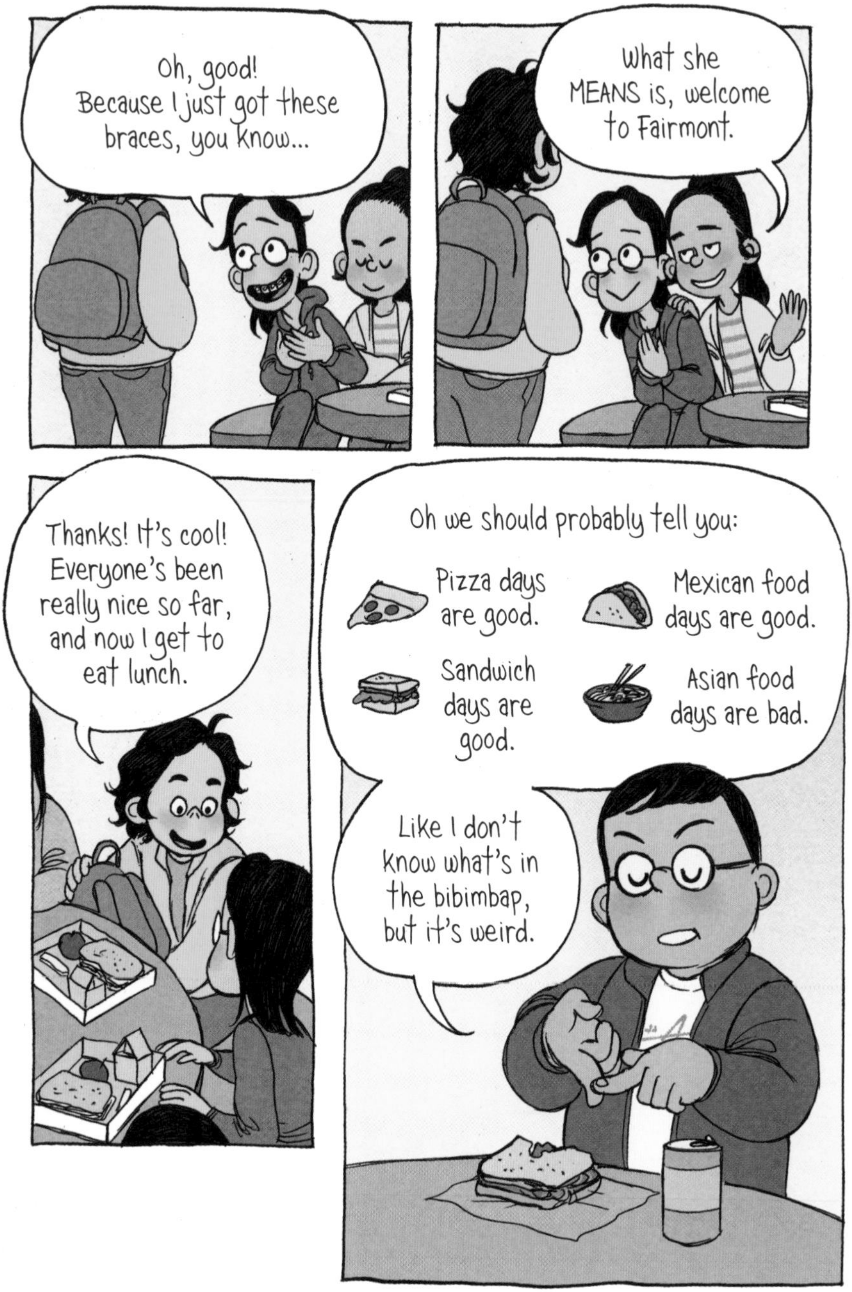
Oh, good! Because I just got these braces, you know...
What she MEANS is, welcome to Fairmont.
Thanks! It's cool! Everyone's been really nice so far, and now I get to eat lunch.
Oh we should probably tell you:
Pizza days are good.
Mexican food days are good.
Sandwich days are good.
Asian food days are bad.
Like I don't know what's in the bibimbap, but it's weird.

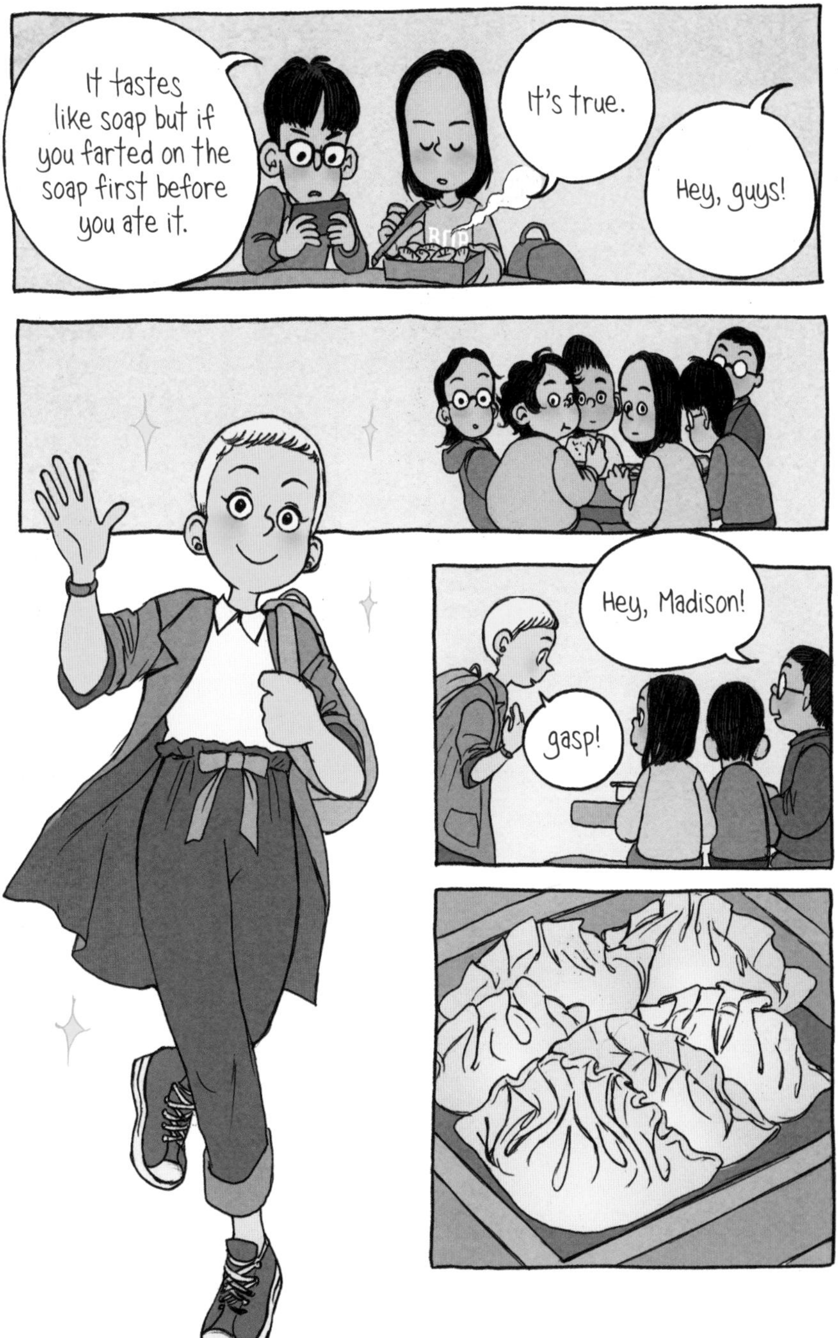
It tastes like soap but if you farted on the soap first before you ate it.
It's true.
Hey, guys!
Hey, Madison!
gasp!

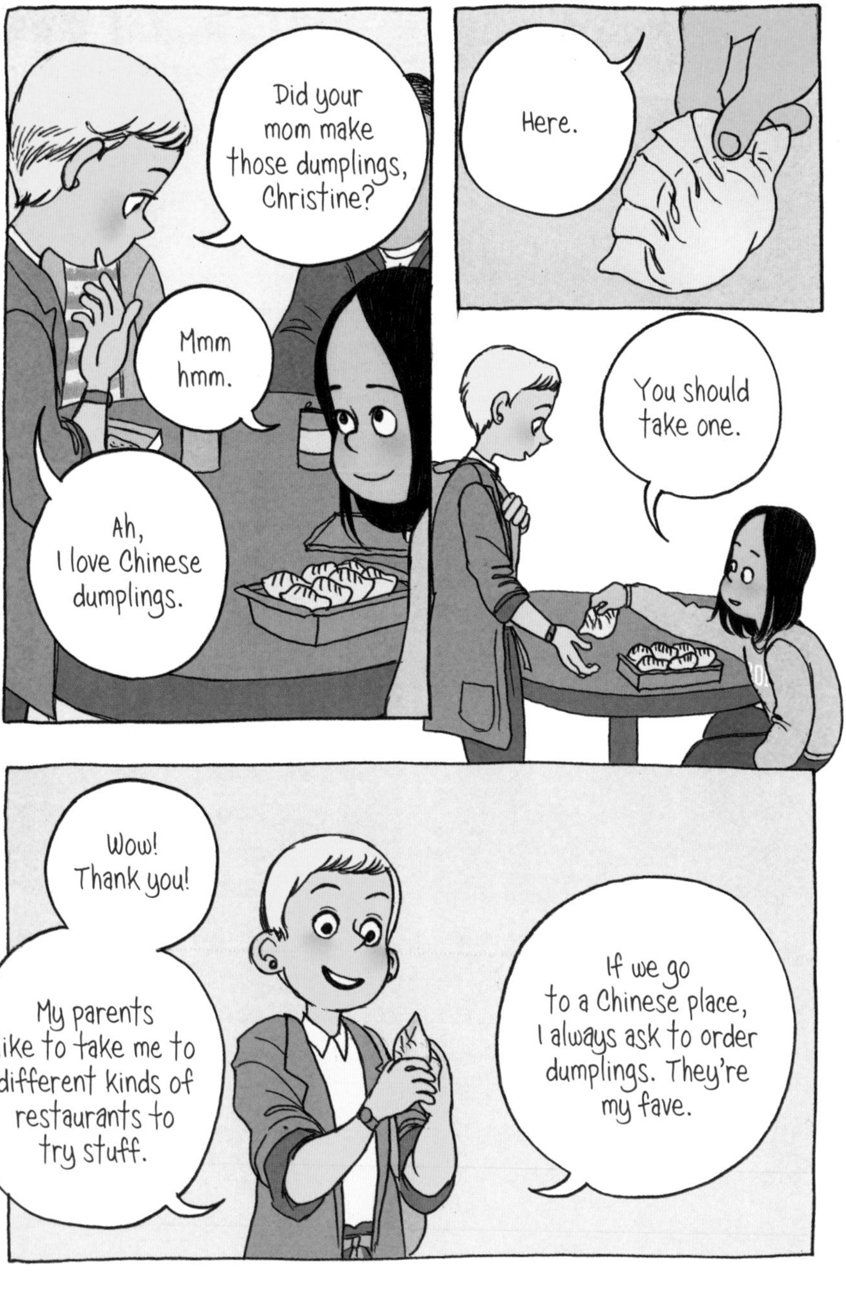
Did your mom make those dumplings, Christine?
Mmm hmm.
Ah, I love Chinese dumplings.
Here.
You should take one.
Wow! Thank you!
My parents like to take me to different kinds of restaurants to try stuff.
If we go to a Chinese place, I always ask to order dumplings. They're my fave.

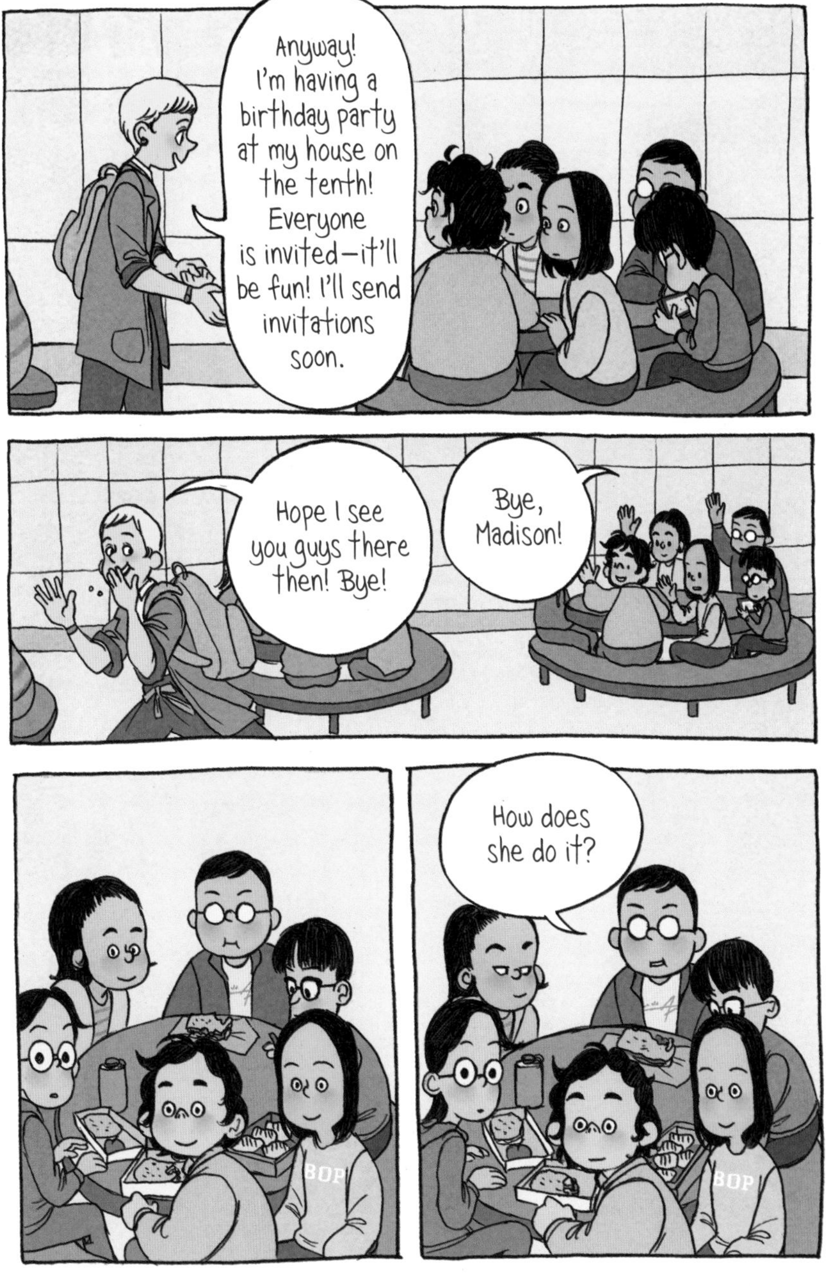
Anyway! I'm having a birthday party at my house on the tenth! Everyone is invited—it'll be fun! I'll send invitations soon.
Hope I see you guys there then! Bye!
Bye, Madison!
BOP
How does she do it?
BOP

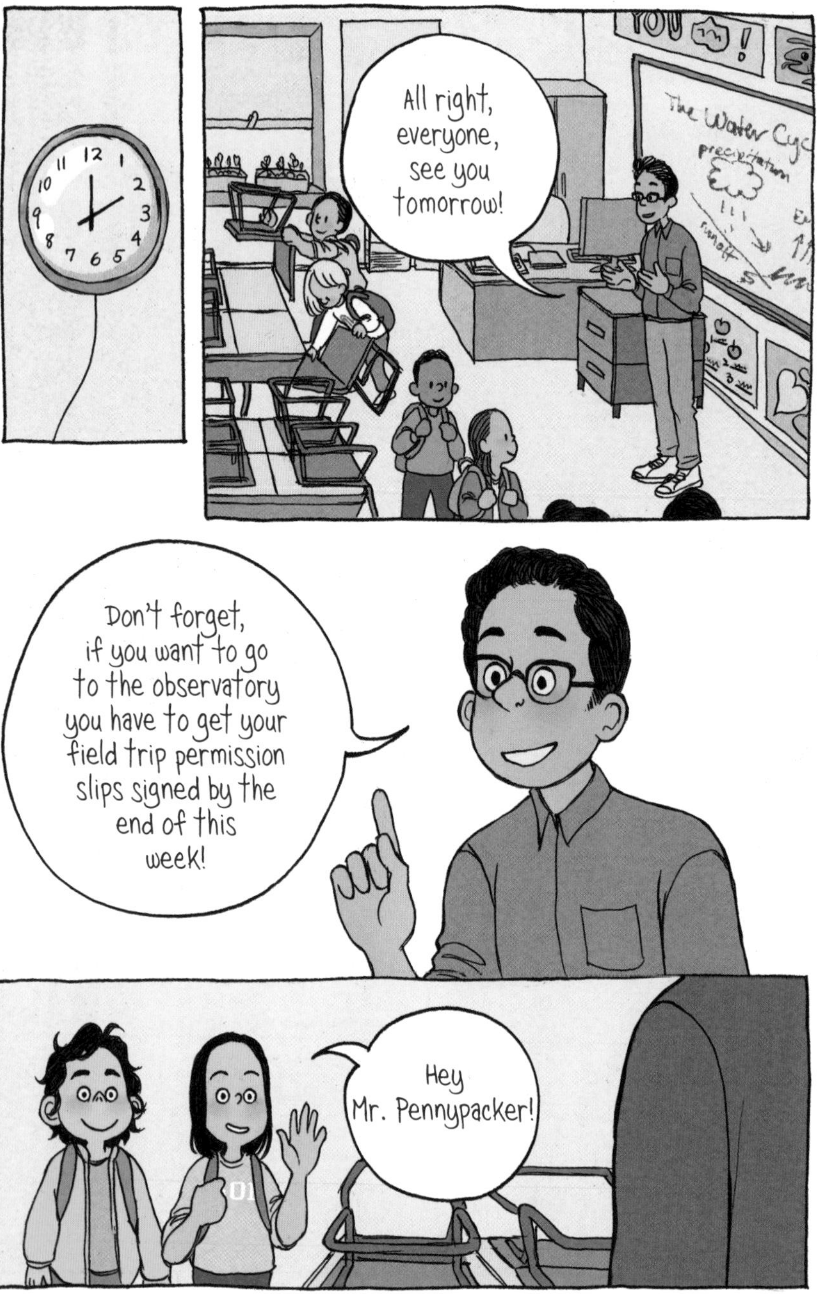
All right, everyone, see you tomorrow!
Don't forget, if you want to go to the observatory you have to get your field trip permission slips signed by the end of this week!
Hey Mr. Pennypacker!

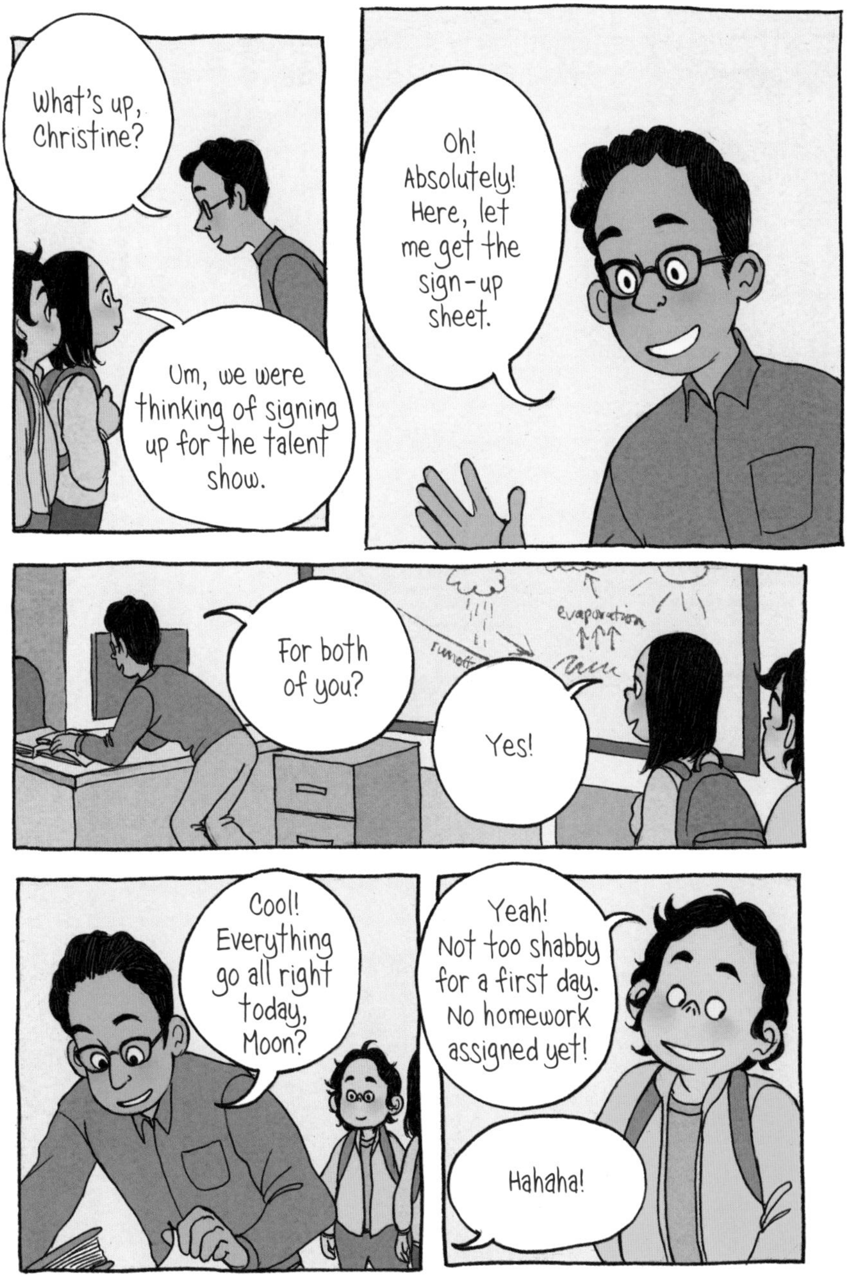
What's up, Christine?
Um, we were thinking of signing up for the talent show.
Oh! Absolutely! Here, let me get the sign-up sheet.
evaporation
runoff
For both of you?
Yes!
Cool! Everything go all right today, Moon?
Yeah! Not too shabby for a first day. No homework assigned yet!
Hahaha!

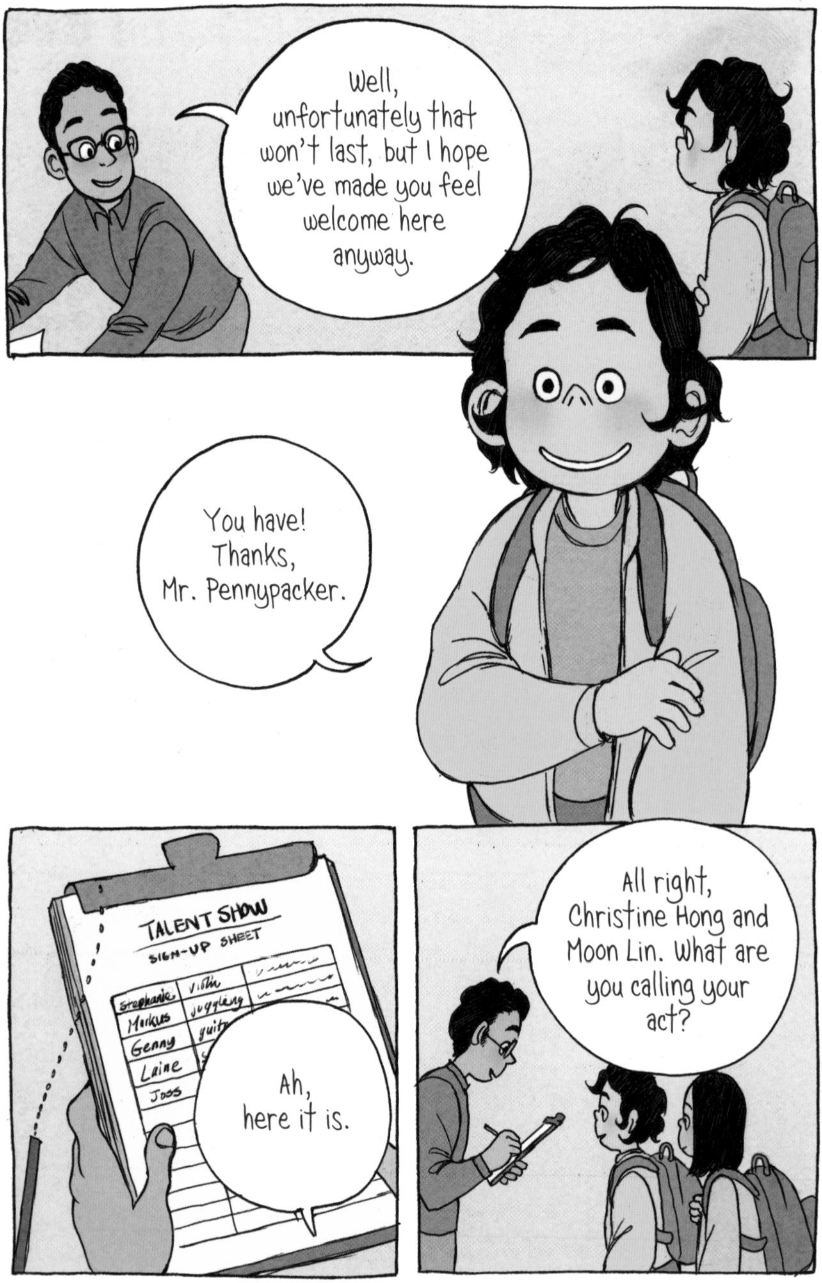
Well, unfortunately that won't last, but I hope we've made you feel welcome here anyway.
You have! Thanks, Mr. Pennypacker.
TALENT SHOW
SIGN-UP SHEET
Ah, here it is.
All right, Christine Hong and Moon Lin. What are you calling your act?

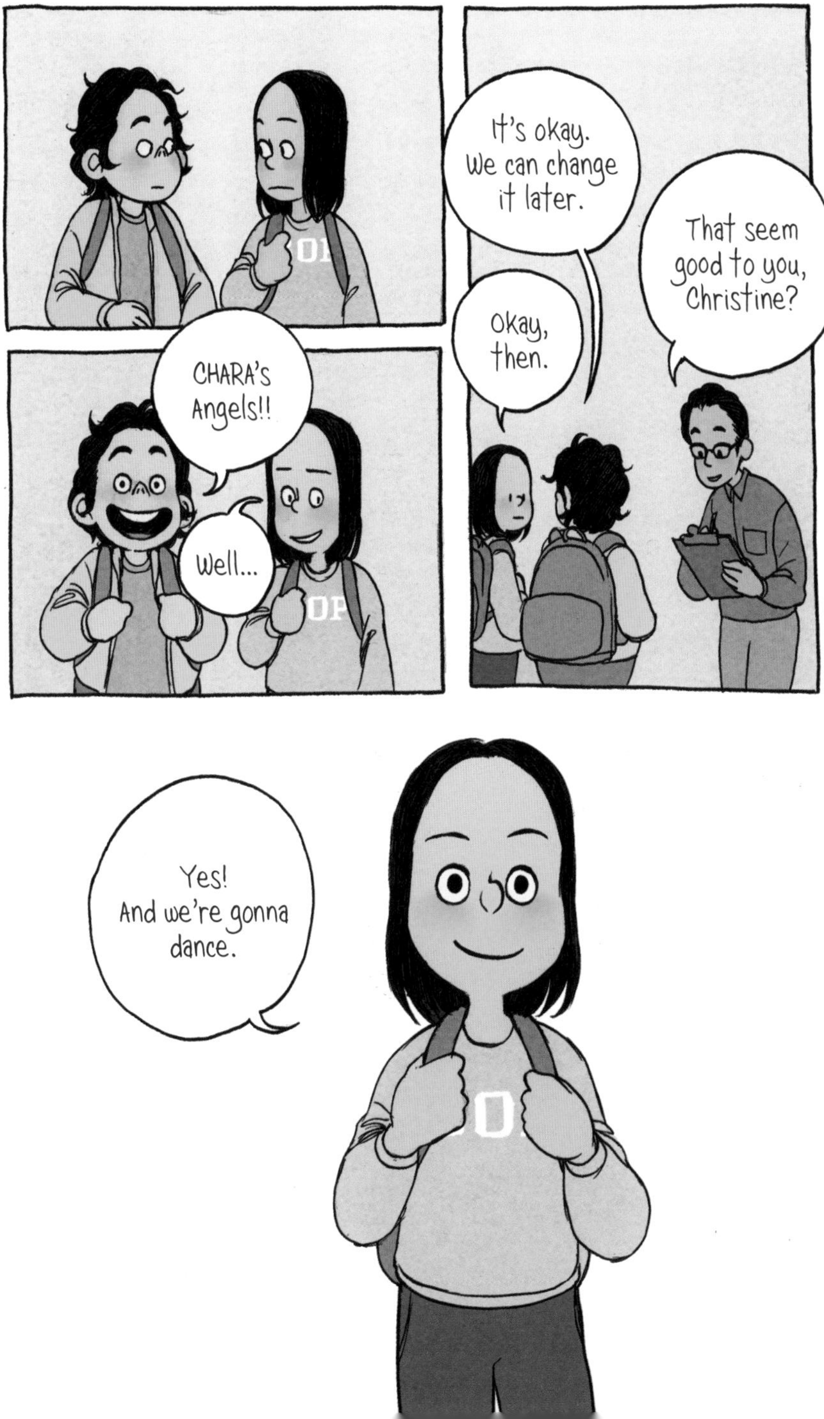
CHARA's Angels!!
Well...
It's okay. We can change it later.
Okay, then.
That seem good to you, Christine?
Yes! And we're gonna dance.

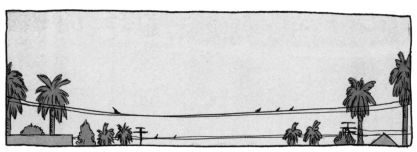

Hey.

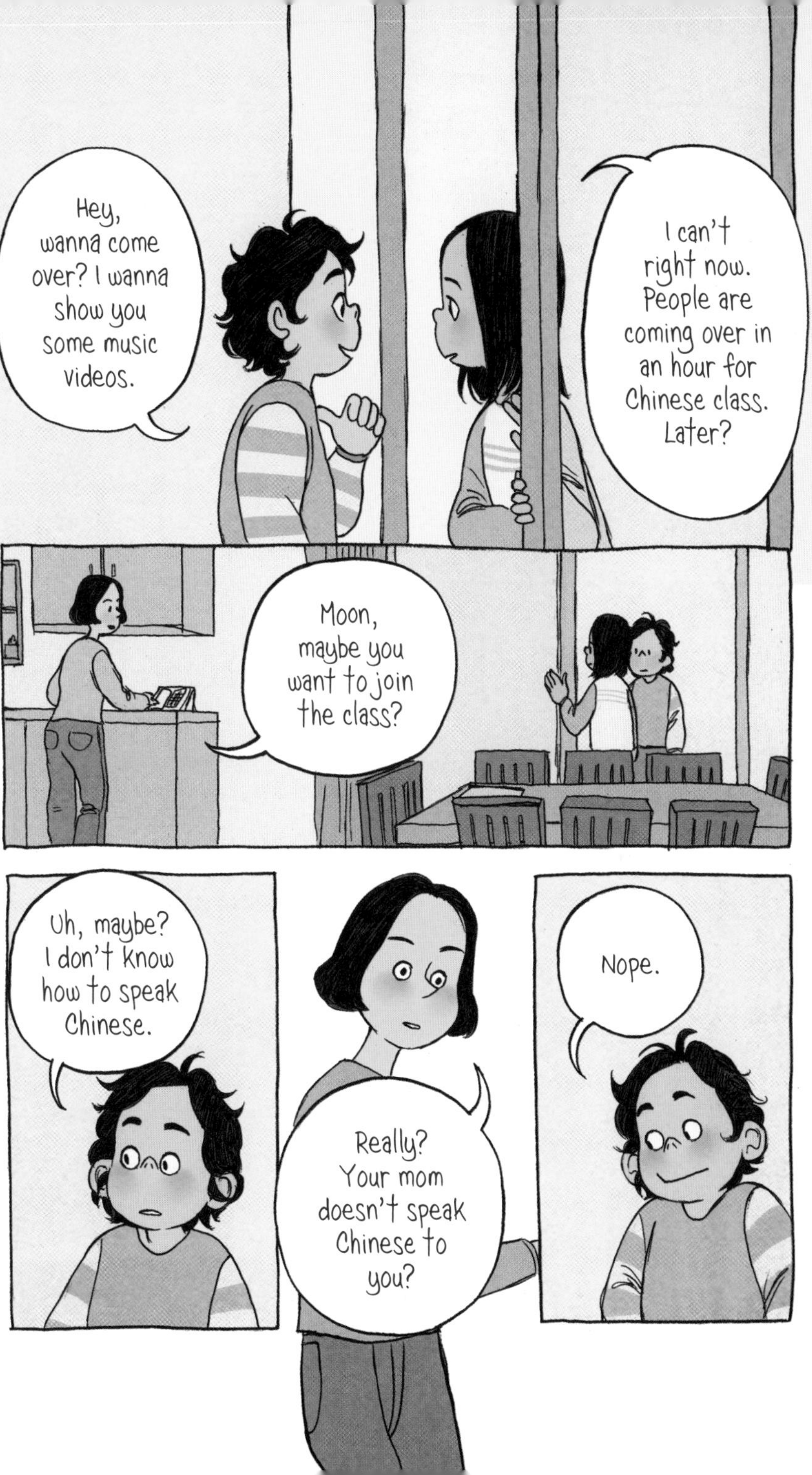
Hey, wanna come over? I wanna show you some music videos.
I can't right now. People are coming over in an hour for Chinese class. Later?
Moon, maybe you want to join the class?
Uh, maybe? I don't know how to speak Chinese.
Really? Your mom doesn't speak Chinese to you?
Nope.

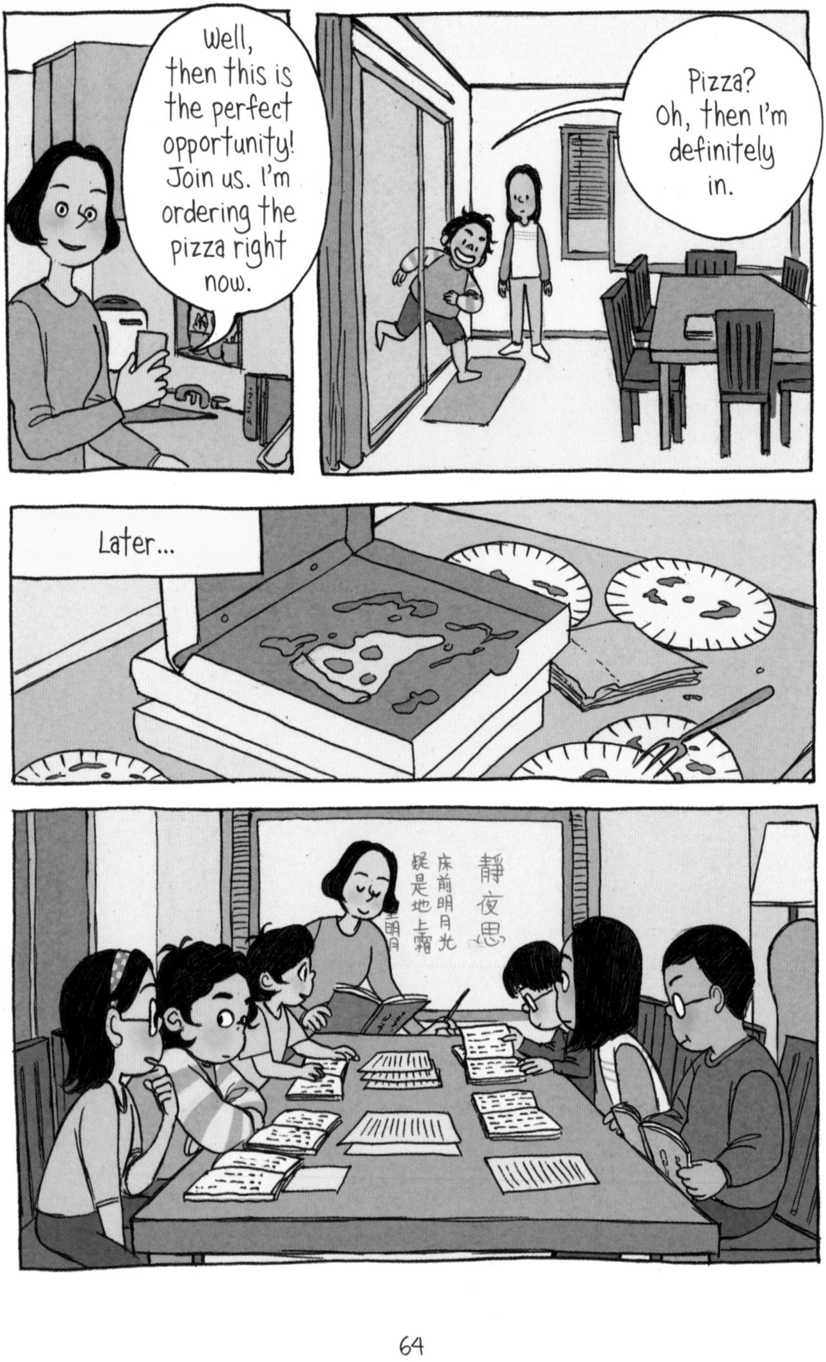

Well, then this is the perfect opportunity! Join us. I'm ordering the pizza right now.
Pizza? Oh, then I'm definitely in.
Later...
靜夜思
床前明月光
疑是地上霜

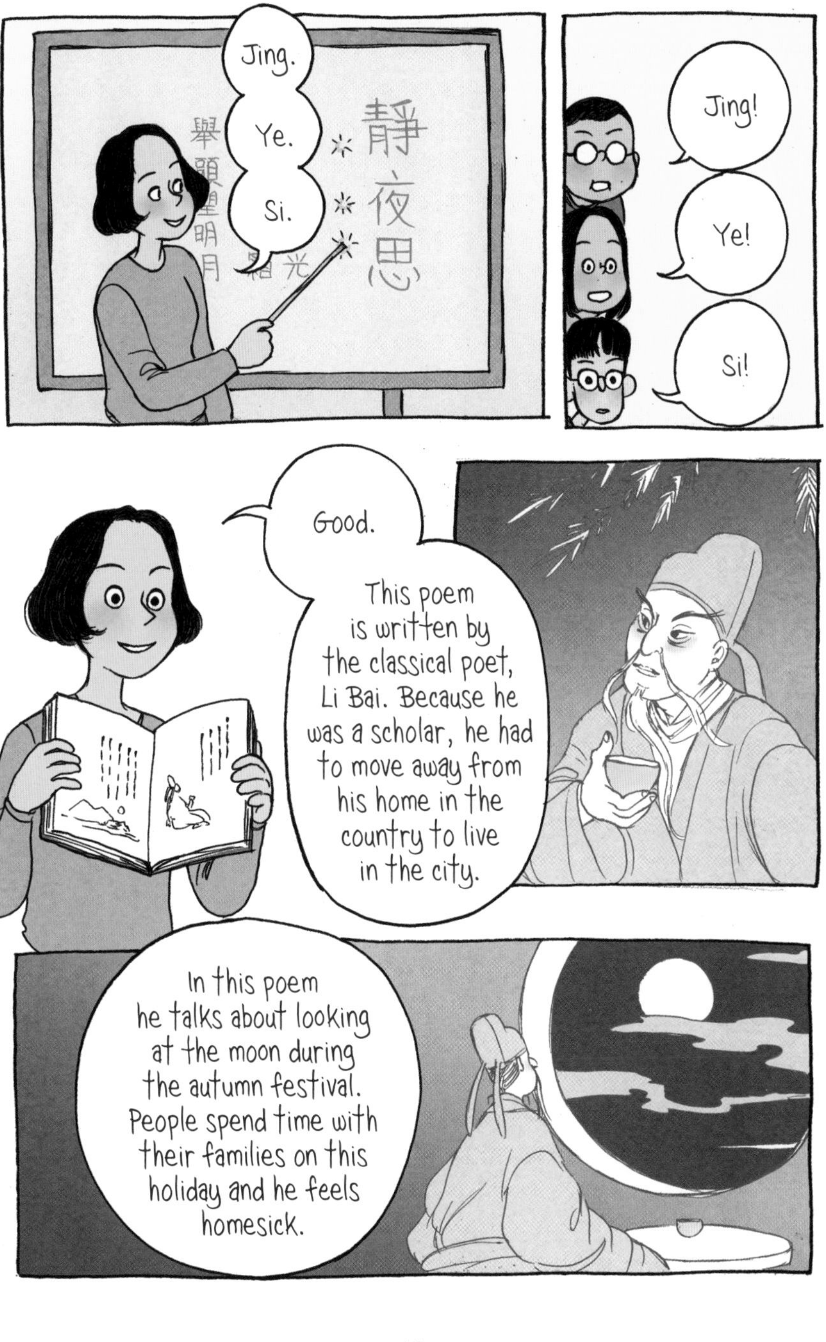

靜夜思
Jing.
Ye.
Si.
Jing!
Ye!
Si!
Good.
This poem is written by the classical poet, Li Bai. Because he was a scholar, he had to move away from his home in the country to live in the city.
In this poem he talks about looking at the moon during the autumn festival. People spend time with their families on this holiday and he feels homesick.

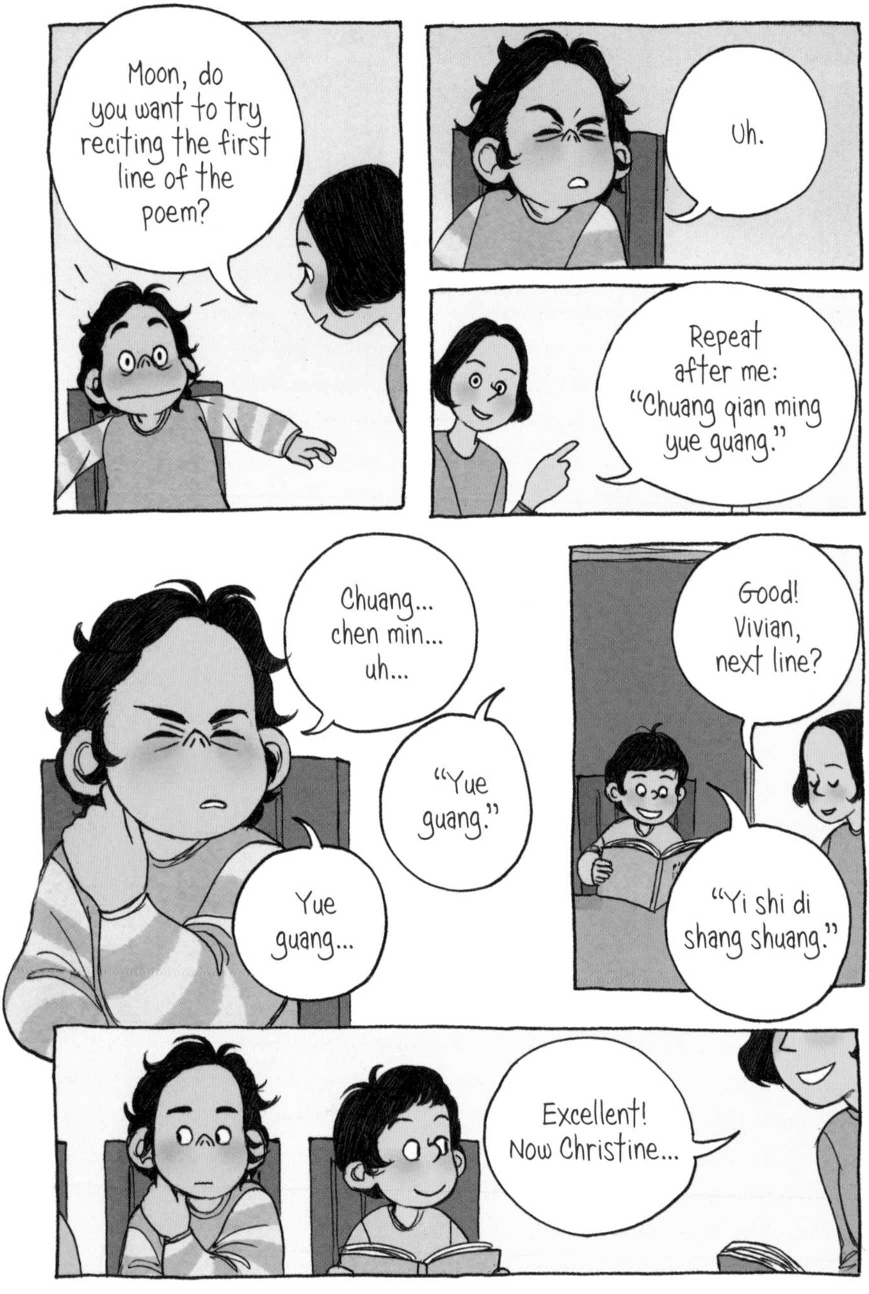
Moon, do you want to try reciting the first line of the poem?
Uh.
Repeat after me: "Chuang qian ming yue guang."
Chuang... chen min... uh...
"Yue guang."
Yue guang...
Good! Vivian, next line?
"Yi shi di shang shuang."
Excellent! Now Christine...

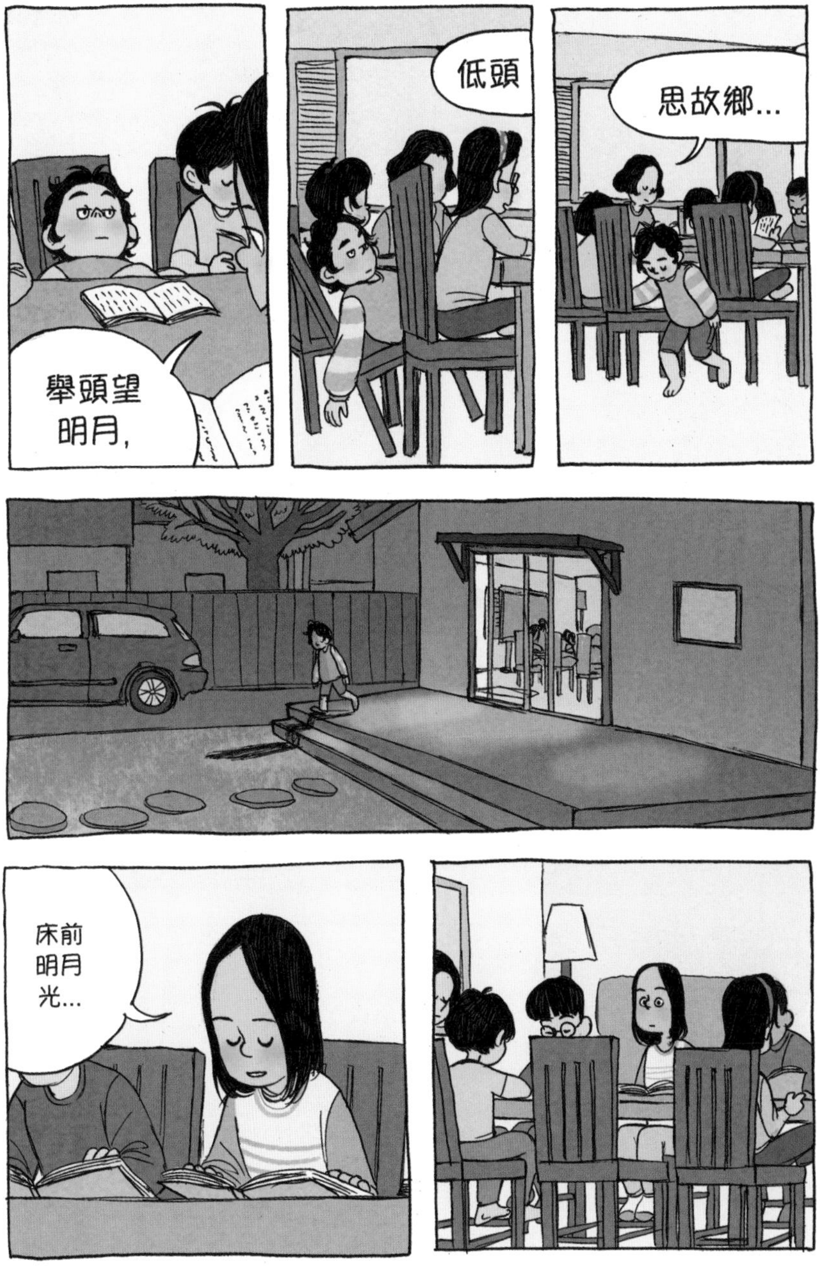
舉頭望
明月,
低頭
思故鄉...
床前
明月
光...

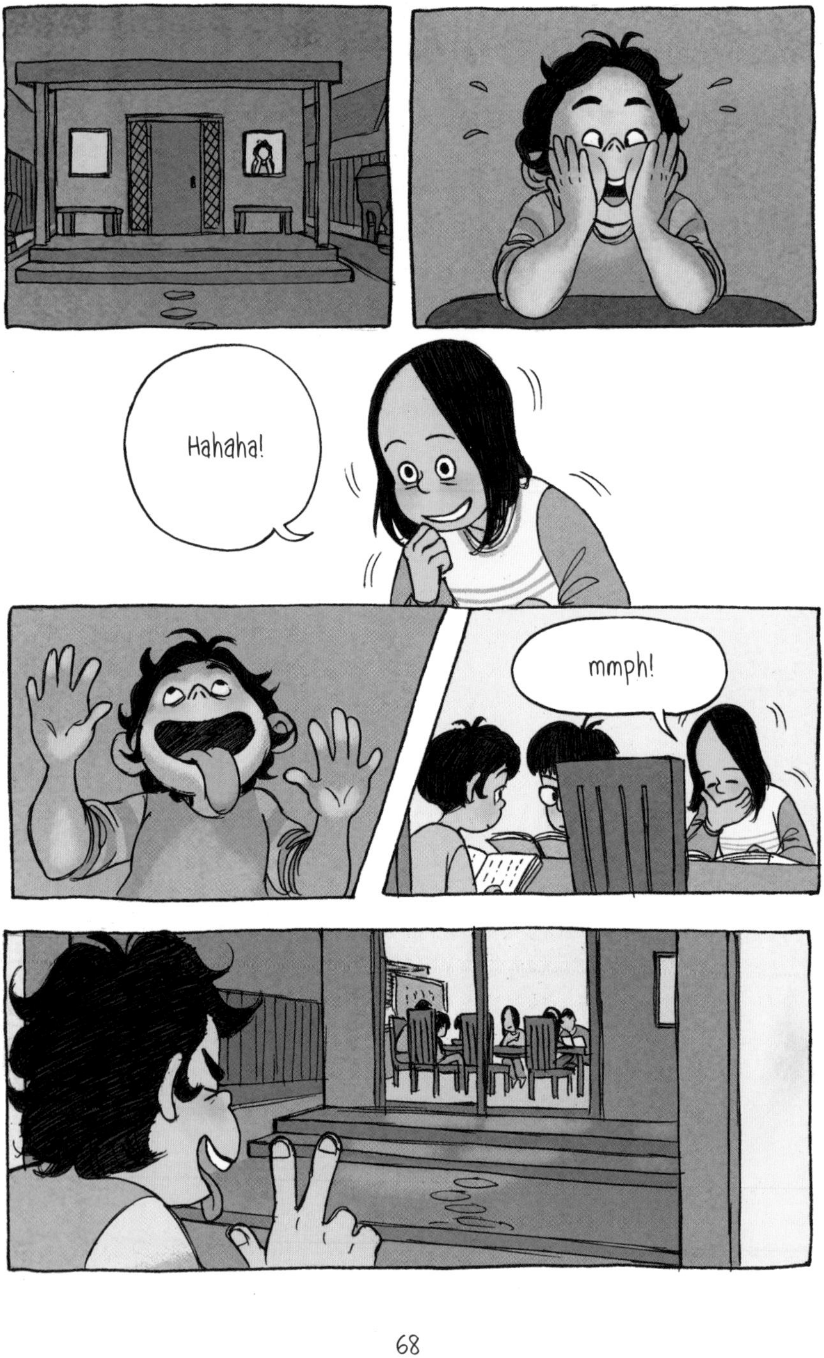
Hahaha!
mmph!

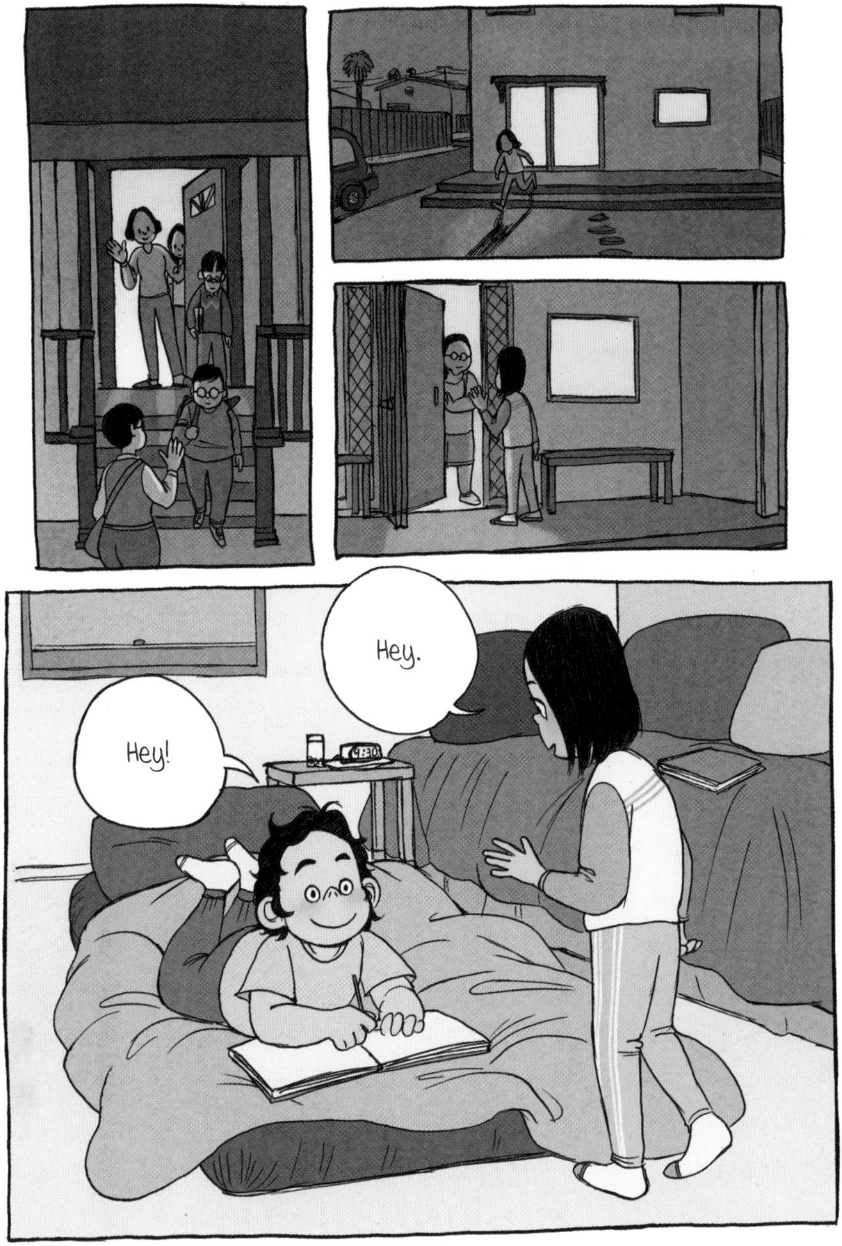
Hey!
Hey.

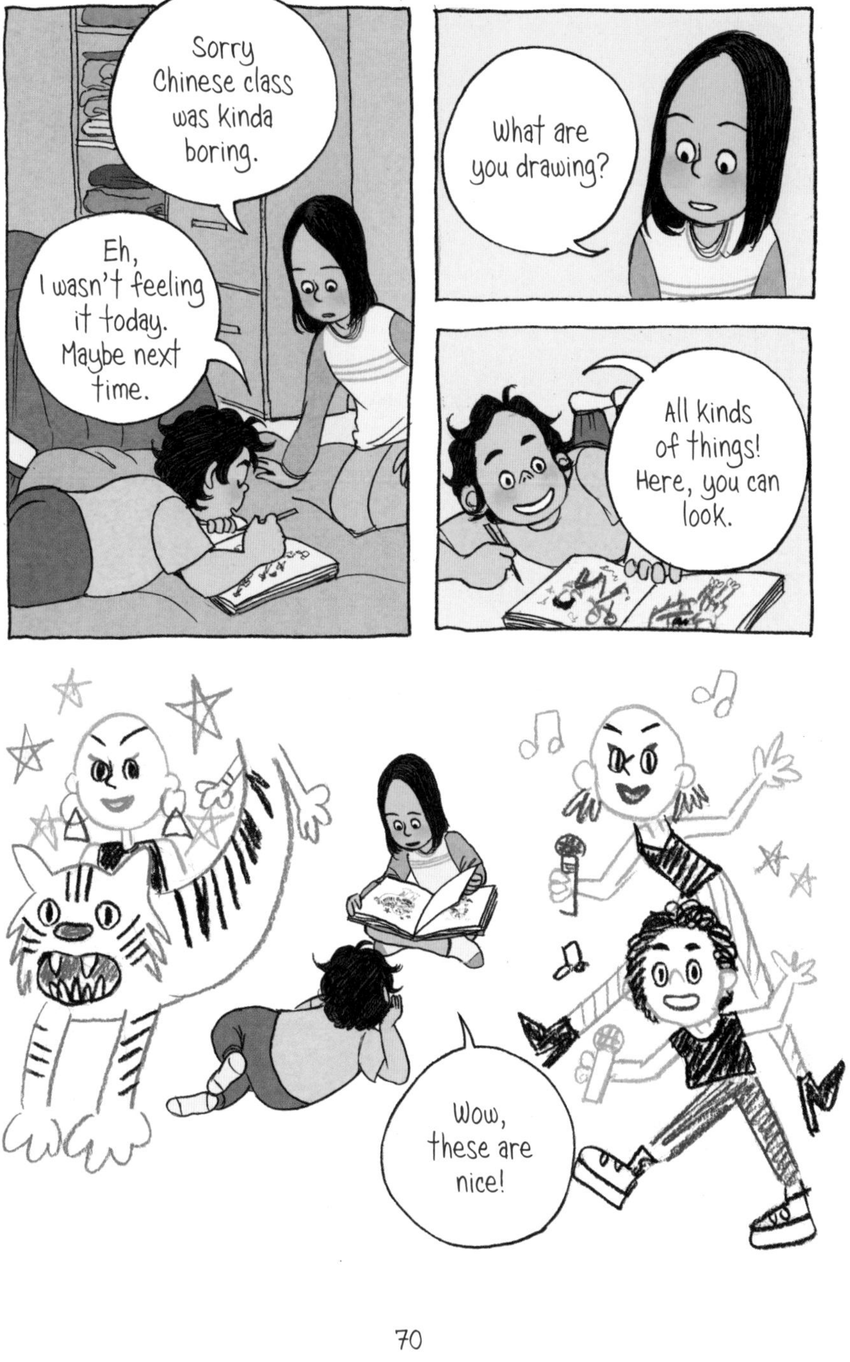
Sorry Chinese class was kinda boring.
Eh, I wasn't feeling it today. Maybe next time.
What are you drawing?
All kinds of things! Here, you can look.
Wow, these are nice!

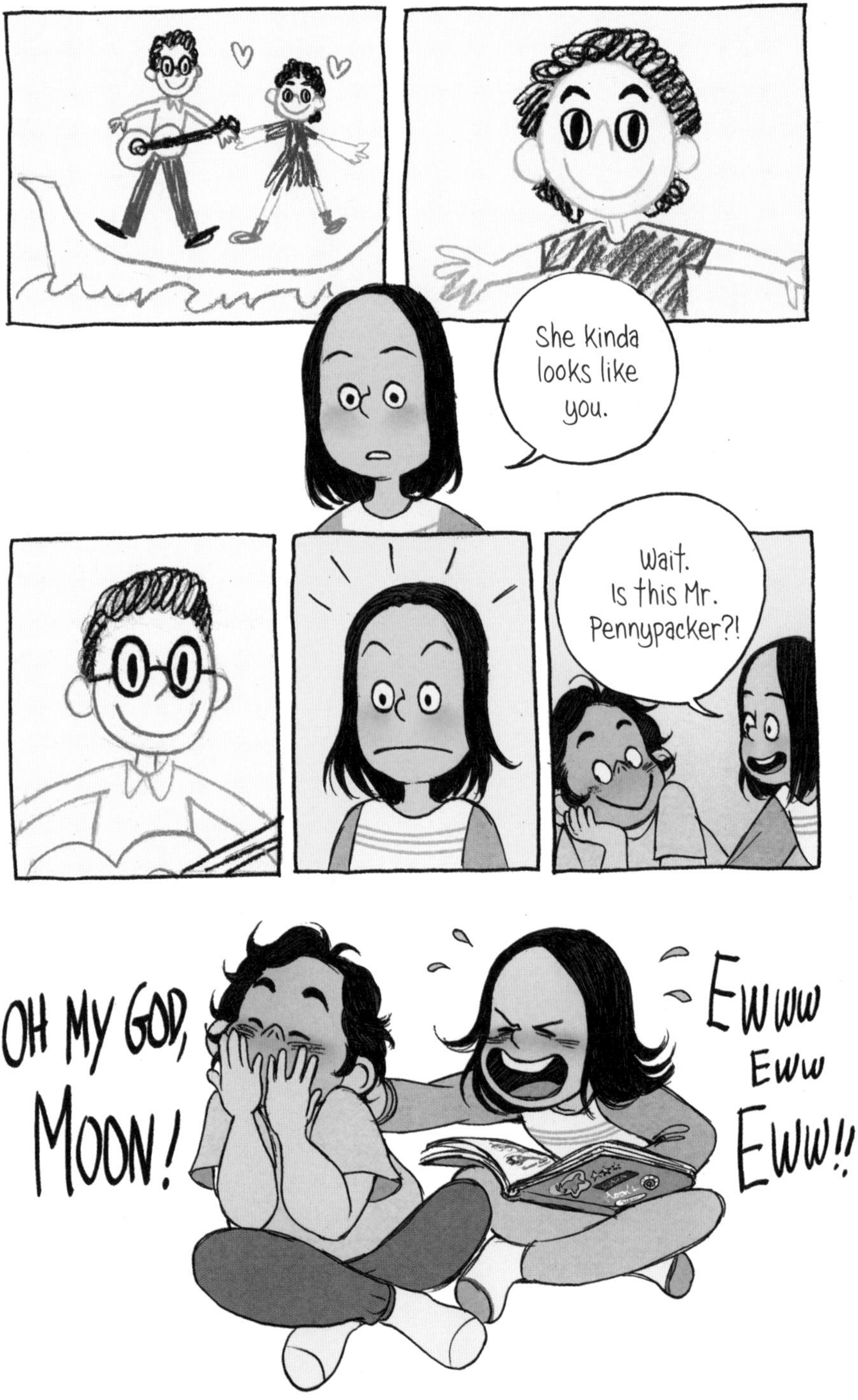
She kinda looks like you.
Wait. Is this Mr. Pennypacker?!
OH MY GOD, MOON!
Ewww Eww Eww!!

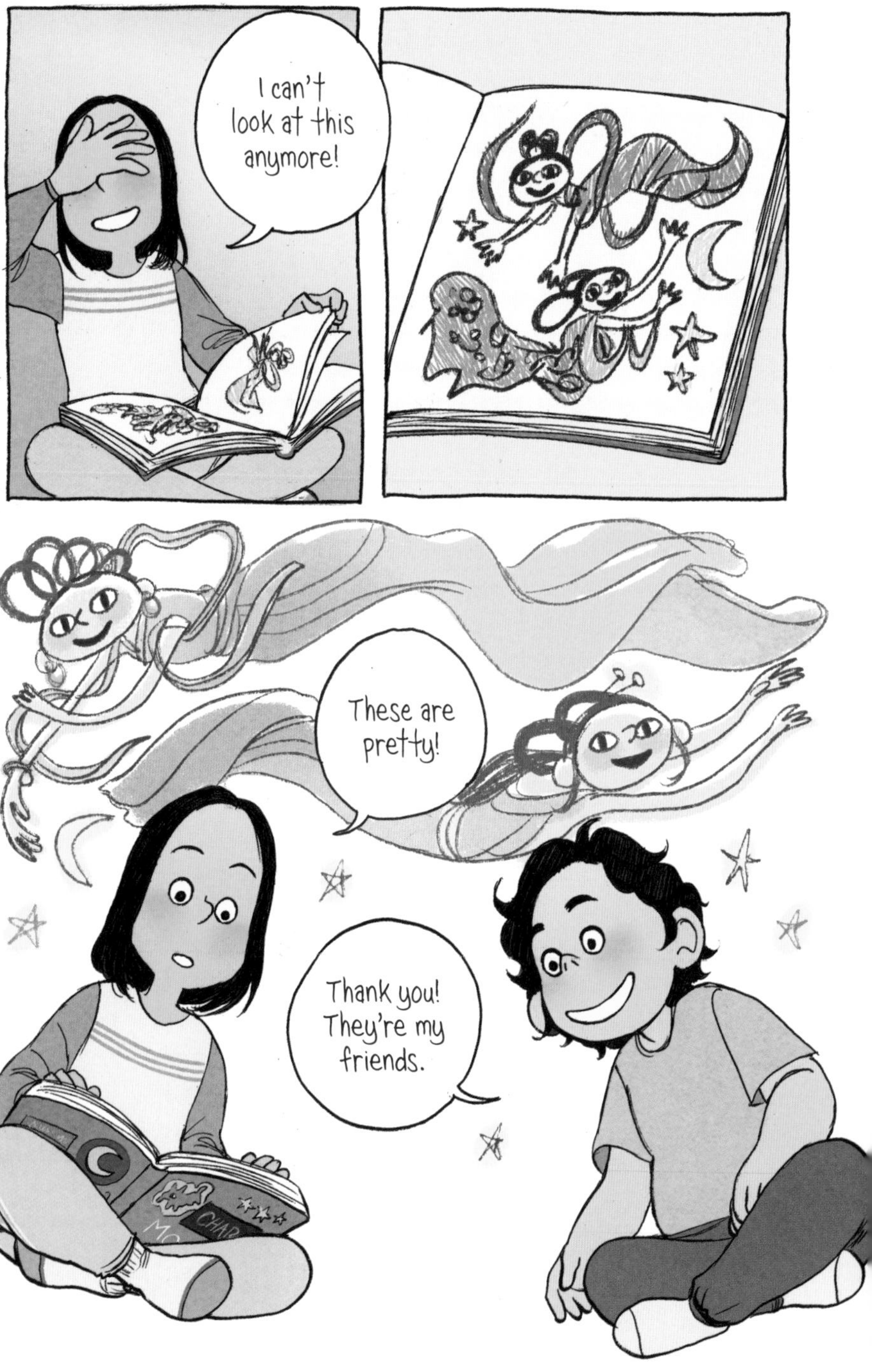
I can't look at this anymore!
These are pretty!
Thank you! They're my friends.

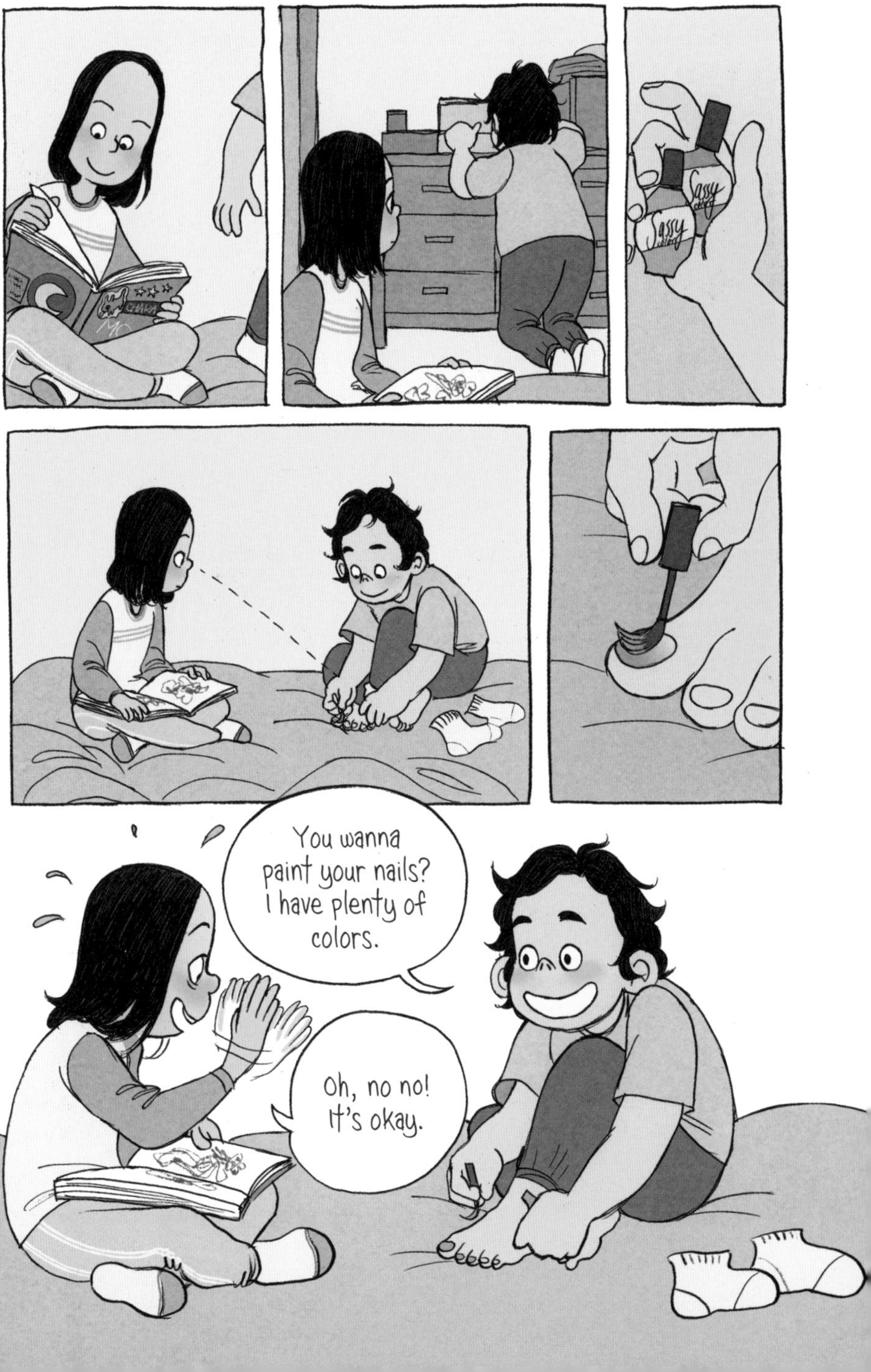
Sassy
Sassy
You wanna paint your nails? I have plenty of colors.
Oh, no no! It's okay.

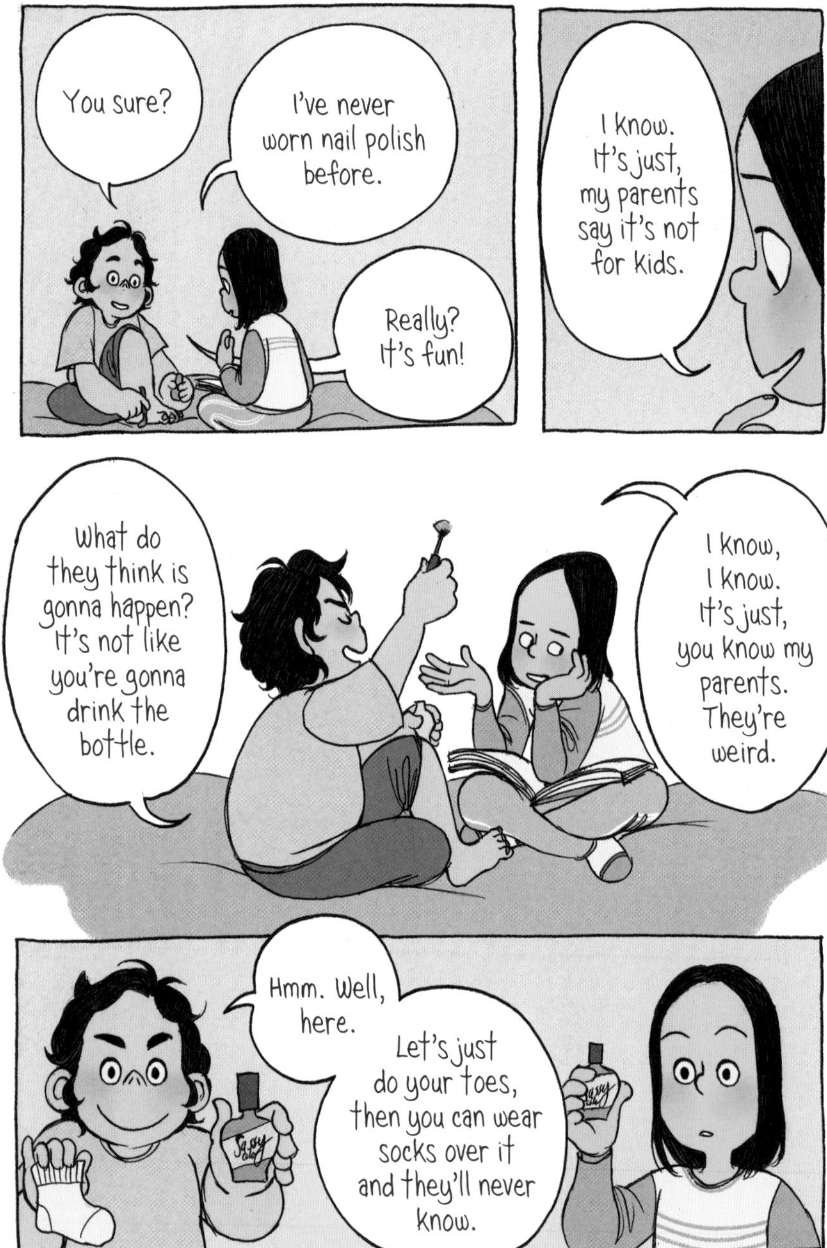
You sure?
I've never worn nail polish before.
Really? It's fun!
I know. It's just, my parents say it's not for kids.
What do they think is gonna happen? It's not like you're gonna drink the bottle.
I know, I know. It's just, you know my parents. They're weird.
Hmm. Well, here.
Let's just do your toes, then you can wear socks over it and they'll never know.

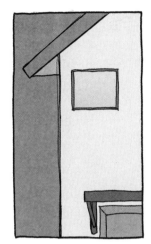

Good night!

Good night, Baba!

Hey, Christine.

I'm really glad you and Moon are becoming friends.

Me, too.

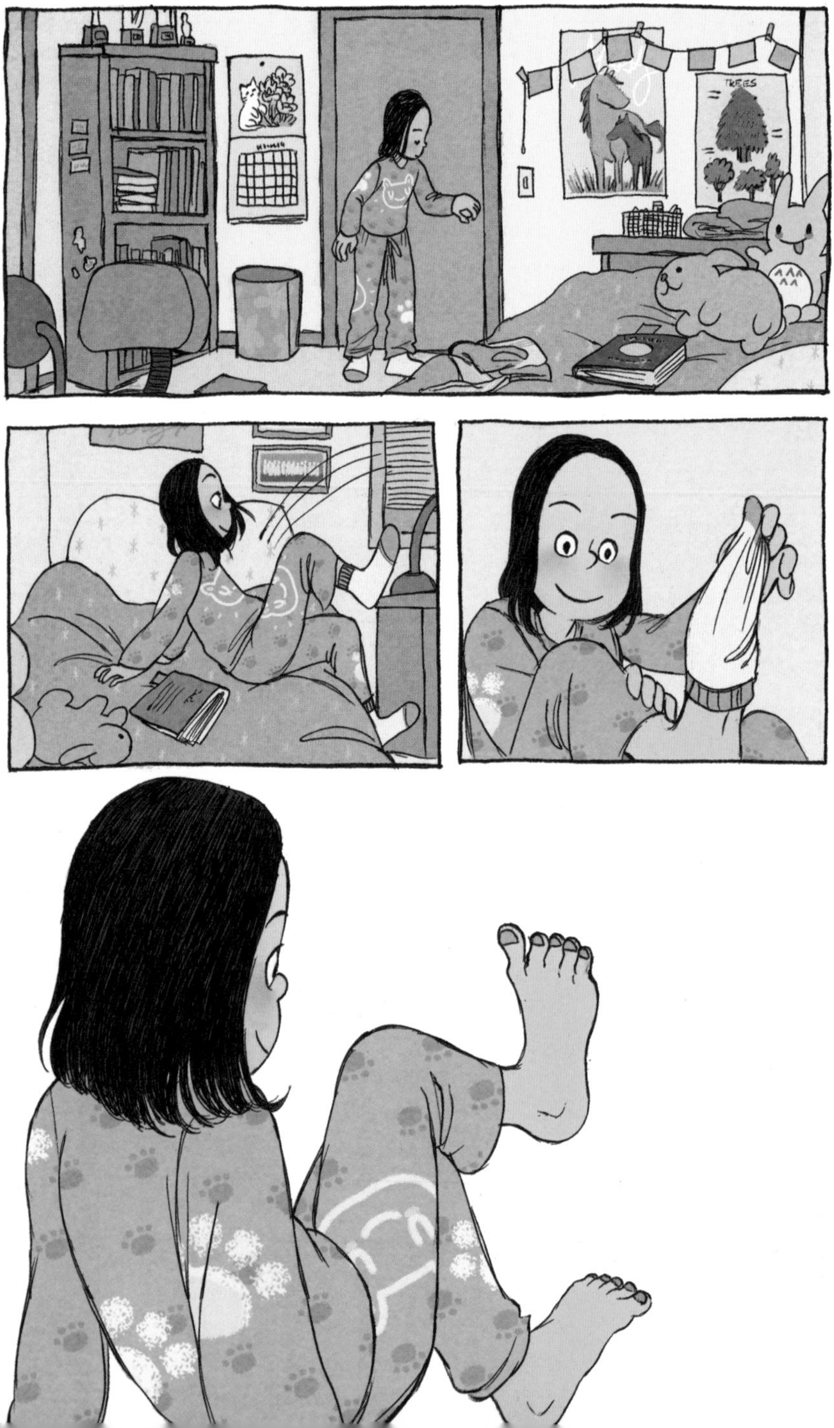
TREES

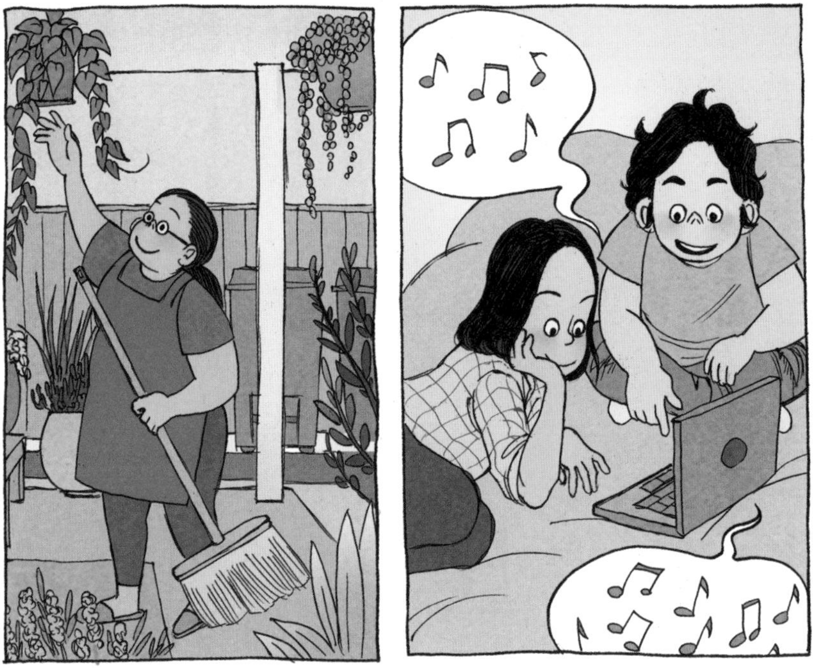

CHAPTER FOUR

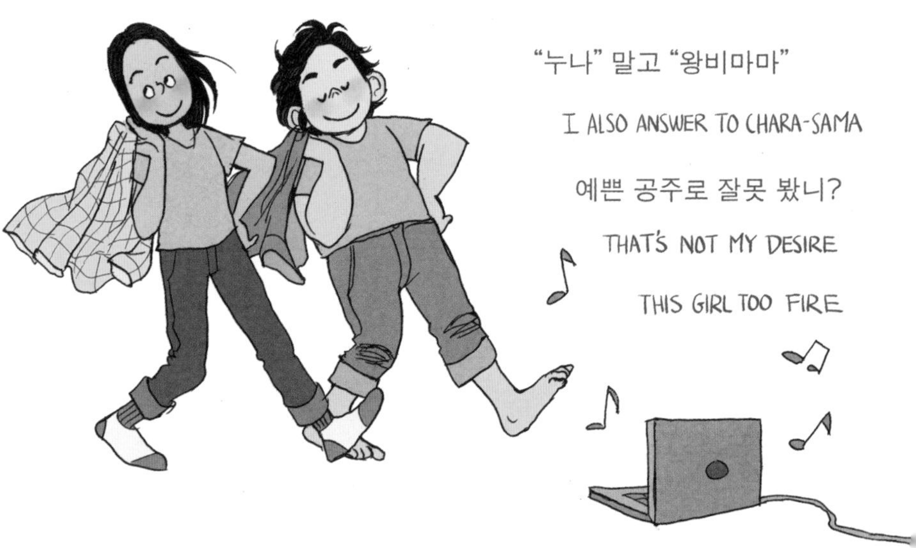
"누나" 말고 "왕비마마"
I ALSO ANSWER TO CHARA-SAMA
예쁜 공주로 잘못 봤니?
THAT'S NOT MY DESIRE
THIS GIRL TOO FIRE

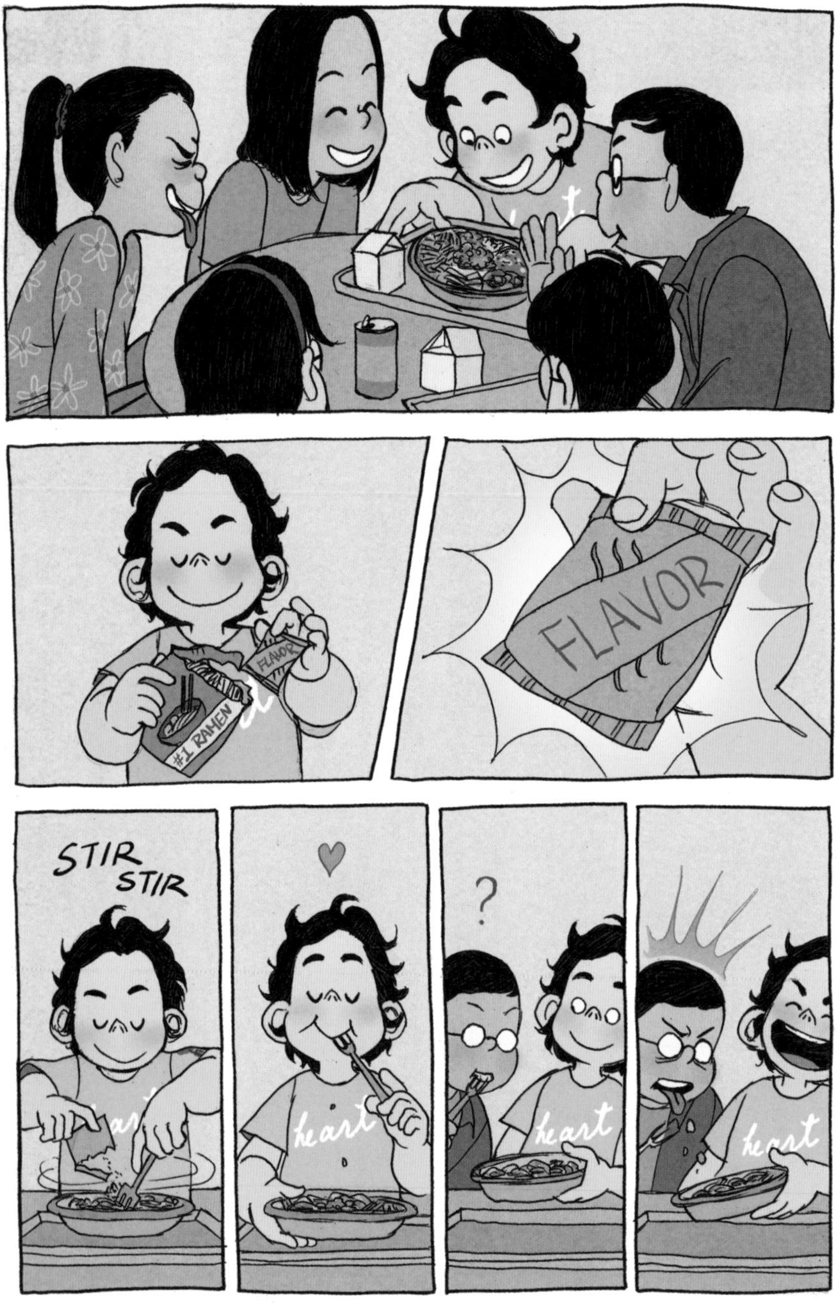
FLAVOR
#1 RAMEN
FLAVOR
STIR
STIR
heart
heart
heart
?

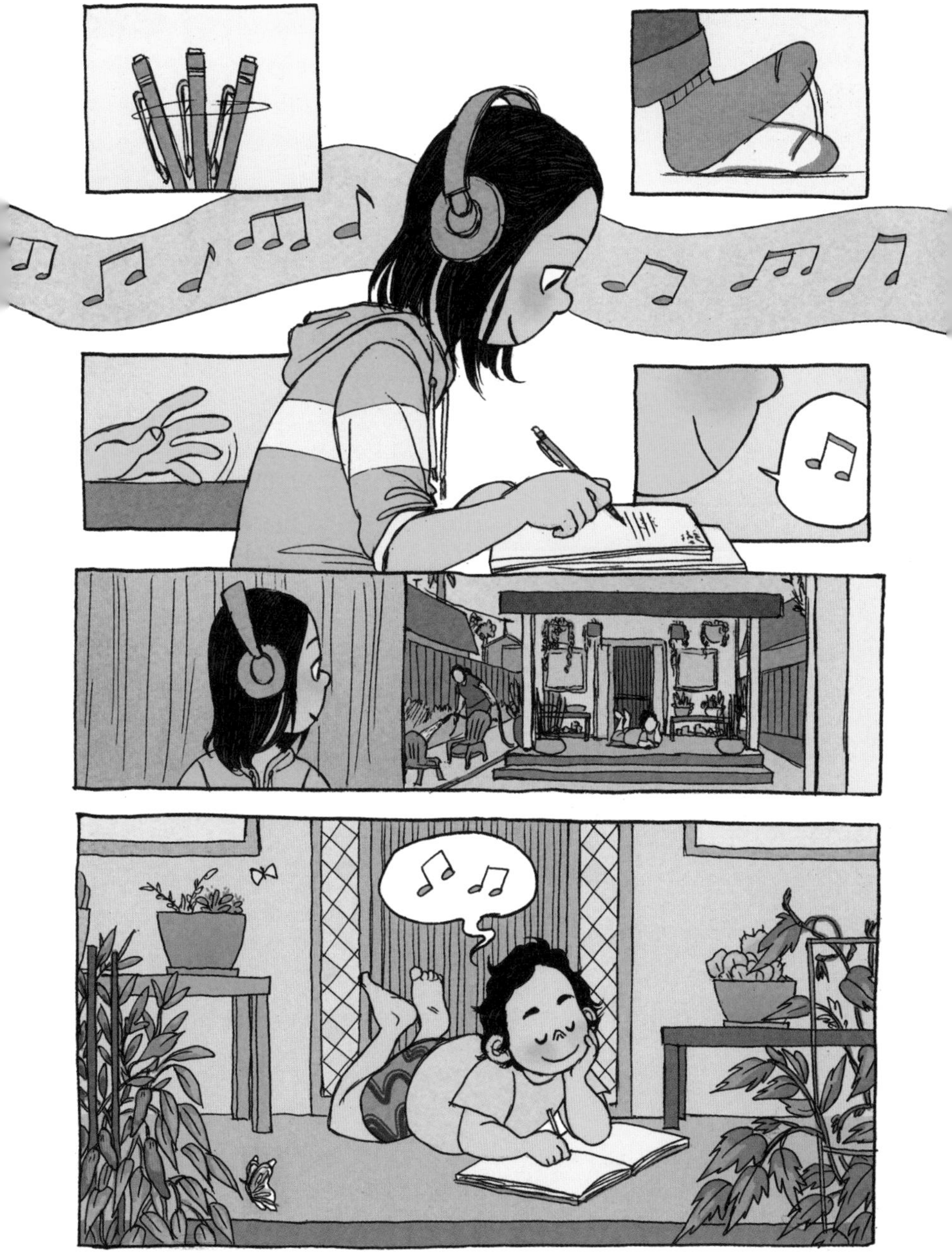

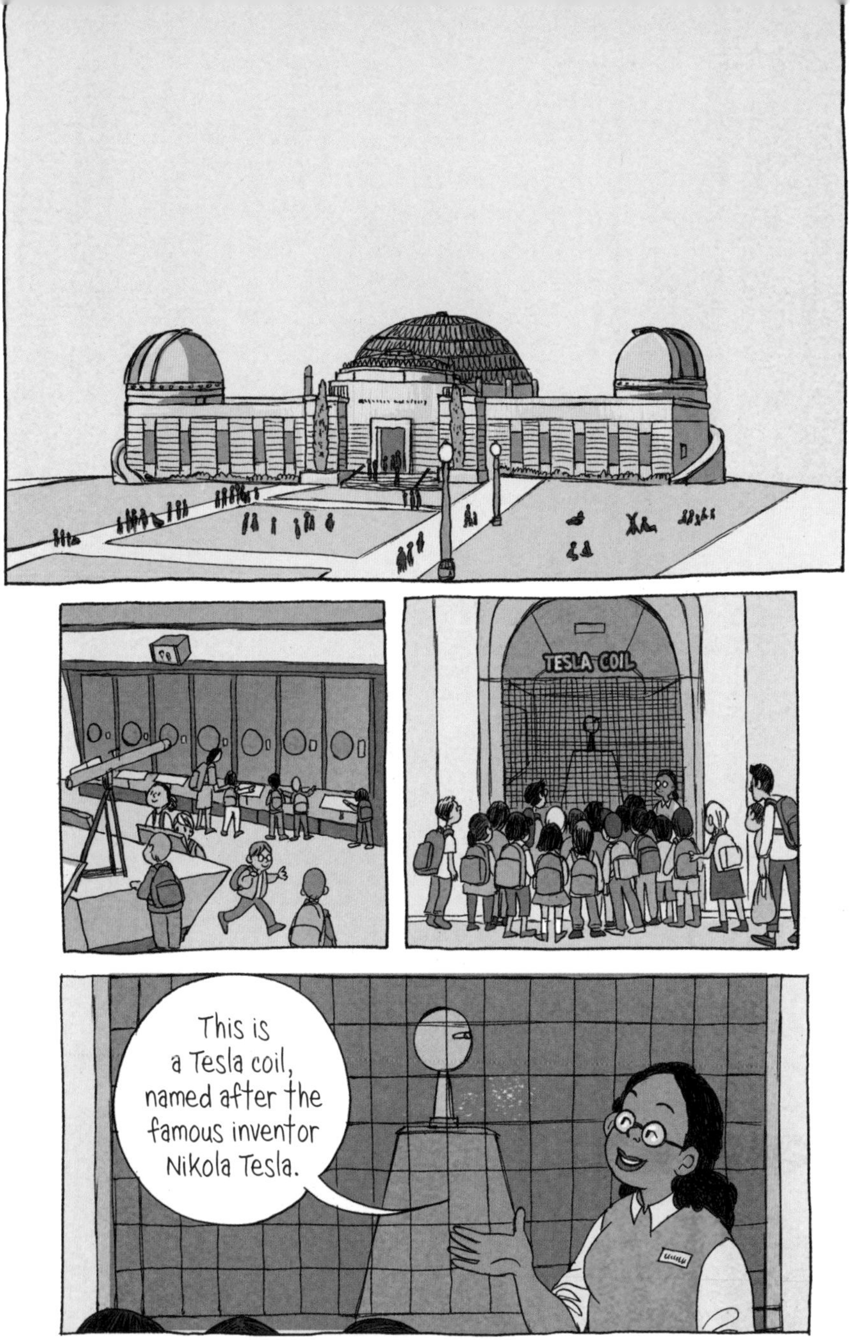
TESLA COIL
This is a Tesla coil, named after the famous inventor Nikola Tesla.

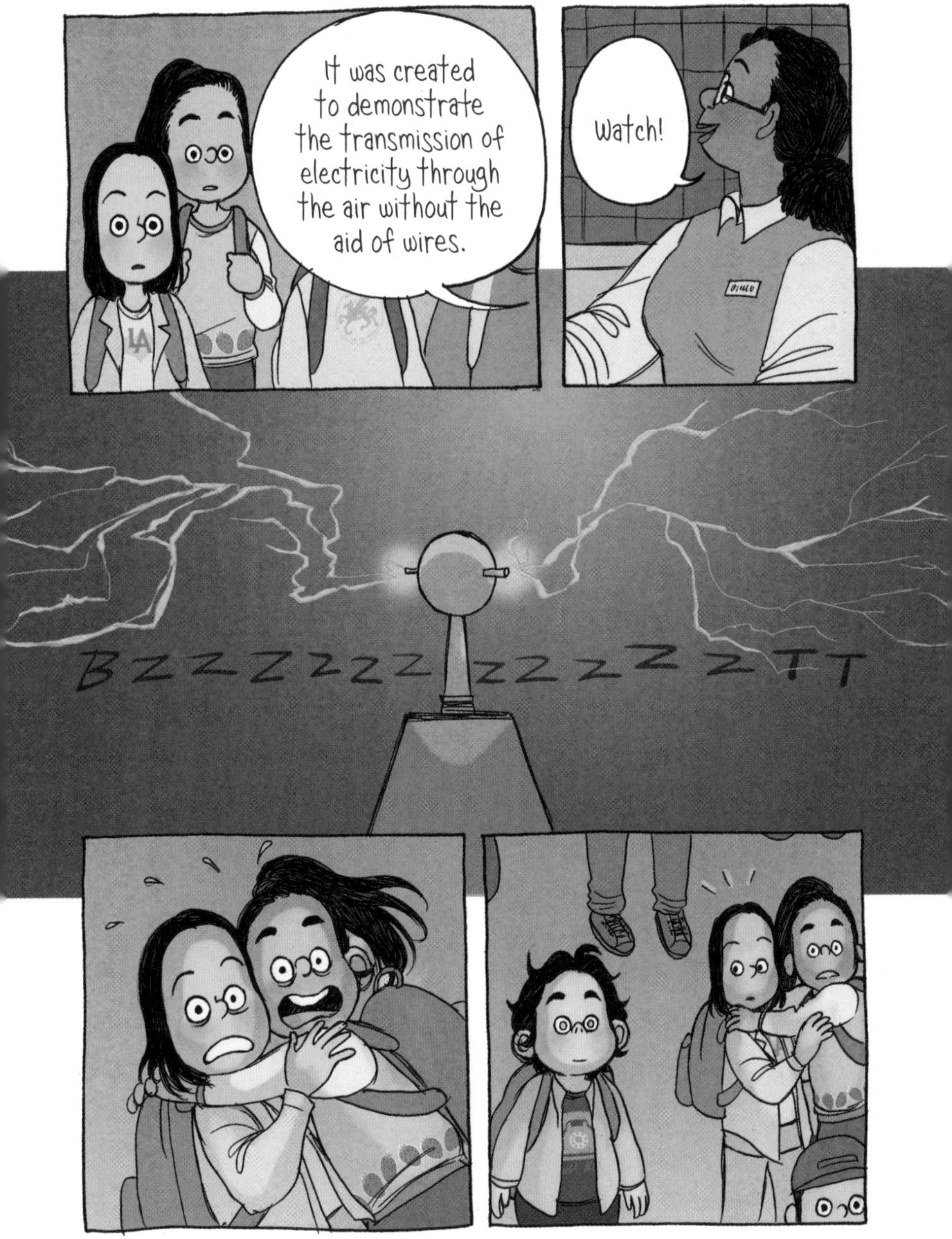
It was created to demonstrate the transmission of electricity through the air without the aid of wires.
Watch!
BZZZZZZZZZZZZZZTT

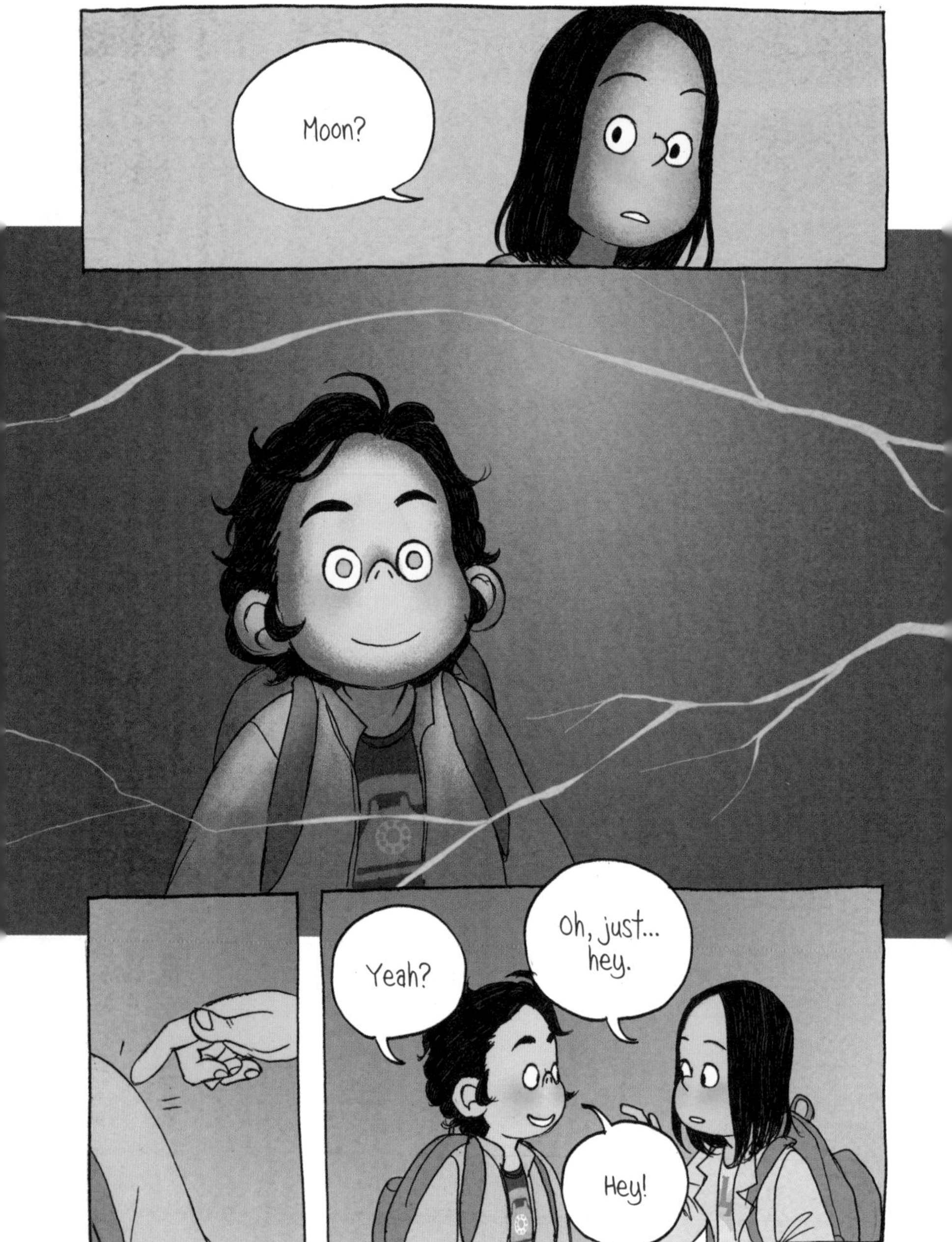
Moon?
Yeah?
Oh, just... hey.
Hey!

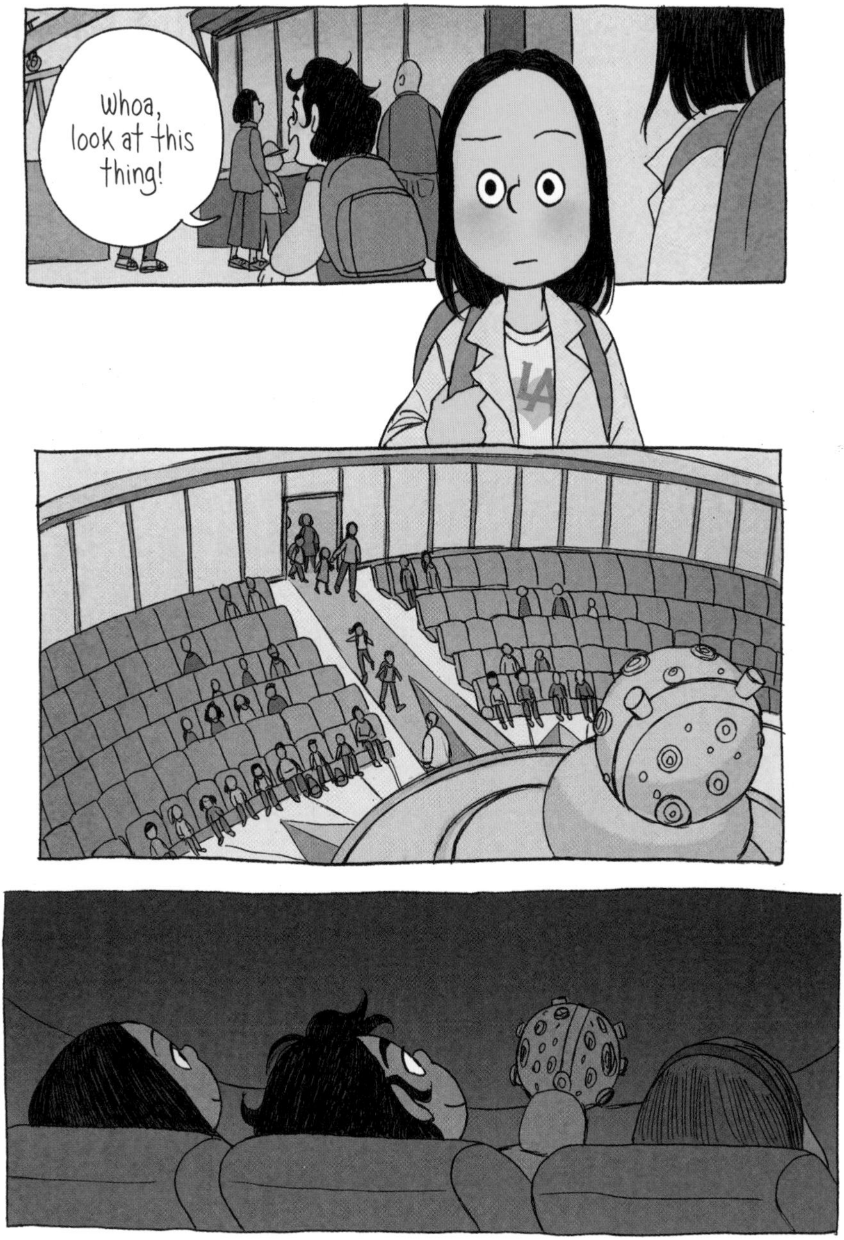
Whoa, look at this thing!

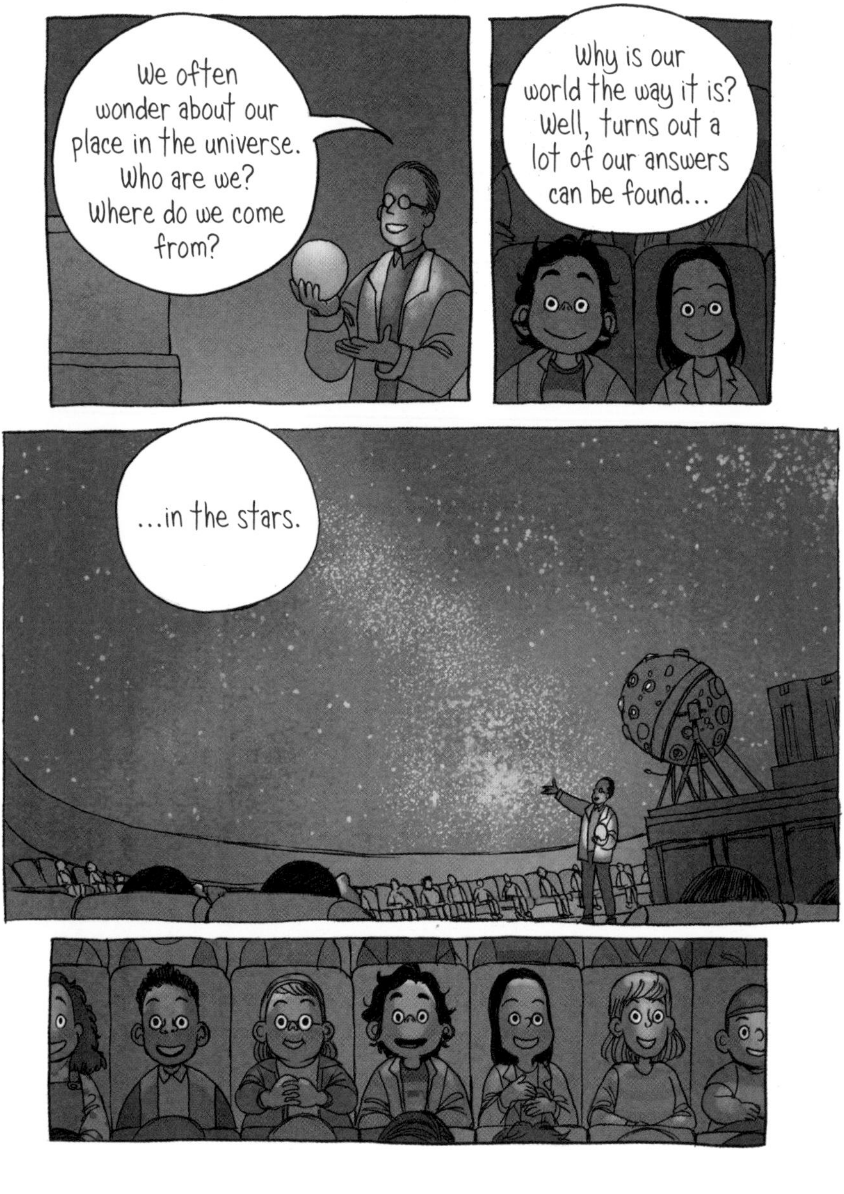
We often wonder about our place in the universe. Who are we? Where do we come from?
Why is our world the way it is? Well, turns out a lot of our answers can be found...
...in the stars.

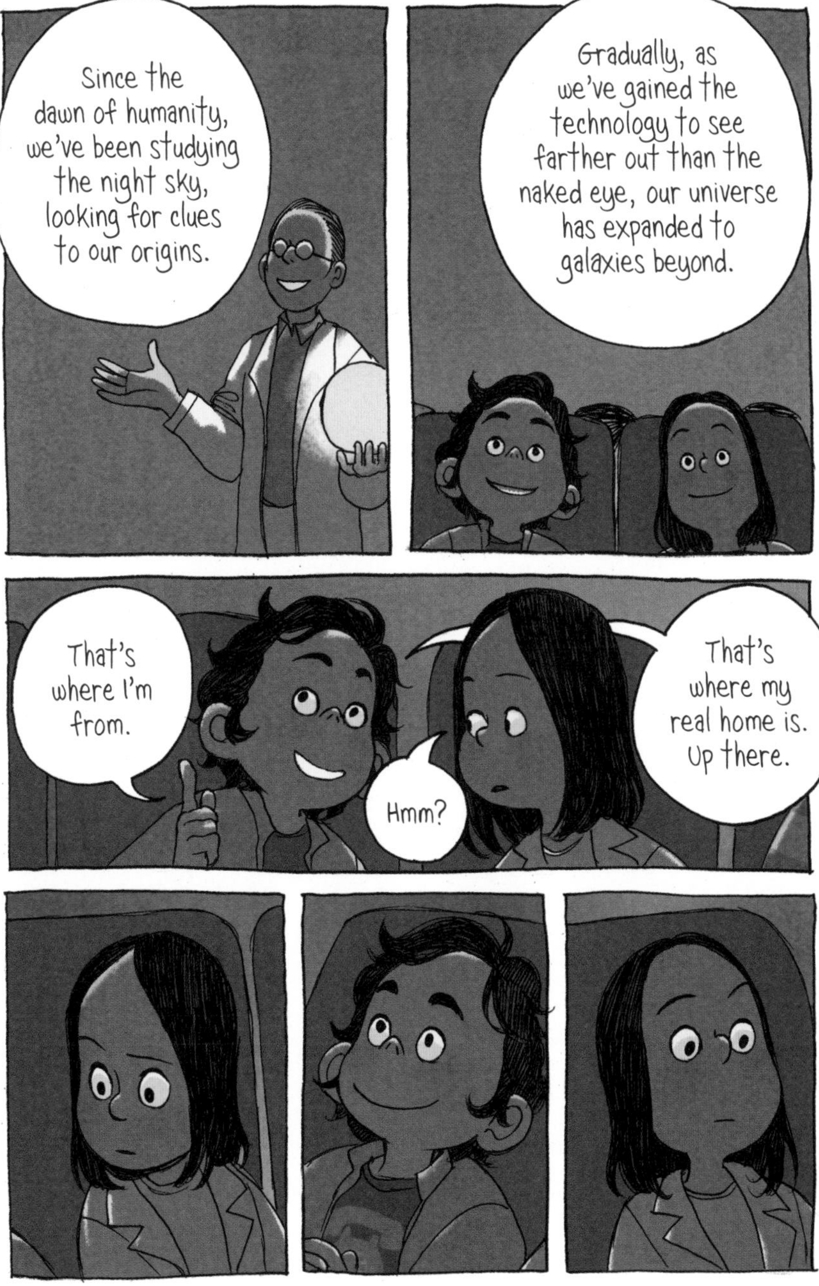
Since the dawn of humanity, we've been studying the night sky, looking for clues to our origins.
Gradually, as we've gained the technology to see farther out than the naked eye, our universe has expanded to galaxies beyond.
That's where I'm from.
Hmm?
That's where my real home is. Up there.

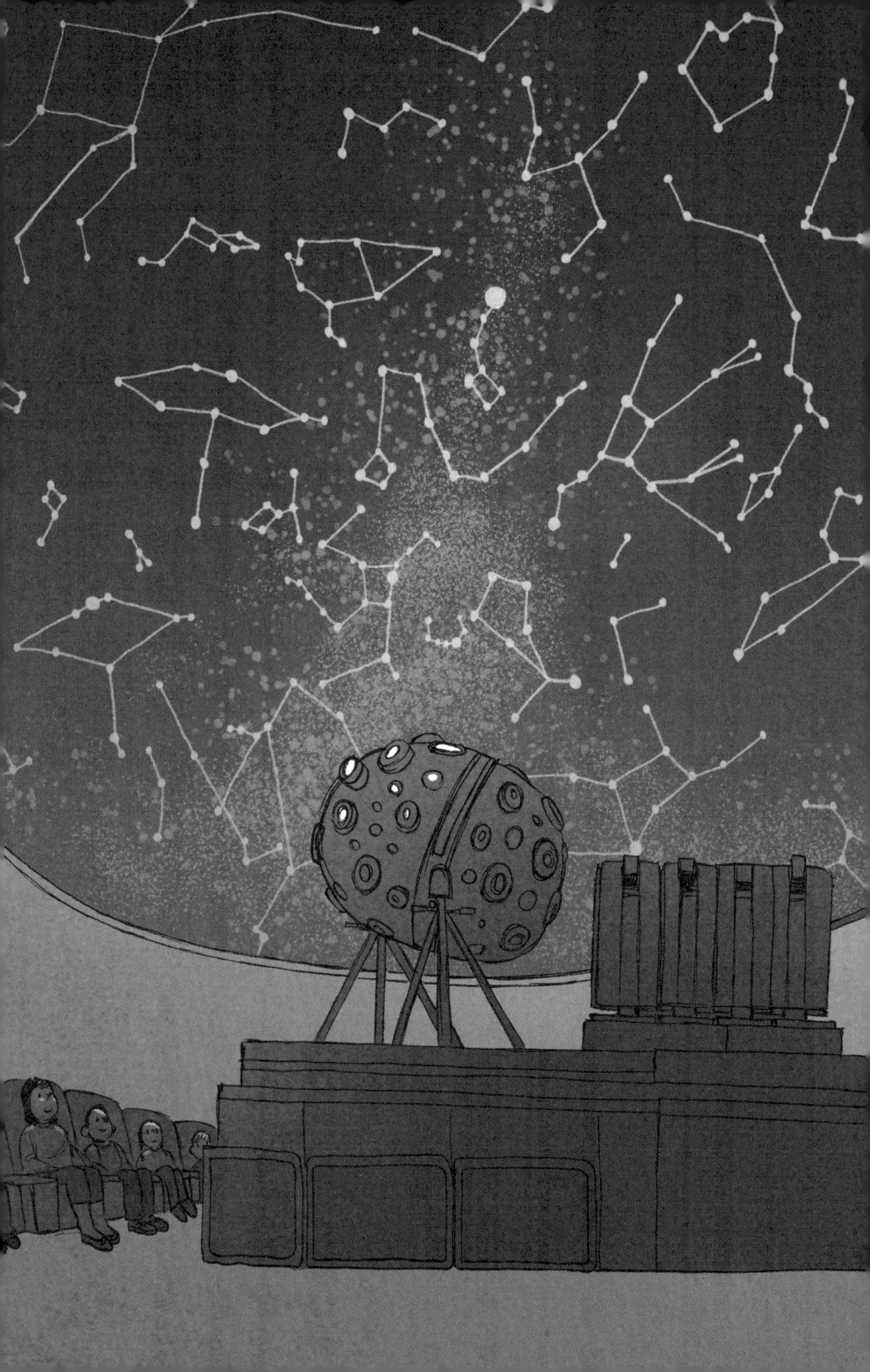

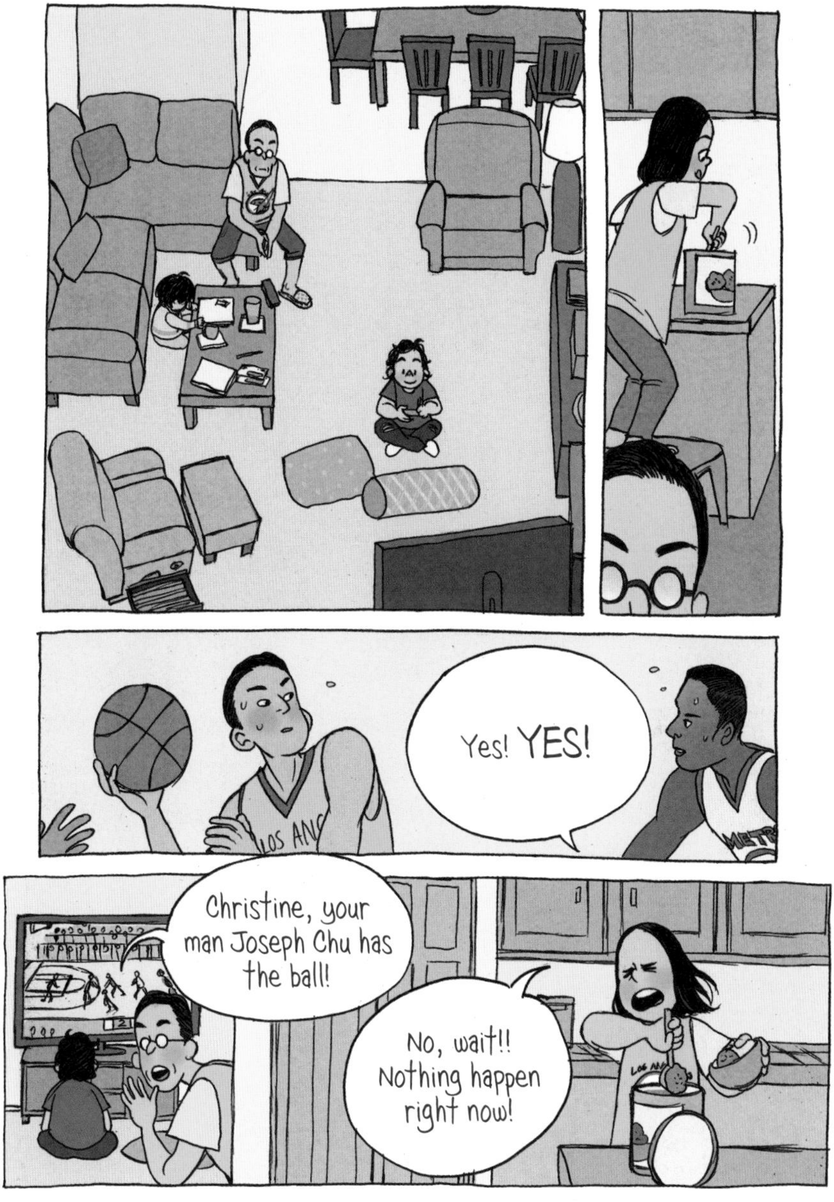
Yes! YES!
Christine, your man Joseph Chu has the ball!
No, wait!! Nothing happen right now!

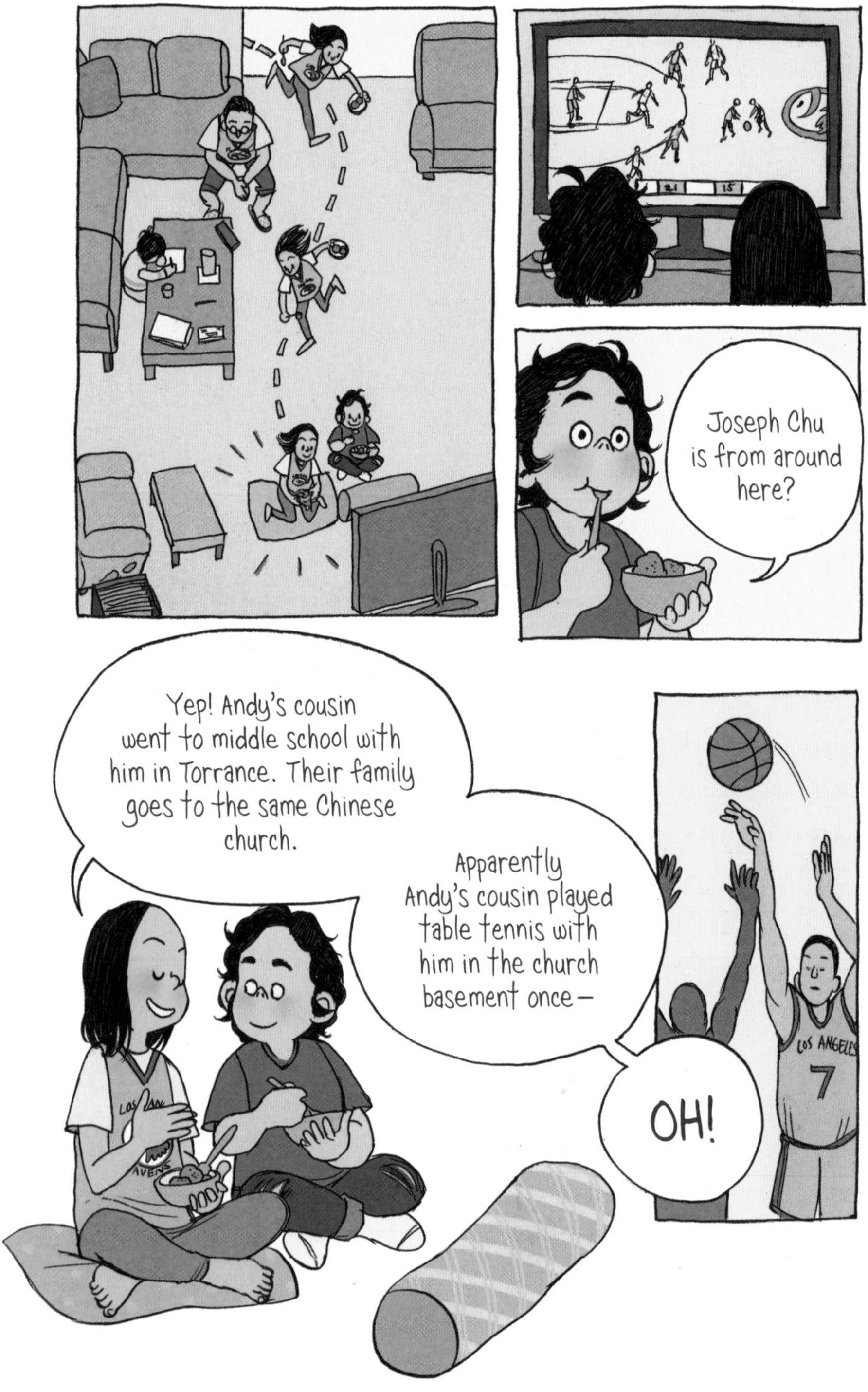

21
15
Joseph Chu is from around here?
Yep! Andy's cousin went to middle school with him in Torrance. Their family goes to the same Chinese church.
Apparently Andy's cousin played table tennis with him in the church basement once—
OH!
LOS ANGELES
7

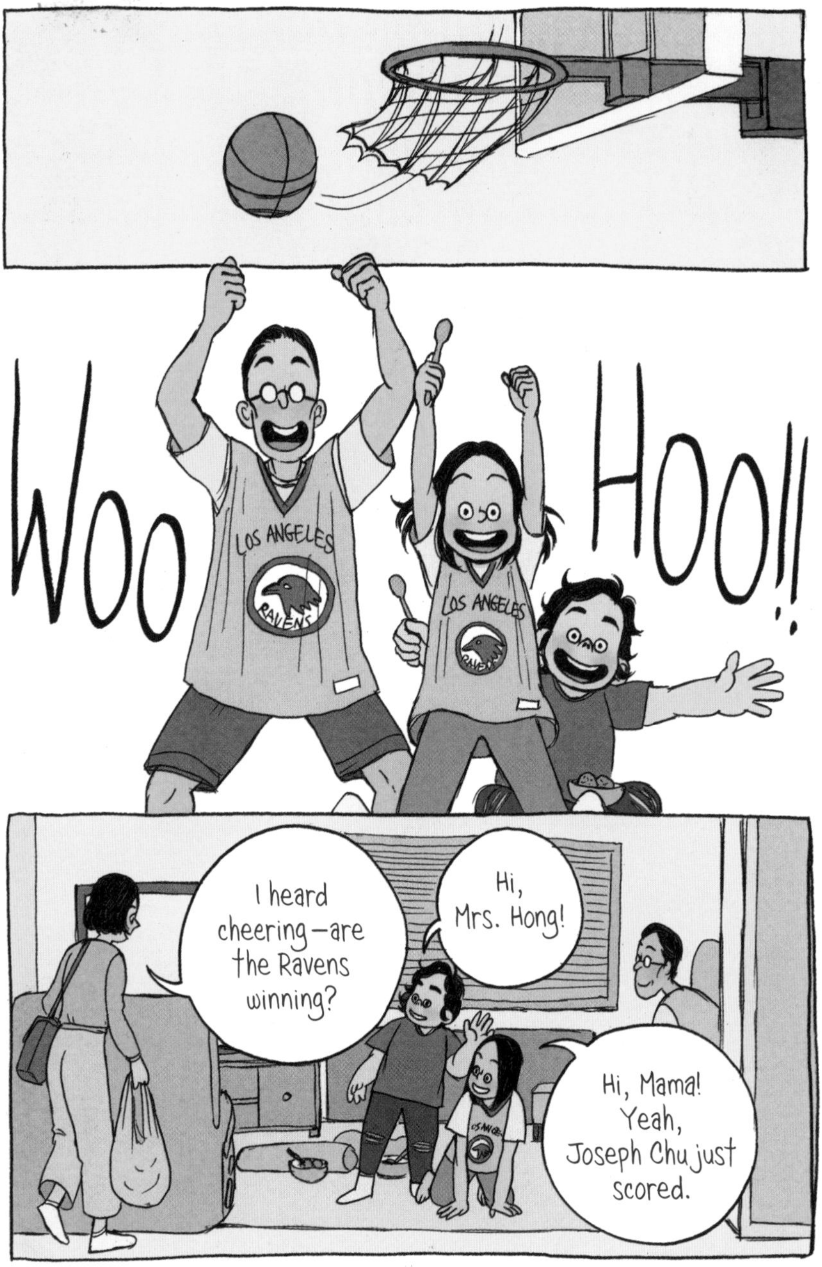
WOO HOO!!
LOS ANGELES
RAVENS
LOS ANGELES
RAVENS
I heard cheering—are the Ravens winning?
Hi, Mrs. Hong!
Hi, Mama! Yeah, Joseph Chu just scored.

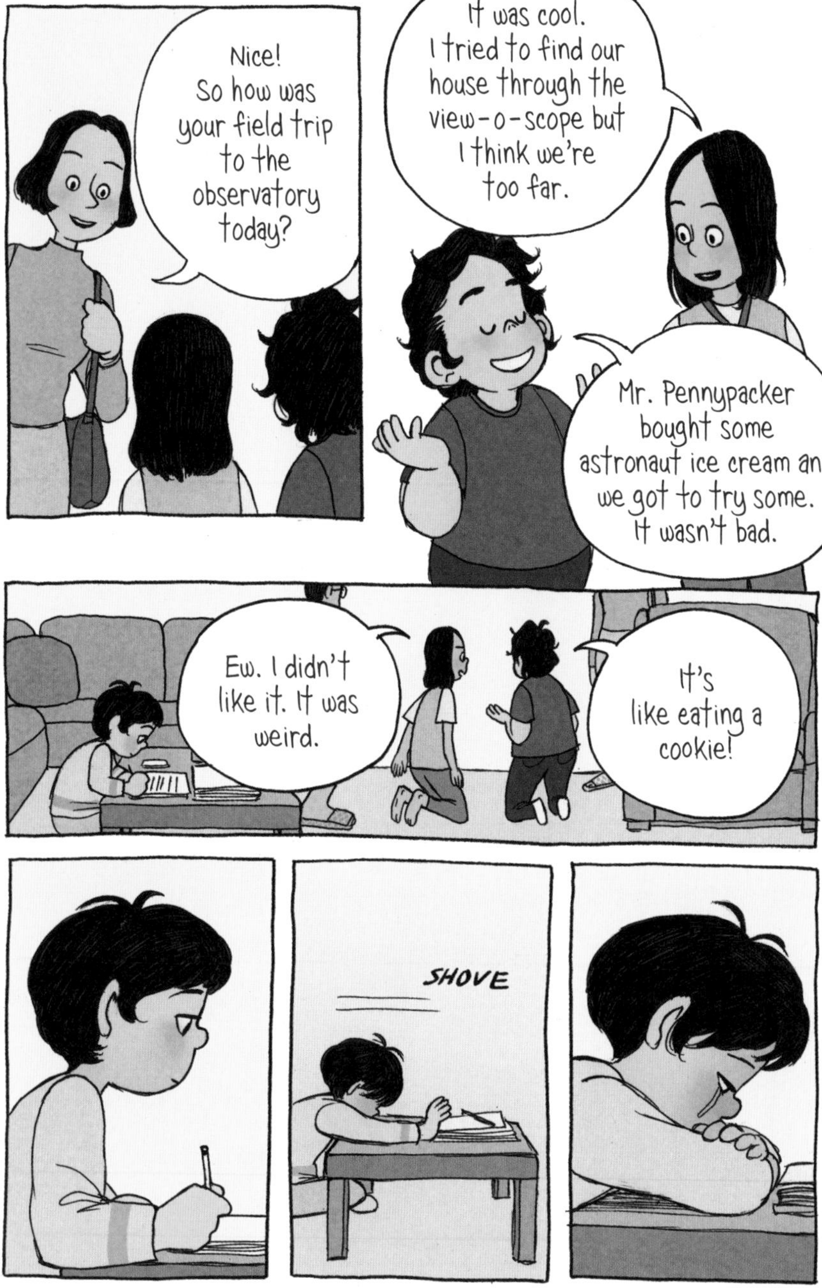
Nice!
So how was your field trip to the observatory today?
It was cool.
I tried to find our house through the view-o-scope but I think we're too far.
Mr. Pennypacker bought some astronaut ice cream and we got to try some.
It wasn't bad.
Ew. I didn't like it. It was weird.
It's like eating a cookie!
SHOVE

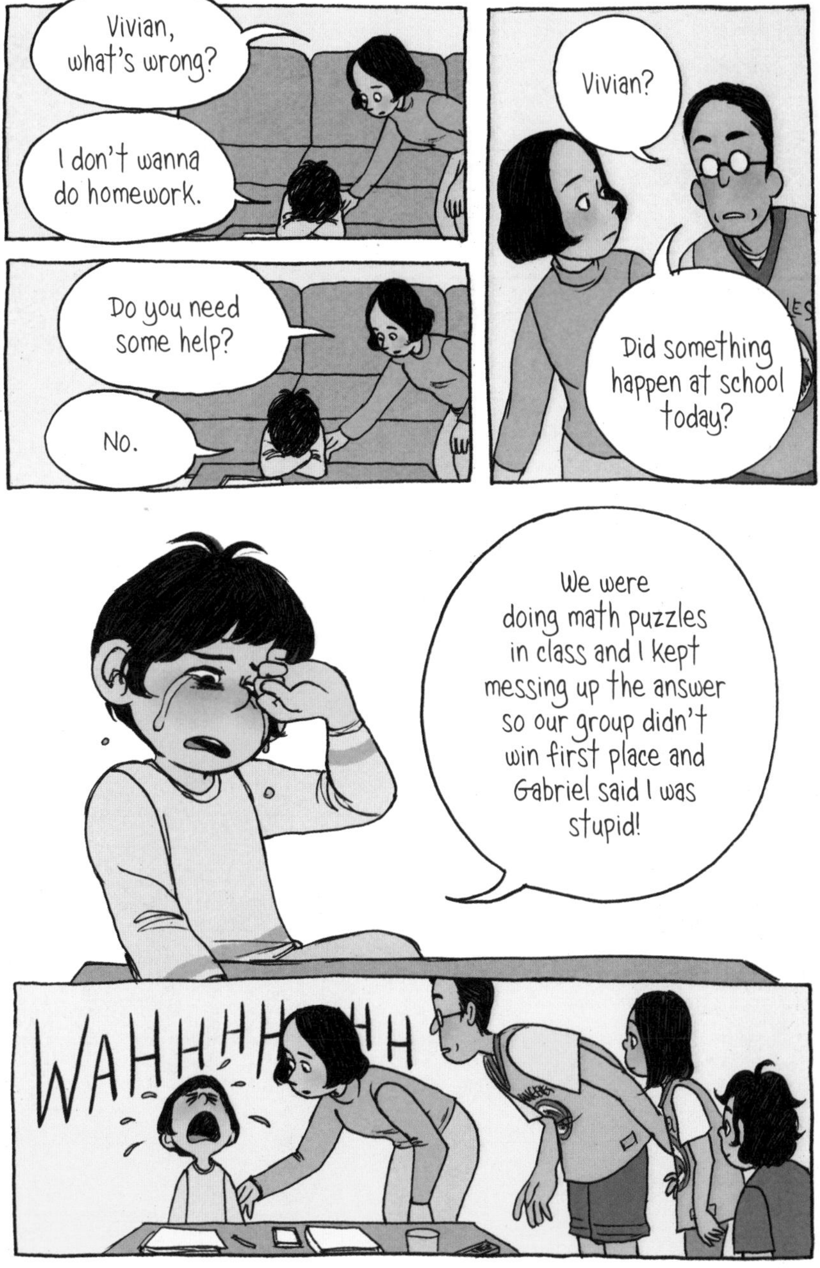
Vivian, what's wrong?
I don't wanna do homework.
Do you need some help?
No.
Vivian?
Did something happen at school today?
We were doing math puzzles in class and I kept messing up the answer so our group didn't win first place and Gabriel said I was stupid!
WAHHHHHHH

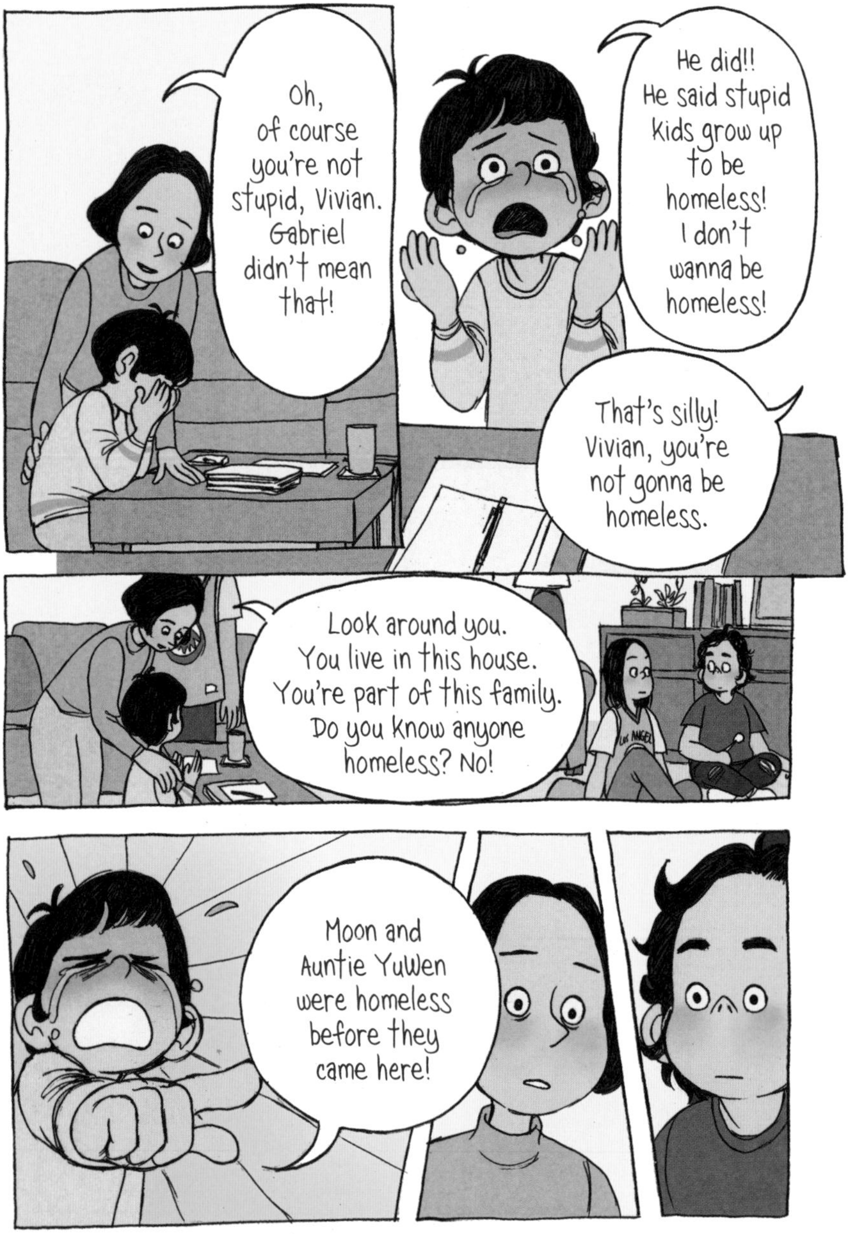

Oh, of course you're not stupid, Vivian. Gabriel didn't mean that!
He did!! He said stupid kids grow up to be homeless! I don't wanna be homeless!
That's silly! Vivian, you're not gonna be homeless.
Look around you. You live in this house. You're part of this family. Do you know anyone homeless? No!
Moon and Auntie YuWen were homeless before they came here!

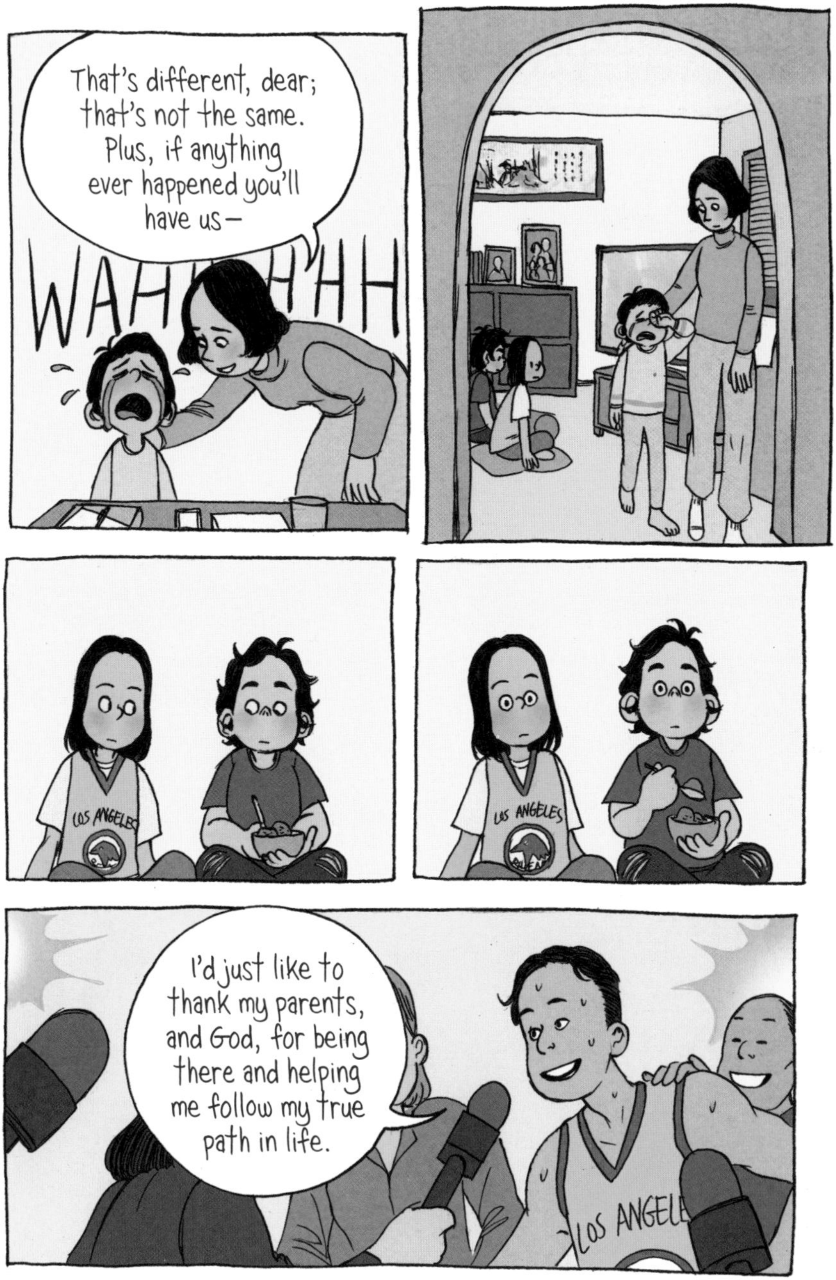
That's different, dear; that's not the same. Plus, if anything ever happened you'll have us—
WAH HHH
LOS ANGELES
LOS ANGELES
I'd just like to thank my parents, and God, for being there and helping me follow my true path in life.
LOS ANGELE

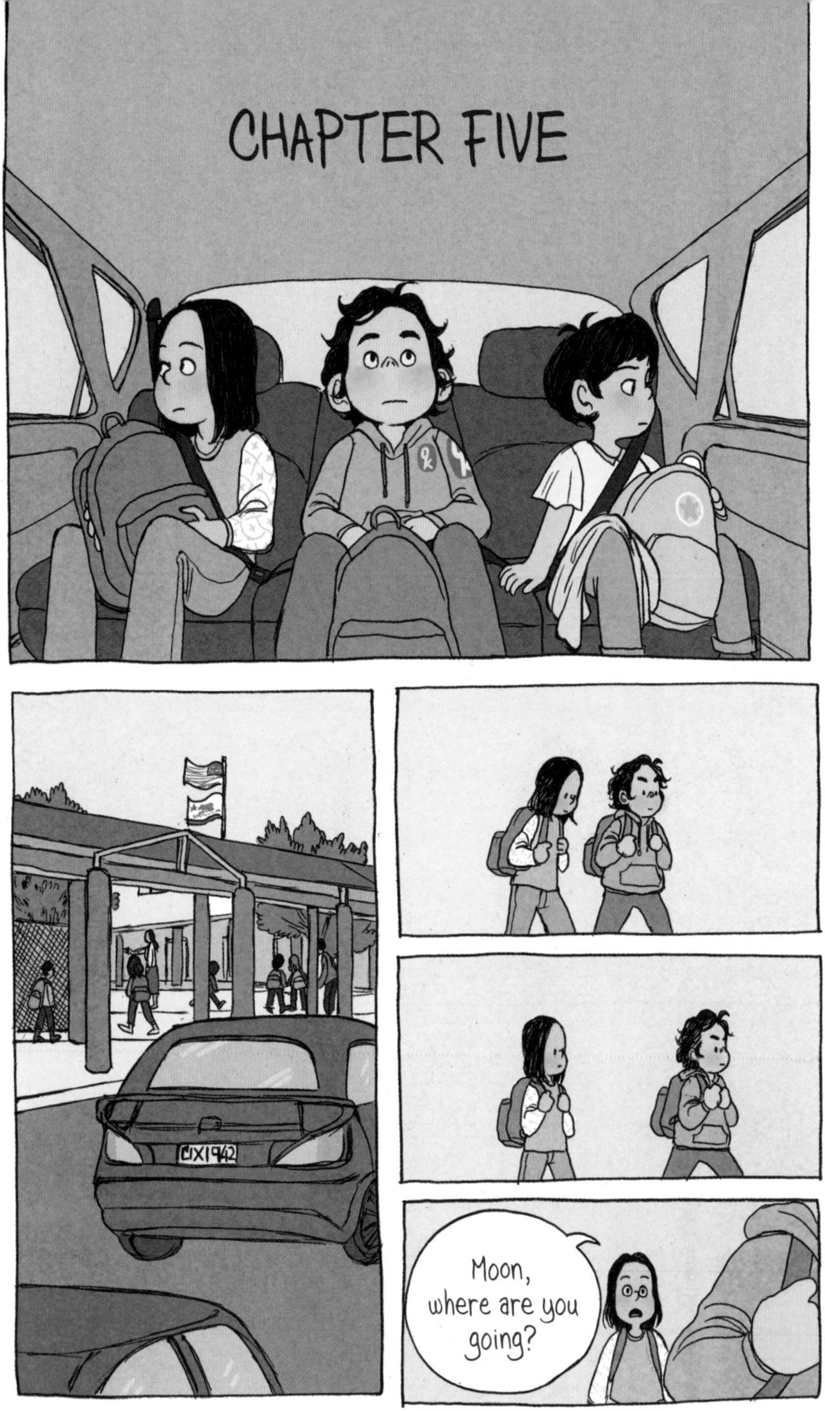
CHAPTER FIVE
CIX1942
Moon, where are you going?

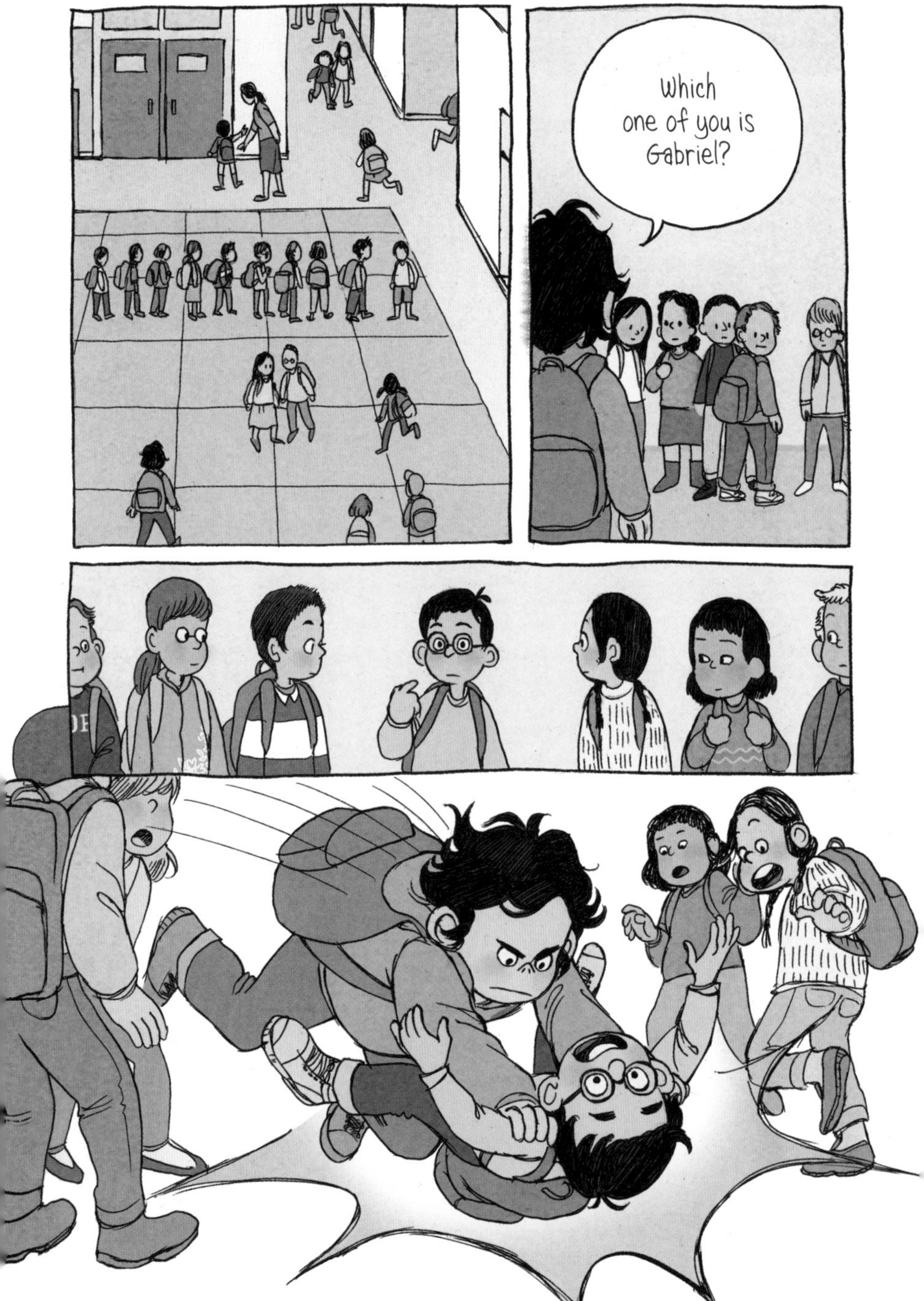
Which one of you is Gabriel?

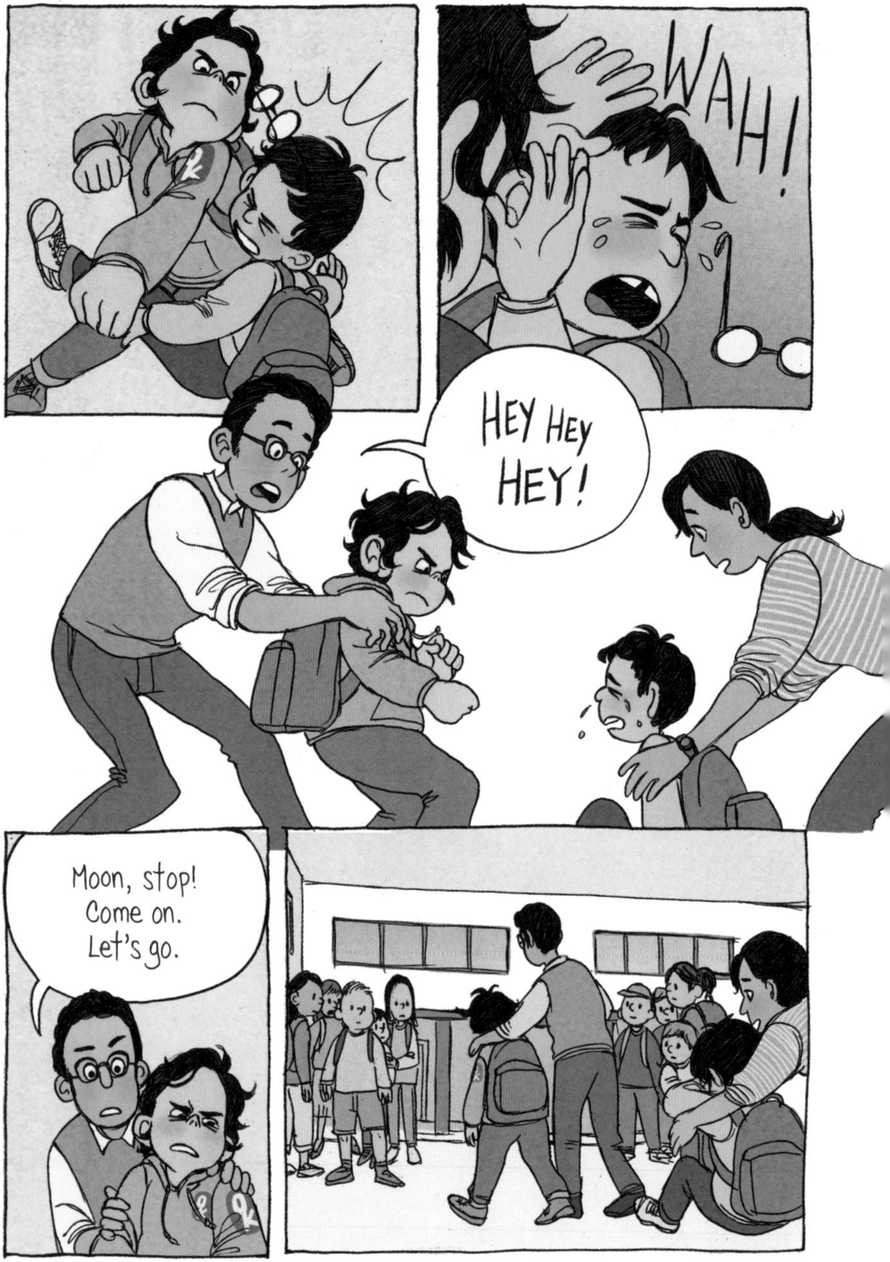
WAH!
HEY HEY HEY!
Moon, stop! Come on. Let's go.

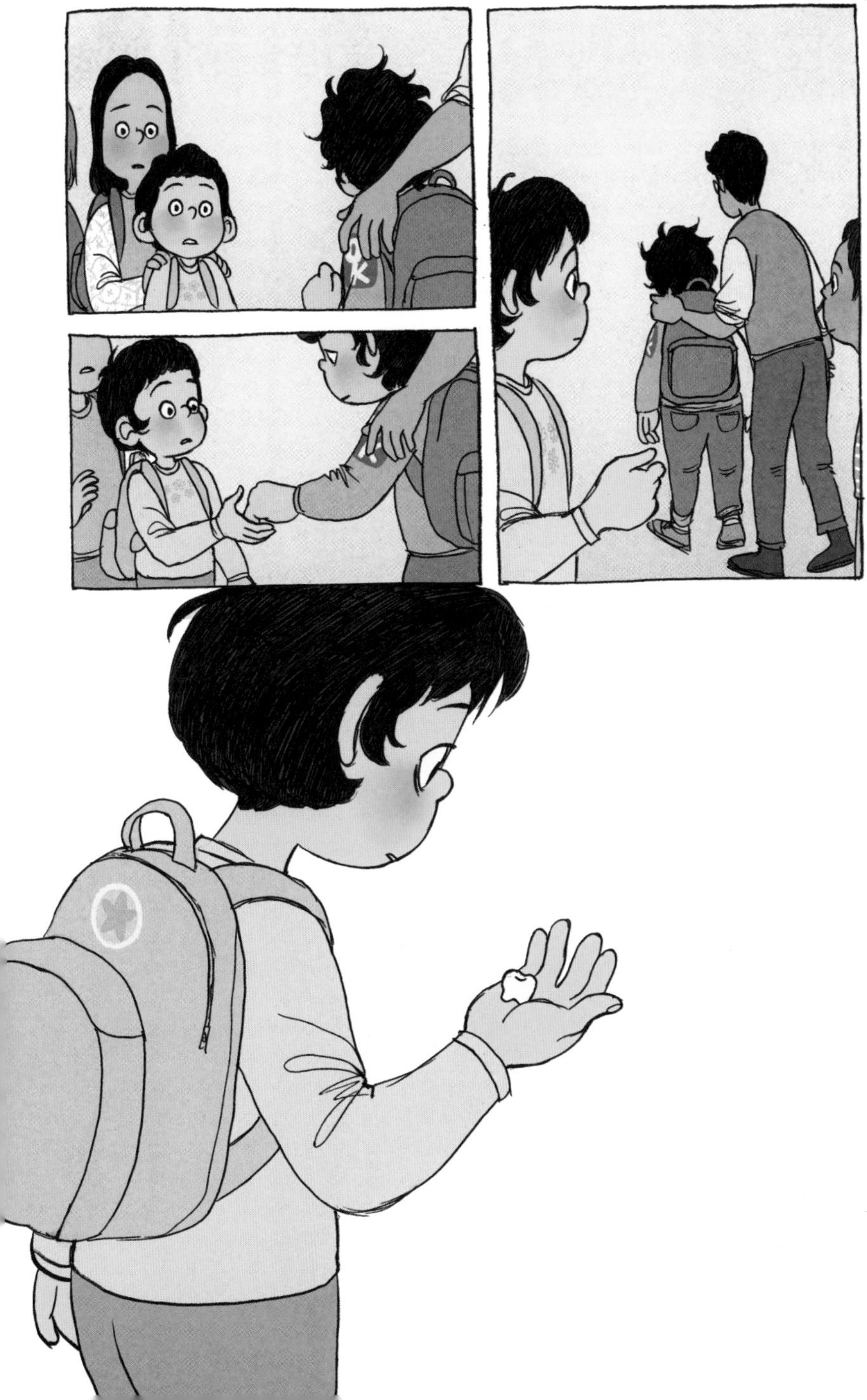

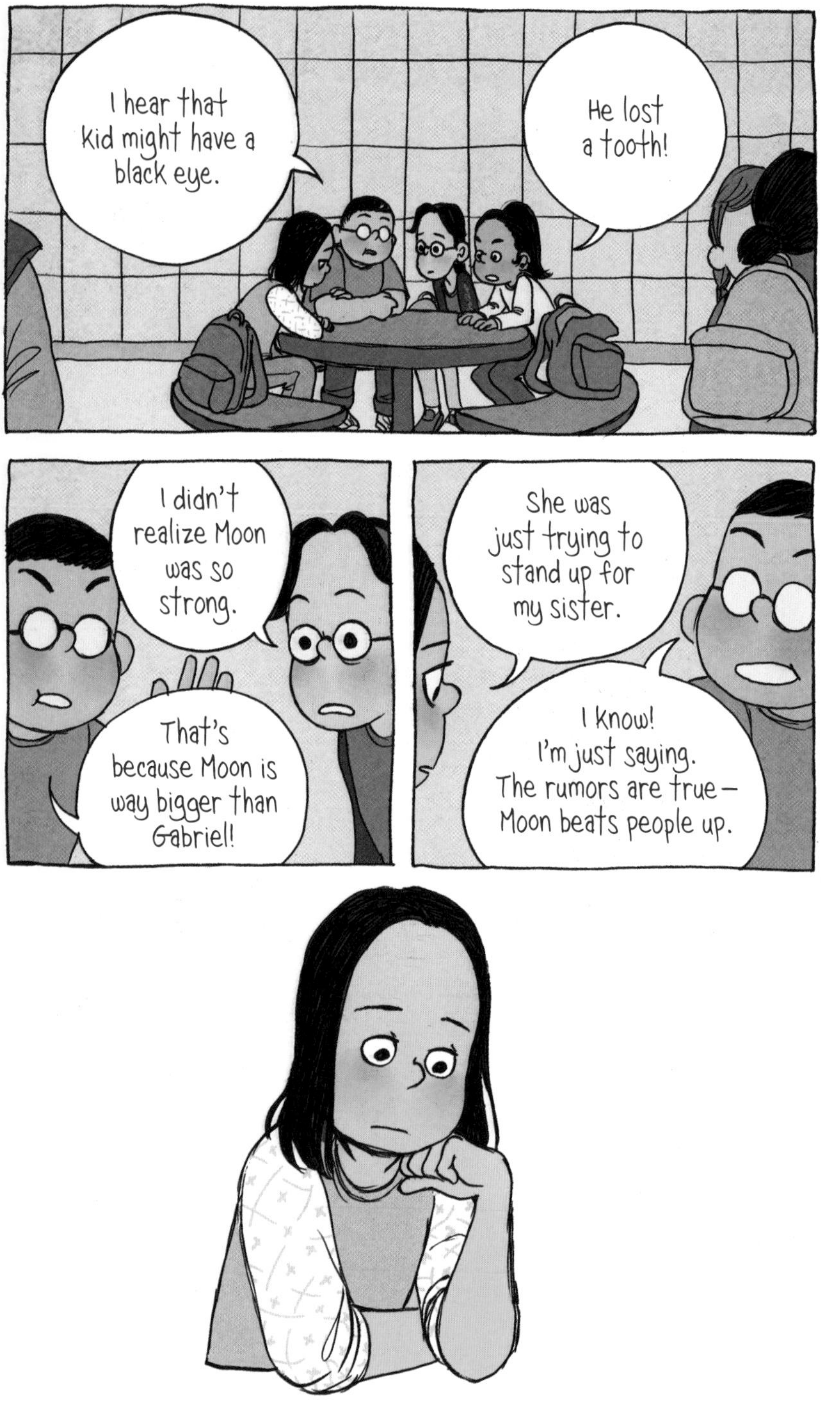
I hear that kid might have a black eye.
He lost a tooth!
I didn't realize Moon was so strong.
That's because Moon is way bigger than Gabriel!
She was just trying to stand up for my sister.
I know! I'm just saying. The rumors are true— Moon beats people up.

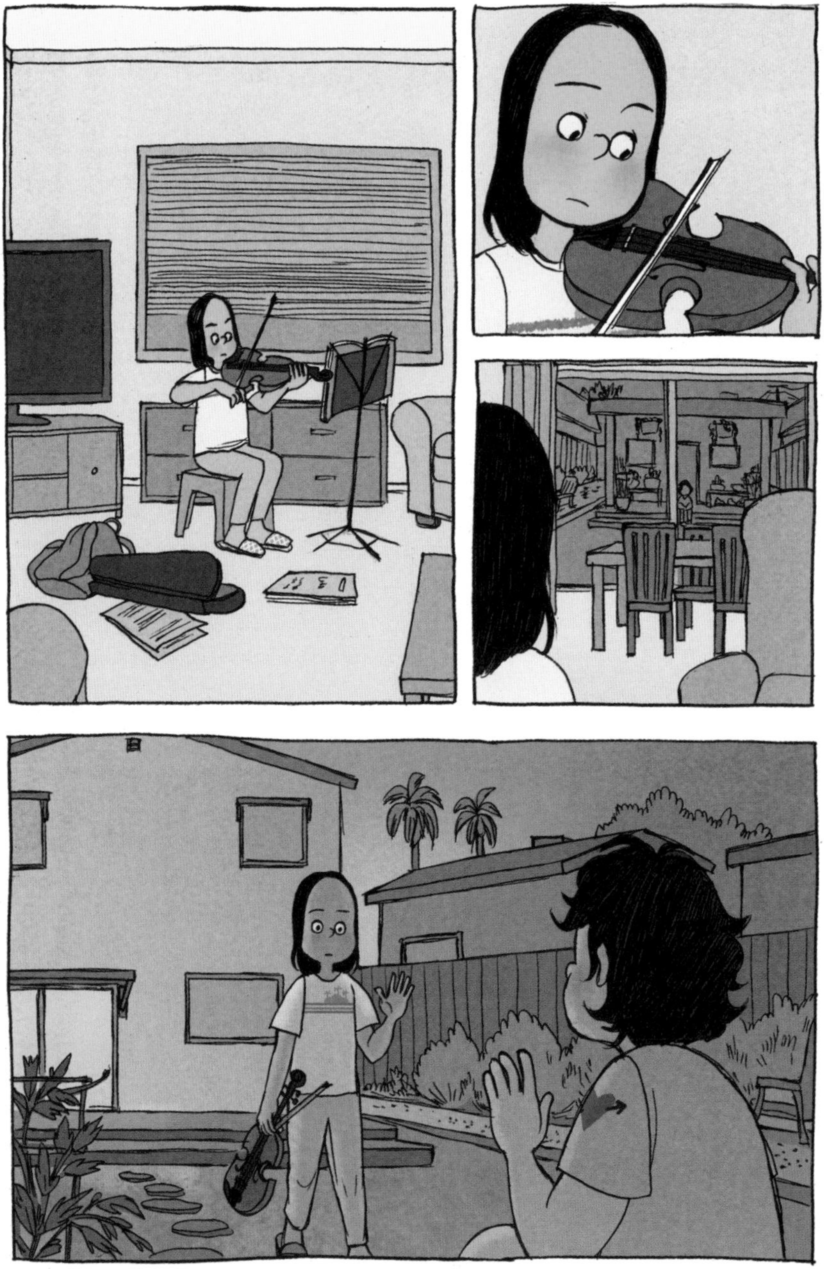

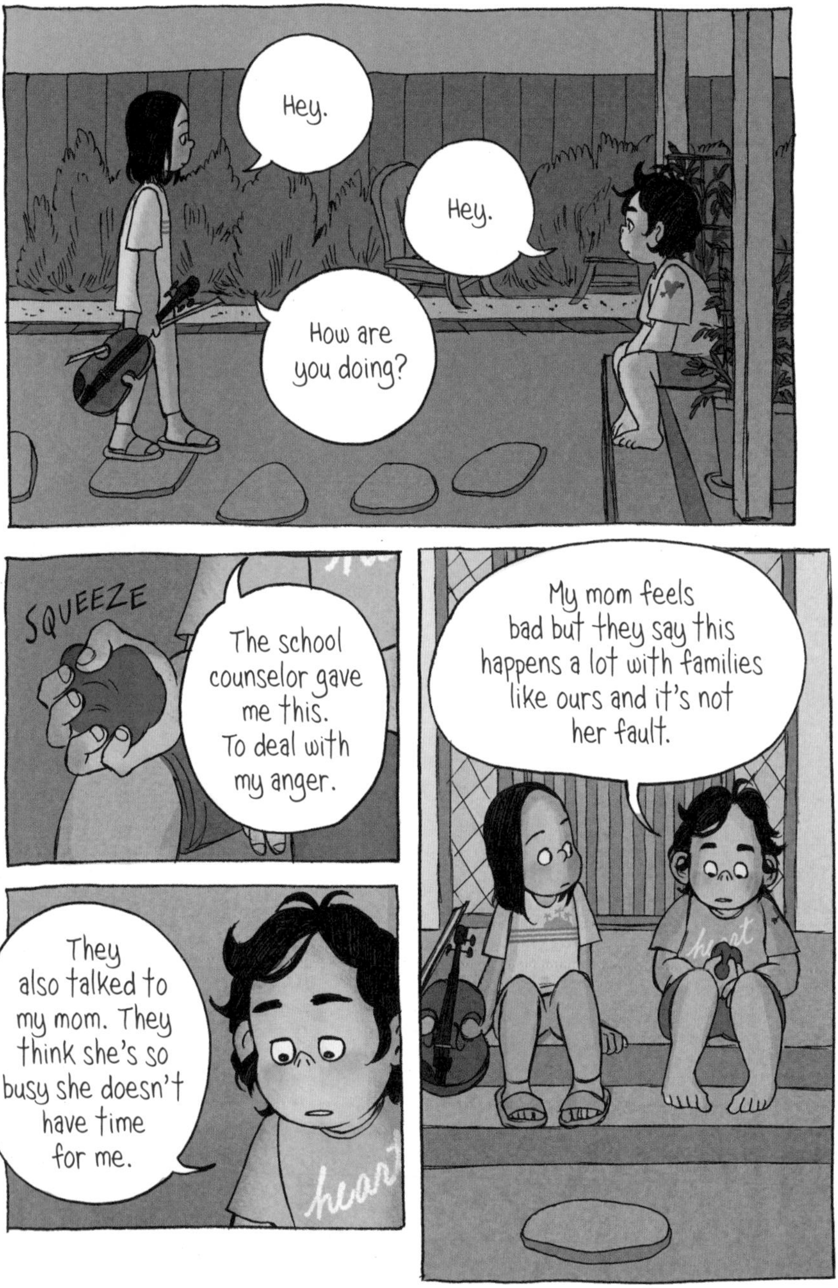
Hey.
Hey.
How are you doing?
SQUEEZE
The school counselor gave me this. To deal with my anger.
My mom feels bad but they say this happens a lot with families like ours and it's not her fault.
They also talked to my mom. They think she's so busy she doesn't have time for me.
heart

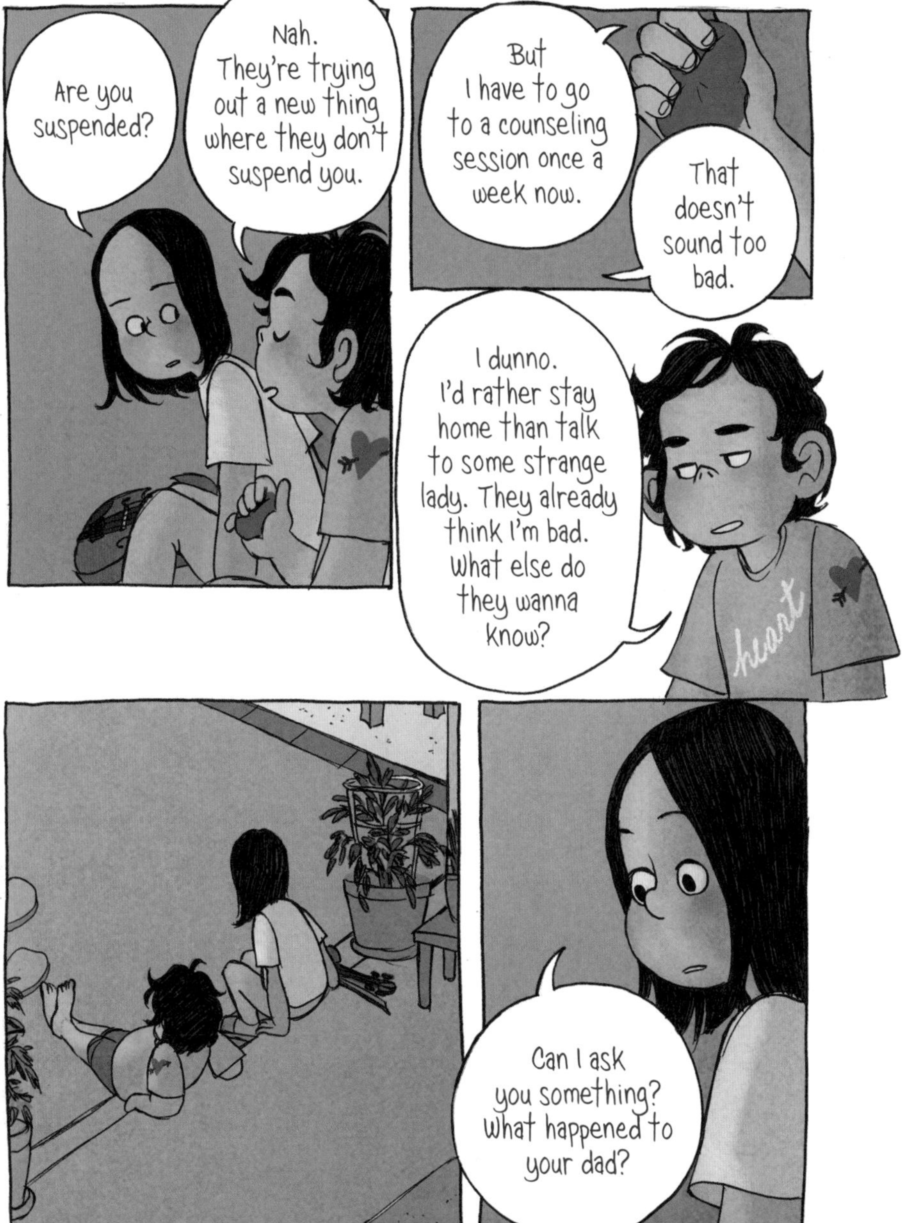
Are you suspended?
Nah. They're trying out a new thing where they don't suspend you.
But I have to go to a counseling session once a week now.
That doesn't sound too bad.
I dunno. I'd rather stay home than talk to some strange lady. They already think I'm bad. What else do they wanna know?
heart
Can I ask you something? What happened to your dad?

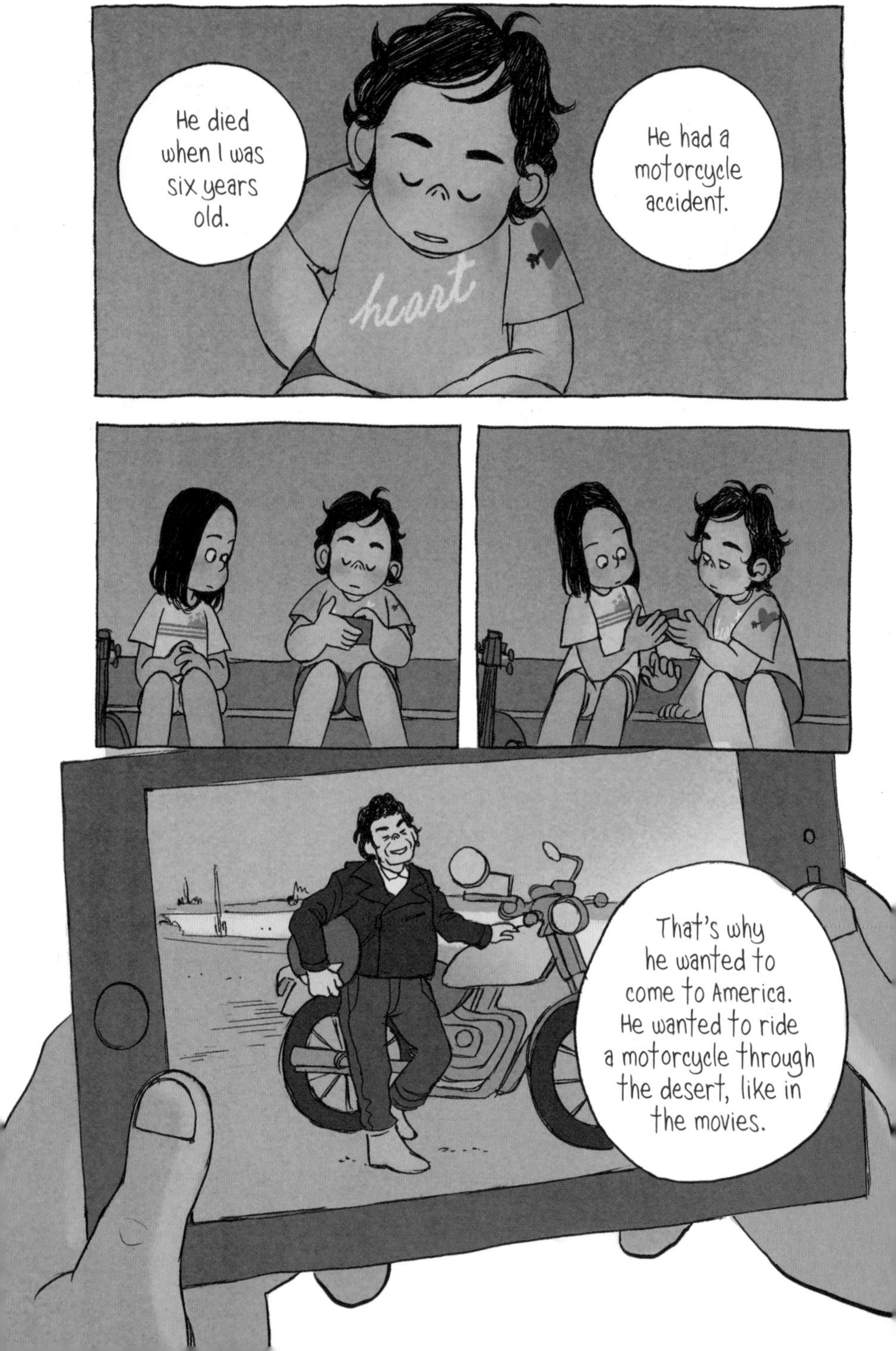
He died when I was six years old.
He had a motorcycle accident.
heart
That's why he wanted to come to America. He wanted to ride a motorcycle through the desert, like in the movies.

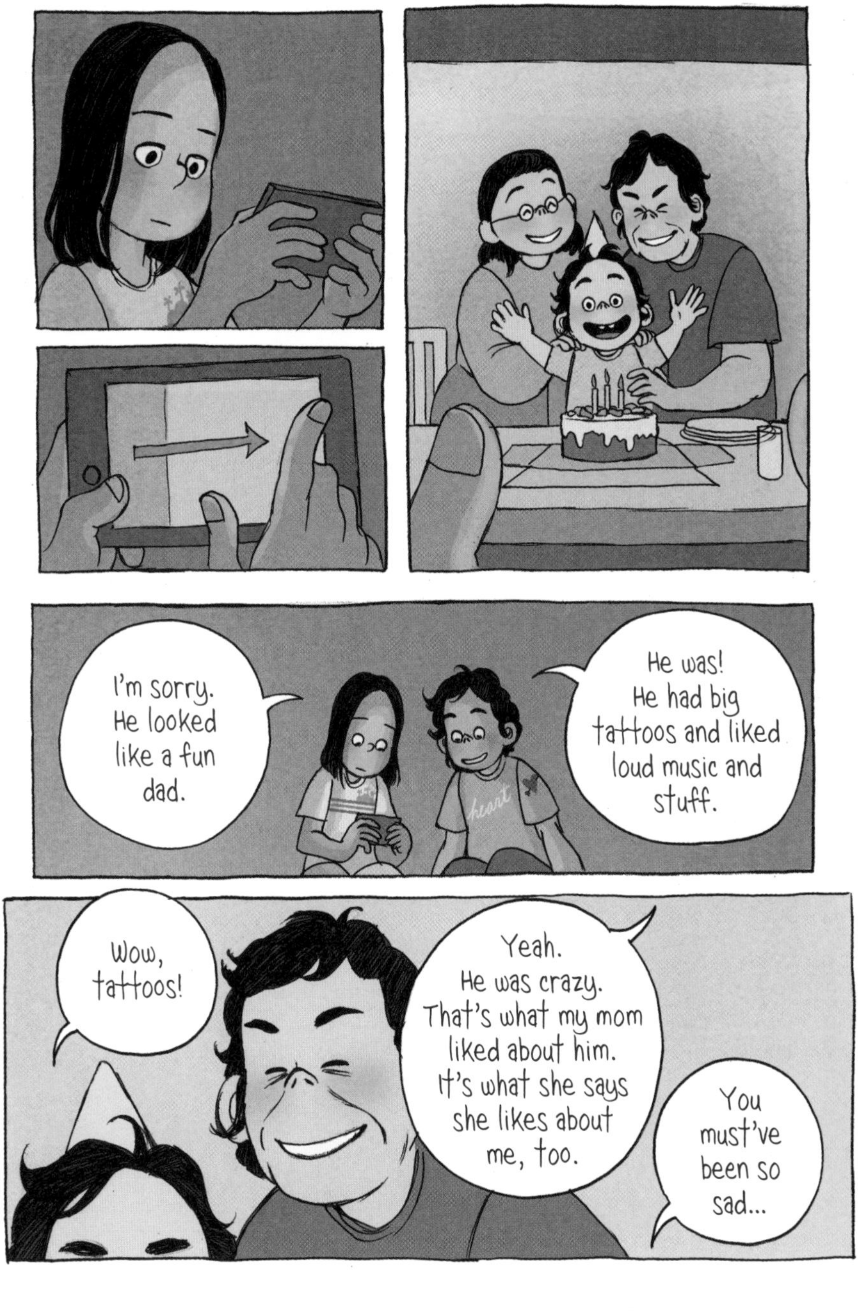
I'm sorry. He looked like a fun dad.
He was! He had big tattoos and liked loud music and stuff.
Wow, tattoos!
Yeah. He was crazy. That's what my mom liked about him. It's what she says she likes about me, too.
You must've been so sad...

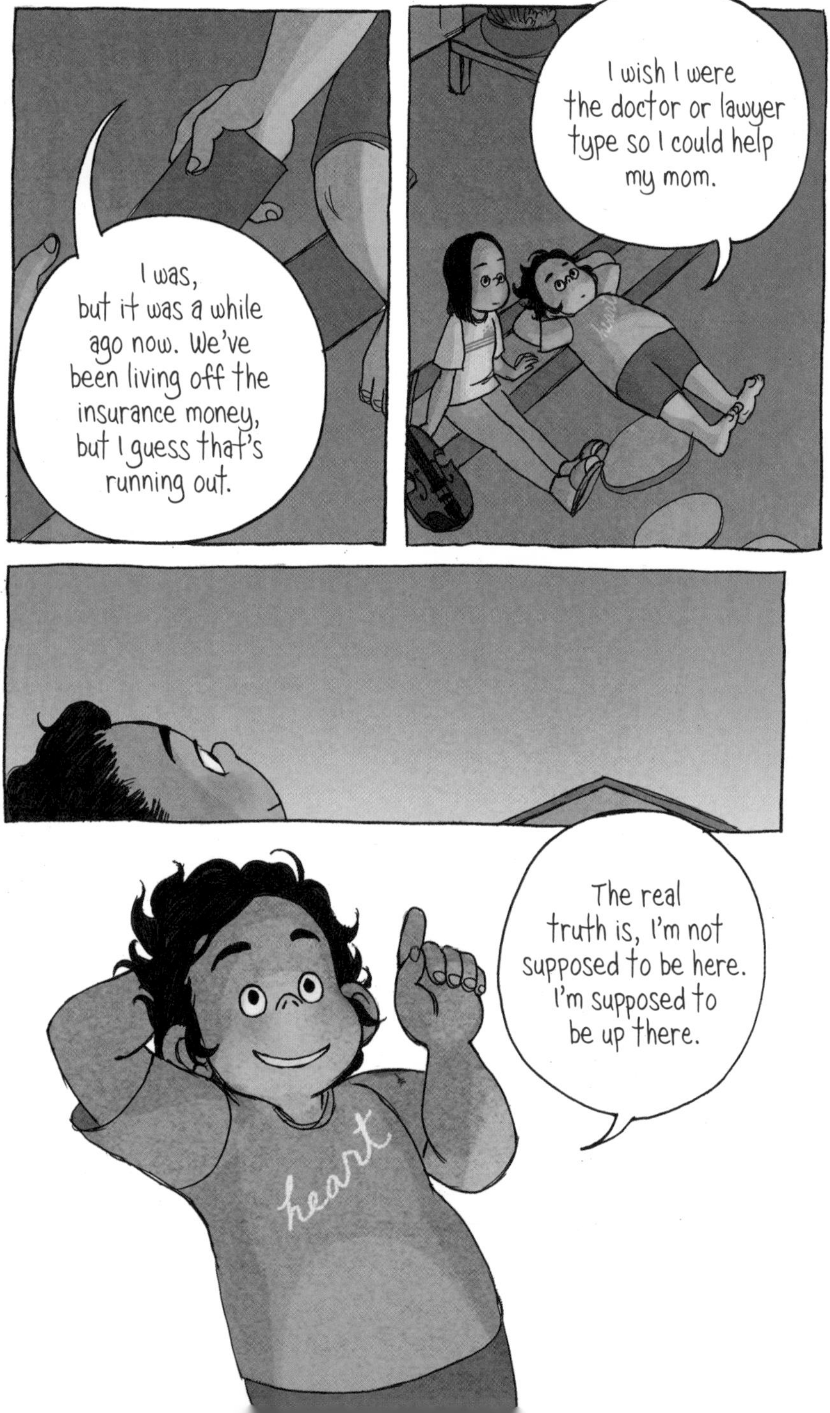
I was, but it was a while ago now. We've been living off the insurance money, but I guess that's running out.
I wish I were the doctor or lawyer type so I could help my mom.
The real truth is, I'm not supposed to be here. I'm supposed to be up there.
heart

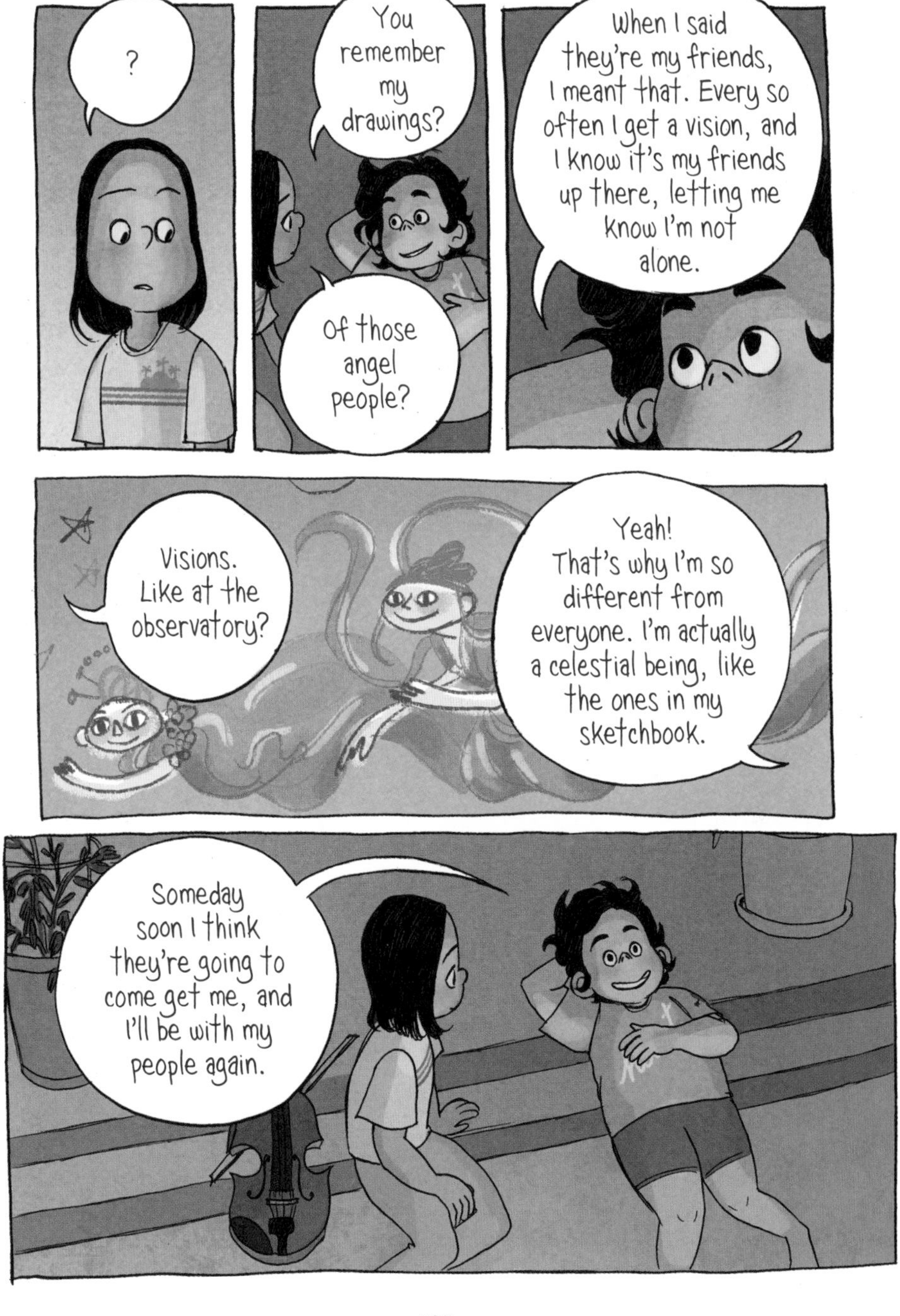
?
You remember my drawings?
Of those angel people?
When I said they're my friends, I meant that. Every so often I get a vision, and I know it's my friends up there, letting me know I'm not alone.
Visions. Like at the observatory?
Yeah! That's why I'm so different from everyone. I'm actually a celestial being, like the ones in my sketchbook.
Someday soon I think they're going to come get me, and I'll be with my people again.

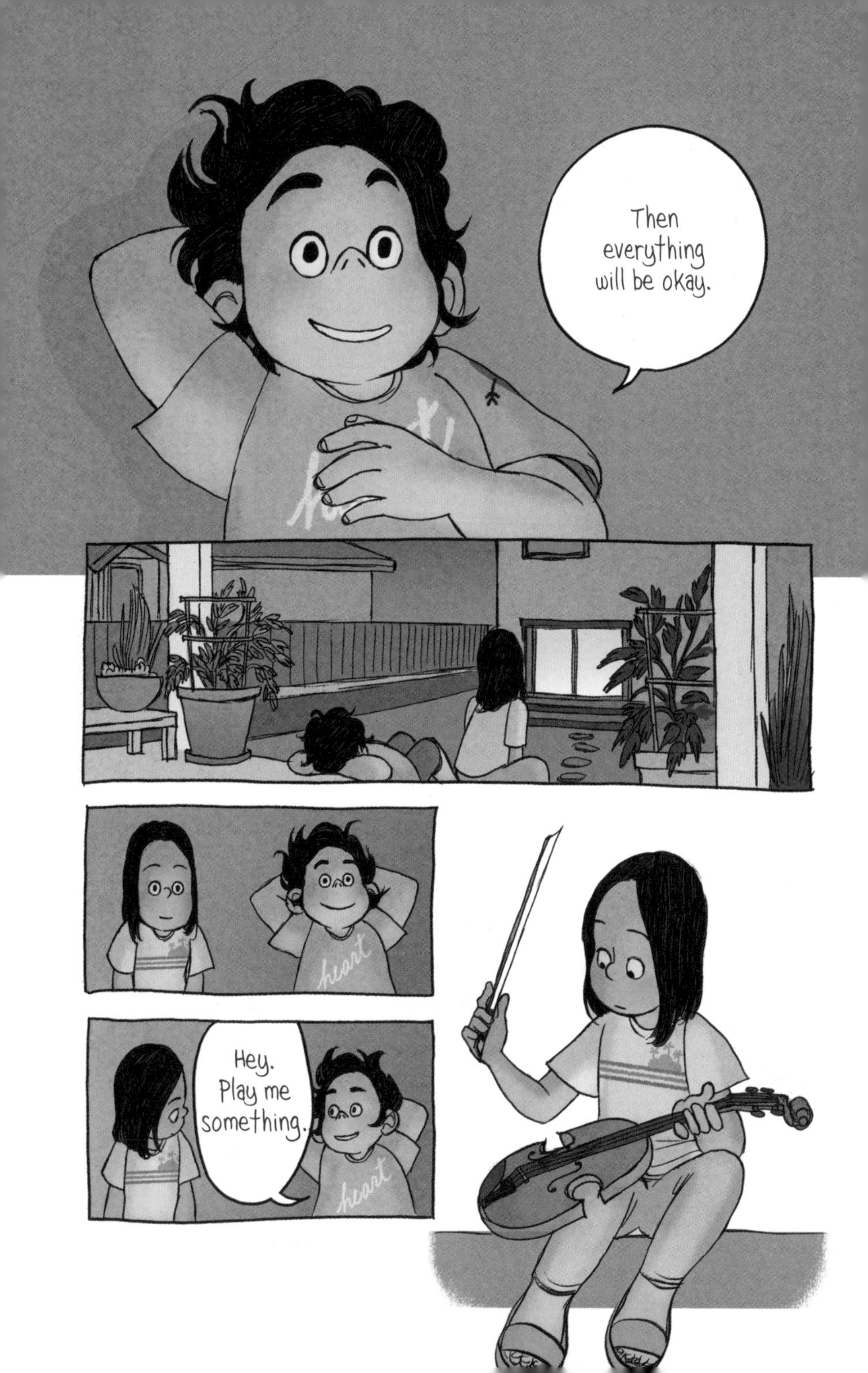
Then everything will be okay.
Hey. Play me something.

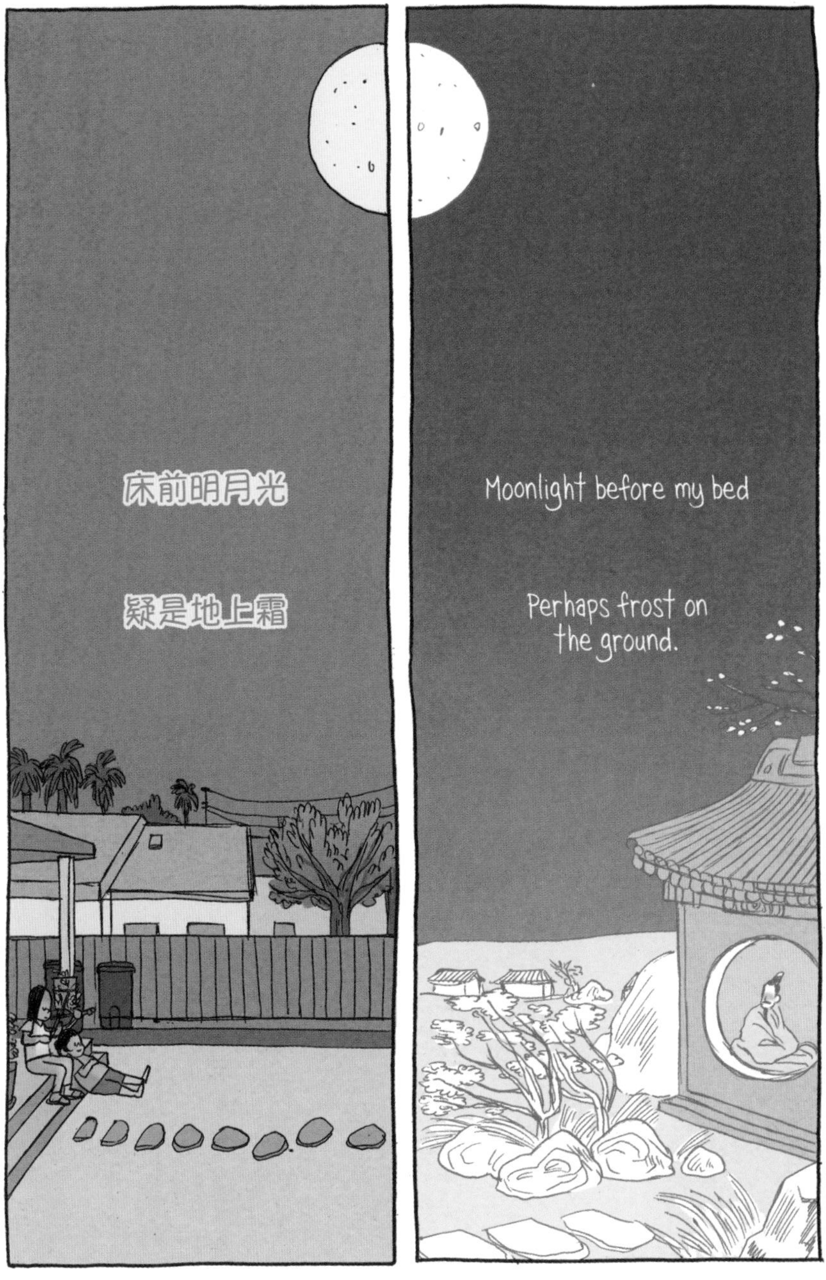
床前明月光
疑是地上霜
Moonlight before my bed
Perhaps frost on the ground.

舉頭望明月

Lift my head and see the moon

低頭思故鄉

Lower my head and
pine for home.

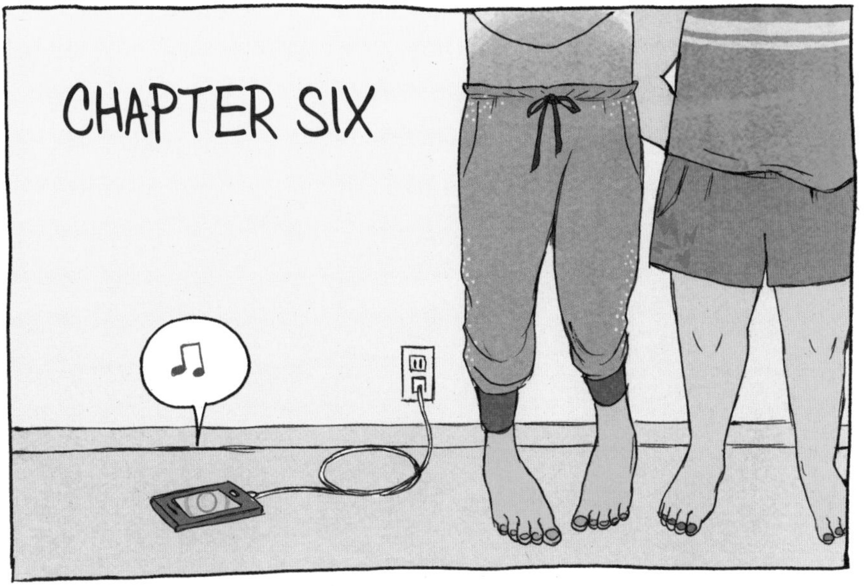
CHAPTER SIX
♫

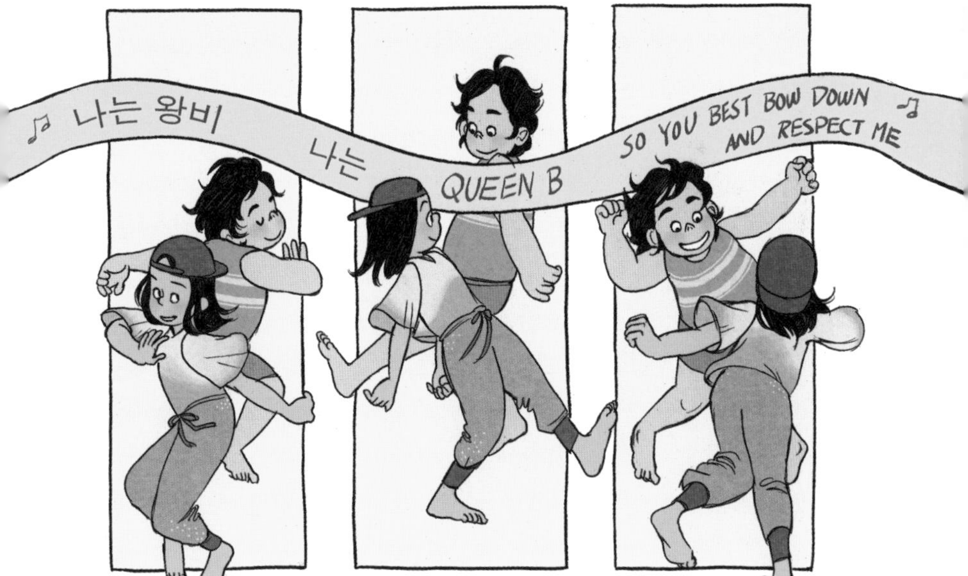
♫ 나는 왕비
나는
QUEEN B
SO YOU BEST BOW DOWN
AND RESPECT ME ♫

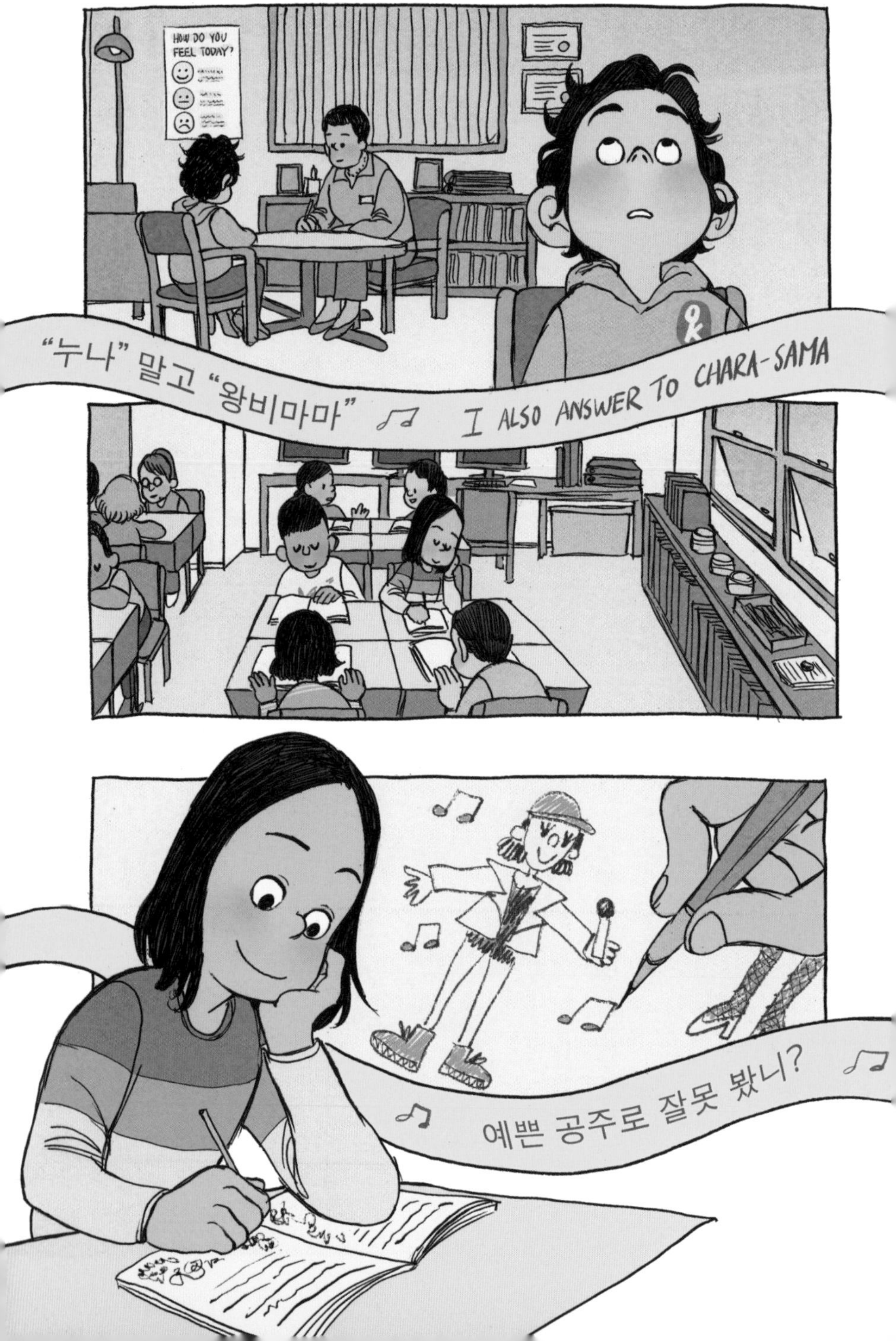
HOW DO YOU FEEL TODAY?
"누나" 말고 "왕비마마" I ALSO ANSWER TO CHARA-SAMA
예쁜 공주로 잘못 봤니?

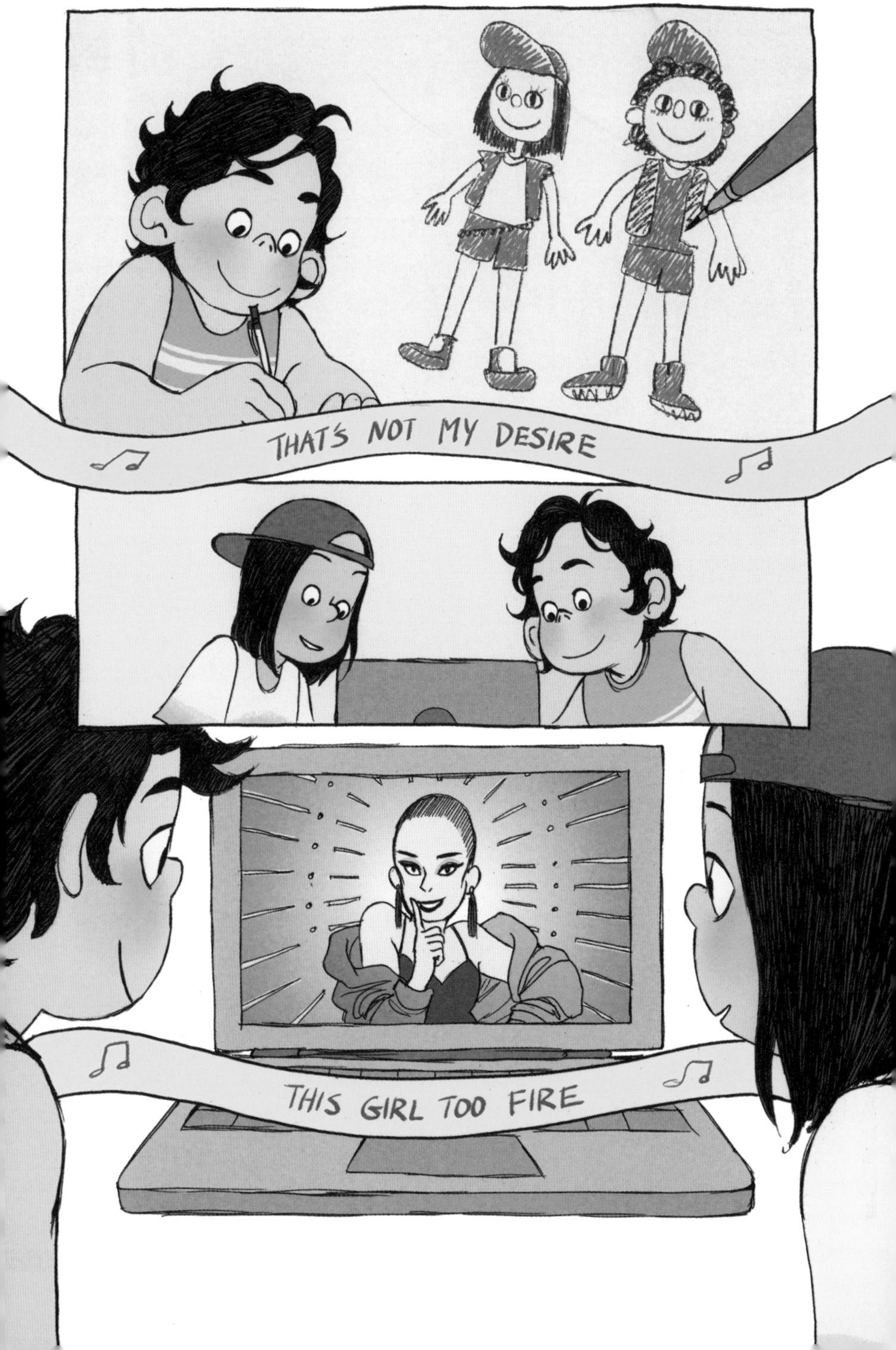
THAT'S NOT MY DESIRE
THIS GIRL TOO FIRE

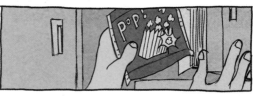

Hey, Christine! Come help your dad.

Stick this in the yellow jack. I'm too big to reach back there.

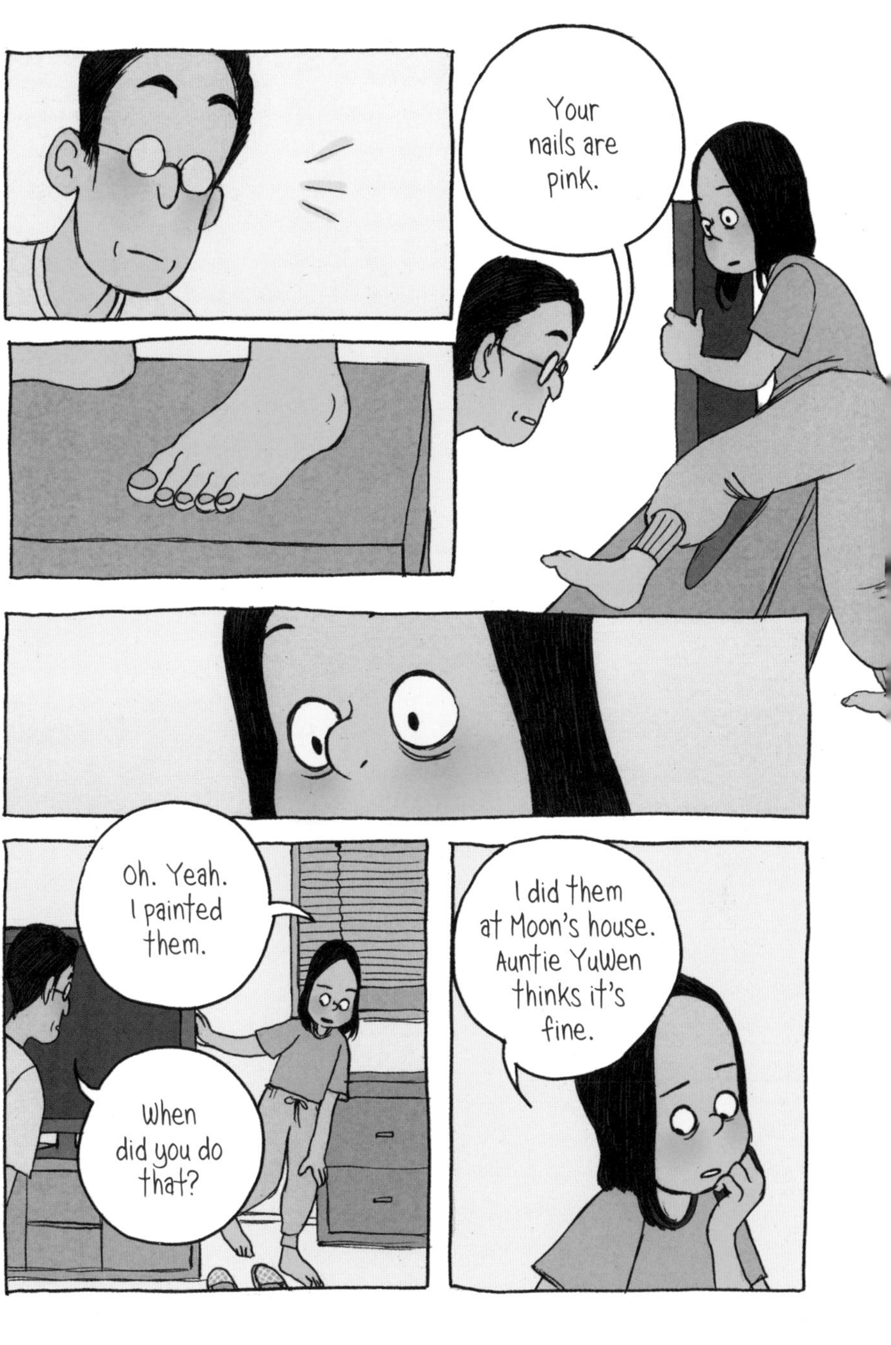

Your nails are pink.
Oh. Yeah. I painted them.
When did you do that?
I did them at Moon's house. Auntie YuWen thinks it's fine.

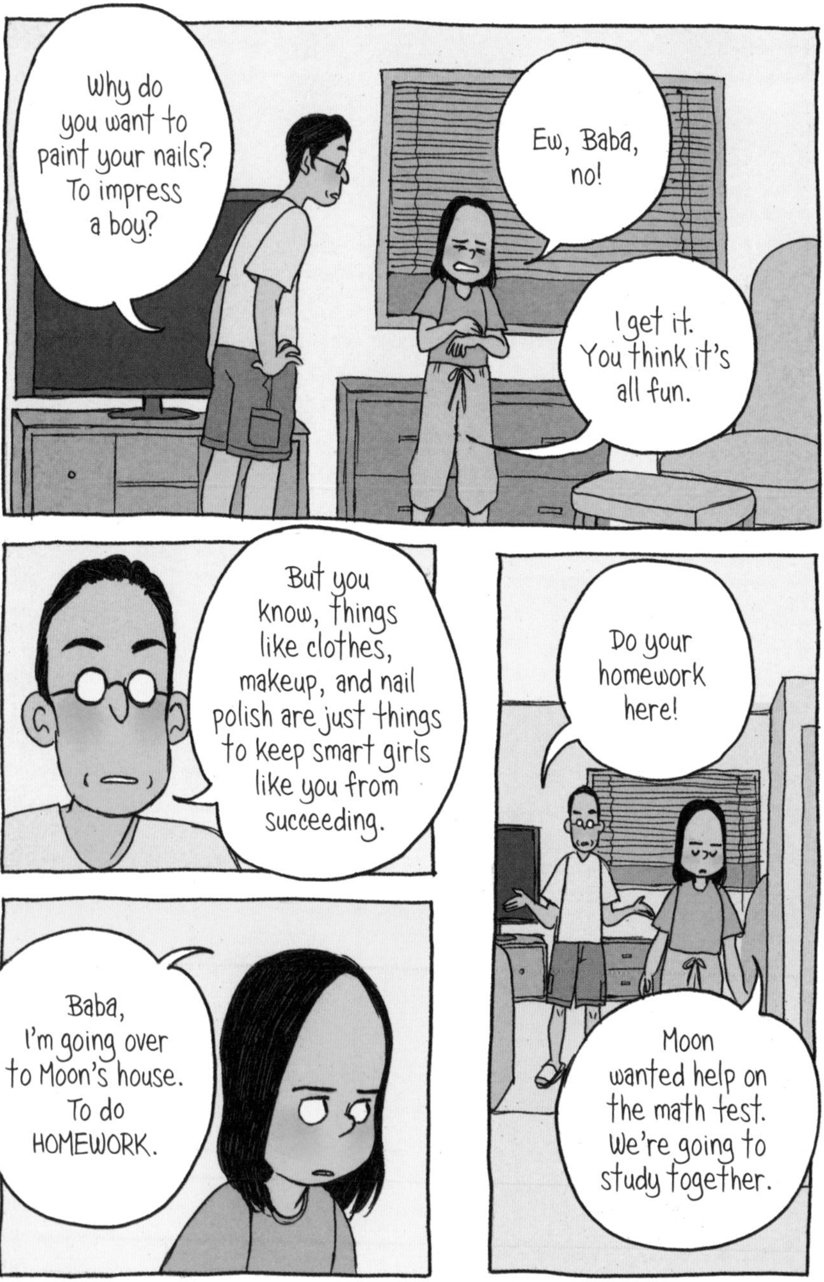
Why do you want to paint your nails? To impress a boy?
Ew, Baba, no!
I get it. You think it's all fun.
But you know, things like clothes, makeup, and nail polish are just things to keep smart girls like you from succeeding.
Baba, I'm going over to Moon's house. To do HOMEWORK.
Do your homework here!
Moon wanted help on the math test. We're going to study together.

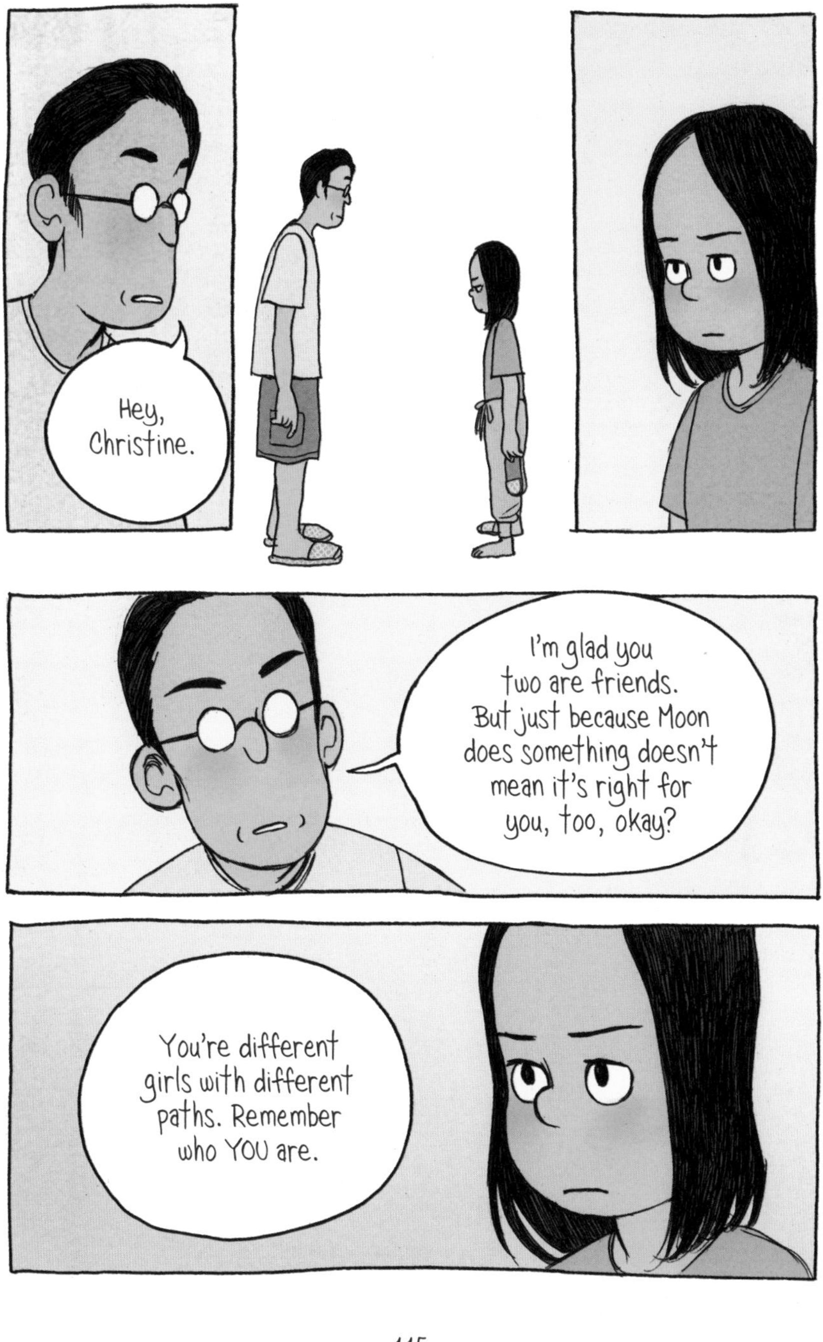
Hey, Christine.
I'm glad you two are friends. But just because Moon does something doesn't mean it's right for you, too, okay?
You're different girls with different paths. Remember who YOU are.

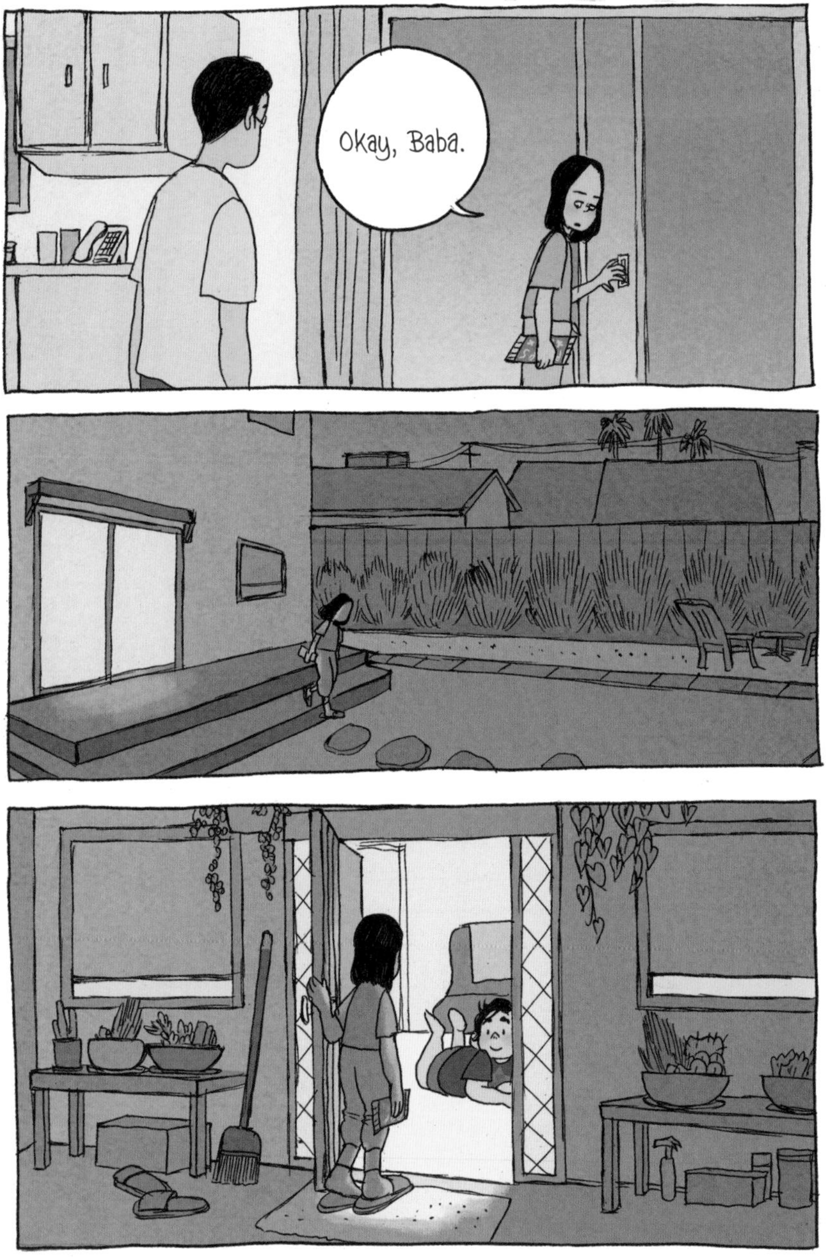
Okay, Baba.

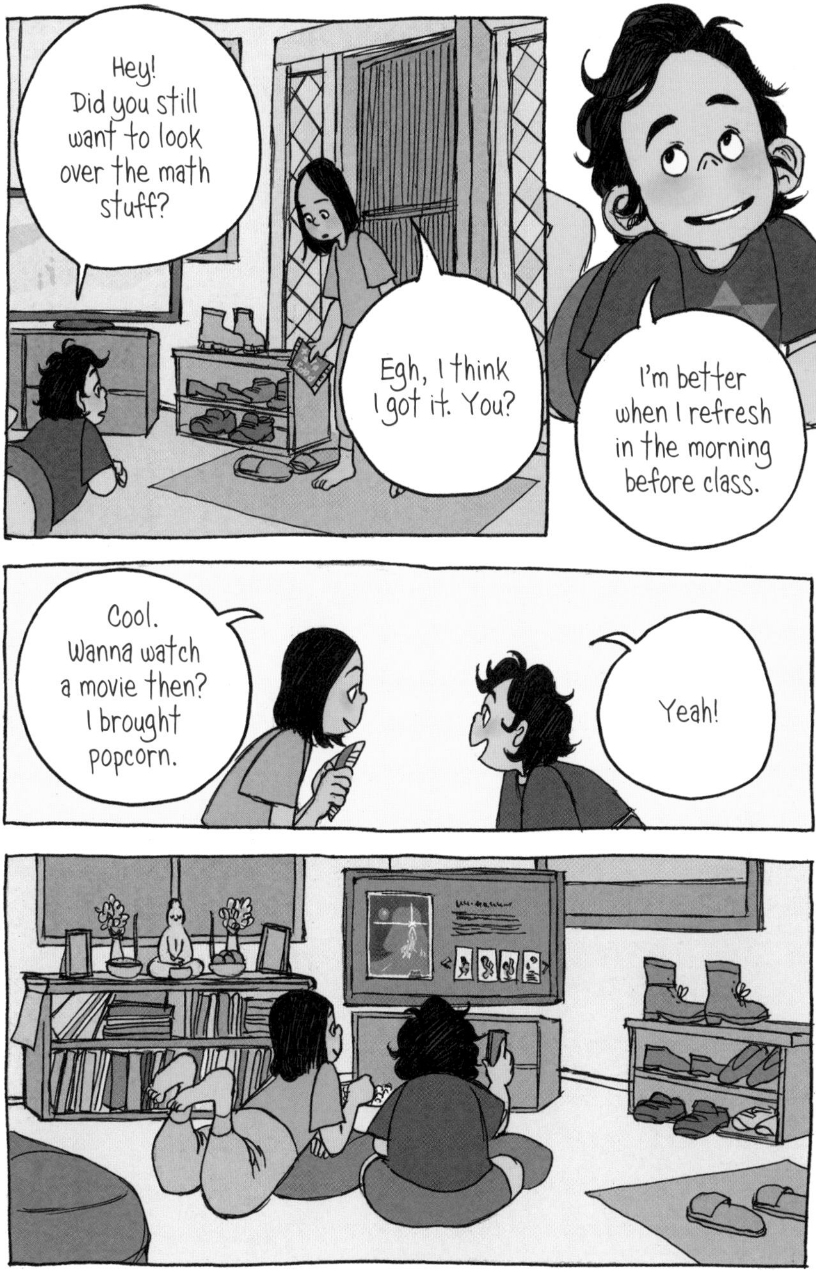
Hey! Did you still want to look over the math stuff?
Egh, I think I got it. You?
I'm better when I refresh in the morning before class.
Cool. Wanna watch a movie then? I brought popcorn.
Yeah!

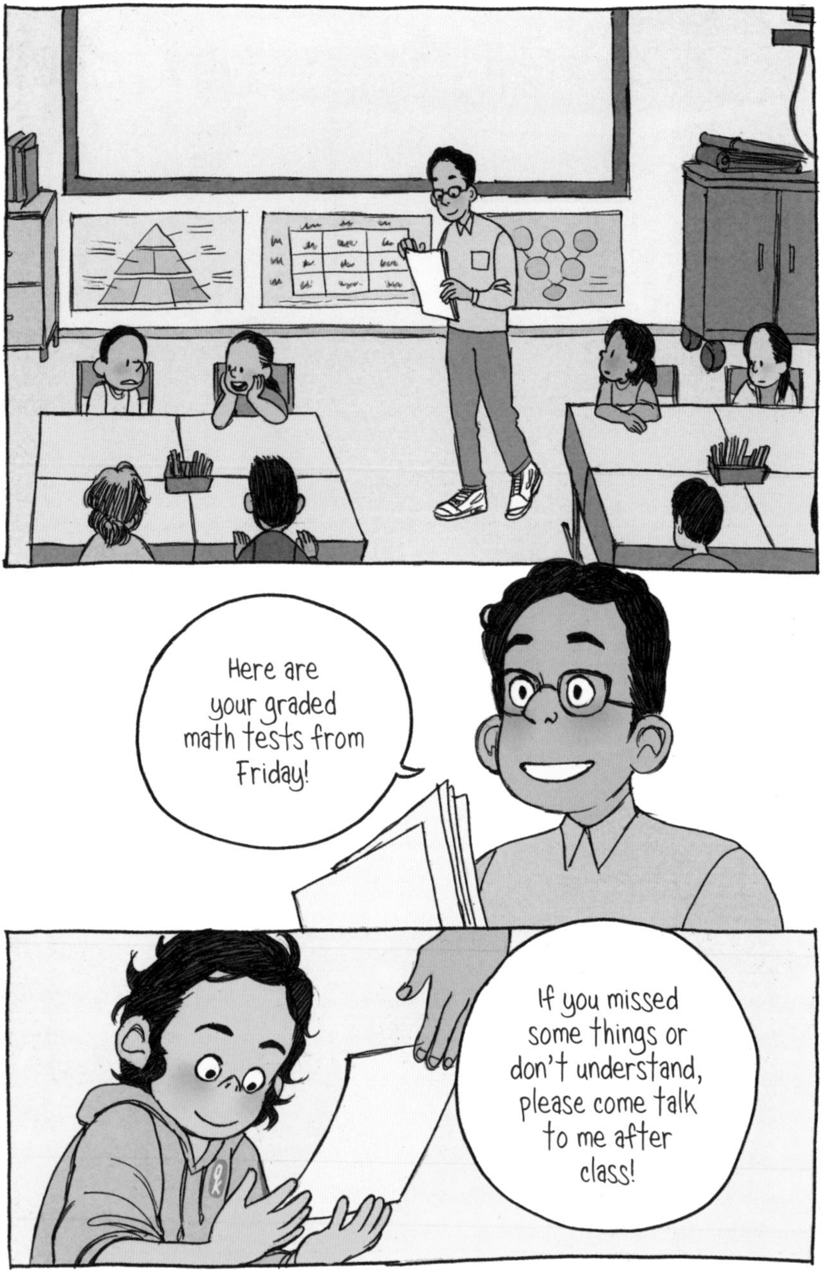
Here are your graded math tests from Friday!
If you missed some things or don't understand, please come talk to me after class!

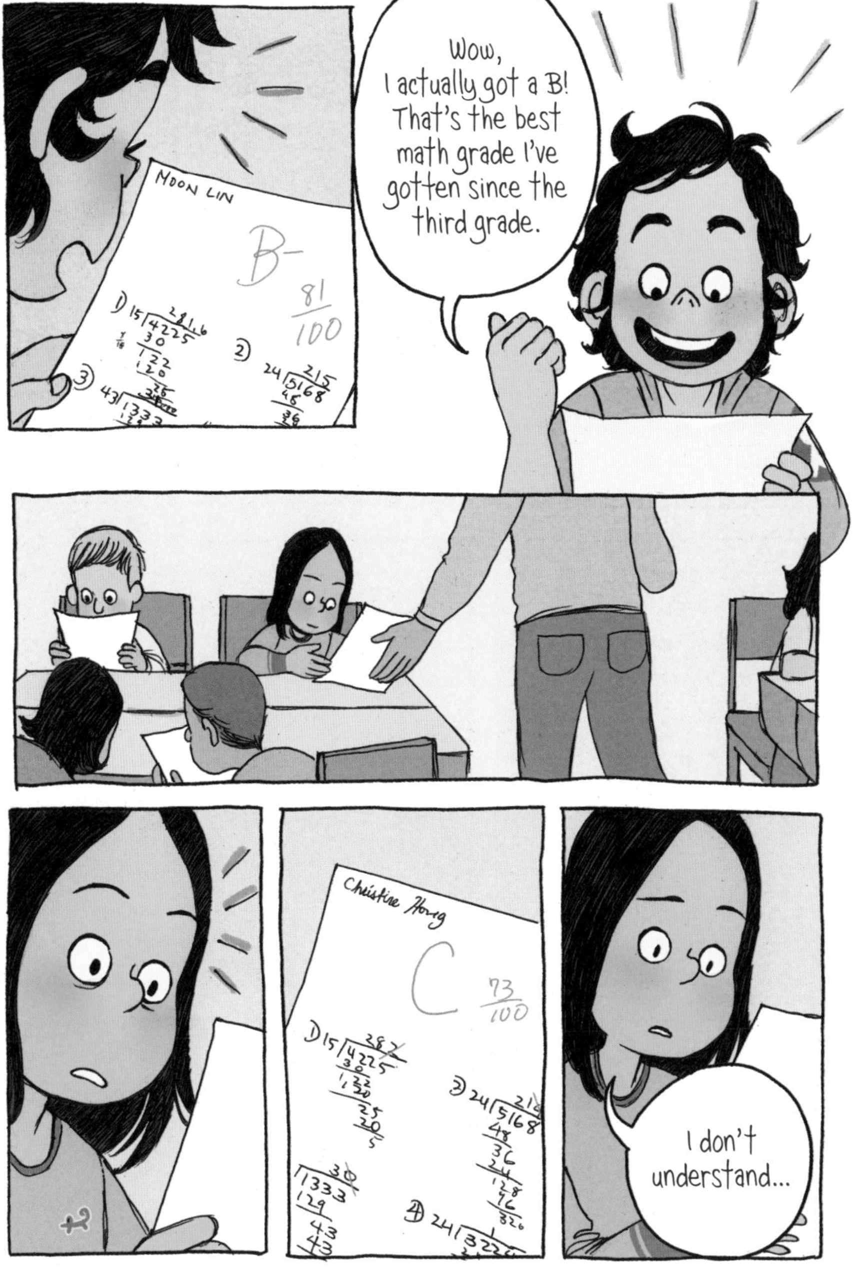
MOON LIN
B-
81/100
Wow, I actually got a B! That's the best math grade I've gotten since the third grade.
Christine Hong
C
73/100
I don't understand...

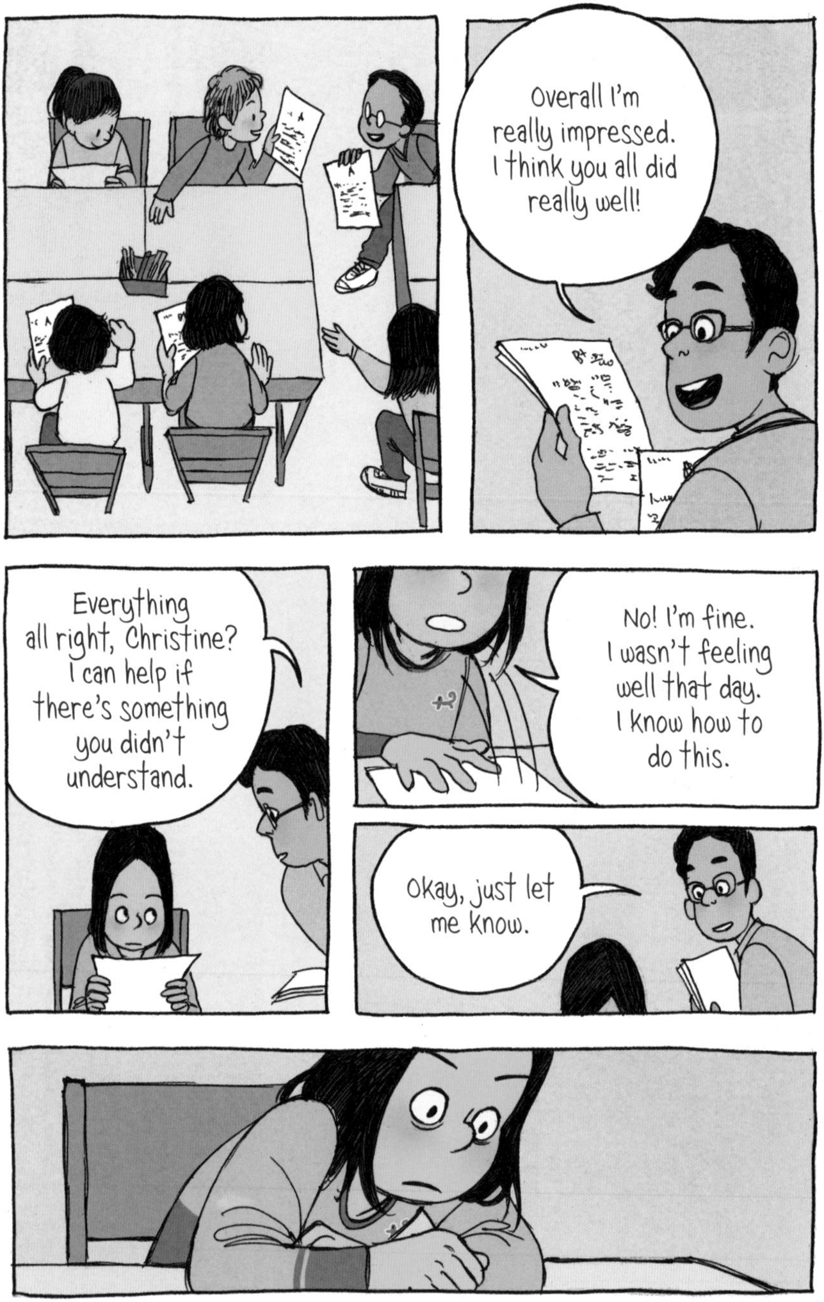
Overall I'm really impressed. I think you all did really well!
Everything all right, Christine? I can help if there's something you didn't understand.
No! I'm fine. I wasn't feeling well that day. I know how to do this.
Okay, just let me know.

RANCH MARKET
花菇
BISCUIT
CANDY
FRUIT
SNACK
CAKE
SALE
1.29
1.29
1.29
4.50
4.50
6.99
6.99
5.99
3.99
2.50
BBQ
4.25
3.29
9.99
MATHLETICS
STUDY ACADEMY
BOOST YOUR ABILITY!
1623 S AZUSA AVE
HACIENDA HEIGHTS
CA, 91745
(626) 717-1142
FREE TRIAL CLASS

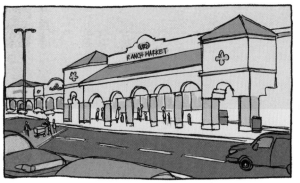

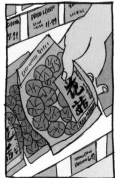

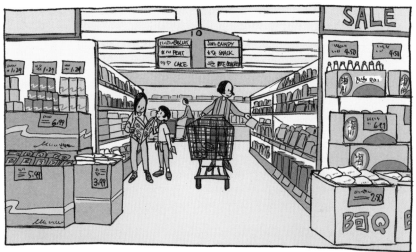

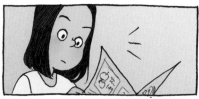

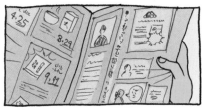

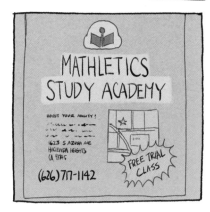

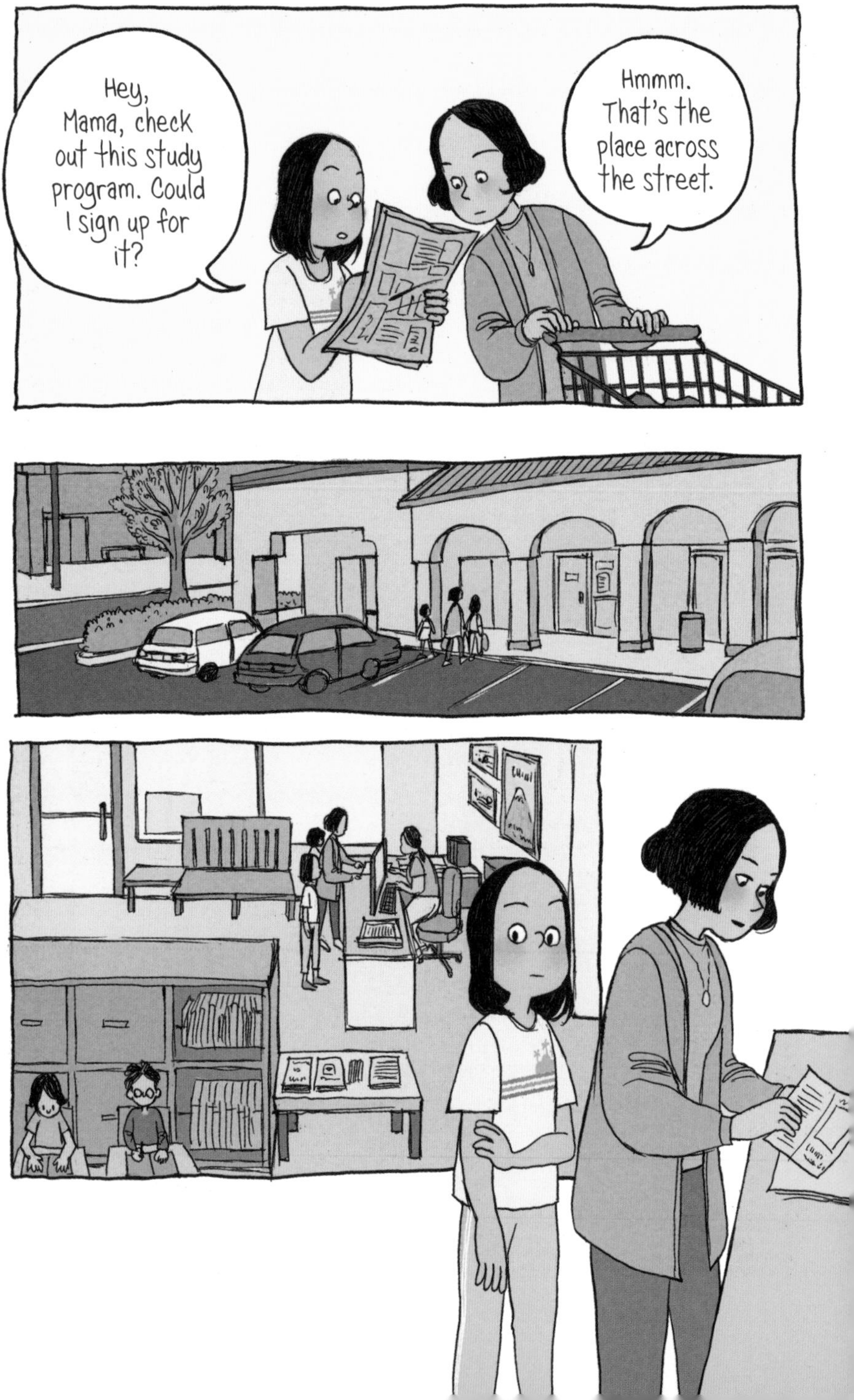
Hey, Mama, check out this study program. Could I sign up for it?
Hmmm. That's the place across the street.

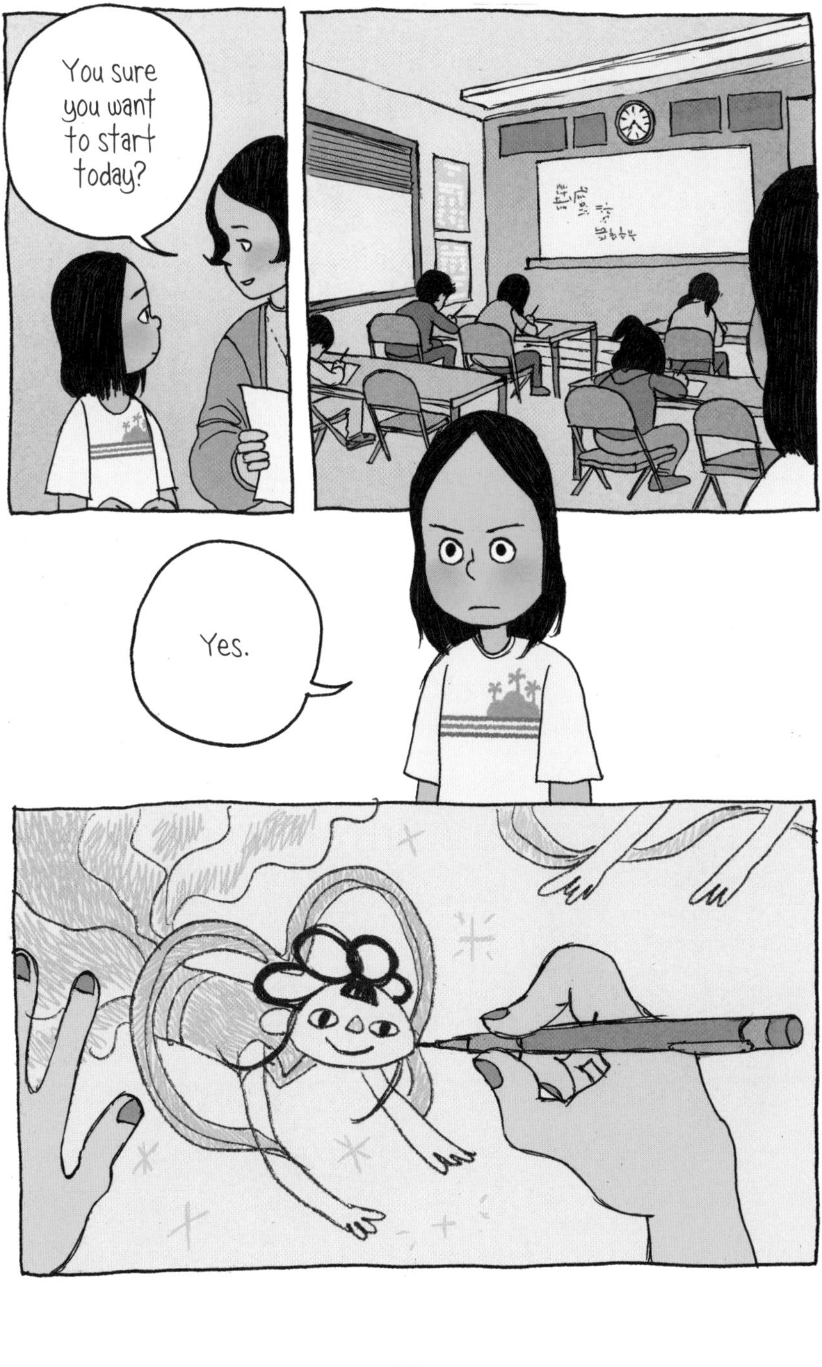
You sure you want to start today?
Yes.

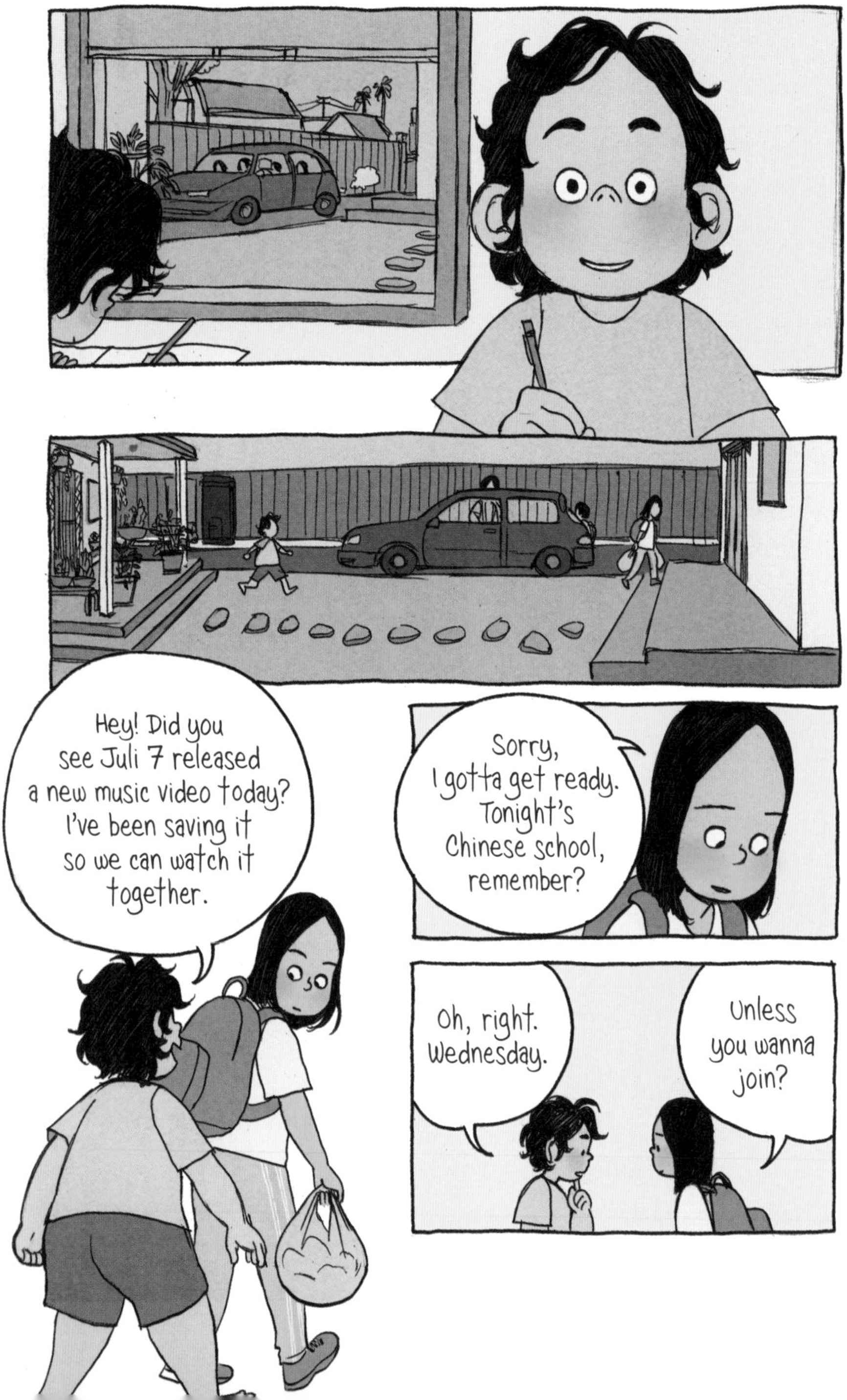
Hey! Did you see Juli 7 released a new music video today? I've been saving it so we can watch it together.
Sorry, I gotta get ready. Tonight's Chinese school, remember?
Oh, right. Wednesday.
Unless you wanna join?

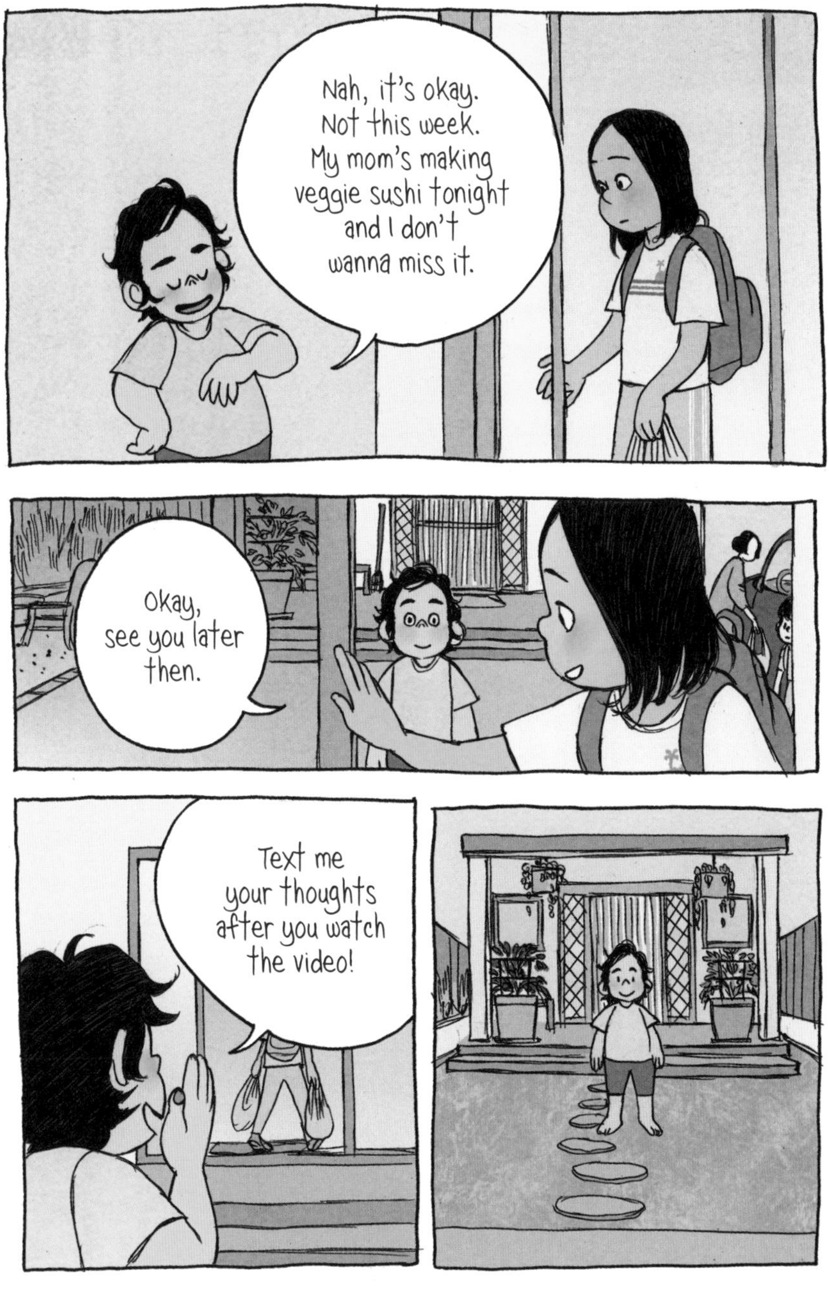
Nah, it's okay. Not this week. My mom's making veggie sushi tonight and I don't wanna miss it.
Okay, see you later then.
Text me your thoughts after you watch the video!

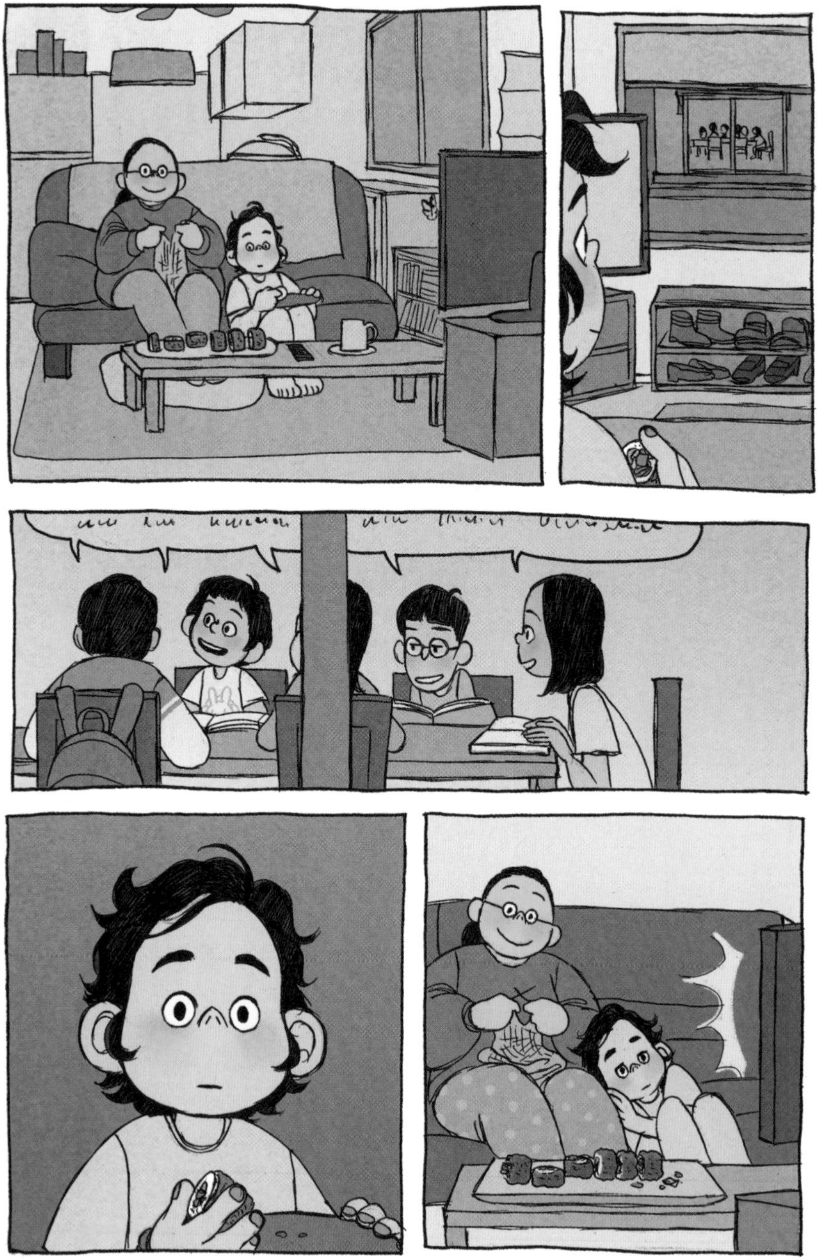

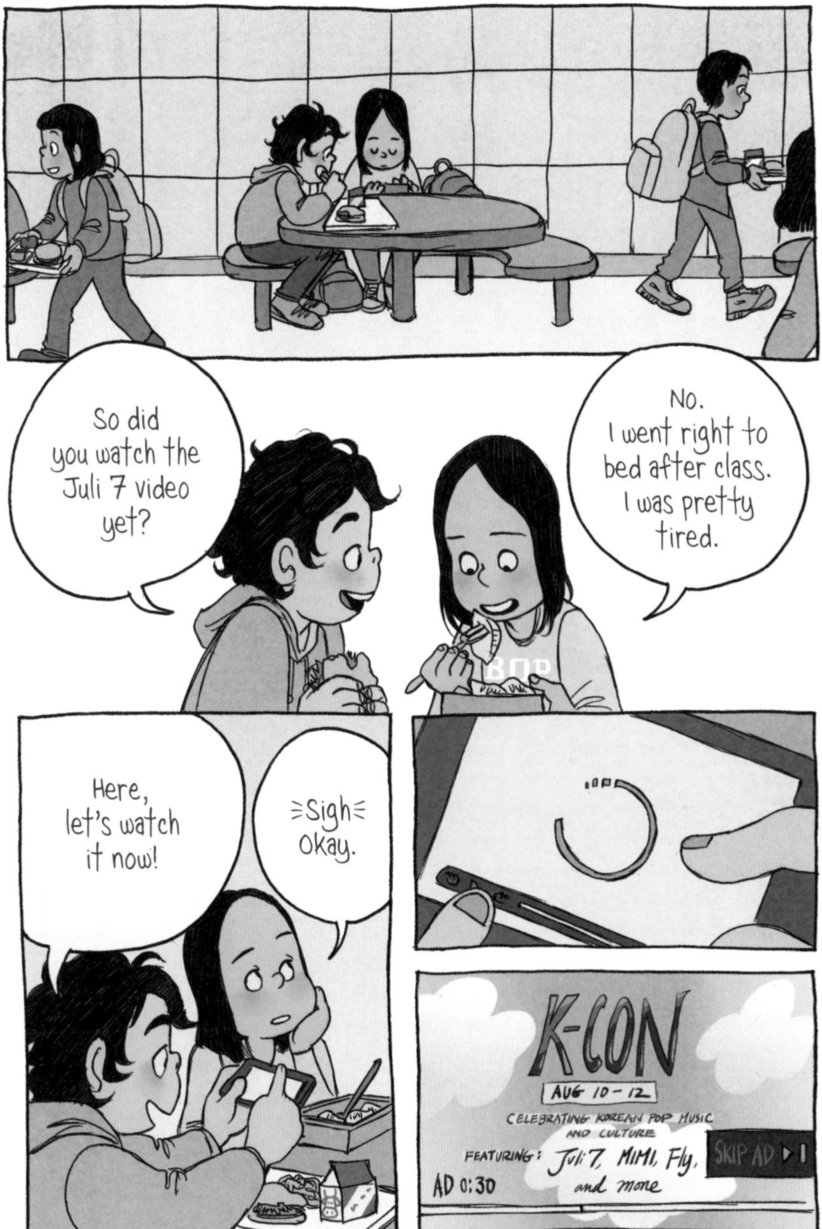
So did you watch the Juli 7 video yet?
No. I went right to bed after class. I was pretty tired.
BOP
Here, let's watch it now!
Sigh Okay.
K-CON
AUG 10 - 12
CELEBRATING KOREAN POP MUSIC AND CULTURE
FEATURING: Juli 7, MIMI, Fly, and more
AD 0:30
SKIP AD

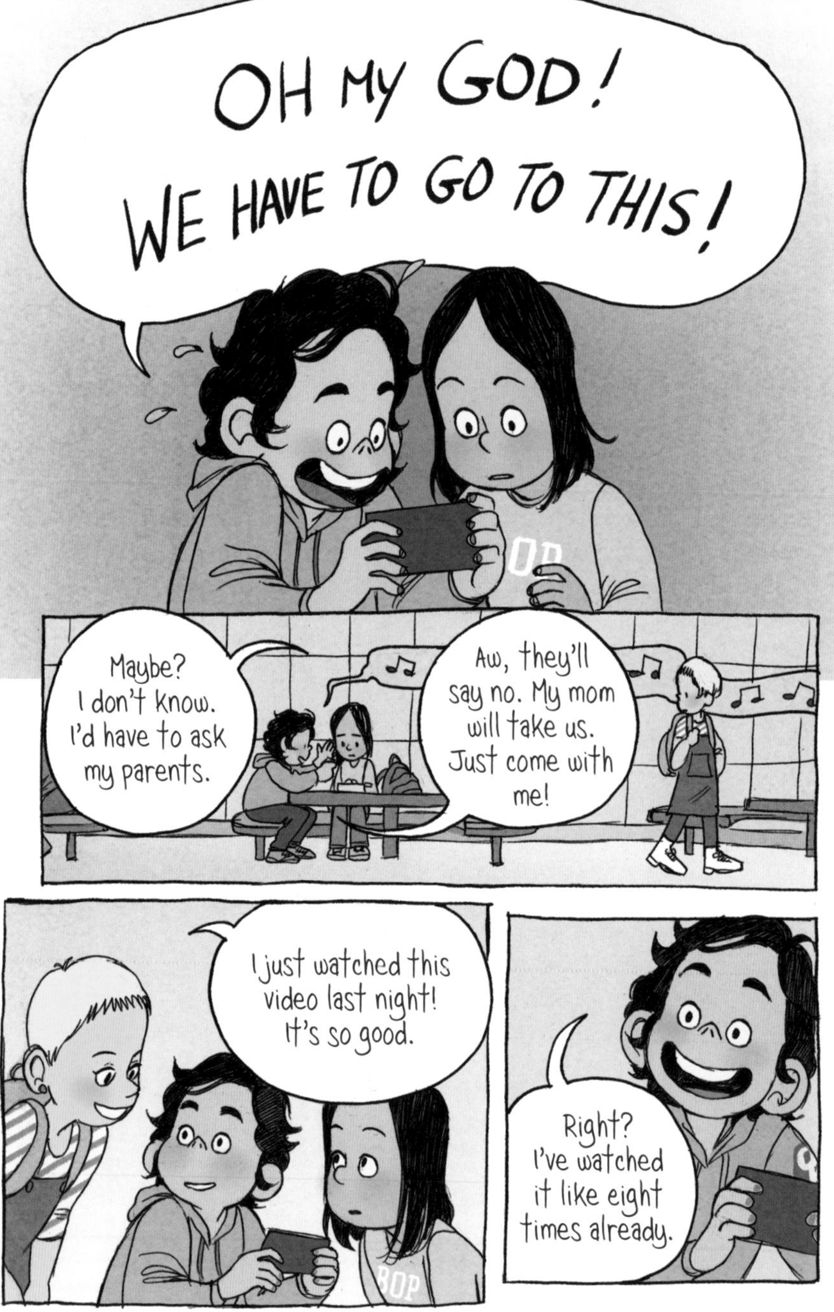
OH MY GOD! WE HAVE TO GO TO THIS!
Maybe? I don't know. I'd have to ask my parents.
Aw, they'll say no. My mom will take us. Just come with me!
I just watched this video last night! It's so good.
Right? I've watched it like eight times already.

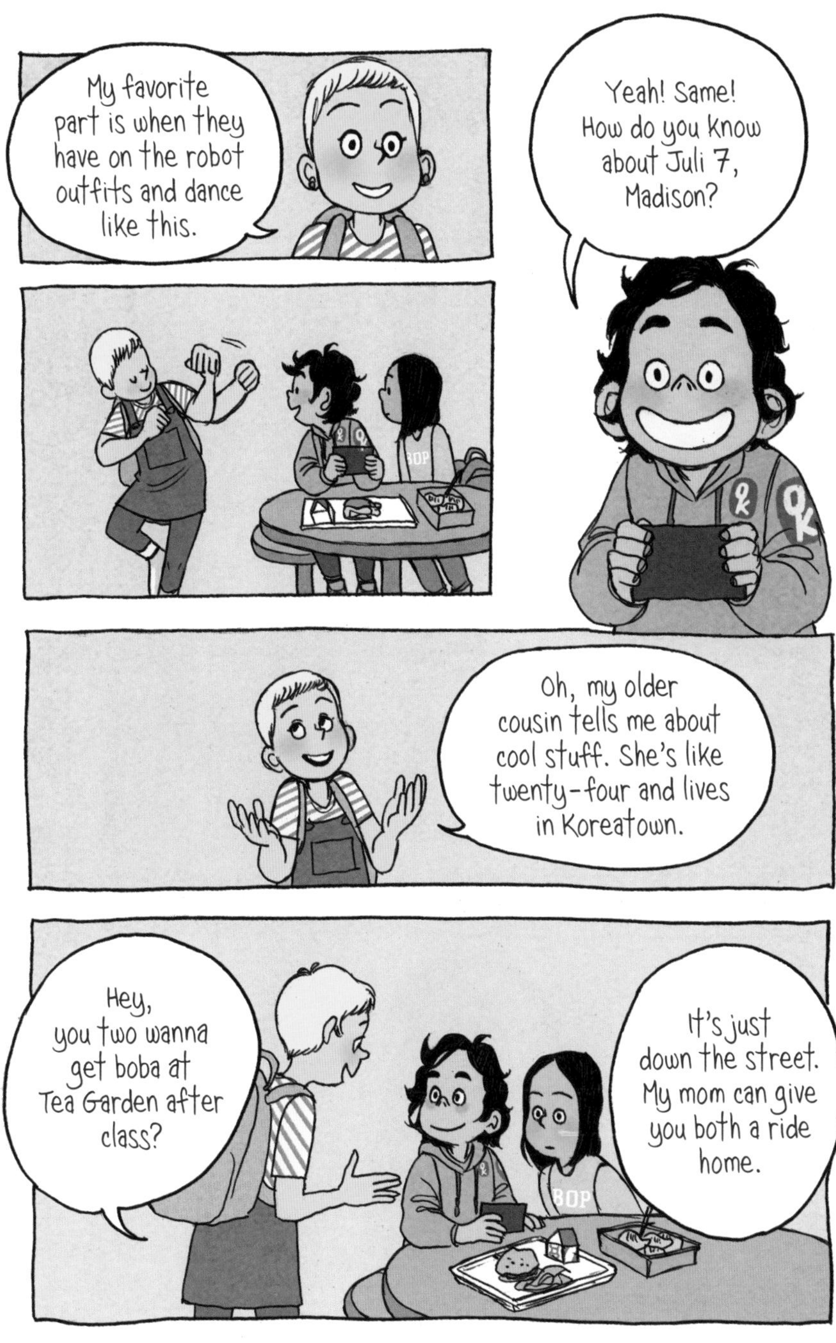
My favorite part is when they have on the robot outfits and dance like this.
Yeah! Same! How do you know about Juli 7, Madison?
OK
BOP
Oh, my older cousin tells me about cool stuff. She's like twenty-four and lives in Koreatown.
Hey, you two wanna get boba at Tea Garden after class?
It's just down the street. My mom can give you both a ride home.
BOP

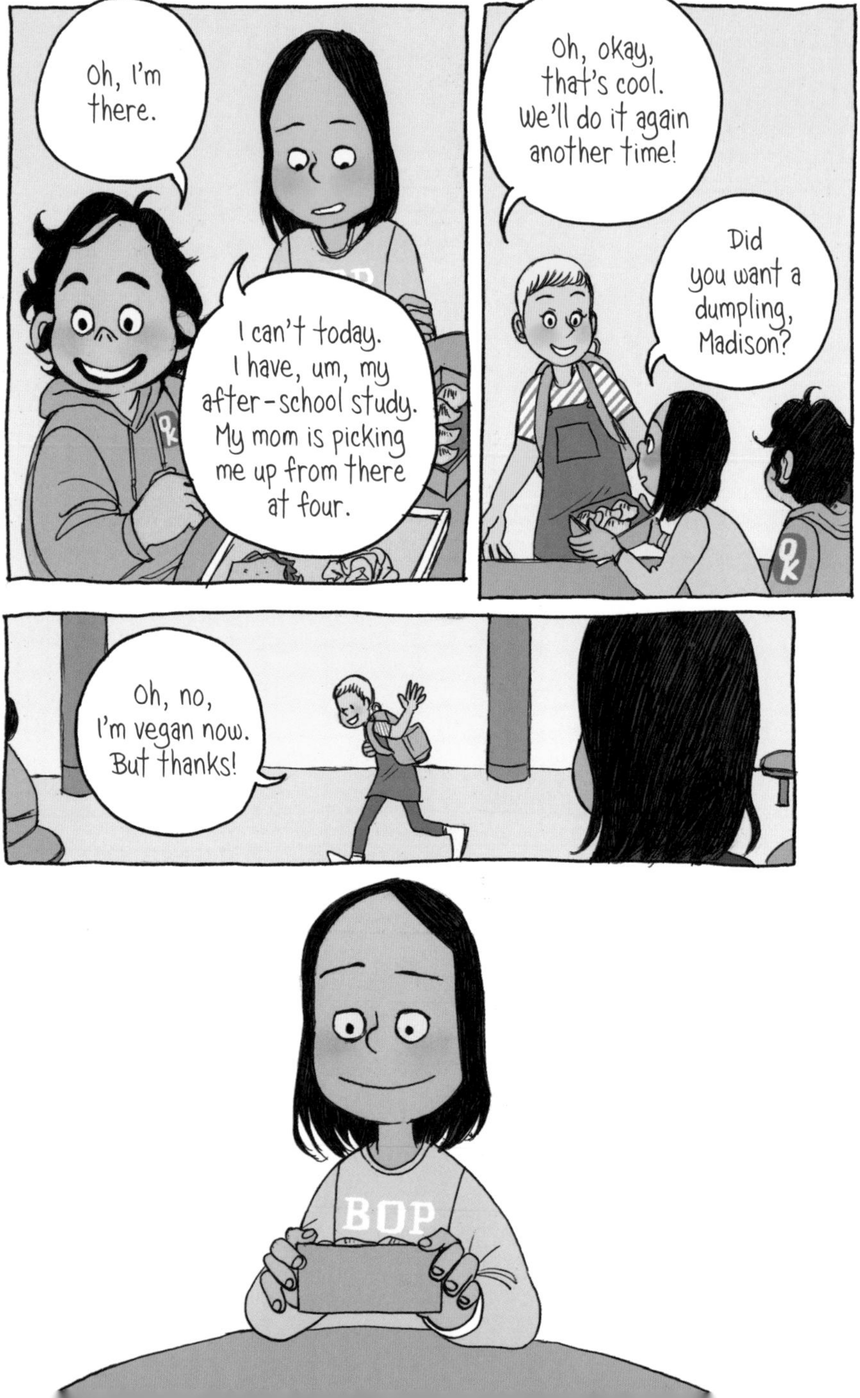
Oh, I'm there.
I can't today. I have, um, my after-school study. My mom is picking me up from there at four.
Oh, okay, that's cool. We'll do it again another time!
Did you want a dumpling, Madison?
Oh, no, I'm vegan now. But thanks!
BOP

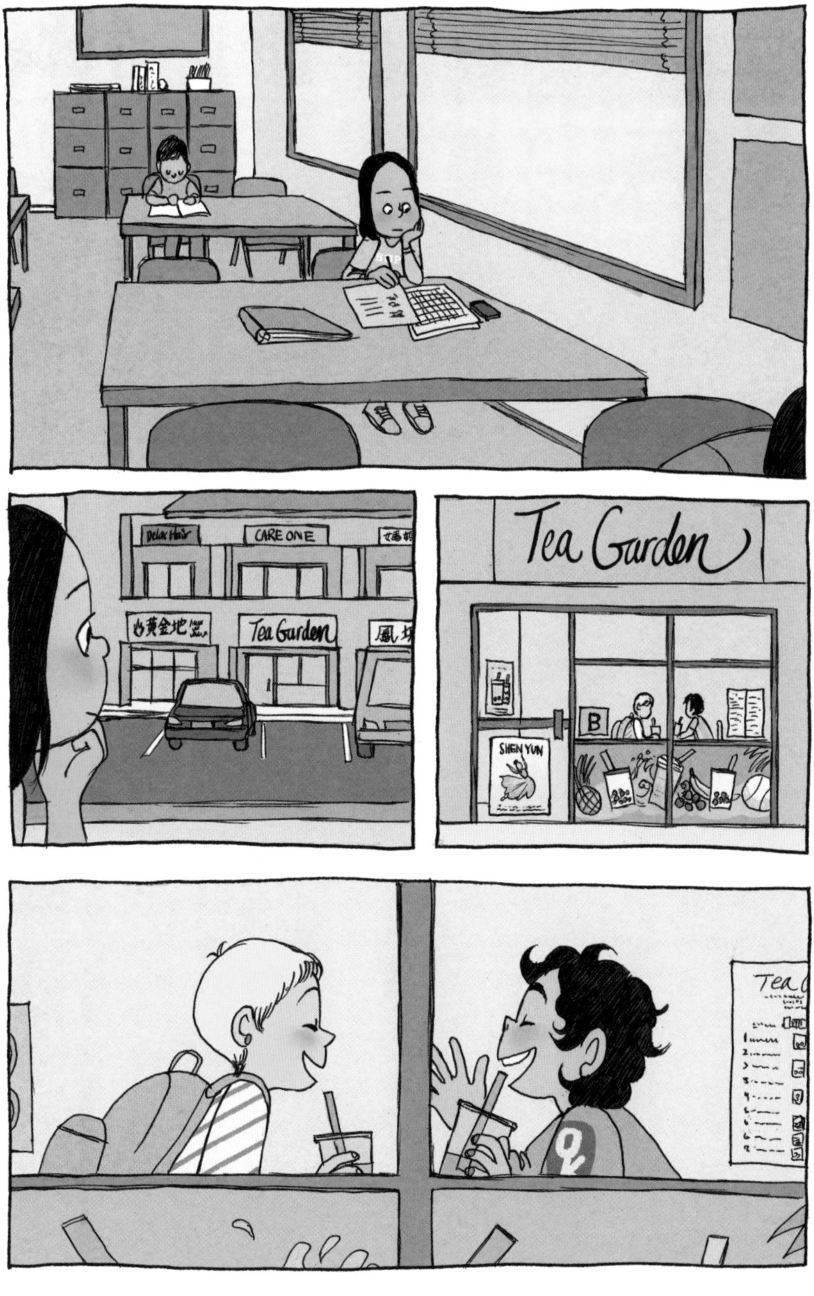
Delac Hair
CARE ONE
黄金地
Tea Garden
Tea Garden
B
SHEN YUN
Tea

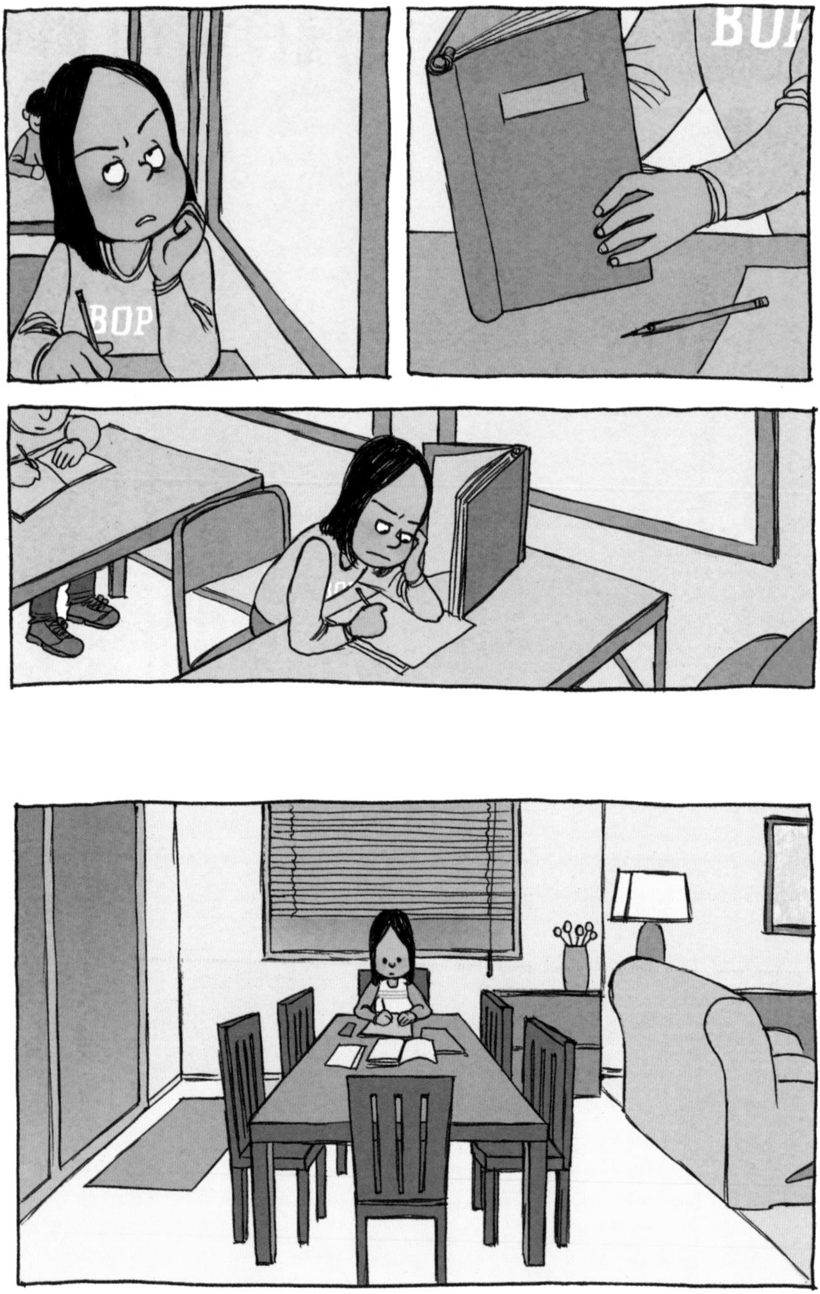
BOP

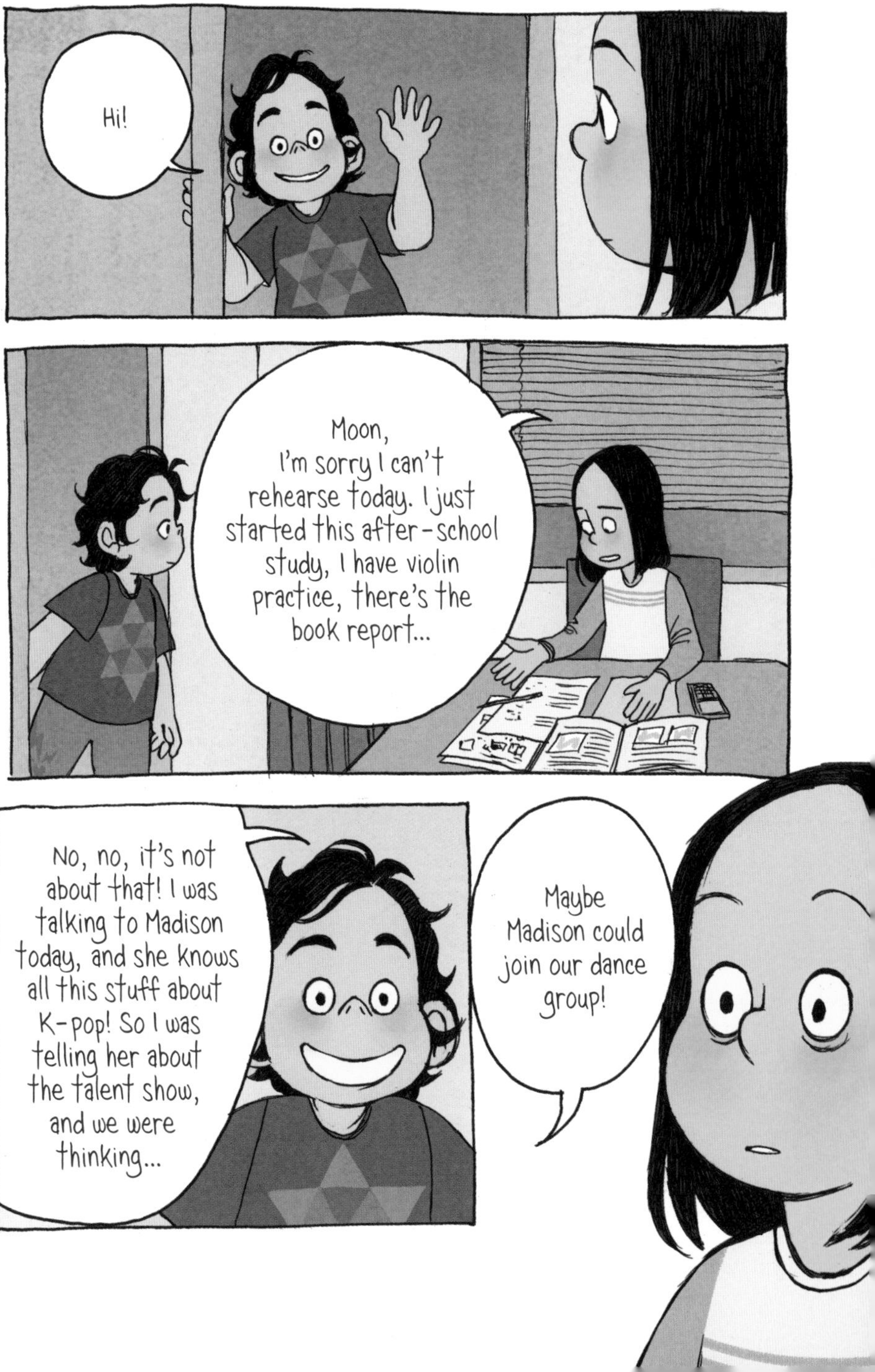
Hi!
Moon, I'm sorry I can't rehearse today. I just started this after-school study, I have violin practice, there's the book report...
No, no, it's not about that! I was talking to Madison today, and she knows all this stuff about K-pop! So I was telling her about the talent show, and we were thinking...
Maybe Madison could join our dance group!

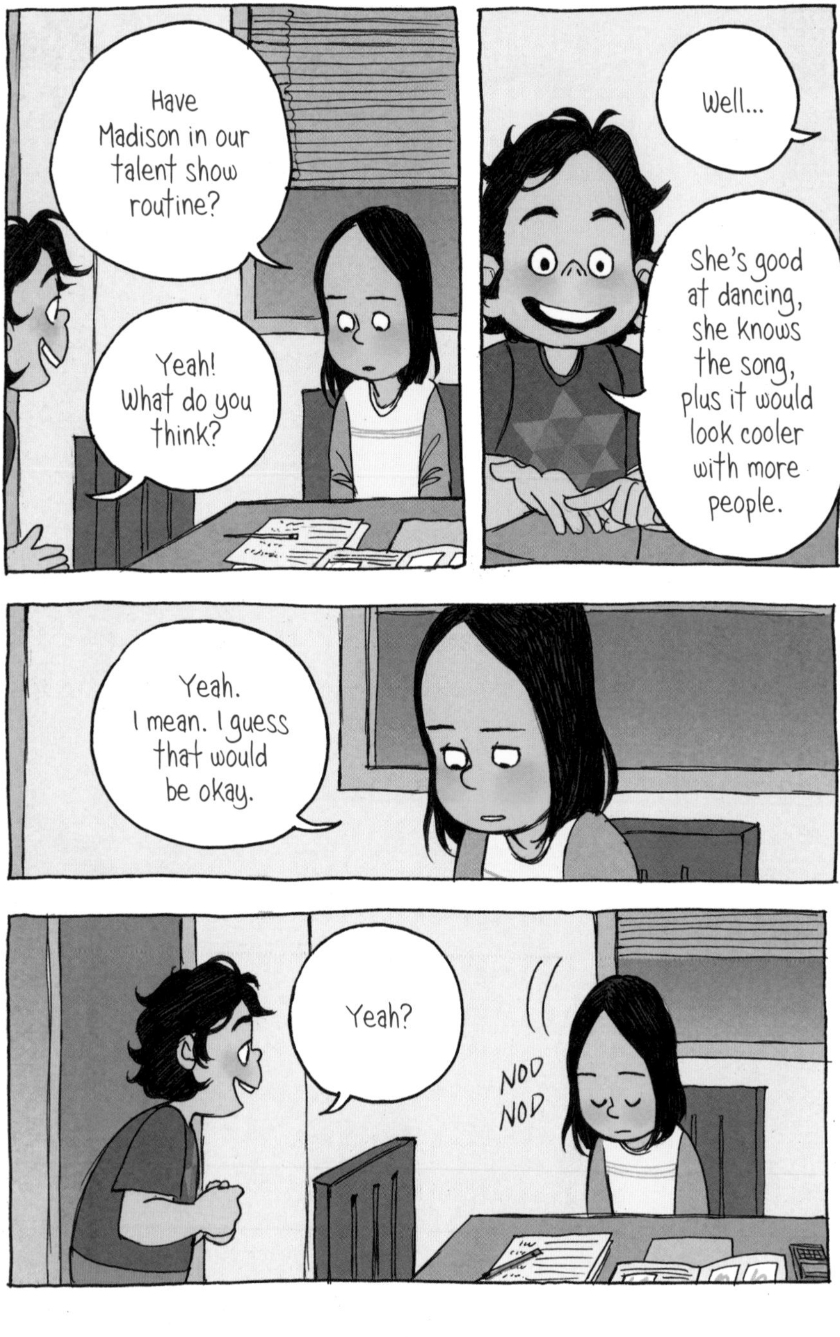
Have Madison in our talent show routine?
Yeah! What do you think?
Well...
She's good at dancing, she knows the song, plus it would look cooler with more people.
Yeah. I mean. I guess that would be okay.
Yeah?
NOD NOD

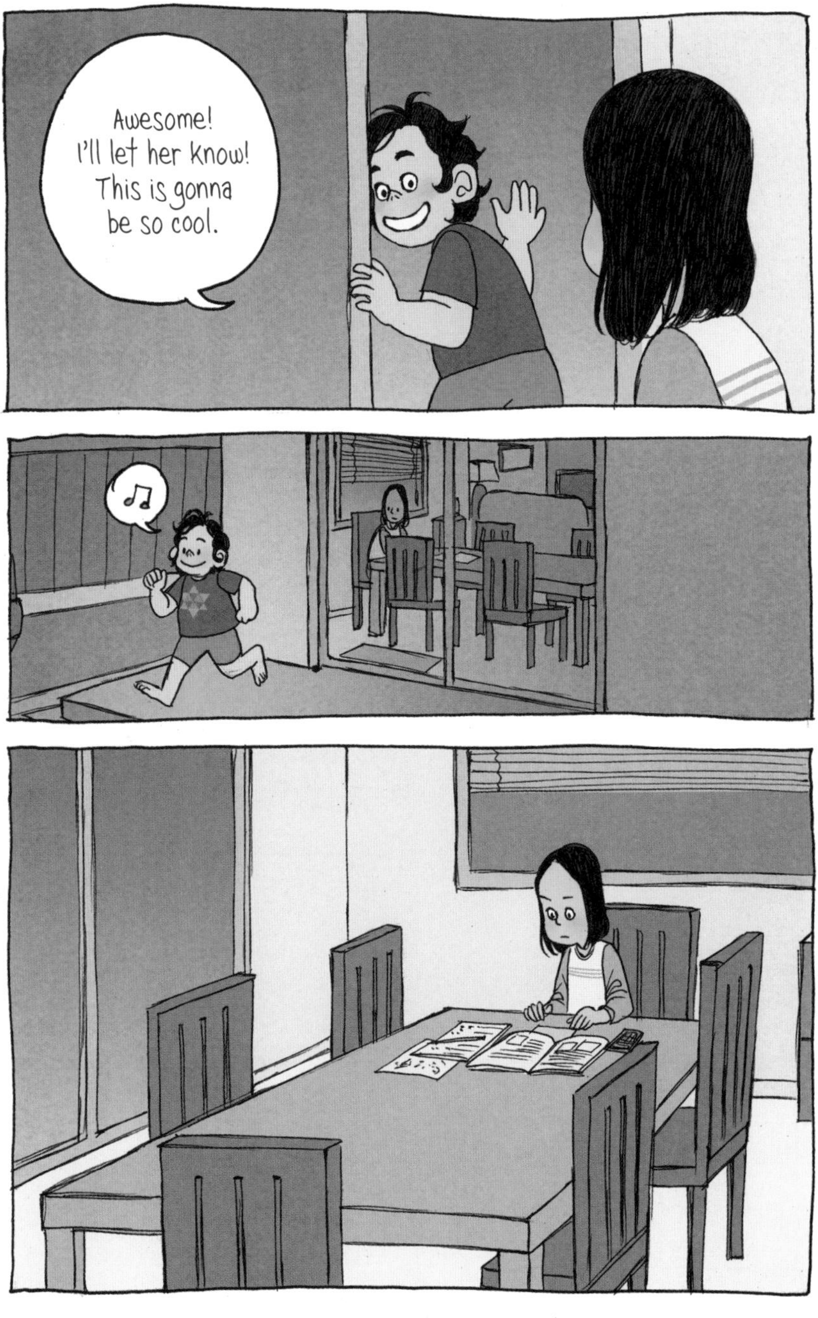
Awesome! I'll let her know! This is gonna be so cool.

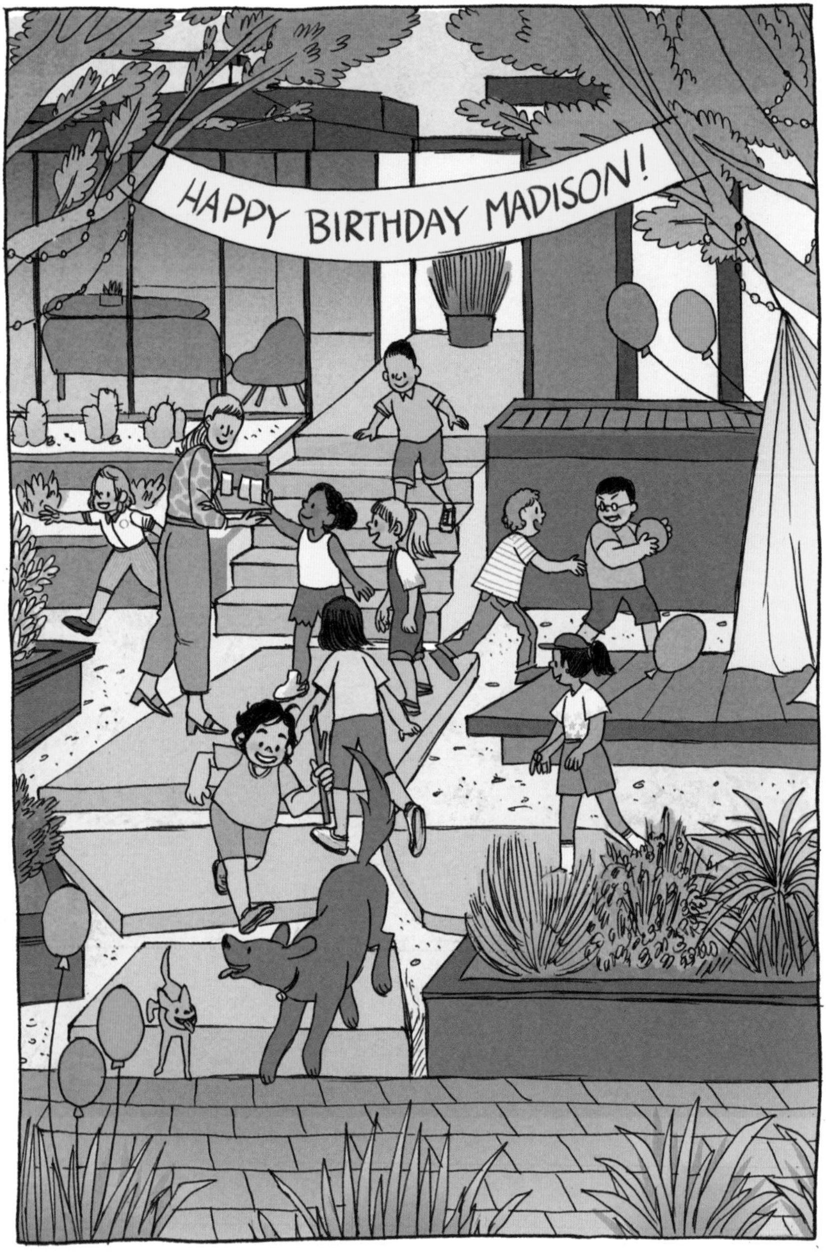
HAPPY BIRTHDAY MADISON!

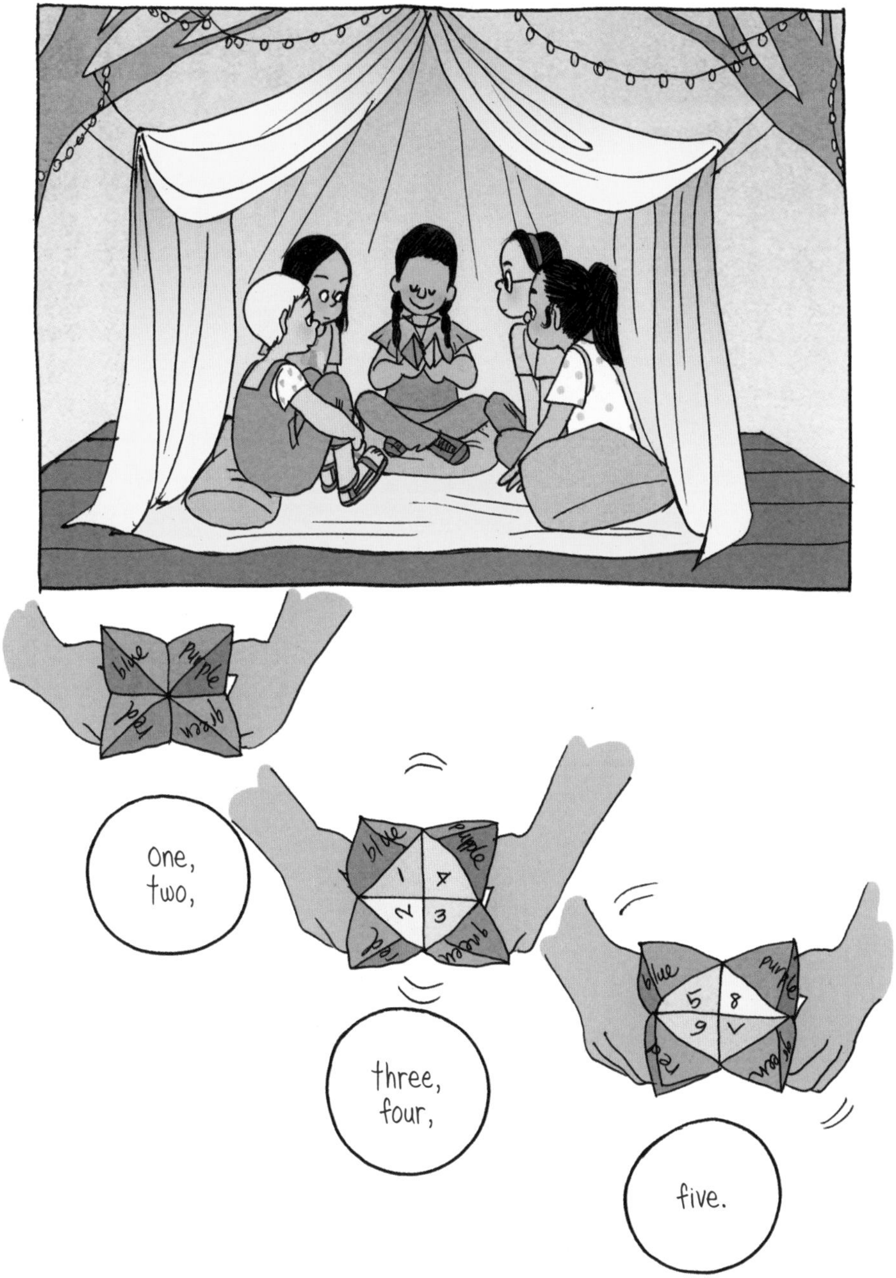
blue
purple
red
green
one, two,
three, four,
five.

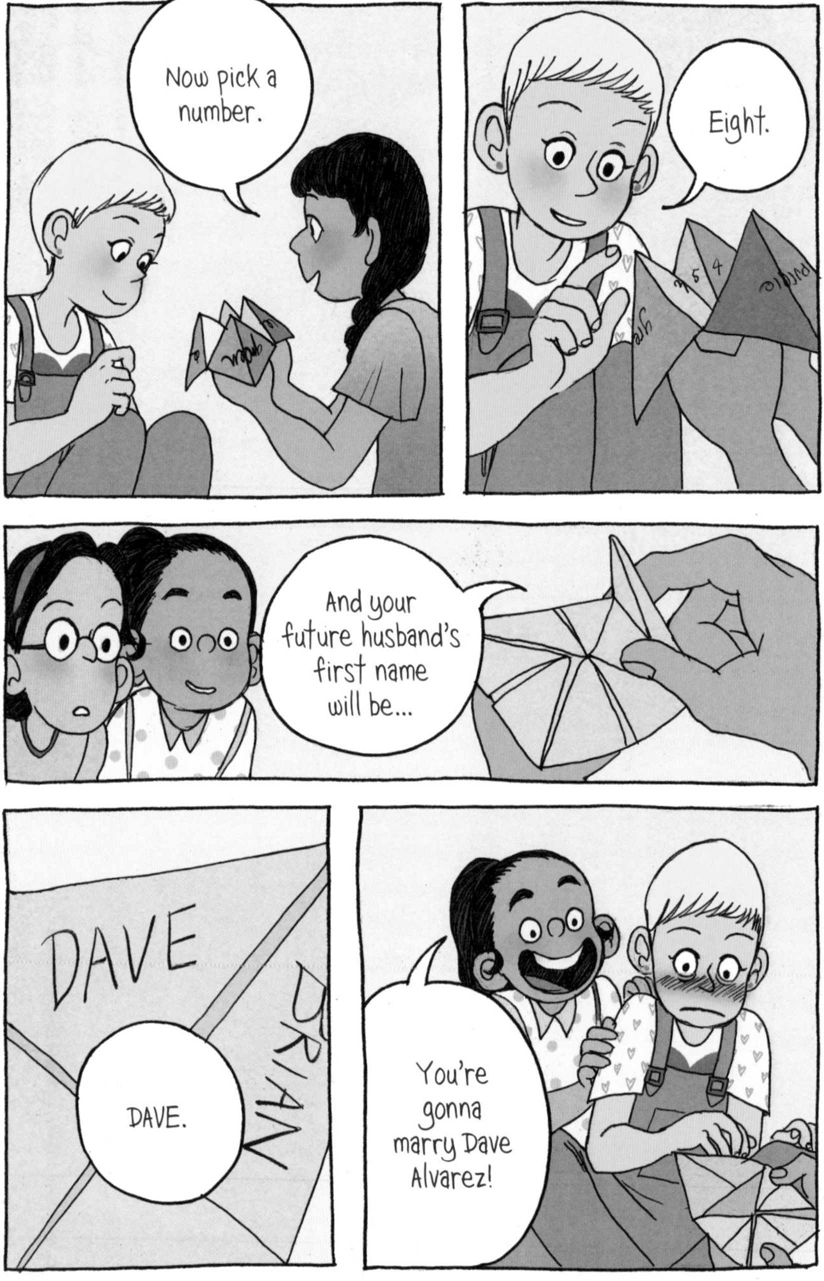
Now pick a number.
Eight.
And your future husband's first name will be...
DAVE
DAVE.
You're gonna marry Dave Alvarez!

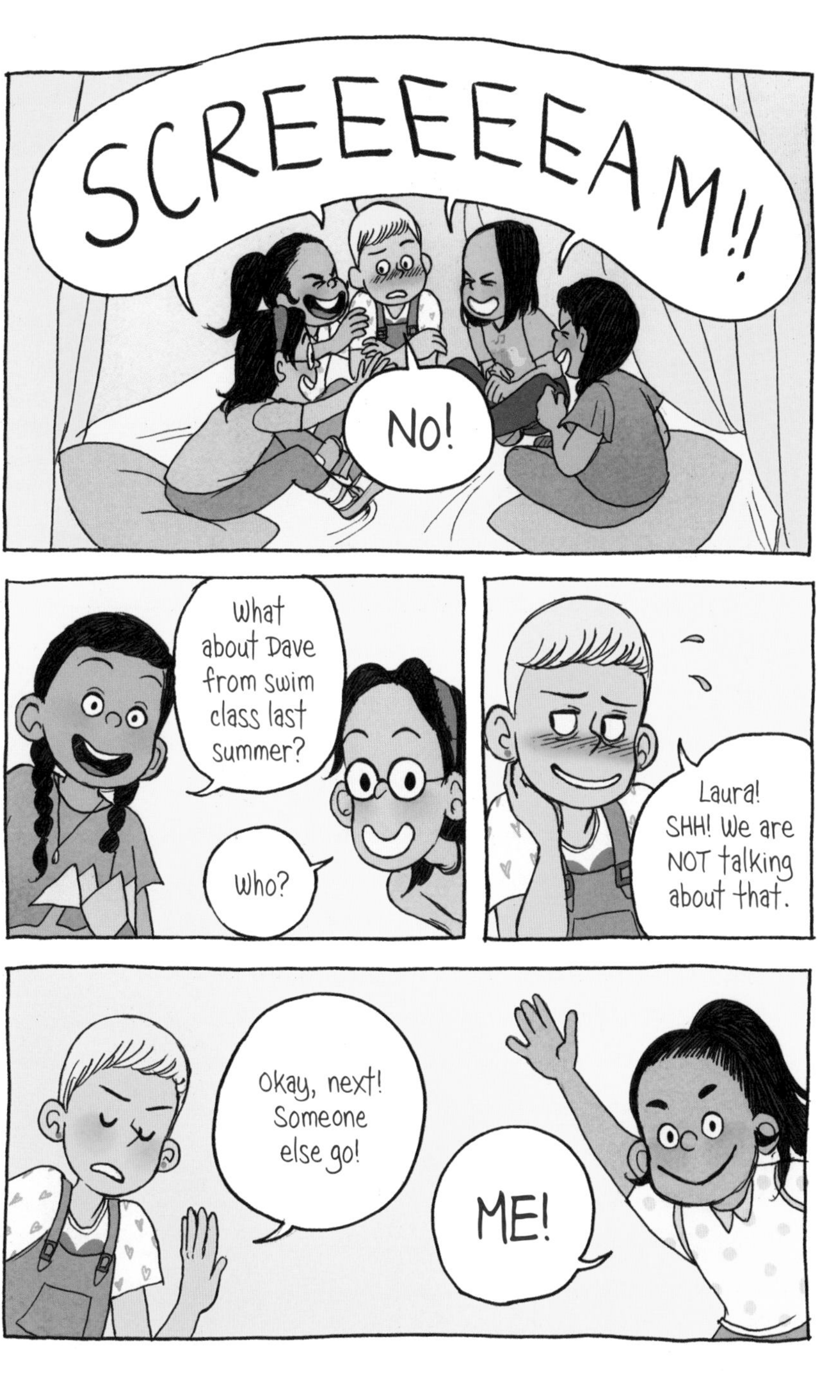
SCREEEEEAM!!
No!
What about Dave from swim class last summer?
Who?
Laura! SHH! We are NOT talking about that.
Okay, next! Someone else go!
ME!

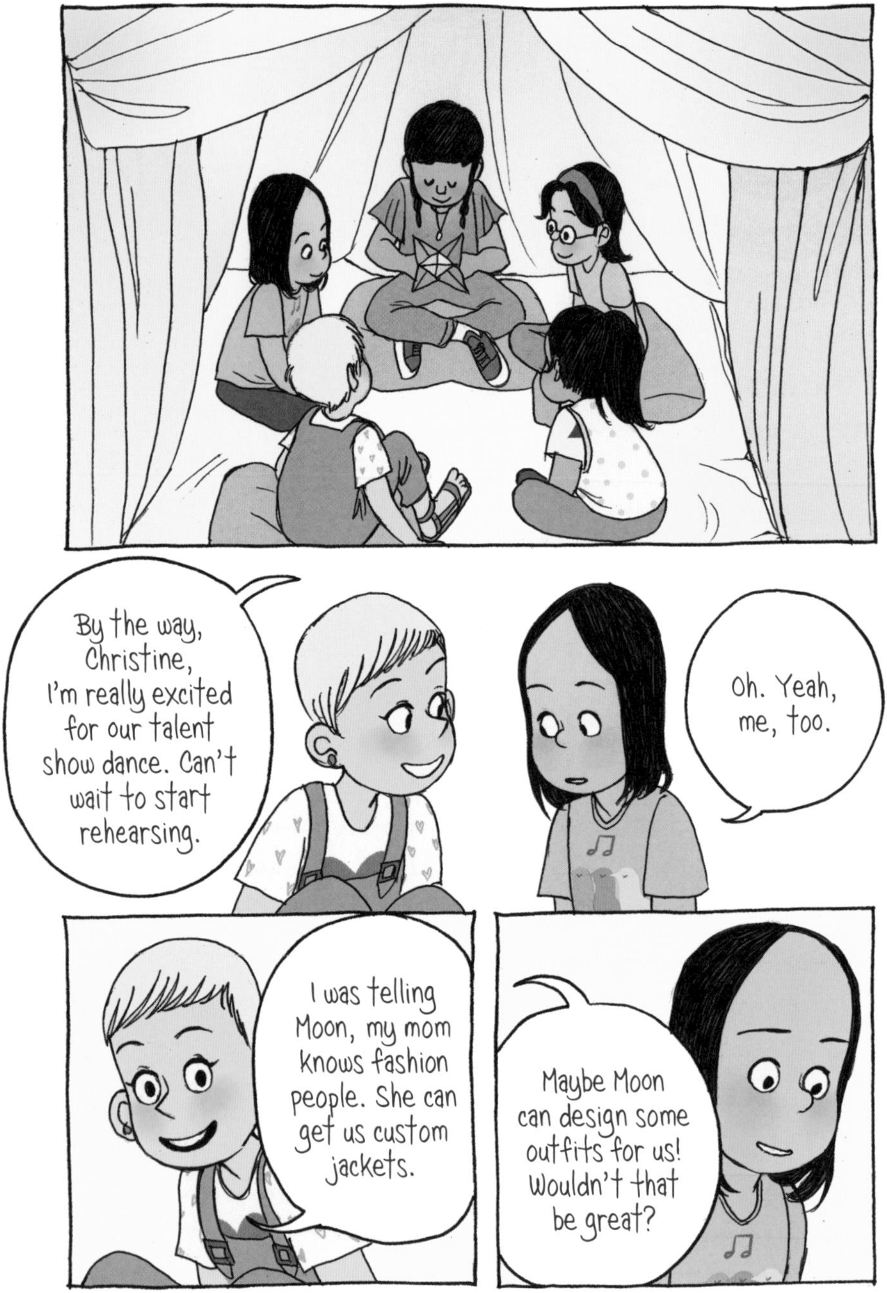
By the way, Christine, I'm really excited for our talent show dance. Can't wait to start rehearsing.
Oh. Yeah, me, too.
I was telling Moon, my mom knows fashion people. She can get us custom jackets.
Maybe Moon can design some outfits for us! Wouldn't that be great?

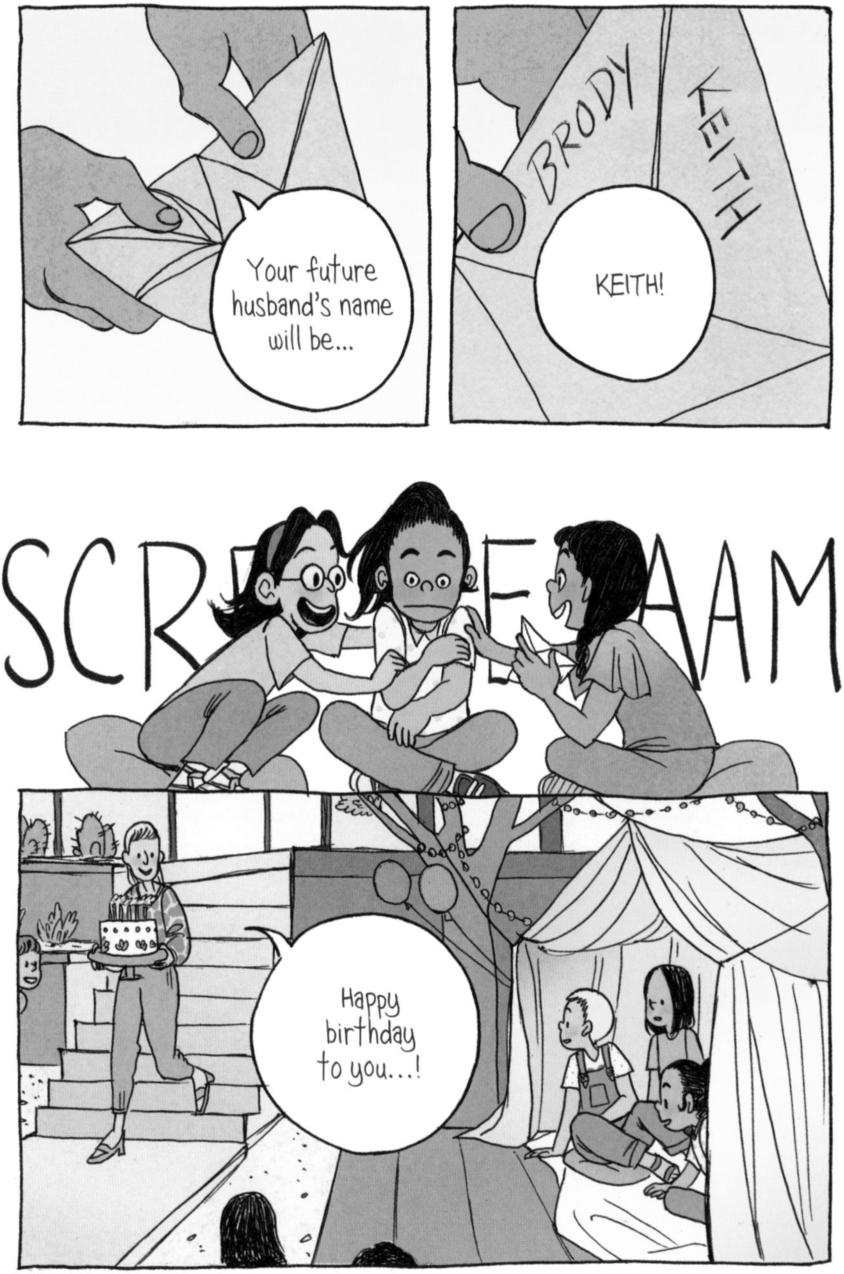
Your future husband's name will be...
BRODY
KEITH
KEITH!
SCREEEAAM
Happy birthday to you...!

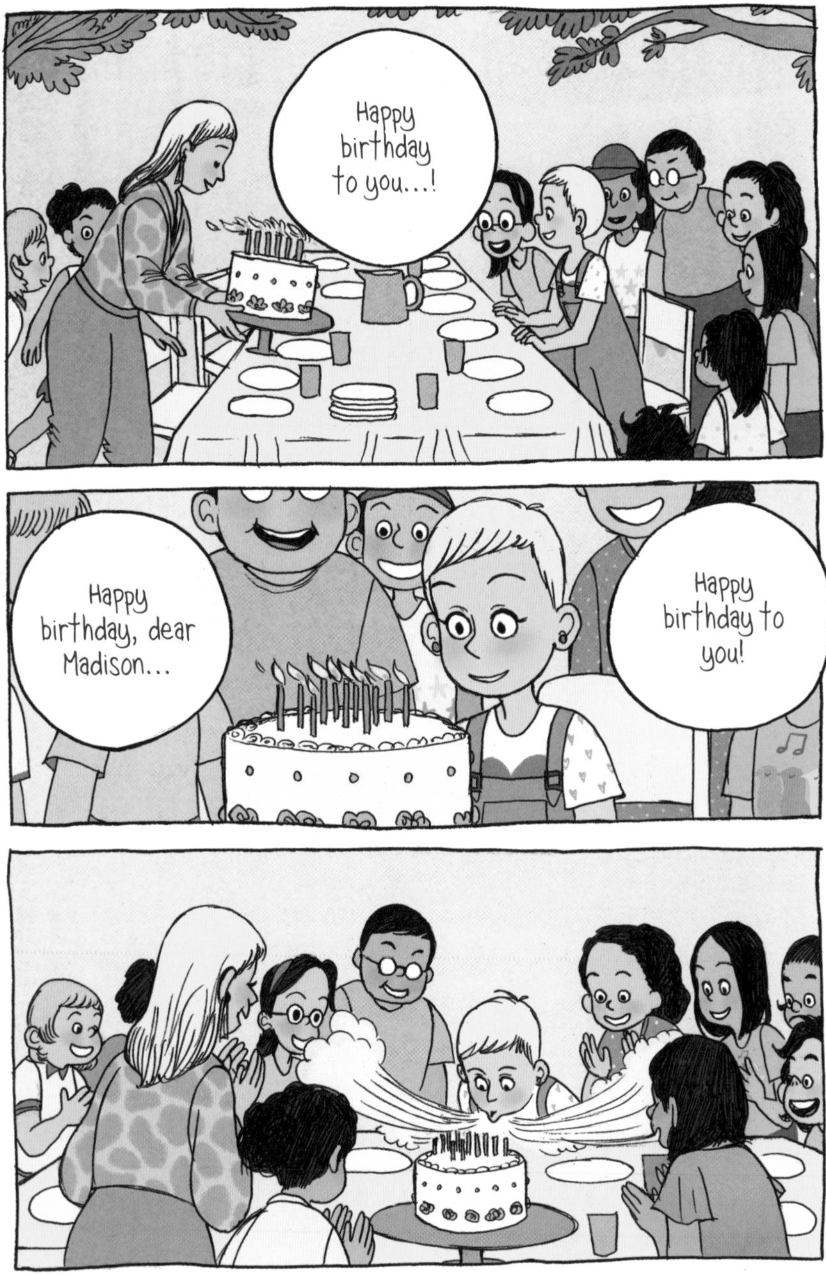
Happy birthday to you...!
Happy birthday, dear Madison...
Happy birthday to you!

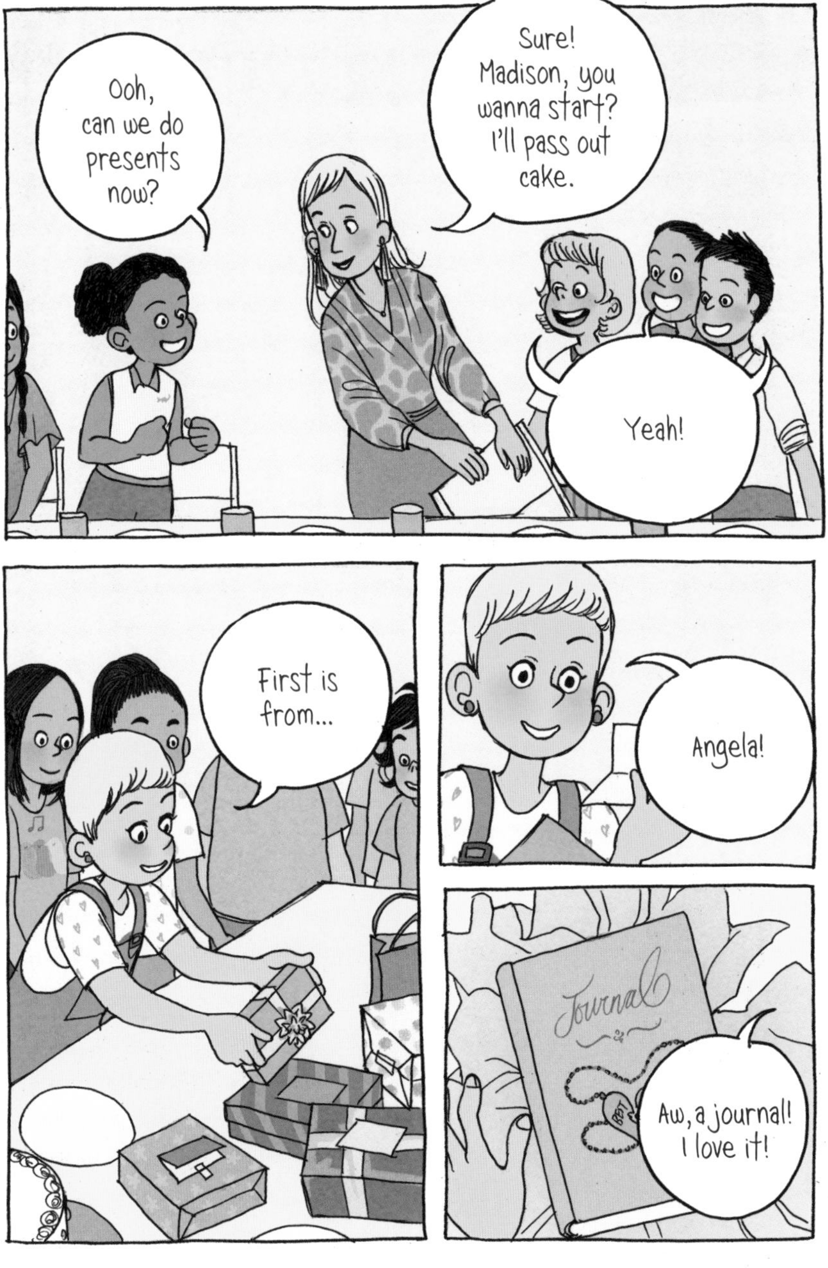
Ooh, can we do presents now?
Sure! Madison, you wanna start? I'll pass out cake.
Yeah!
First is from...
Angela!
Journal
Aw, a journal! I love it!

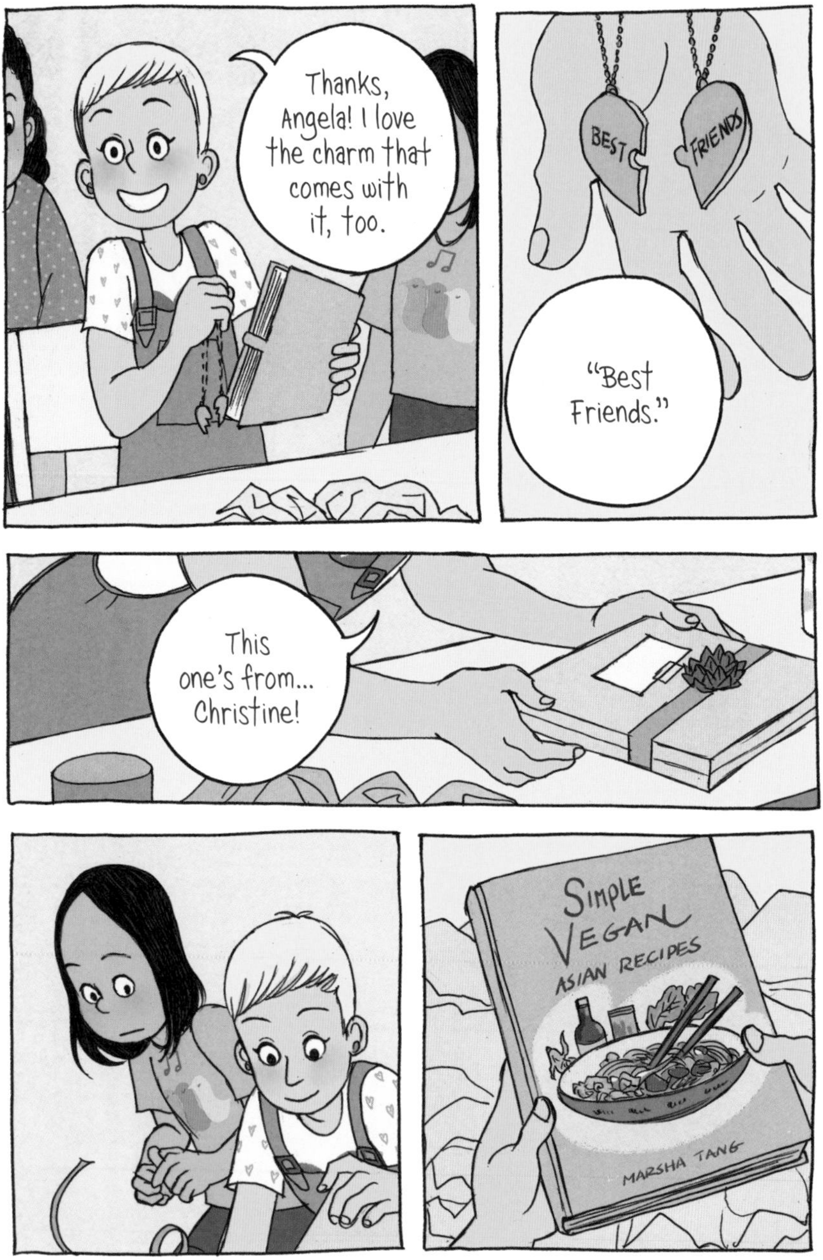
Thanks, Angela! I love the charm that comes with it, too.
BEST
FRIENDS
"Best Friends."
This one's from... Christine!
SIMPLE VEGAN
ASIAN RECIPES
MARSHA TANG

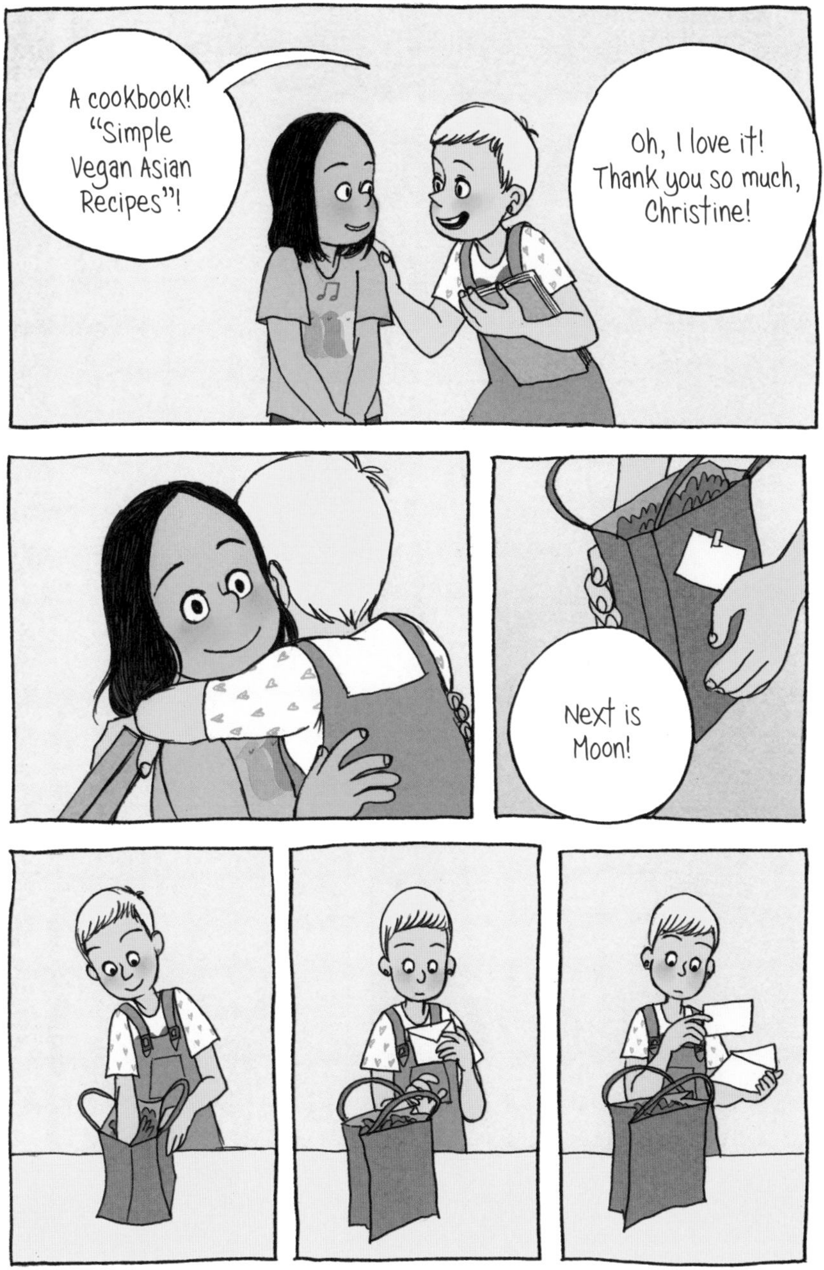
A cookbook! "Simple Vegan Asian Recipes"!
Oh, I love it! Thank you so much, Christine!
Next is Moon!

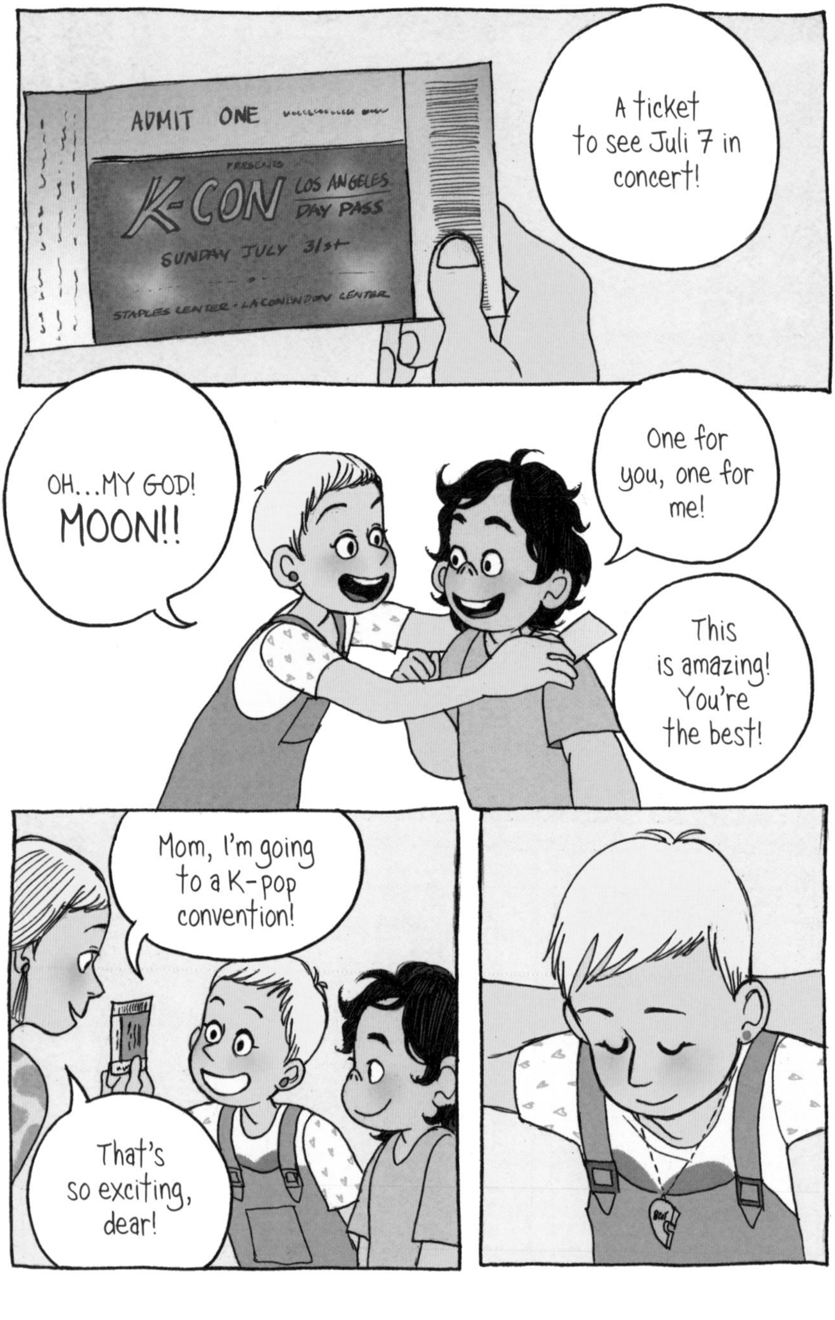
ADMIT ONE
PRESENTS
K-CON
LOS ANGELES
DAY PASS
SUNDAY JULY 31st
STAPLES CENTER · LA CONVENTION CENTER
A ticket to see Juli 7 in concert!
OH...MY GOD! MOON!!
One for you, one for me!
This is amazing! You're the best!
Mom, I'm going to a K-pop convention!
That's so exciting, dear!

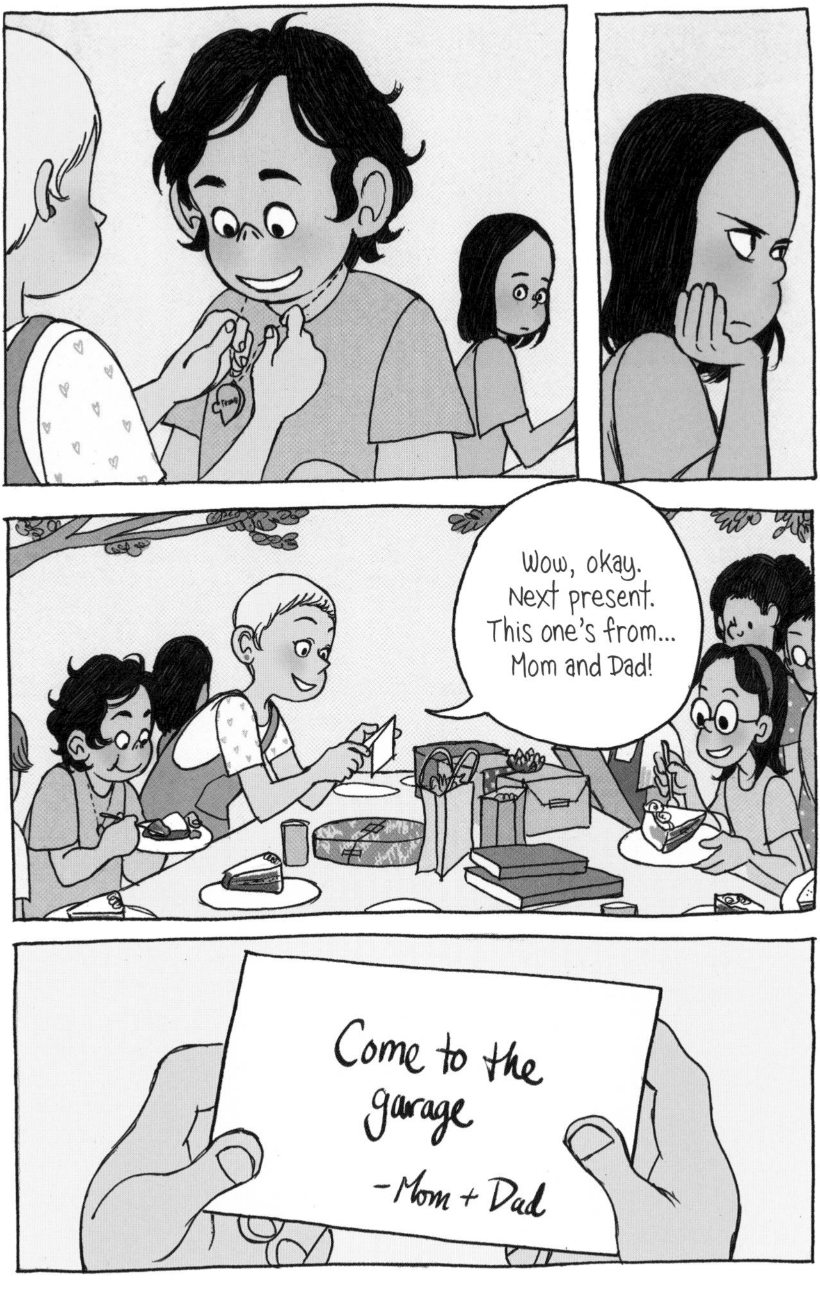
Wow, okay. Next present. This one's from... Mom and Dad!
Come to the garage
-Mom + Dad

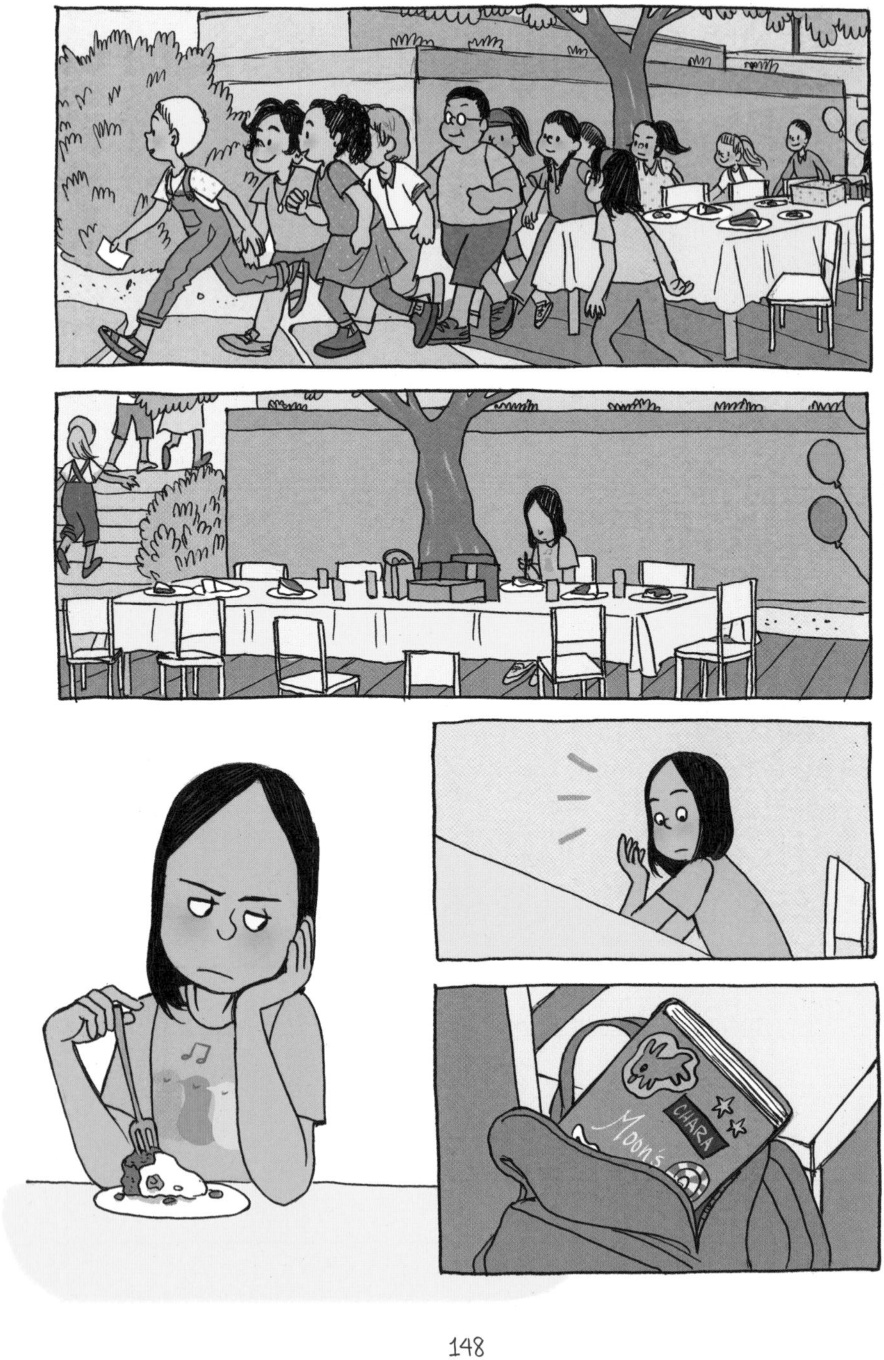
CHARA
Moon's

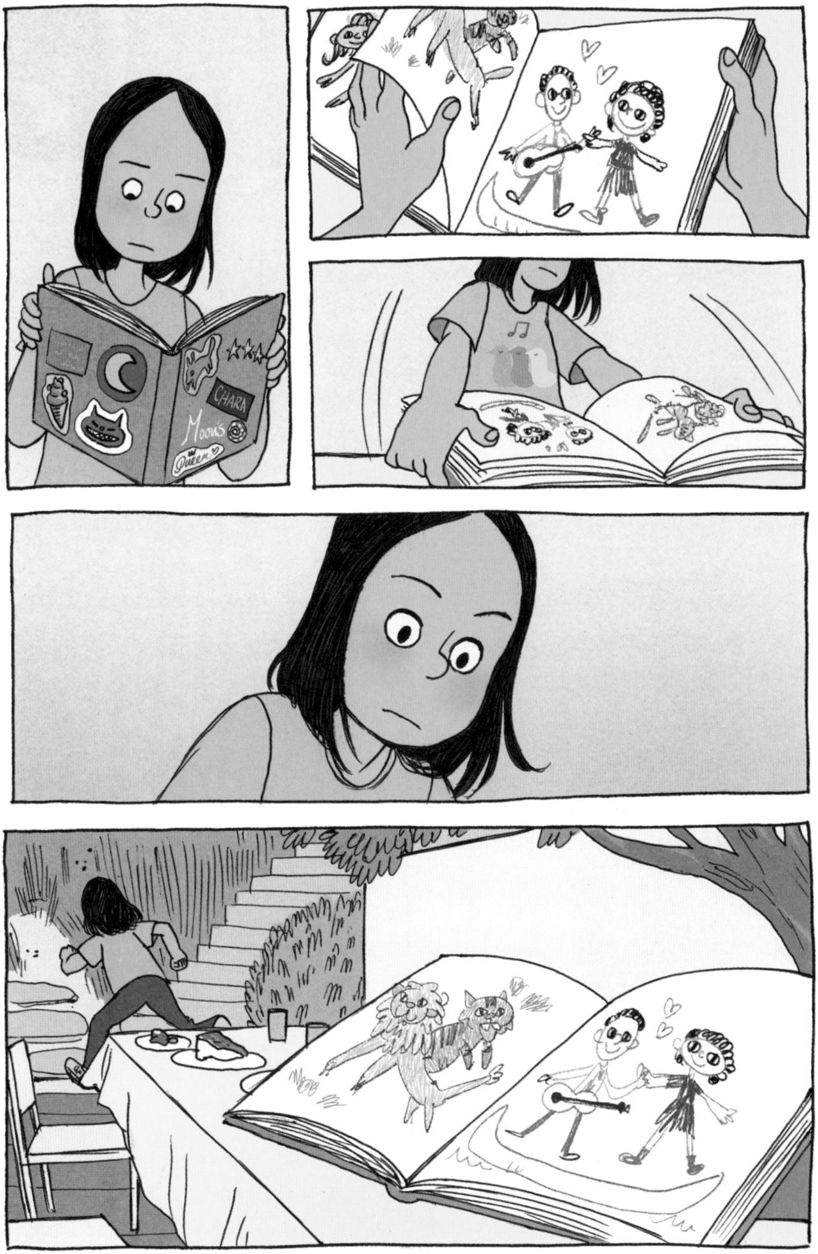
CHARA
Moon's
Queen

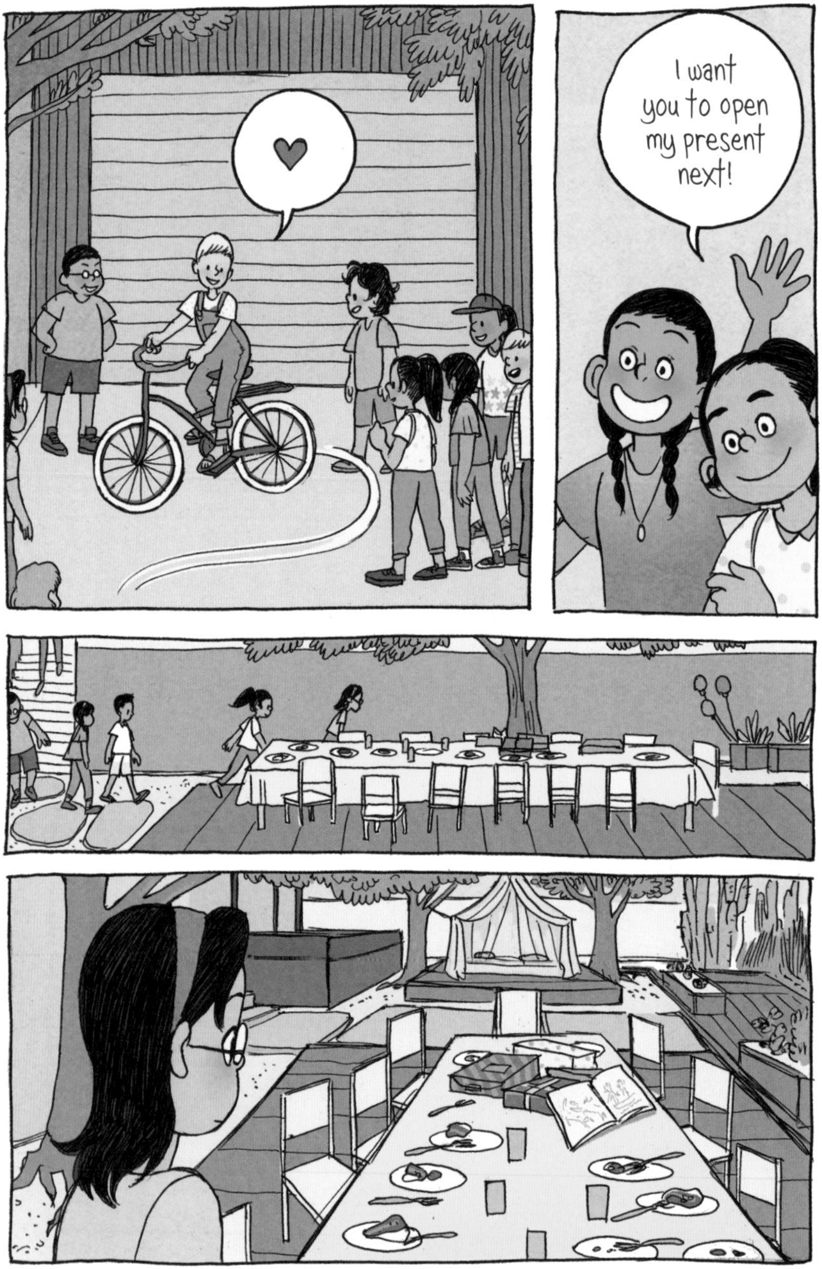
I want you to open my present next!

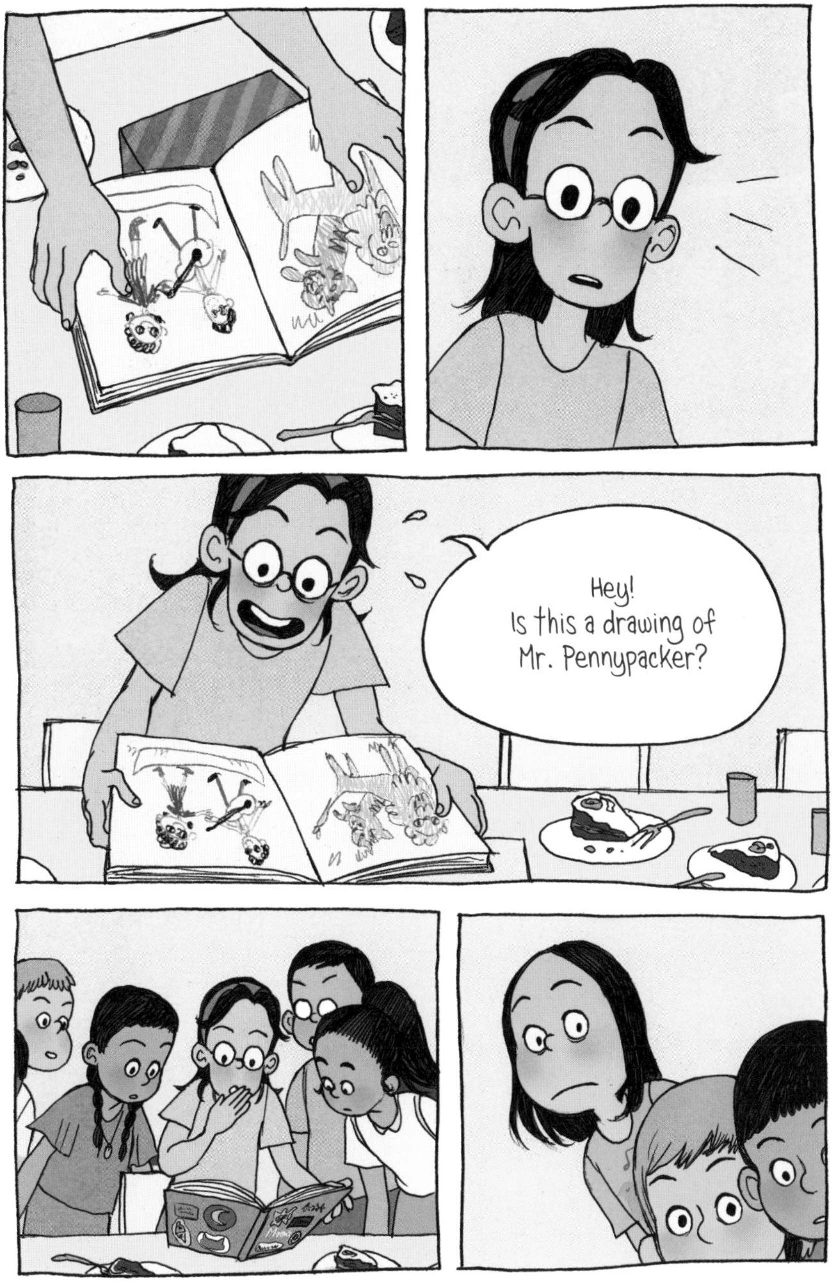
Hey!
Is this a drawing of
Mr. Pennypacker?

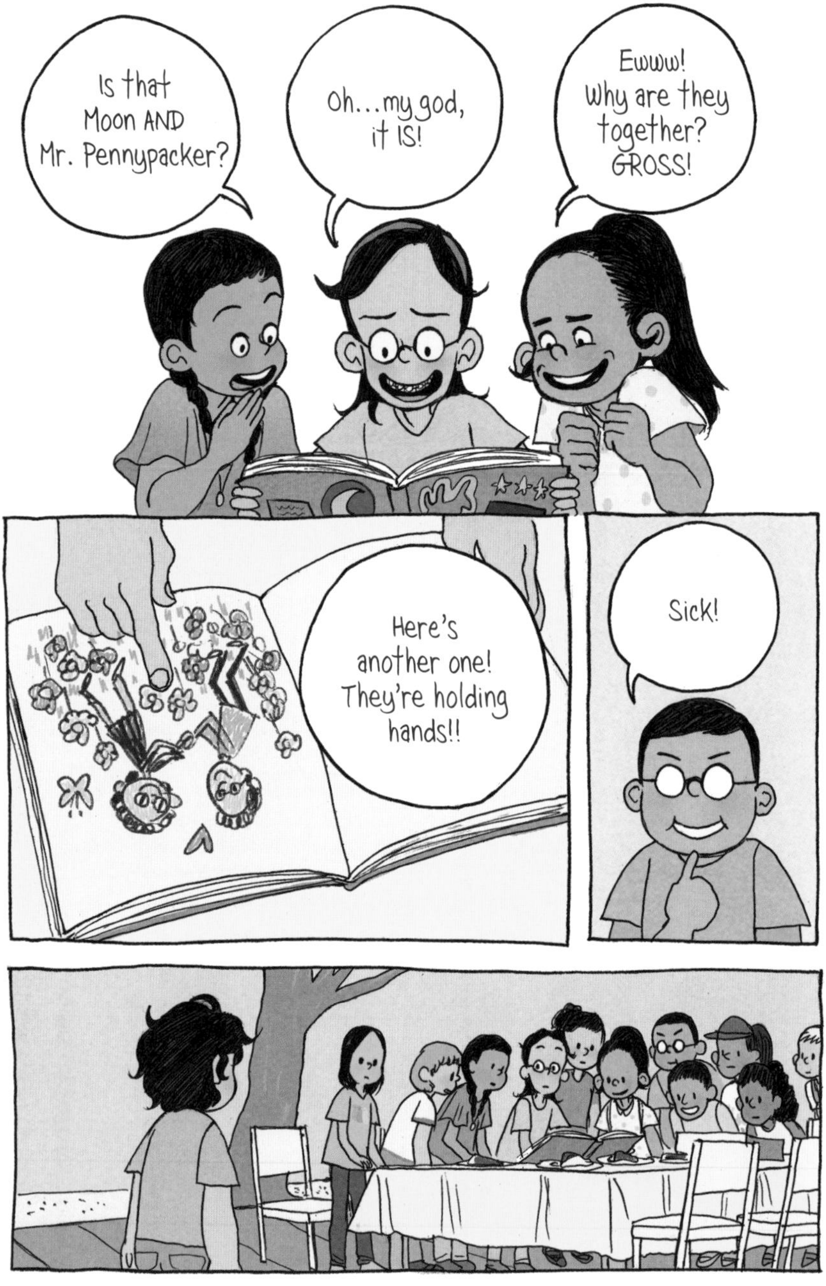
Is that Moon AND Mr. Pennypacker?
Oh...my god, it IS!
Ewww! Why are they together? GROSS!
Here's another one! They're holding hands!!
Sick!

Sorry.

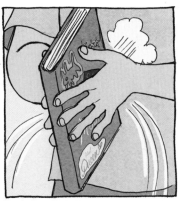

Here you go, Mrs. Pennypacker.

SMACK

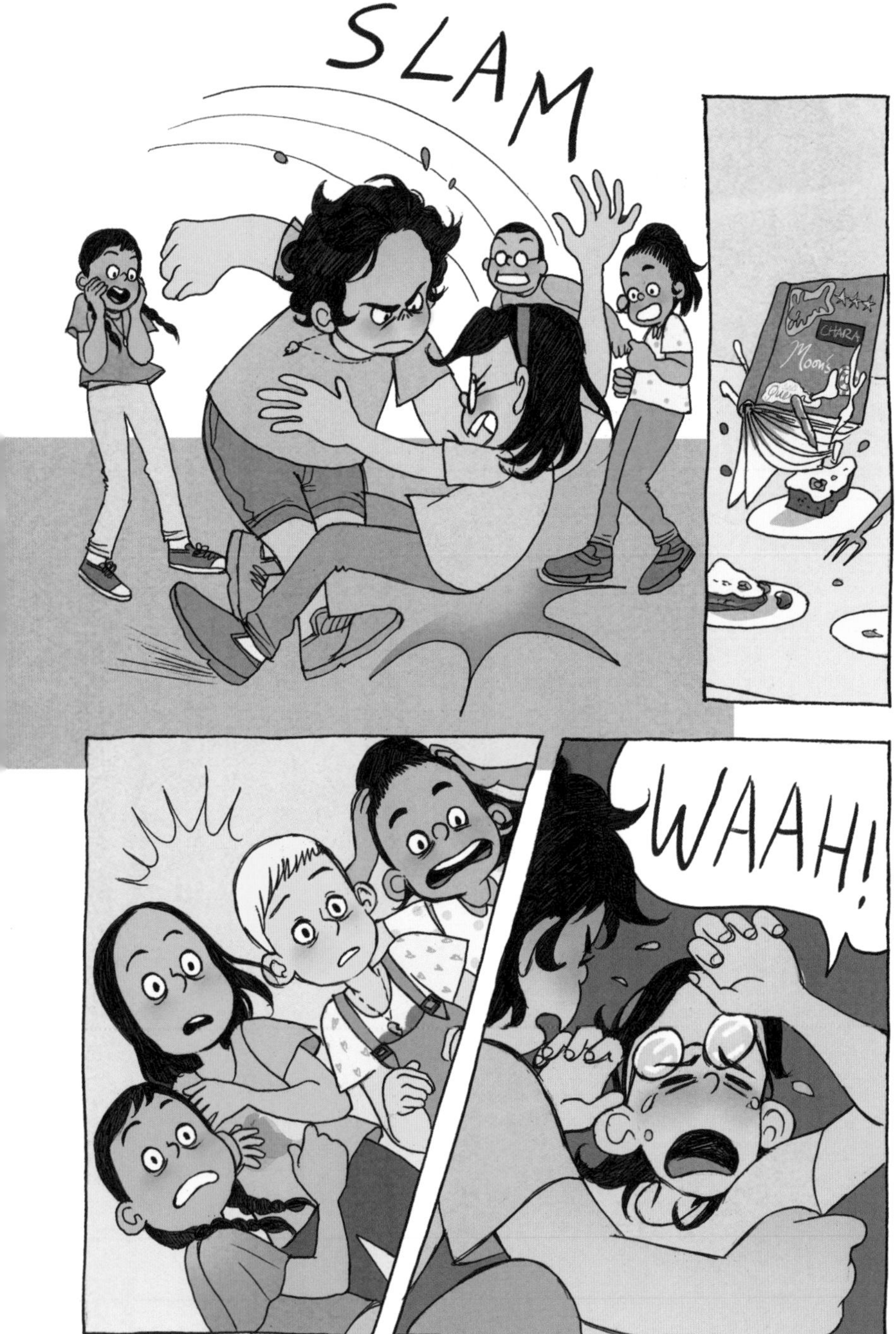
SLAM
CHARA
Moon's
WAAH!

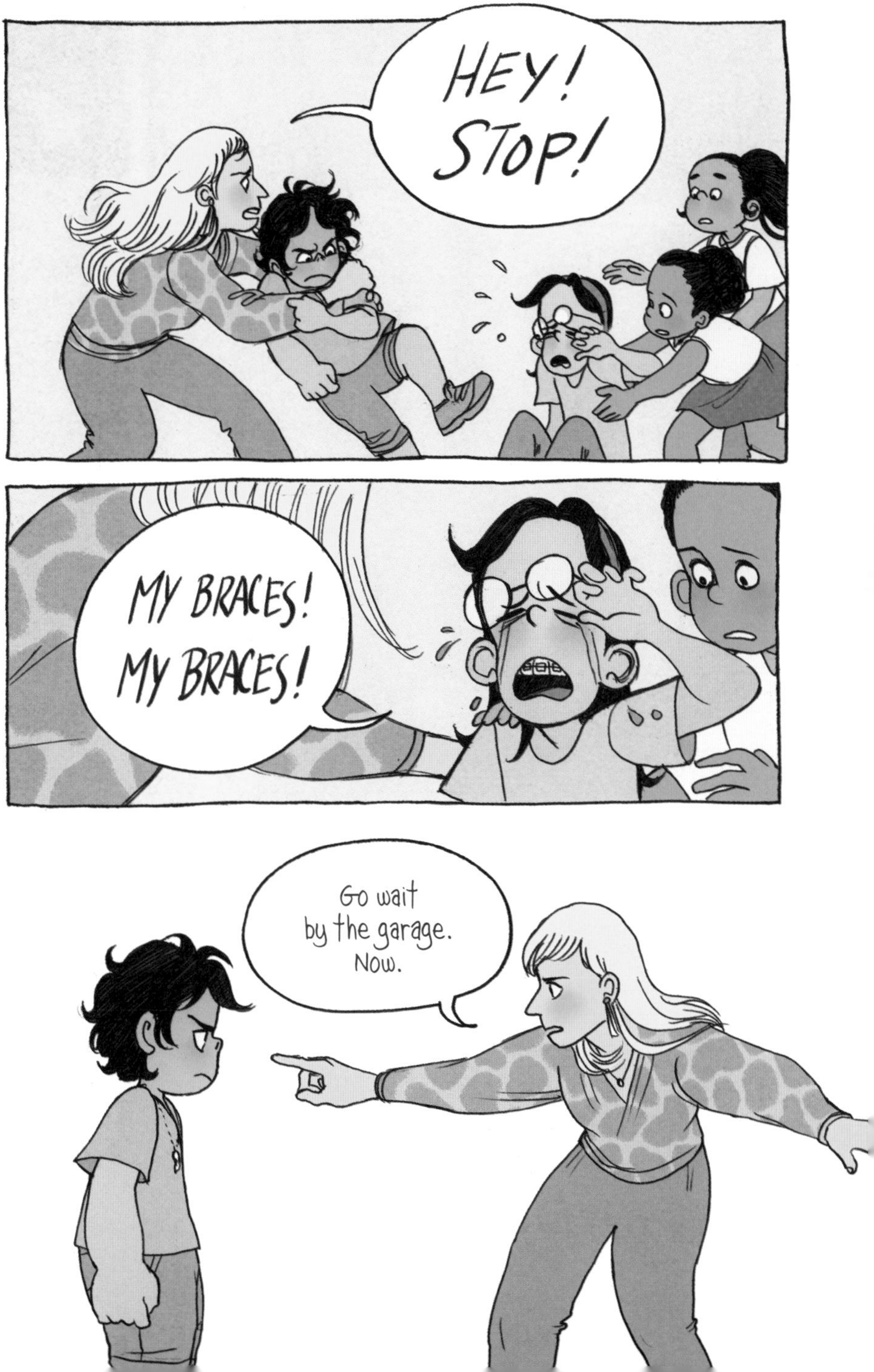
HEY! STOP!
MY BRACES! MY BRACES!
Go wait by the garage. Now.

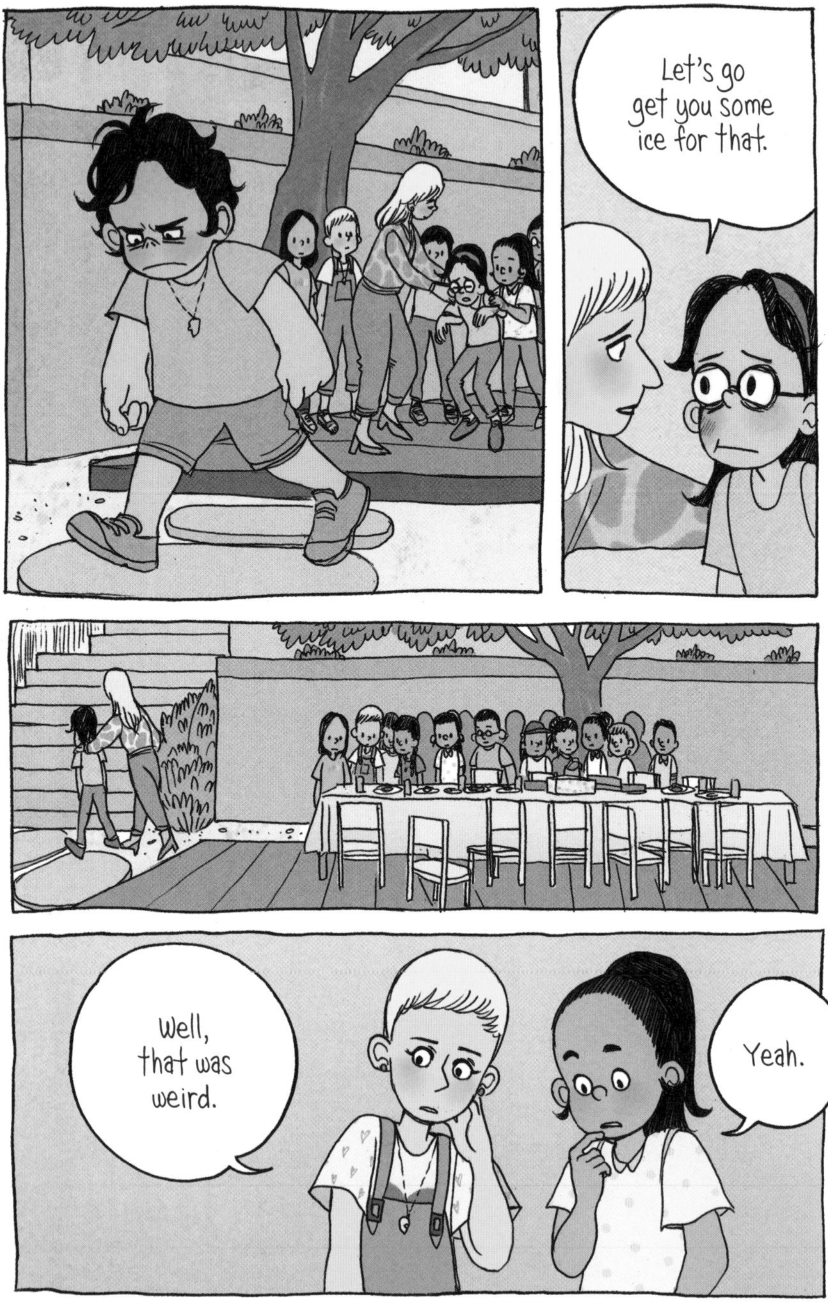
Let's go get you some ice for that.
Well, that was weird.
Yeah.

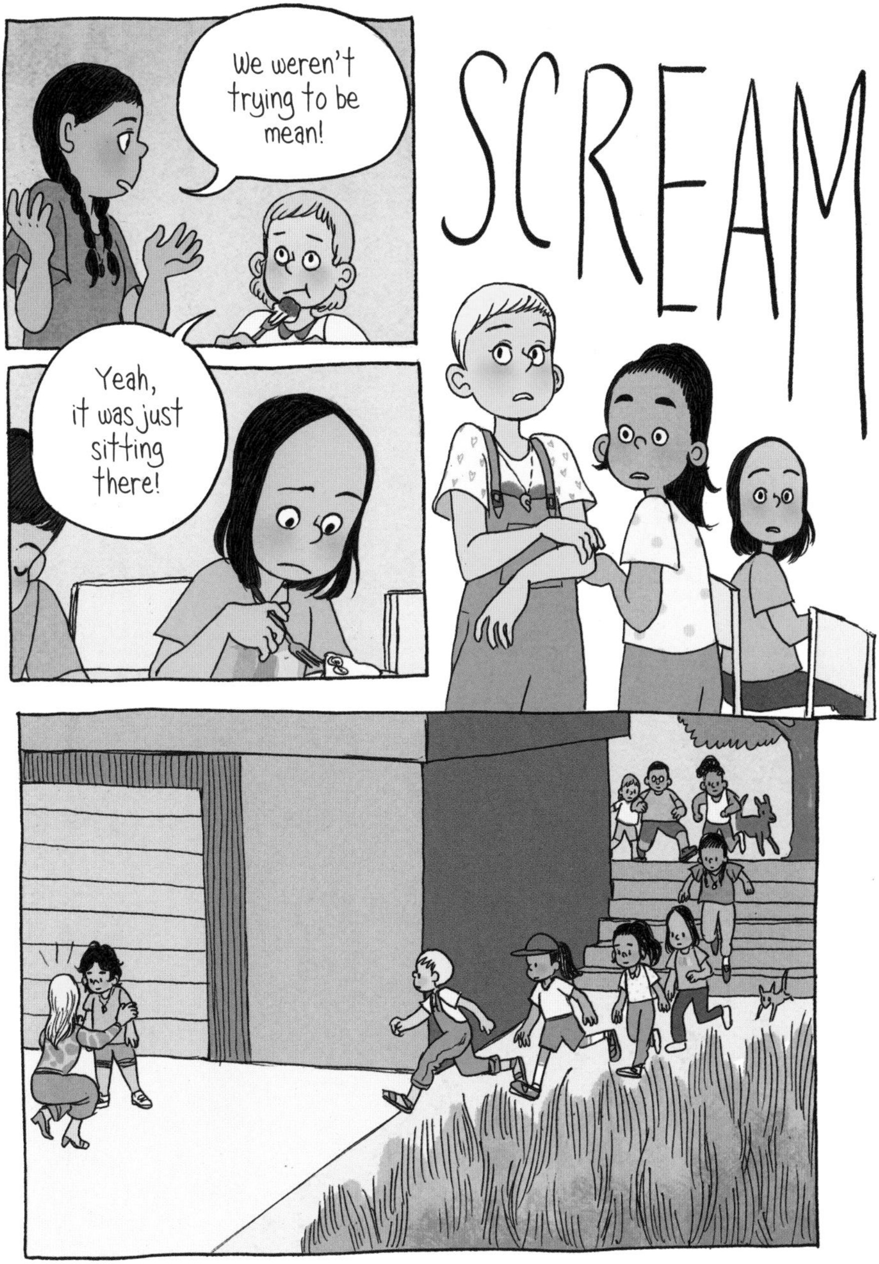
We weren't trying to be mean!
Yeah, it was just sitting there!
SCREAM

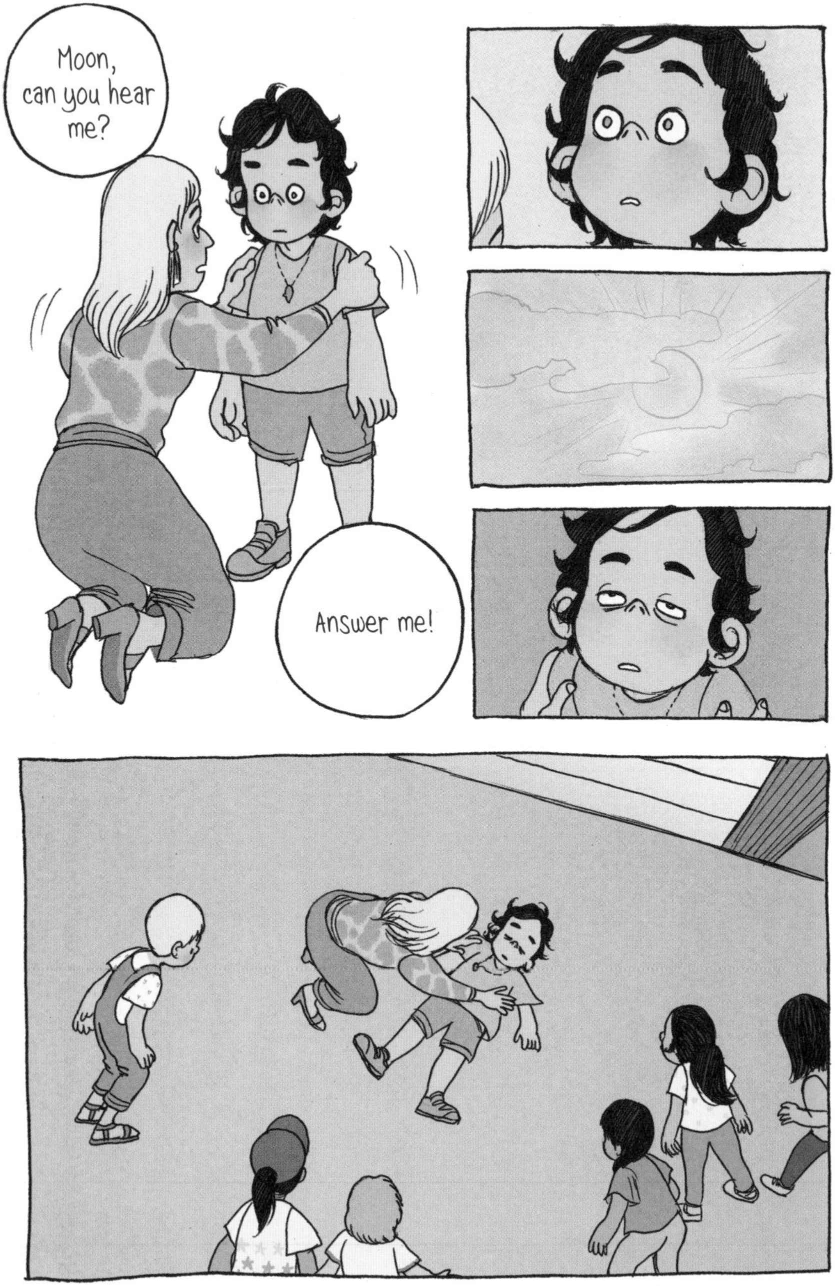
Moon,
can you hear
me?
Answer me!

CHAPTER SEVEN

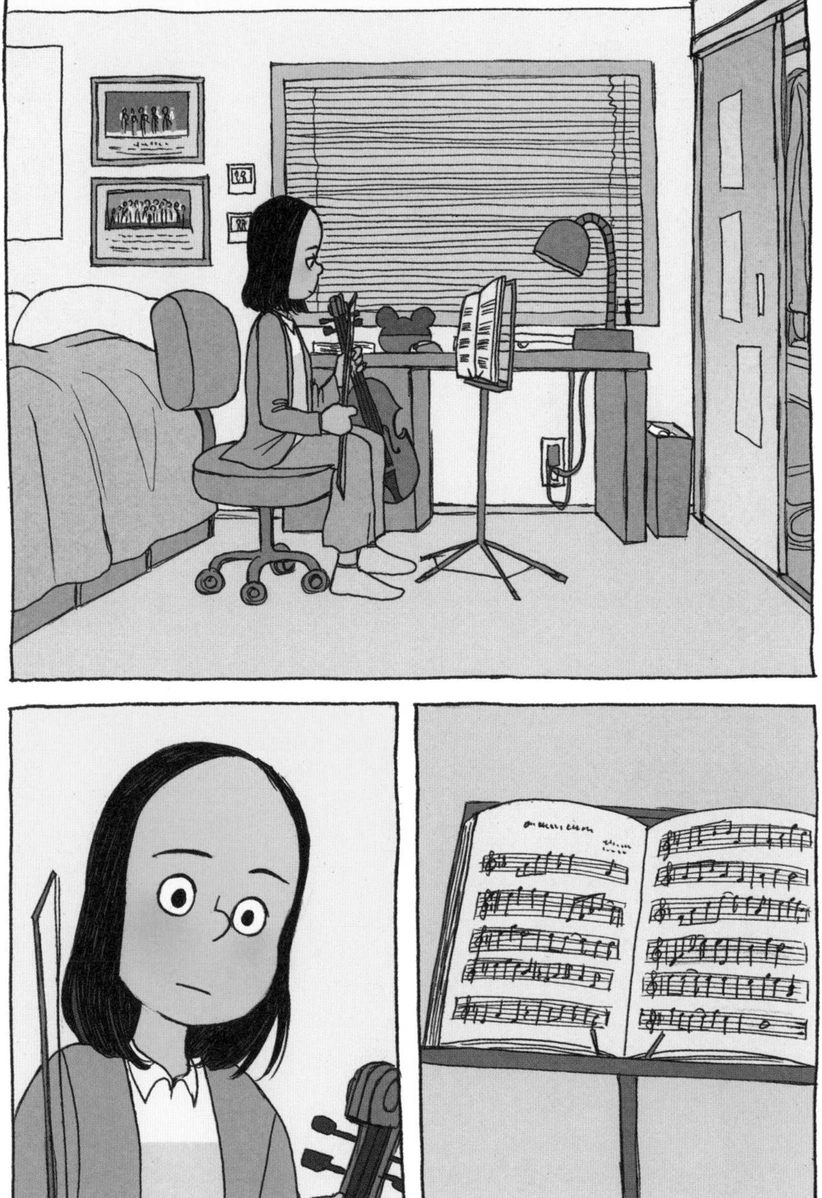

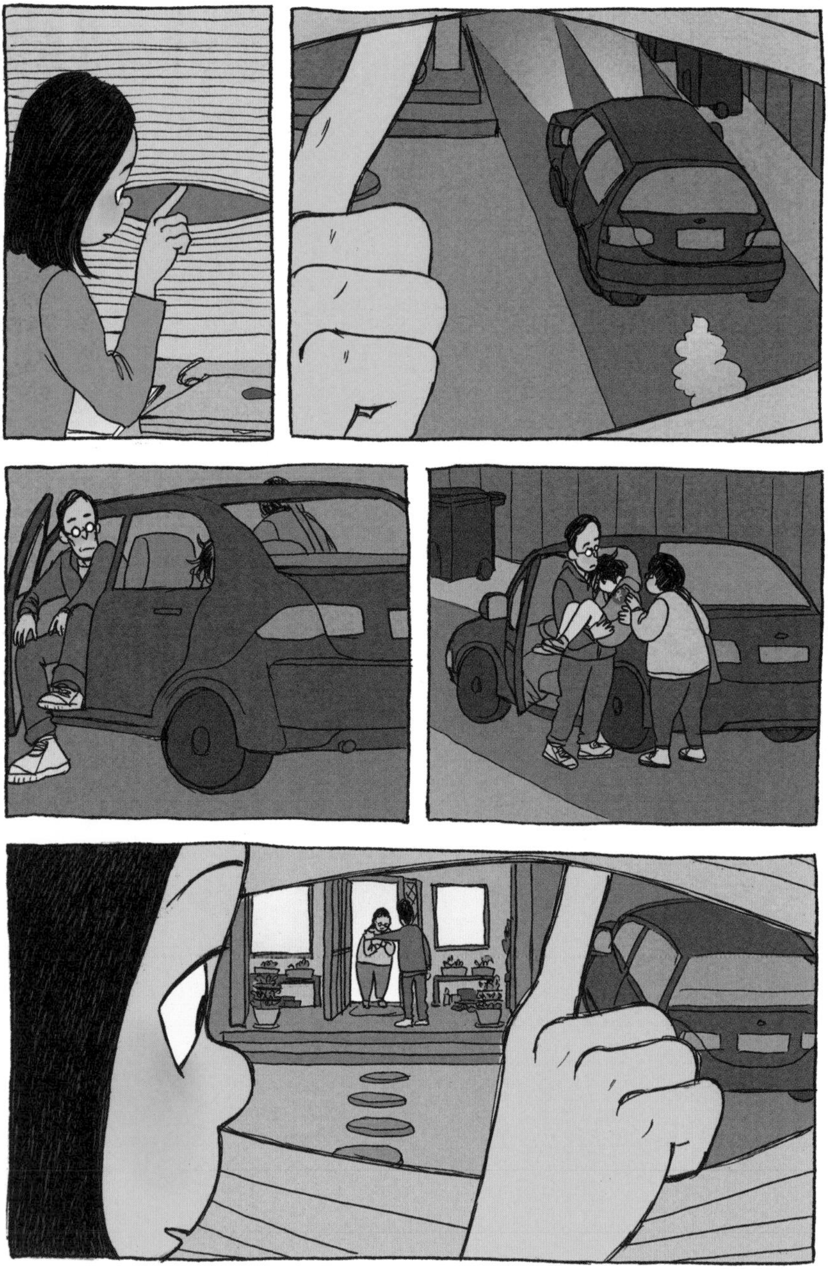

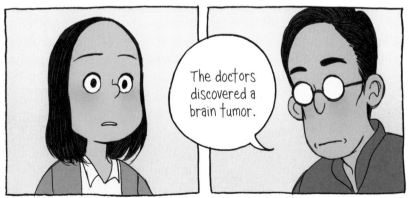

The doctors discovered a brain tumor.

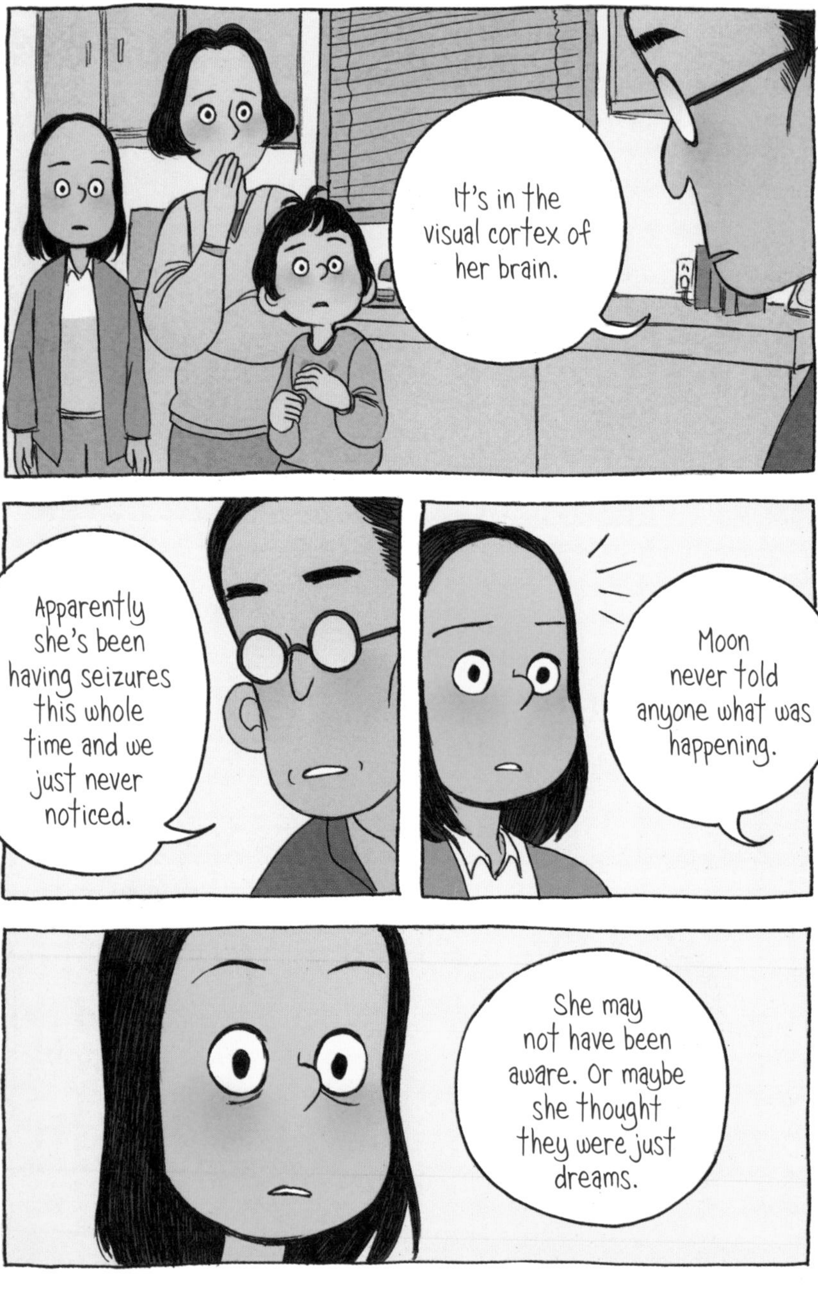
It's in the visual cortex of her brain.
Apparently she's been having seizures this whole time and we just never noticed.
Moon never told anyone what was happening.
She may not have been aware. Or maybe she thought they were just dreams.

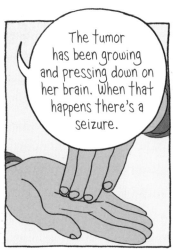

The tumor has been growing and pressing down on her brain. When that happens there's a seizure.

At first it would've only affected her vision. Now it's gotten stronger. That's why she collapsed today.

What are they gonna do?

They're gonna try to operate and remove it as soon as possible.

Is Moon gonna be okay?

I think so. We hope so.

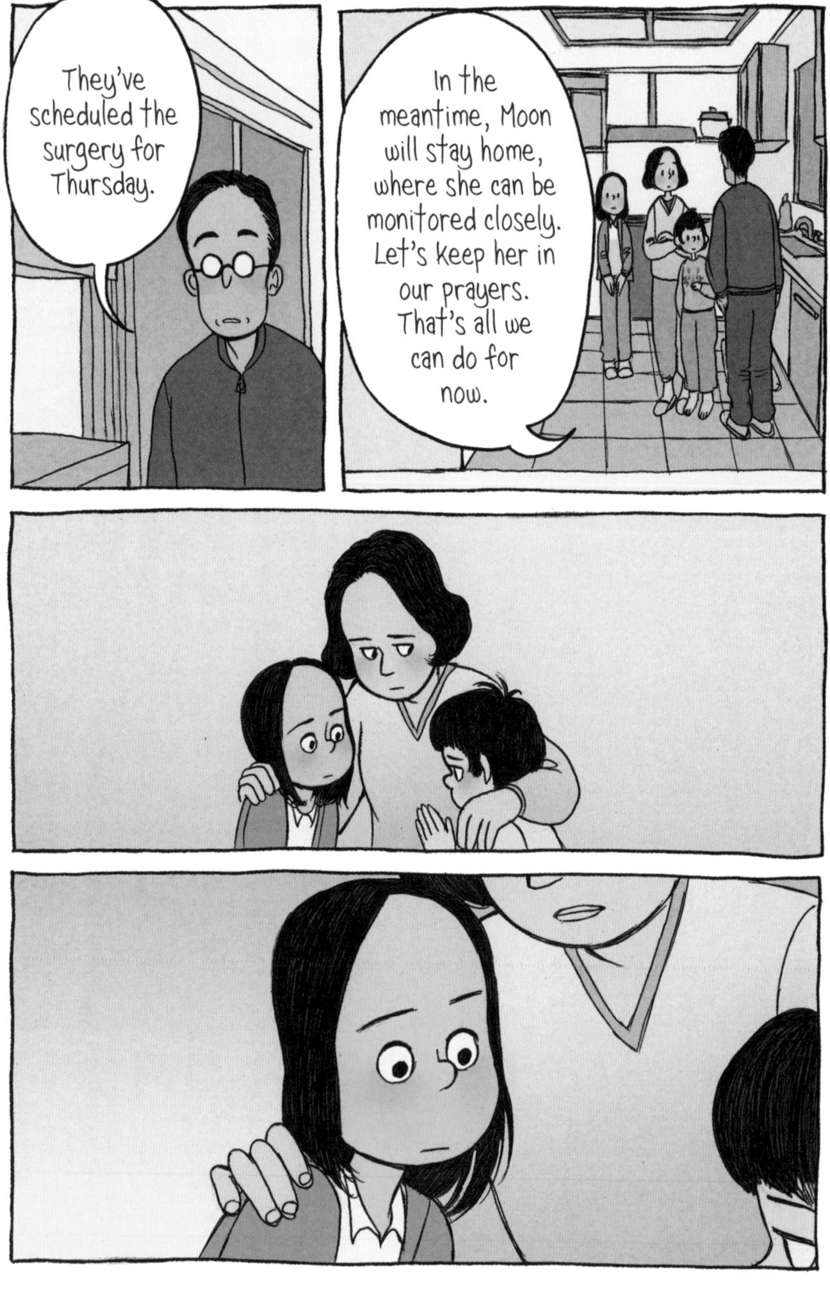
They've scheduled the surgery for Thursday.
In the meantime, Moon will stay home, where she can be monitored closely. Let's keep her in our prayers. That's all we can do for now.

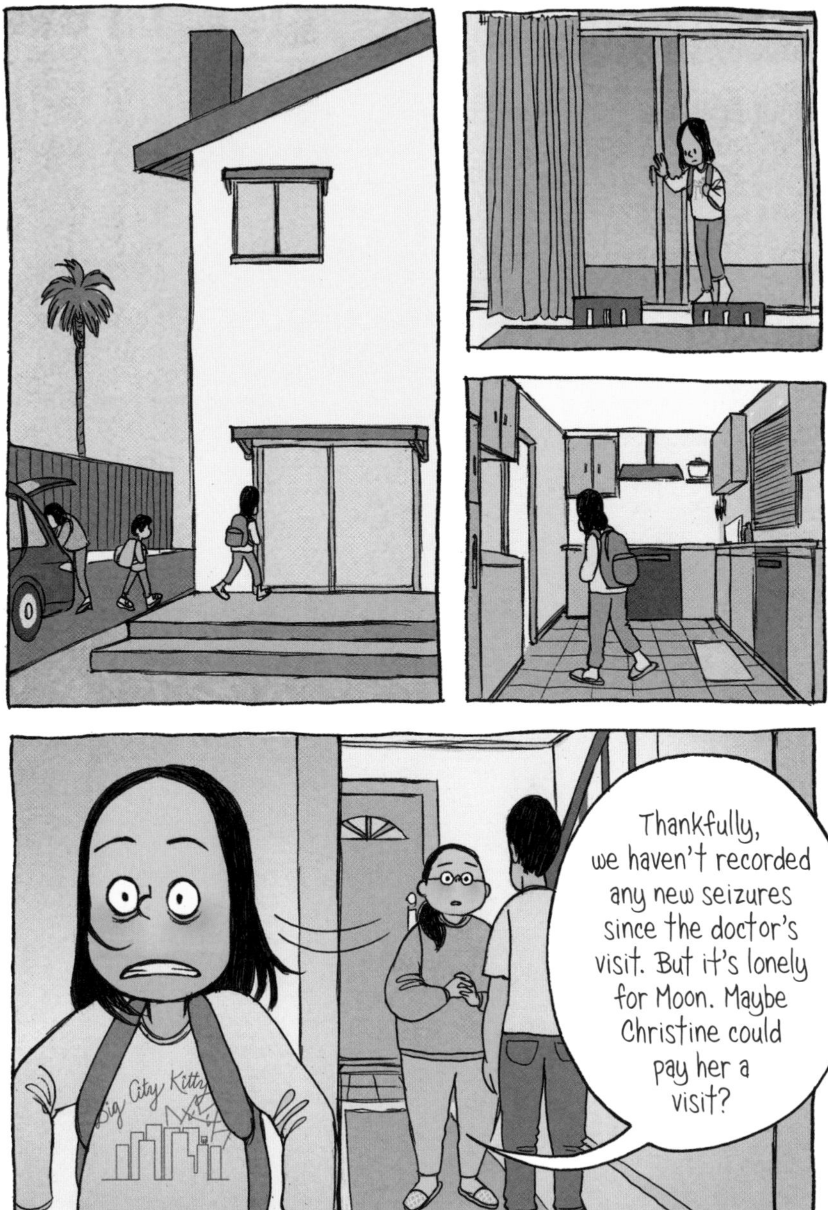
Thankfully, we haven't recorded any new seizures since the doctor's visit. But it's lonely for Moon. Maybe Christine could pay her a visit?
Big City Kitty

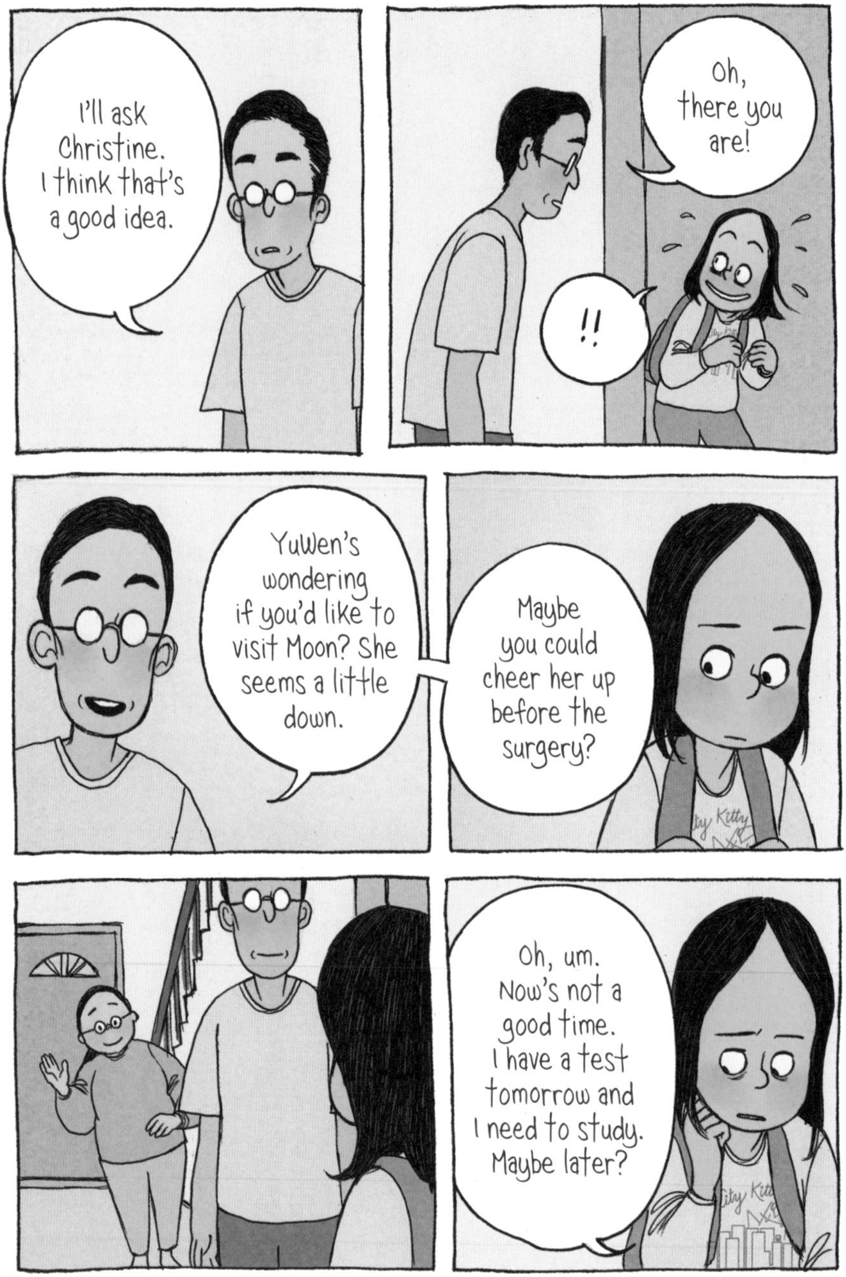
I'll ask Christine. I think that's a good idea.
Oh, there you are!
!!
YuWen's wondering if you'd like to visit Moon? She seems a little down.
Maybe you could cheer her up before the surgery?
Oh, um. Now's not a good time. I have a test tomorrow and I need to study. Maybe later?

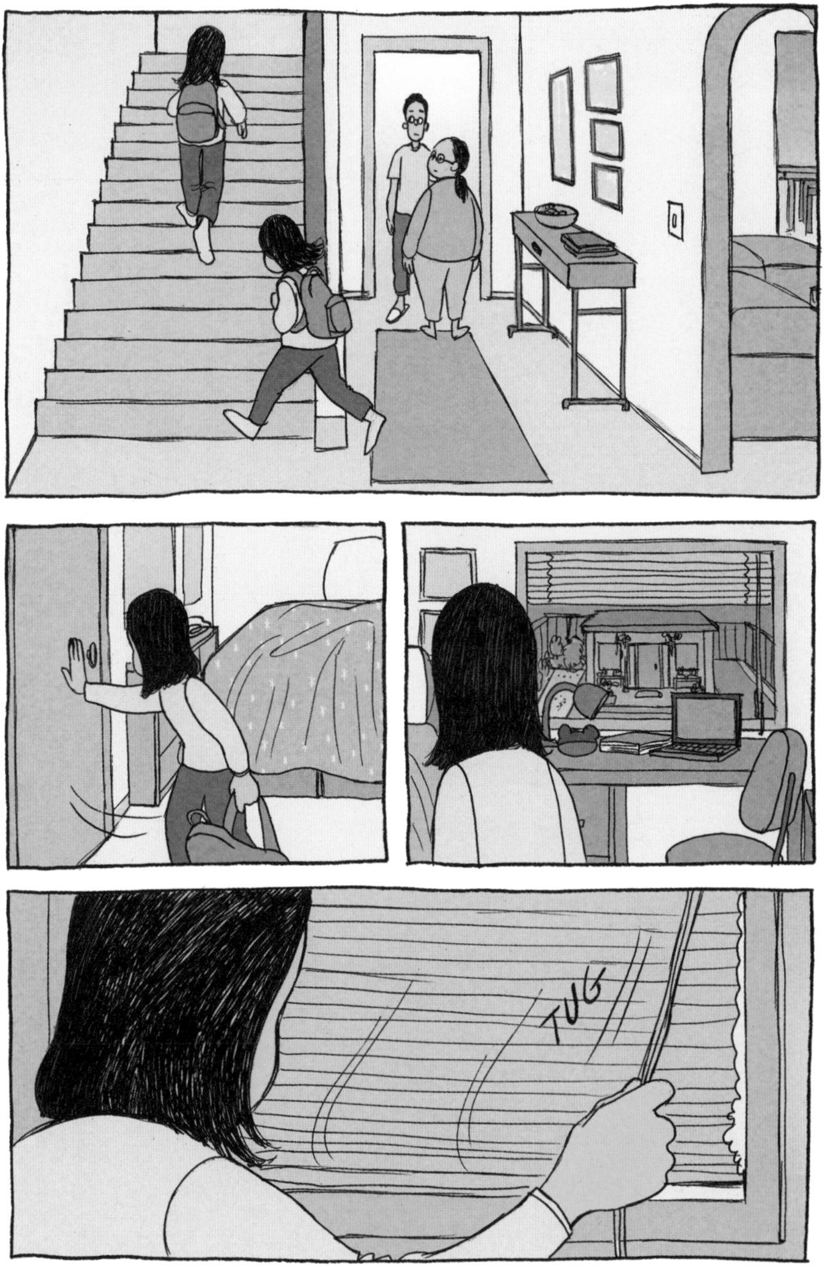
TUG

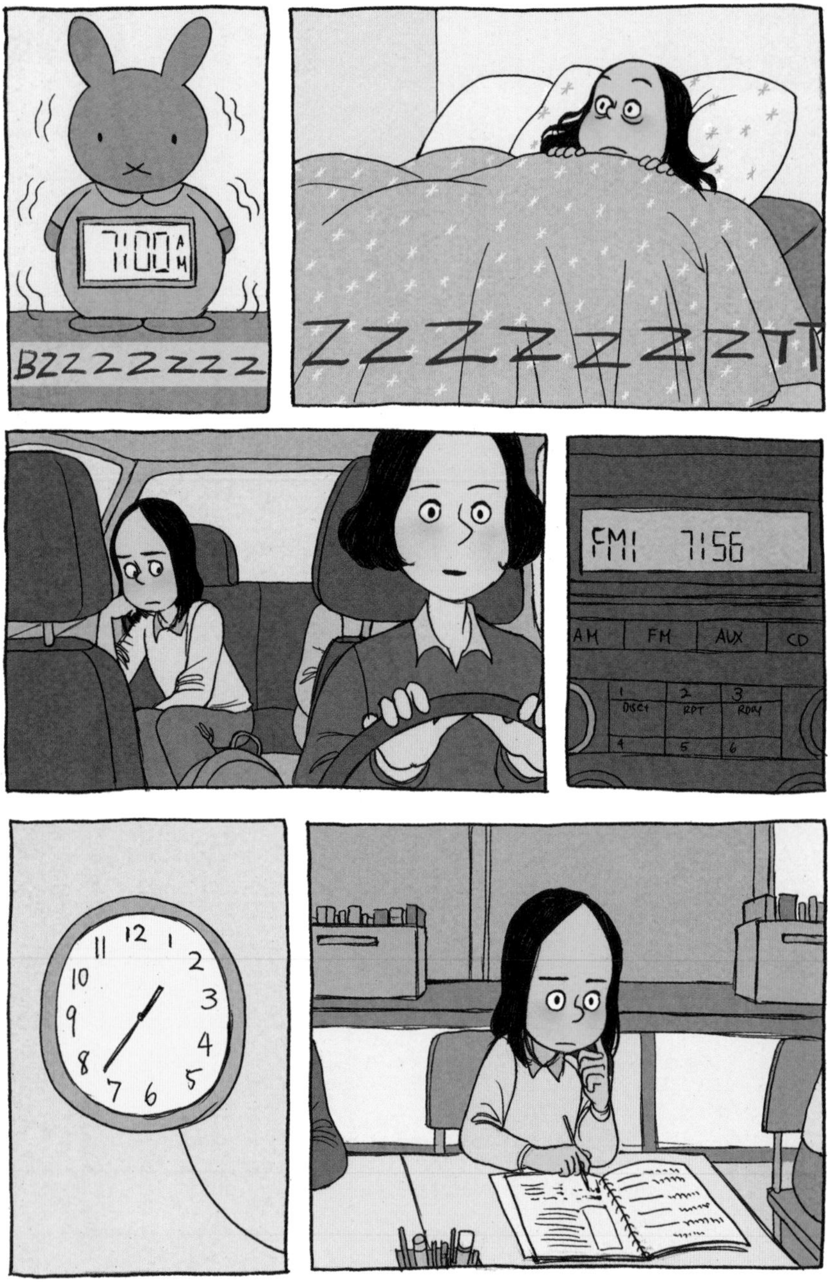
7:00 AM
BZZZZZZZZ
ZZZZZZZZTT
FM1 7:56
AM
FM
AUX
CD
1
DISC+
2
RPT
3
RDM
4
5
6

2:35
1 2 3
4 5 6
6:05 PM
12:31 AM

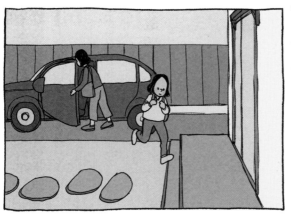

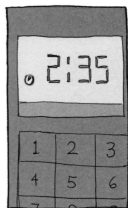

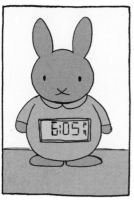

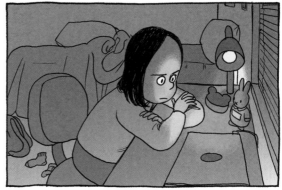

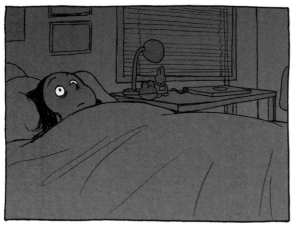

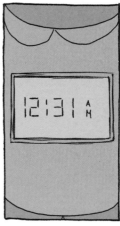

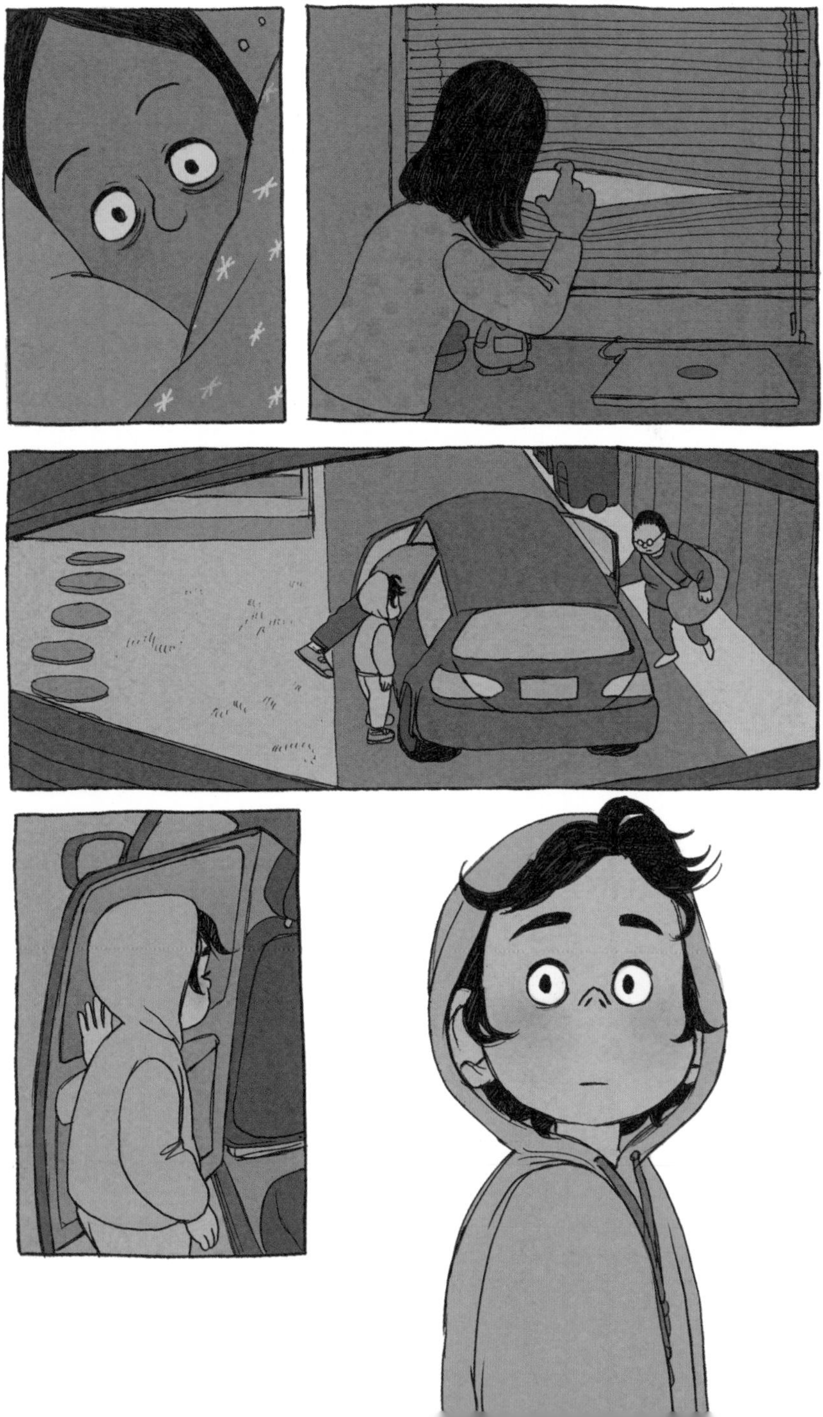

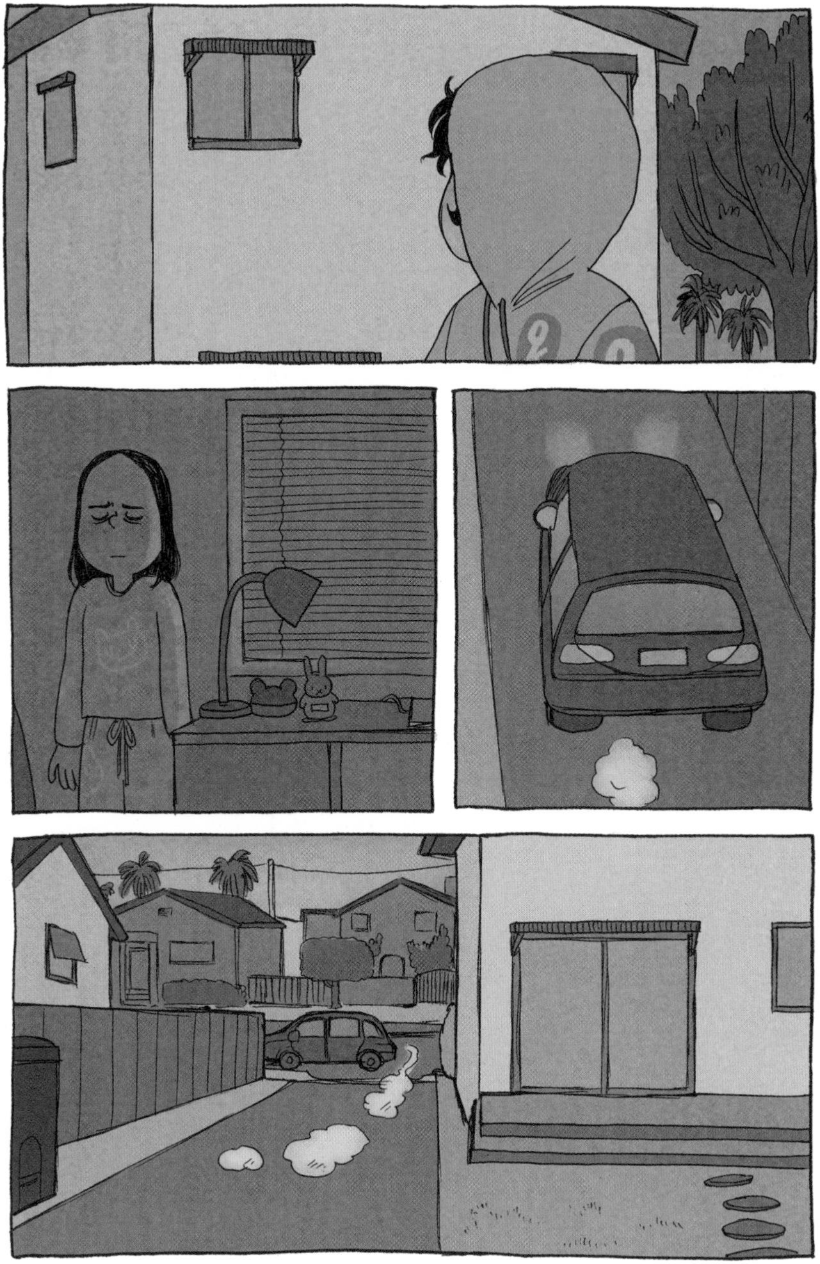

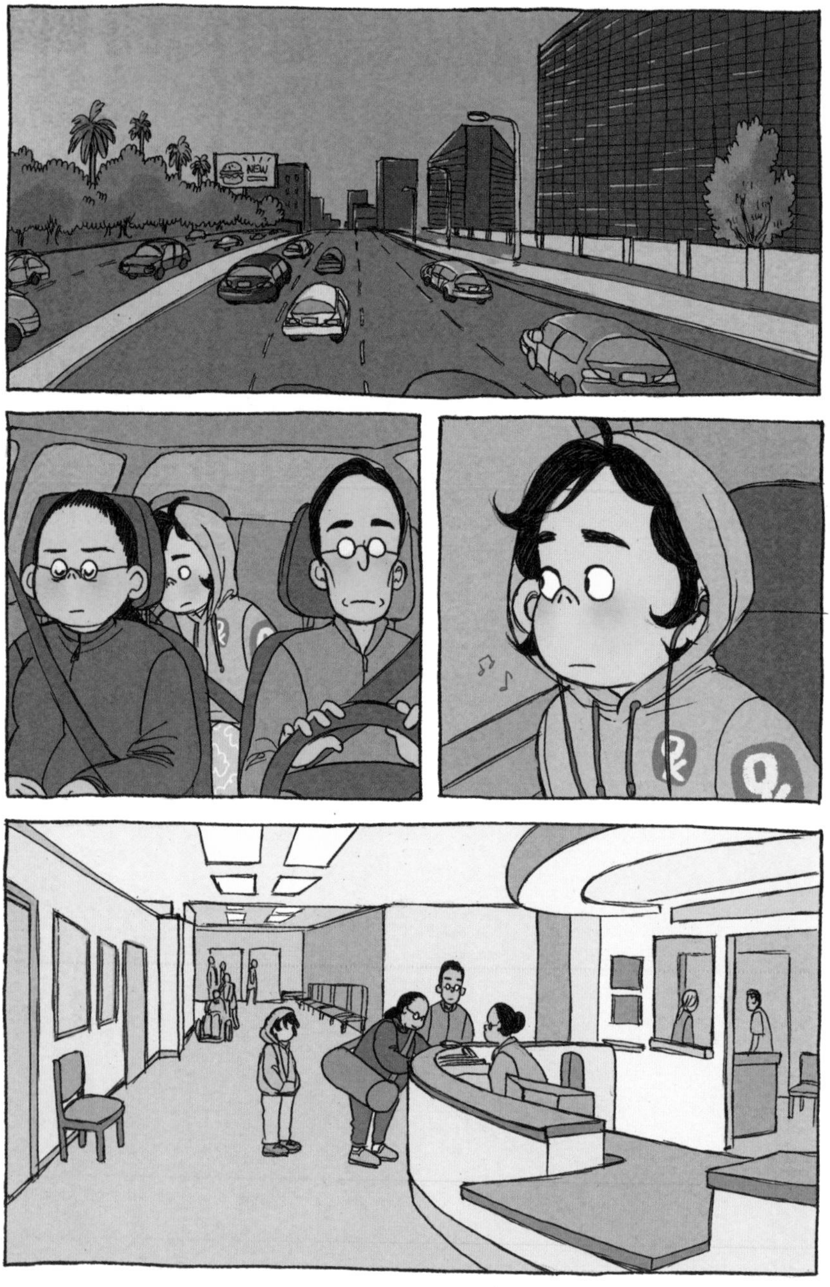
NEW

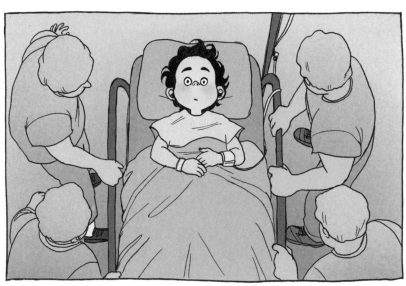

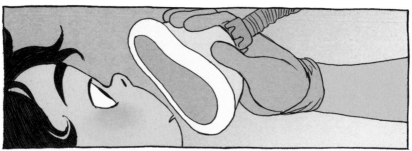

Okay, Moon, you're going to take some deep breaths. Just relax!

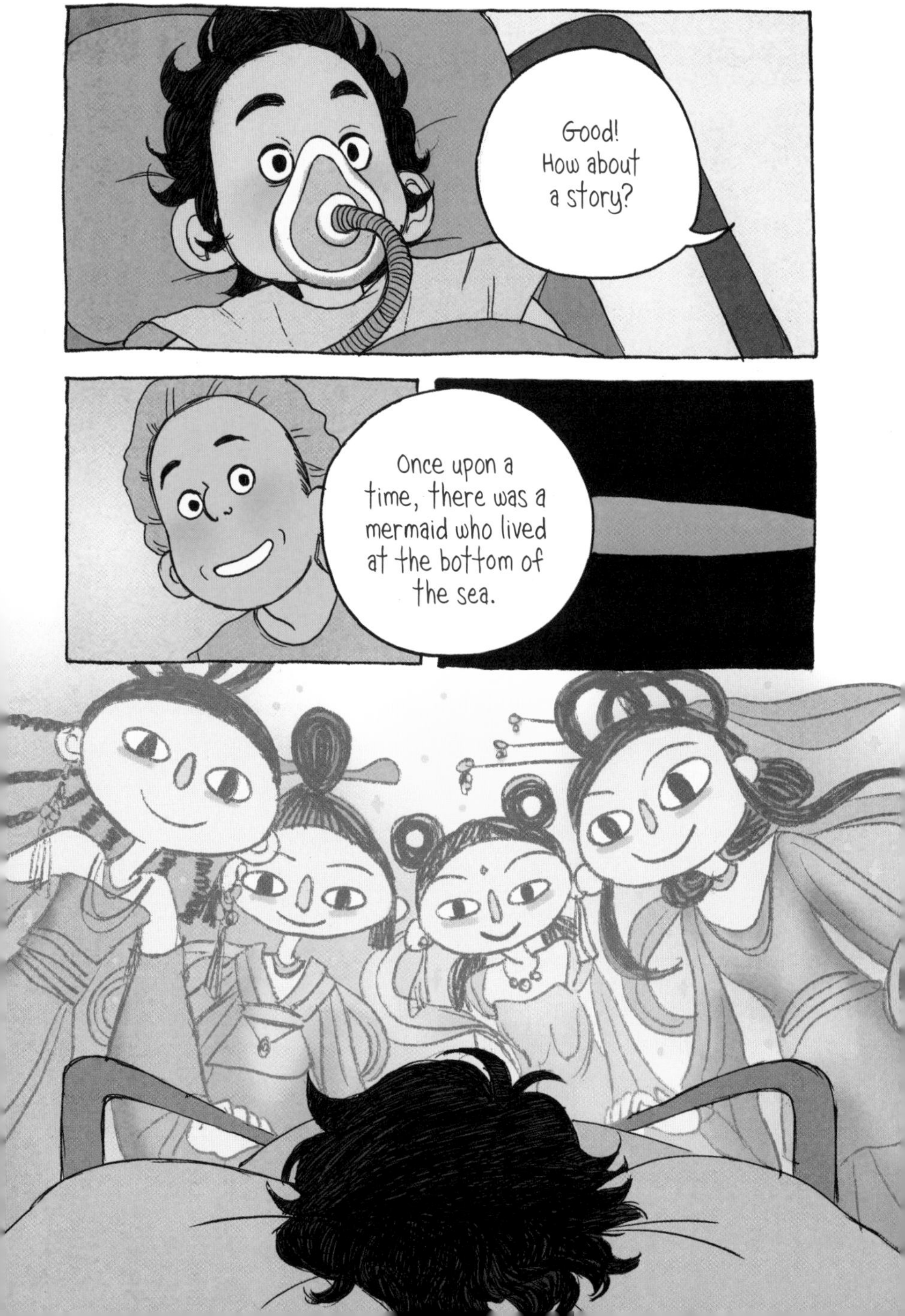
Good! How about a story?
Once upon a time, there was a mermaid who lived at the bottom of the sea.

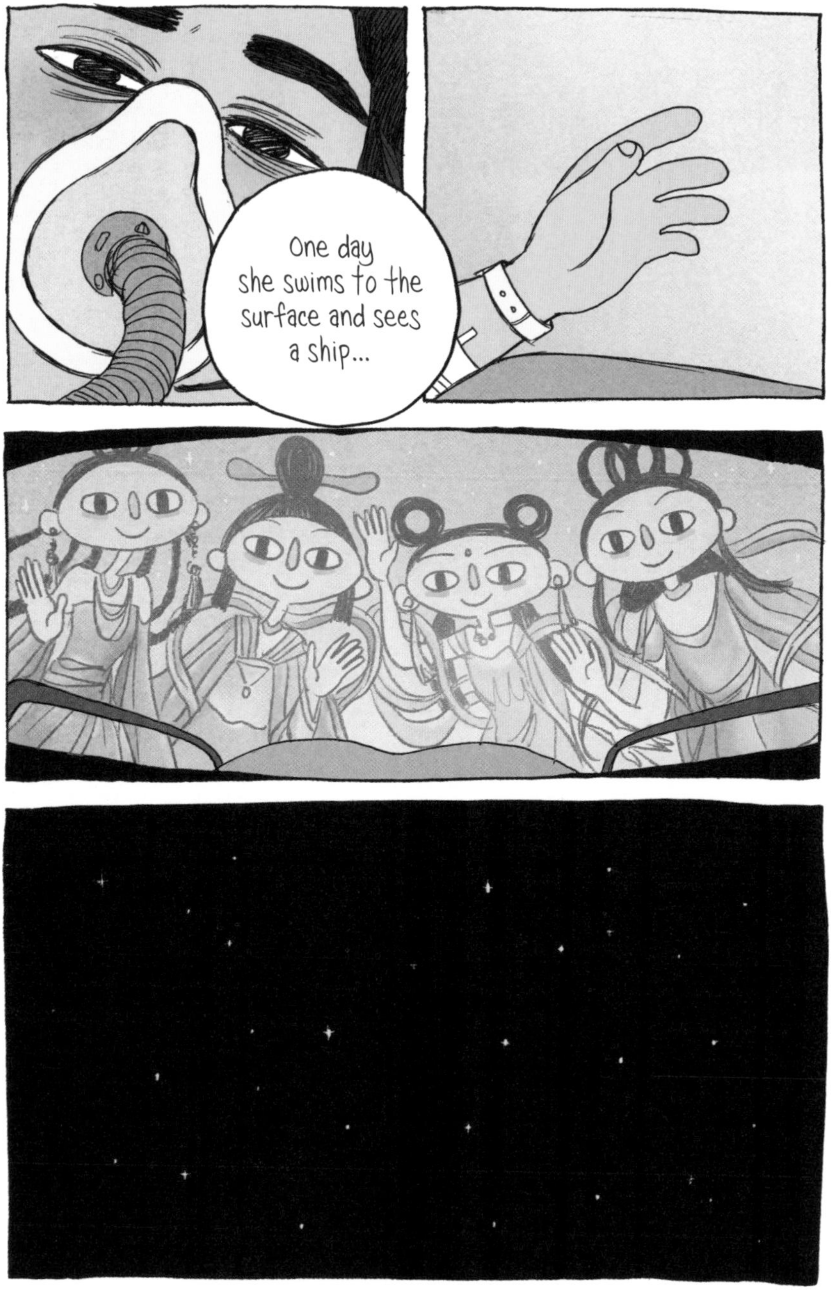
One day she swims to the surface and sees a ship...

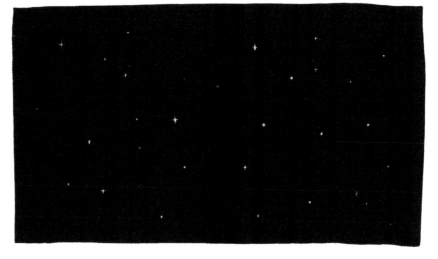

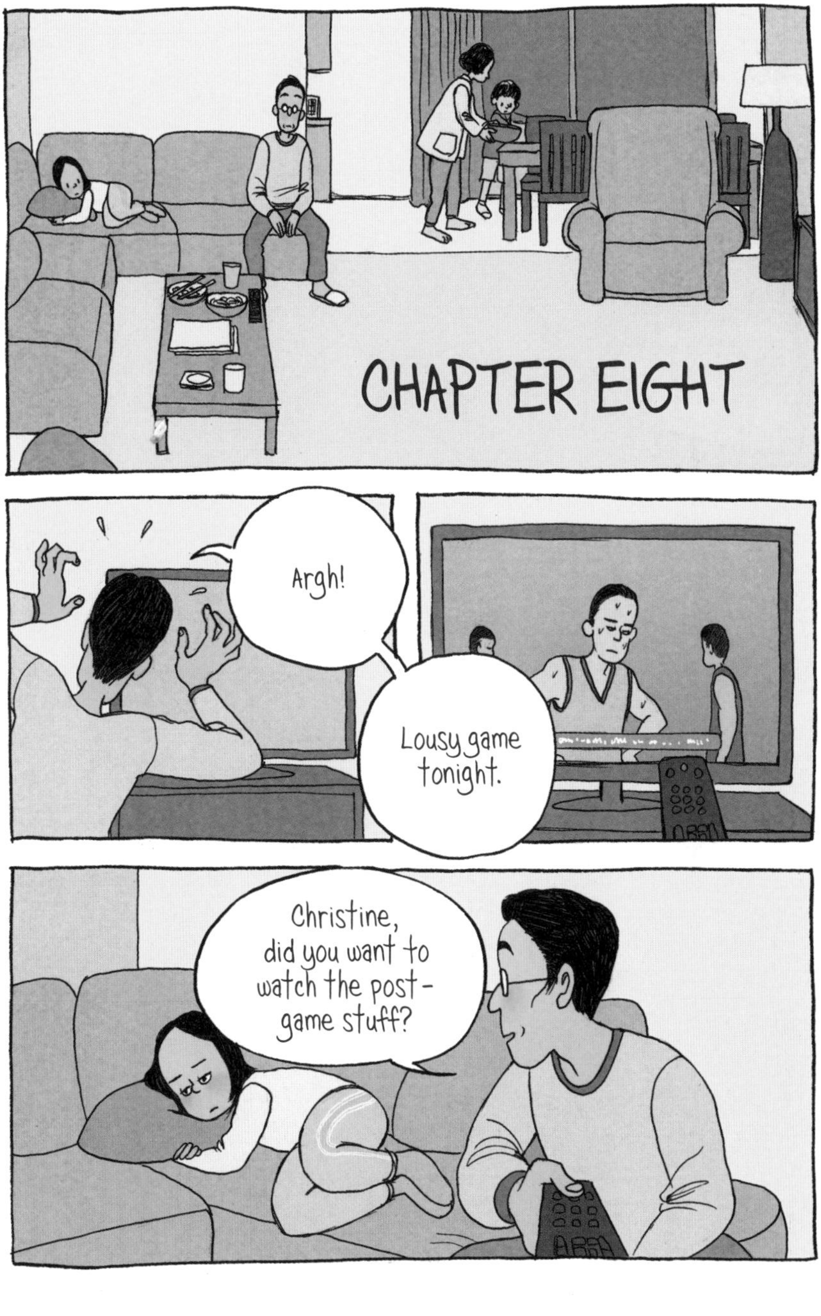
CHAPTER EIGHT
Argh!
Lousy game tonight.
Christine, did you want to watch the post-game stuff?

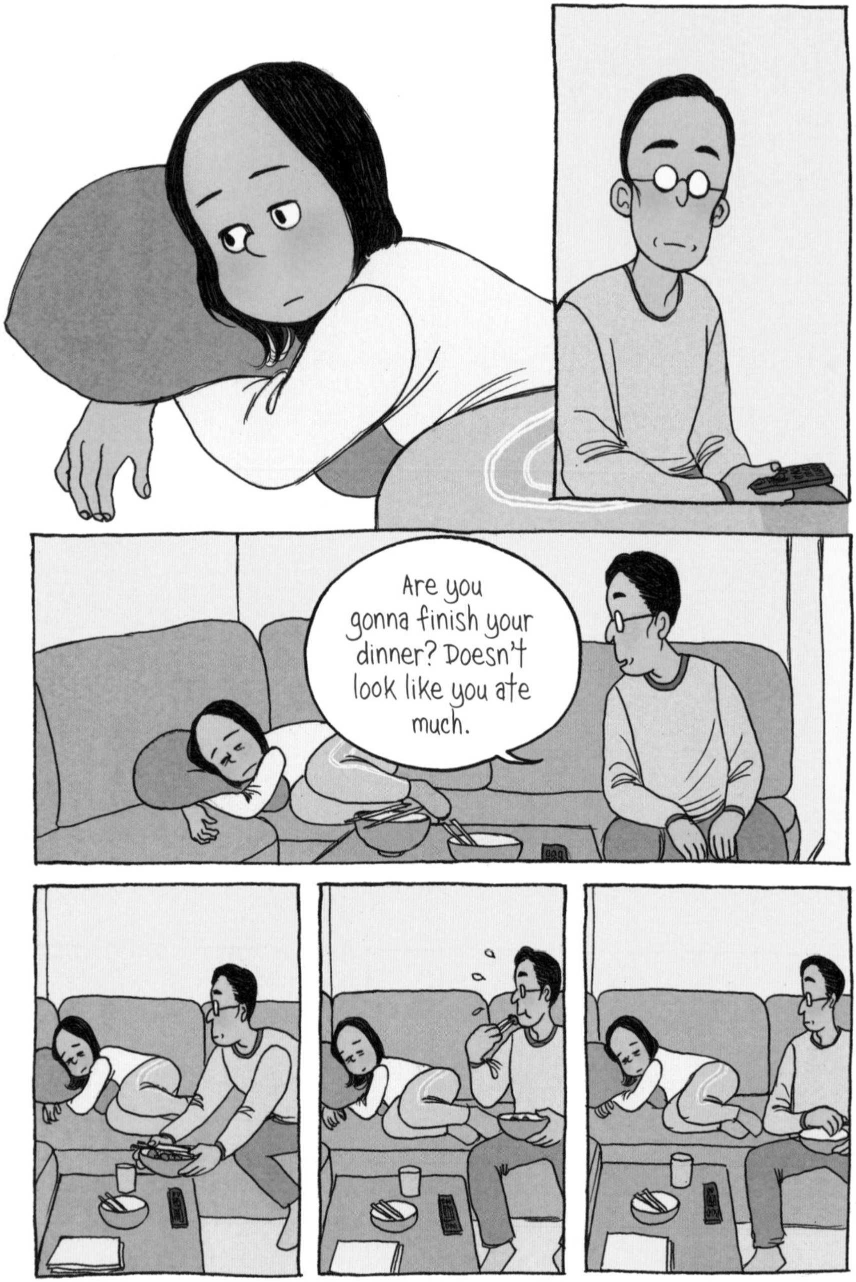
Are you gonna finish your dinner? Doesn't look like you ate much.

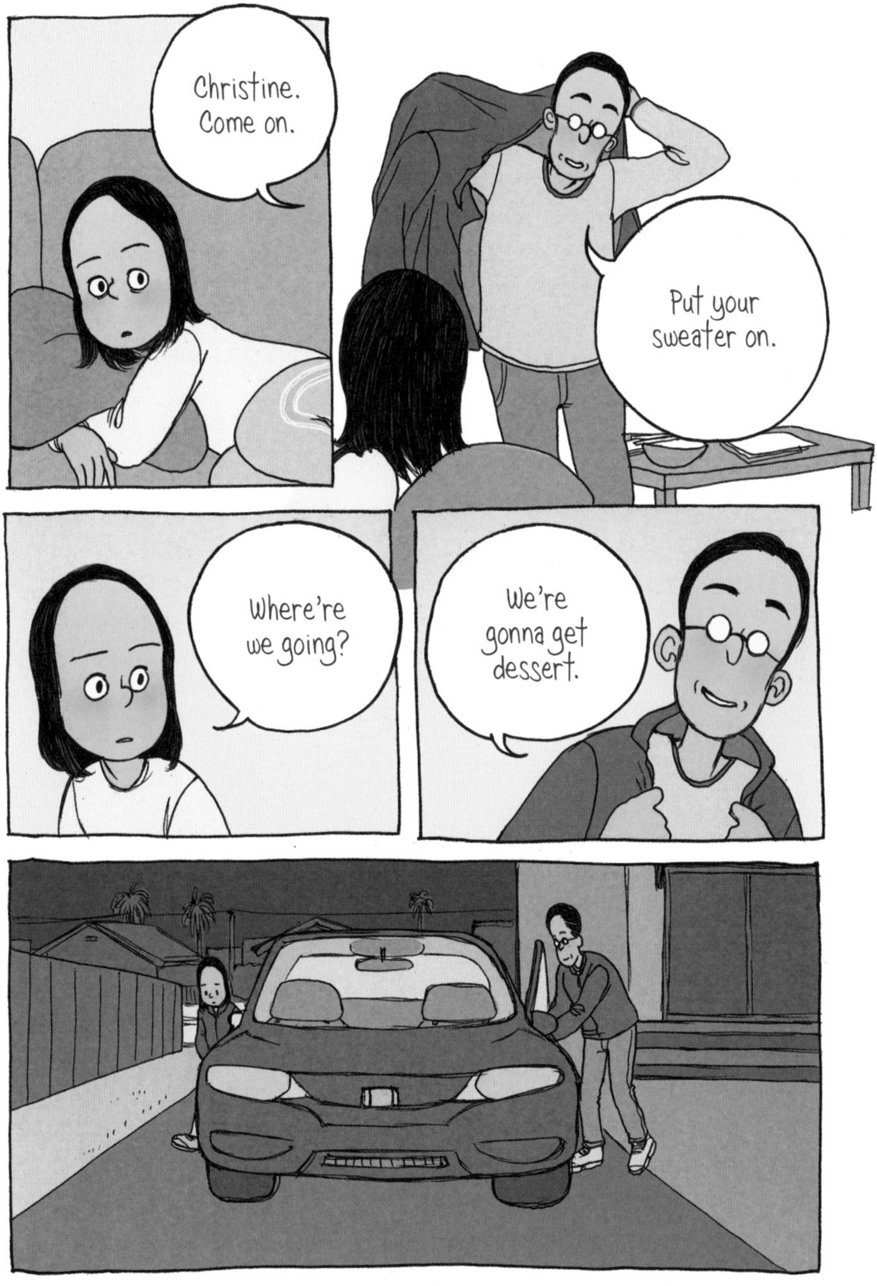
Christine. Come on.
Put your sweater on.
Where're we going?
We're gonna get dessert.

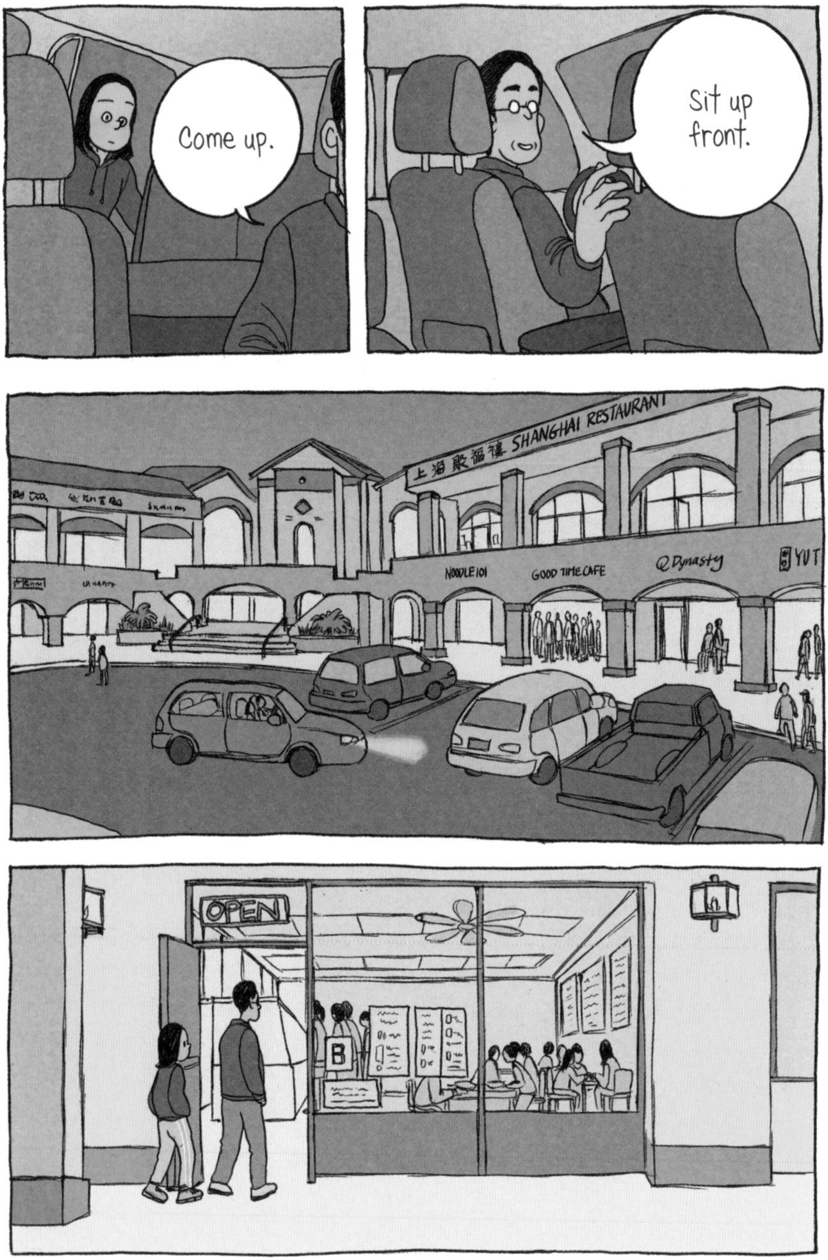
Come up.
Sit up front.
SHANGHAI RESTAURANT
NOODLE 101
GOOD TIME CAFE
Dynasty
OPEN

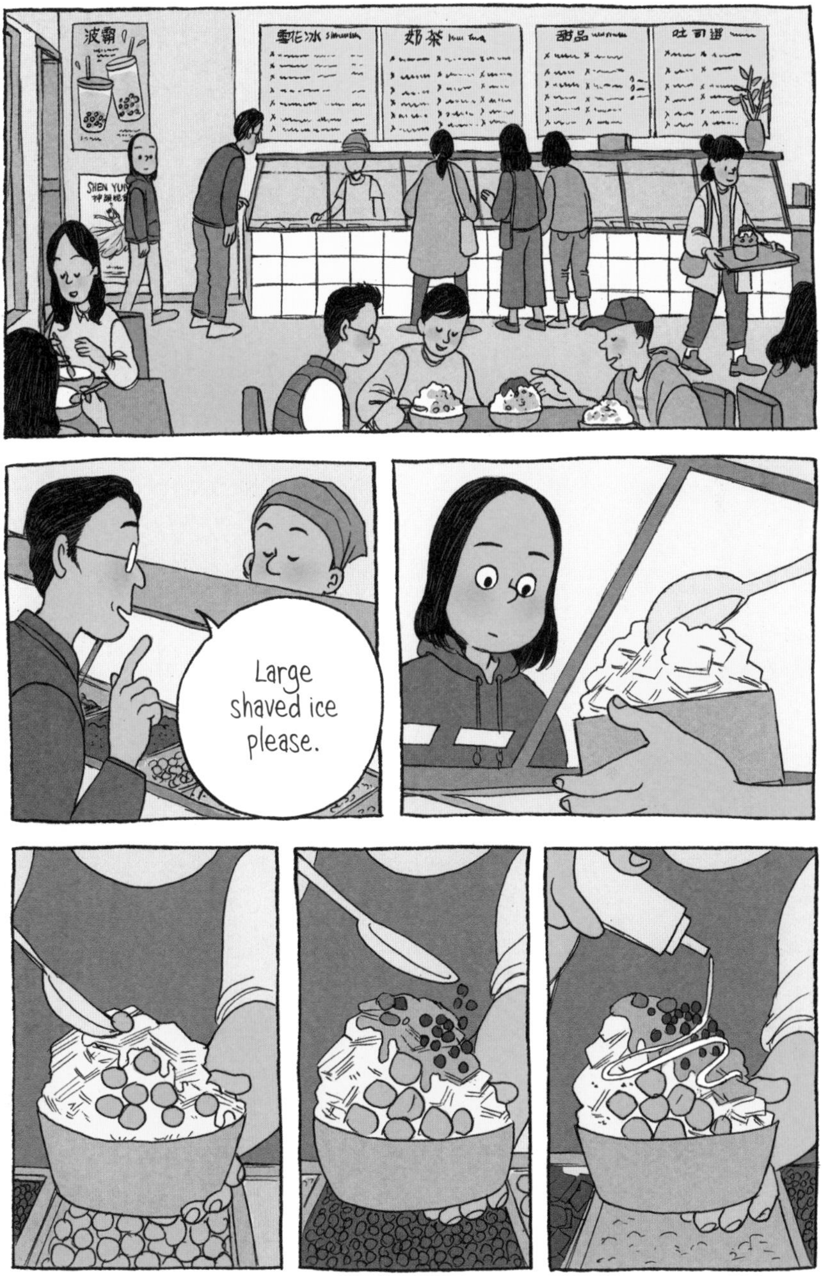
波霸
雪花冰
奶茶
甜品
Large shaved ice please.

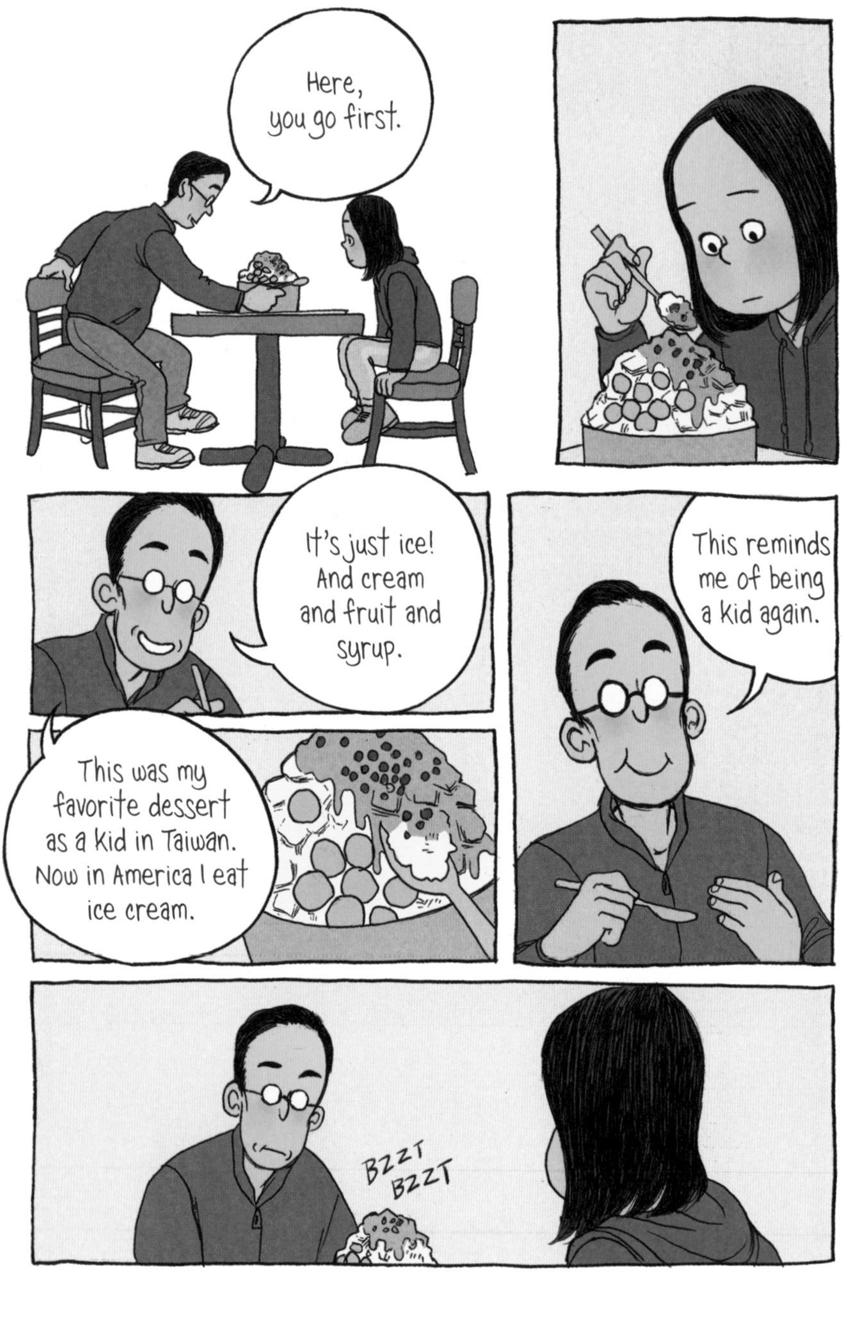
Here, you go first.
It's just ice! And cream and fruit and syrup.
This reminds me of being a kid again.
This was my favorite dessert as a kid in Taiwan. Now in America I eat ice cream.
BZZT BZZT

It's YuWen.

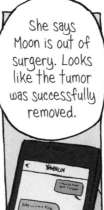

She says Moon is out of surgery. Looks like the tumor was successfully removed.

She is resting now.

Well, that's a relief. Let's hope we keep getting good news.

Baba. Is Moon going to be...

...different?

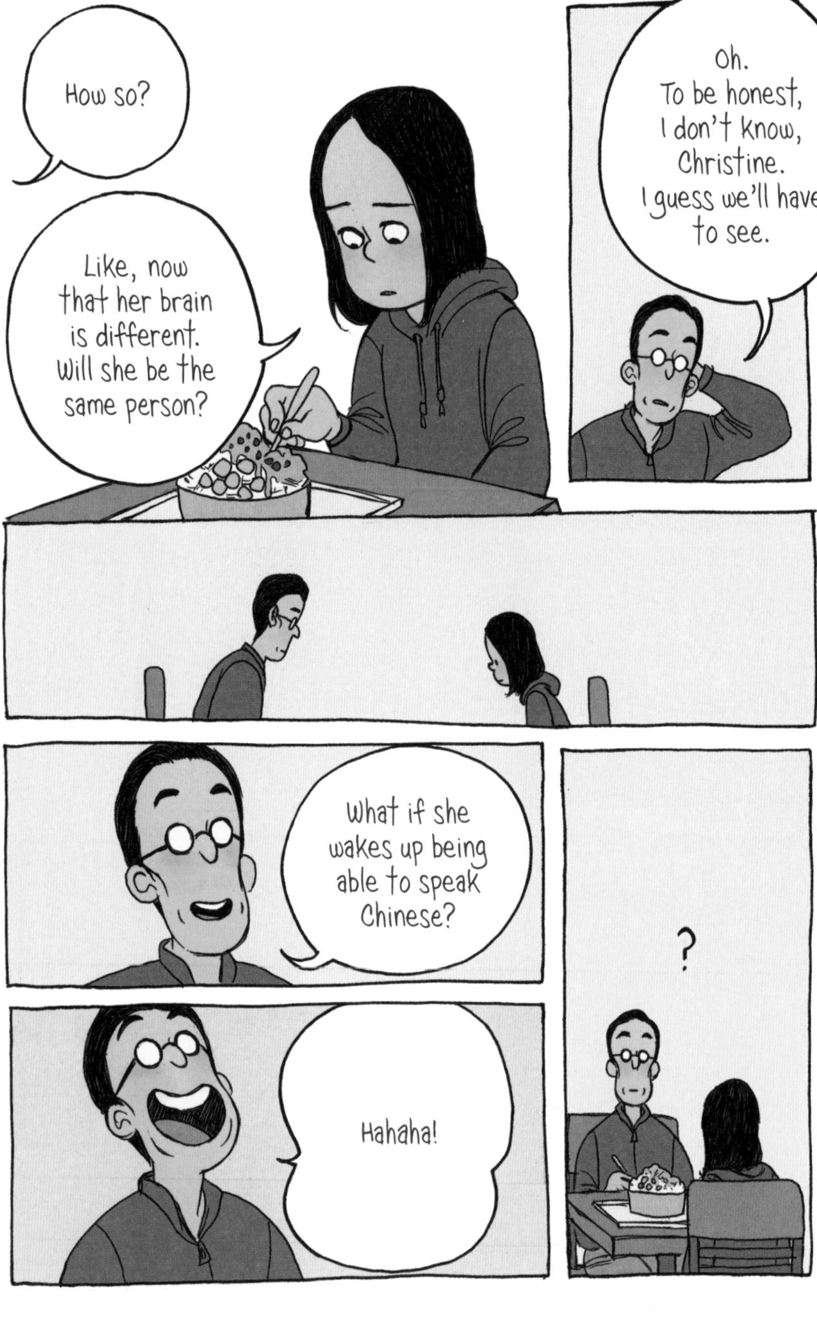
How so?
Like, now that her brain is different. Will she be the same person?
Oh. To be honest, I don't know, Christine. I guess we'll have to see.
What if she wakes up being able to speak Chinese?
Hahaha!
?

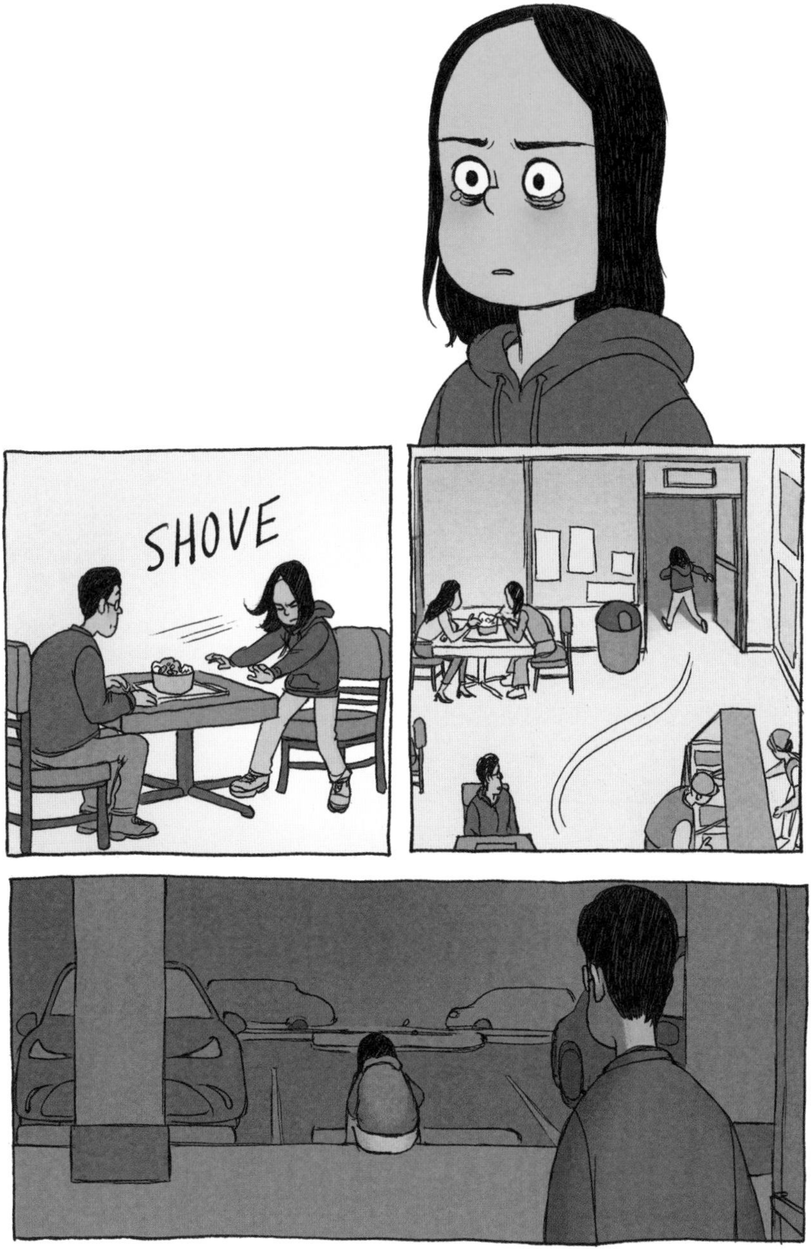
SHOVE

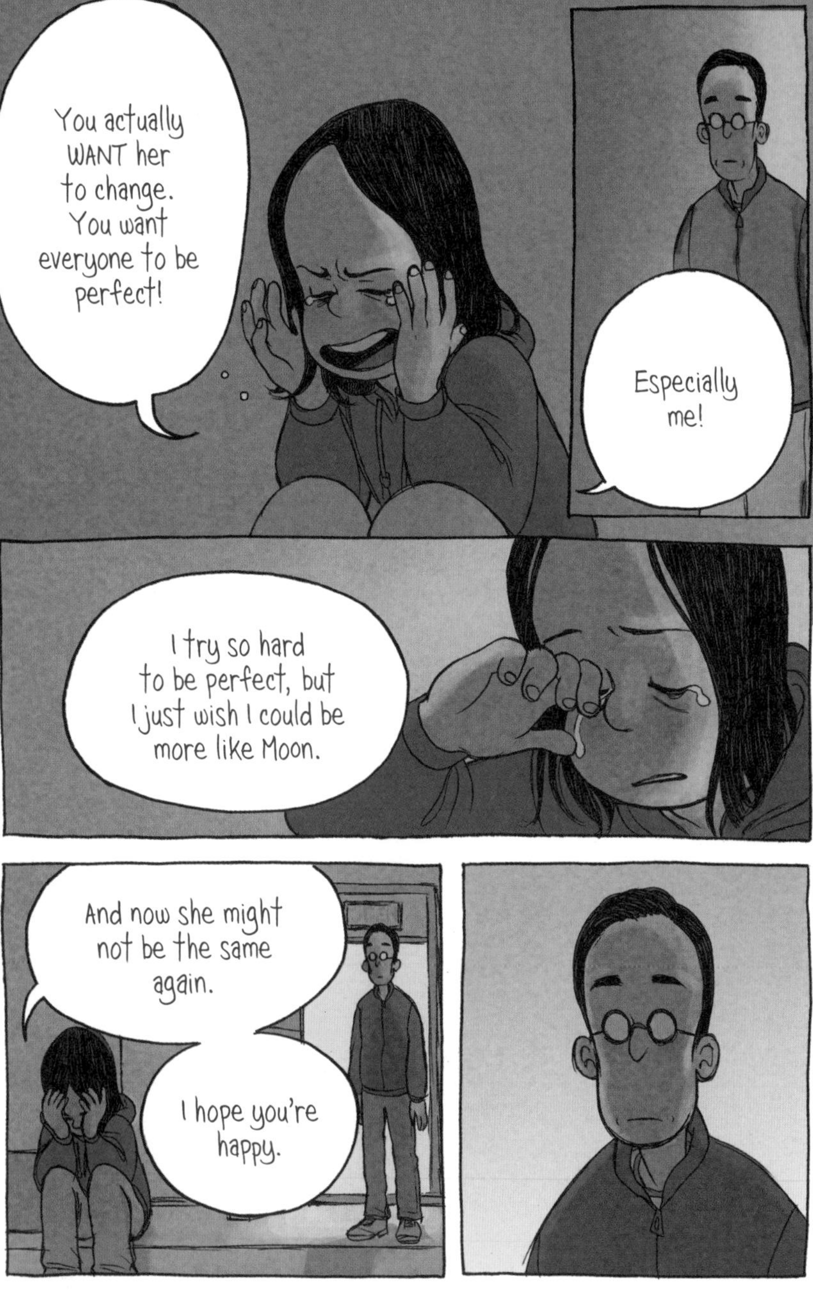
You actually WANT her to change. You want everyone to be perfect!
Especially me!
I try so hard to be perfect, but I just wish I could be more like Moon.
And now she might not be the same again.
I hope you're happy.

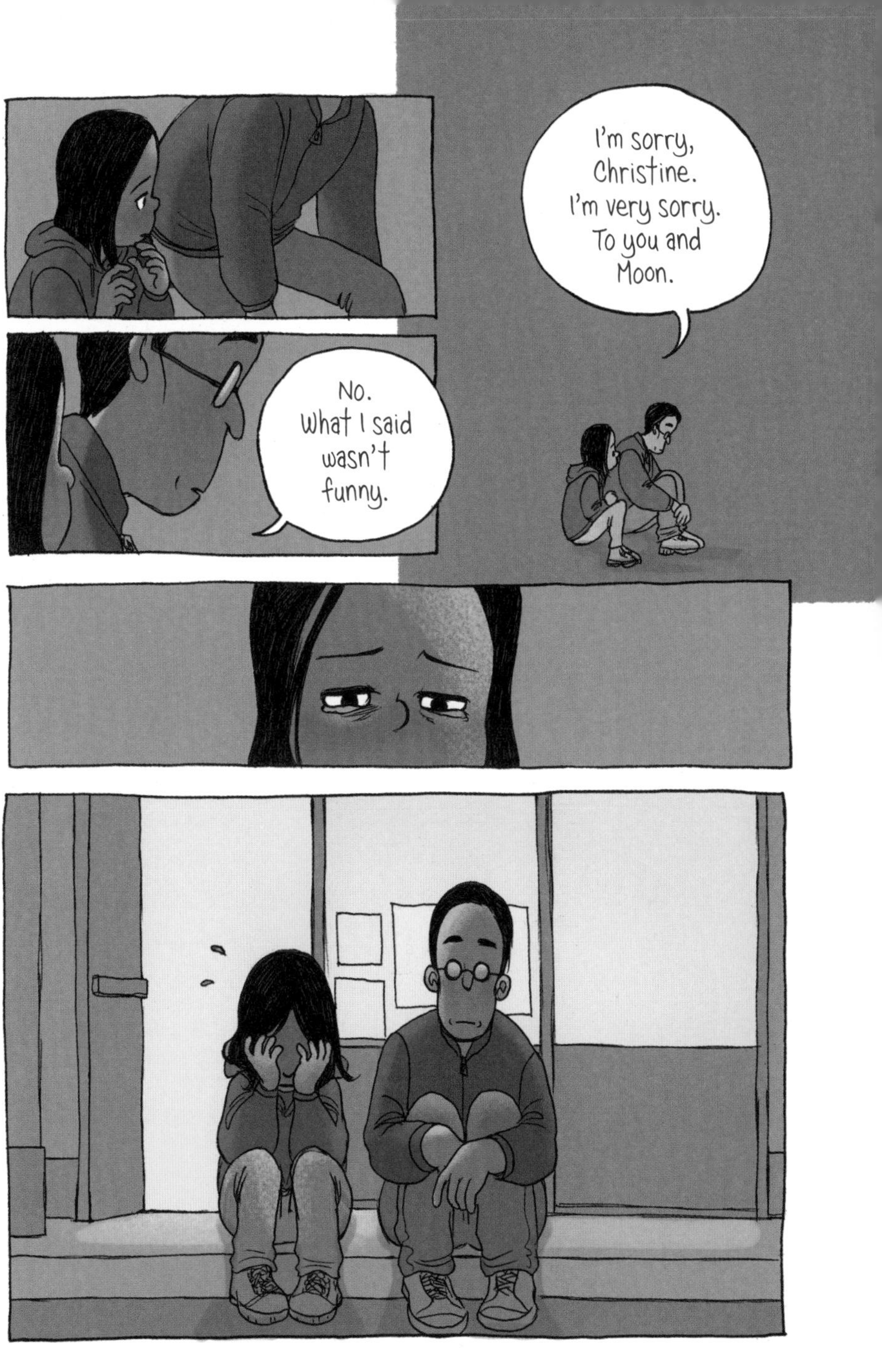
I'm sorry, Christine. I'm very sorry. To you and Moon.
No. What I said wasn't funny.

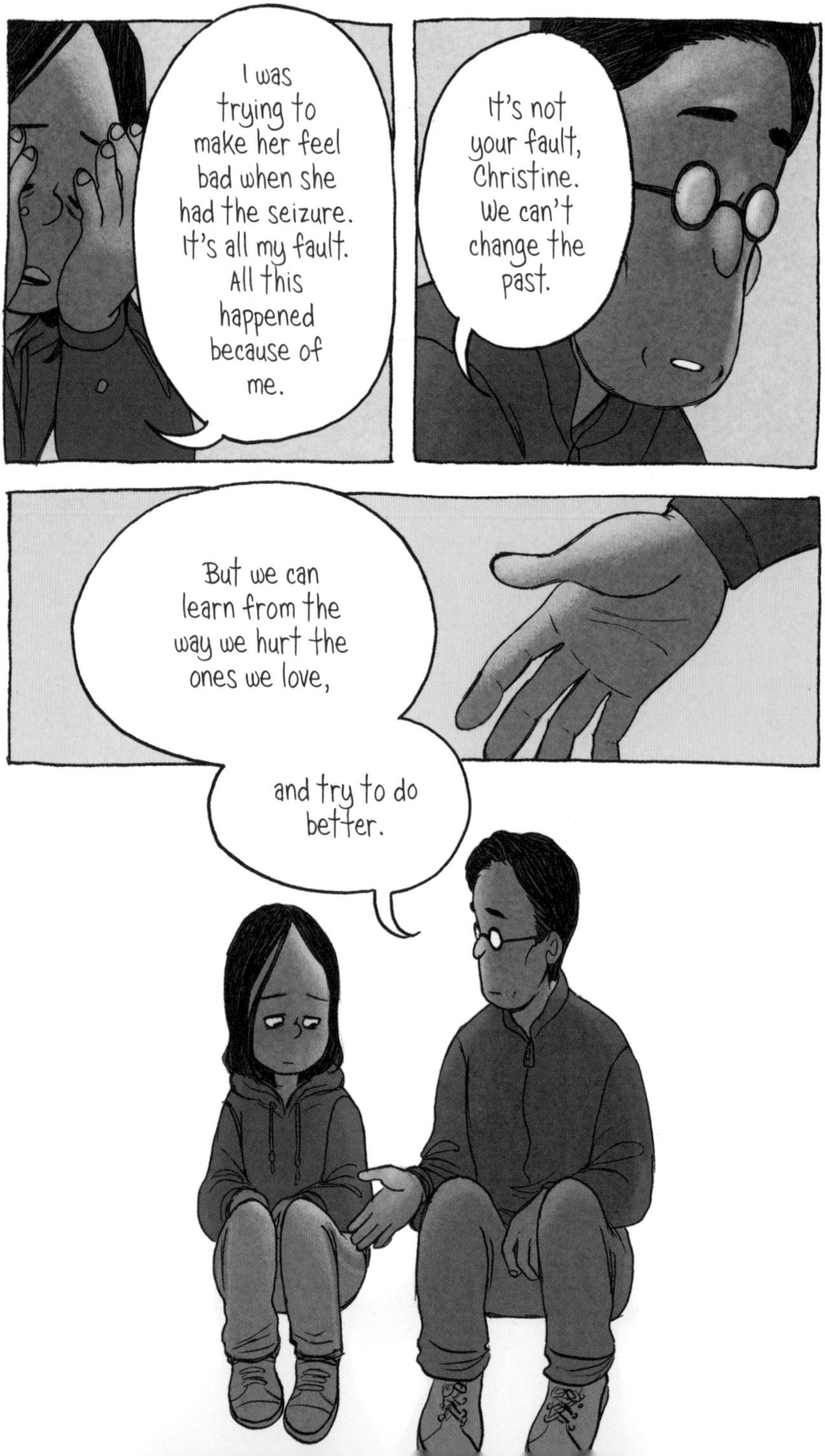
I was trying to make her feel bad when she had the seizure. It's all my fault. All this happened because of me.
It's not your fault, Christine. We can't change the past.
But we can learn from the way we hurt the ones we love,
and try to do better.

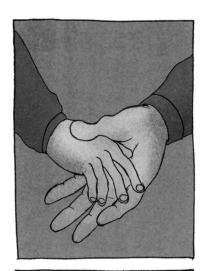

Let's go see her when she wakes up, huh?

Come on. Let's finish our shaved ice before it melts.

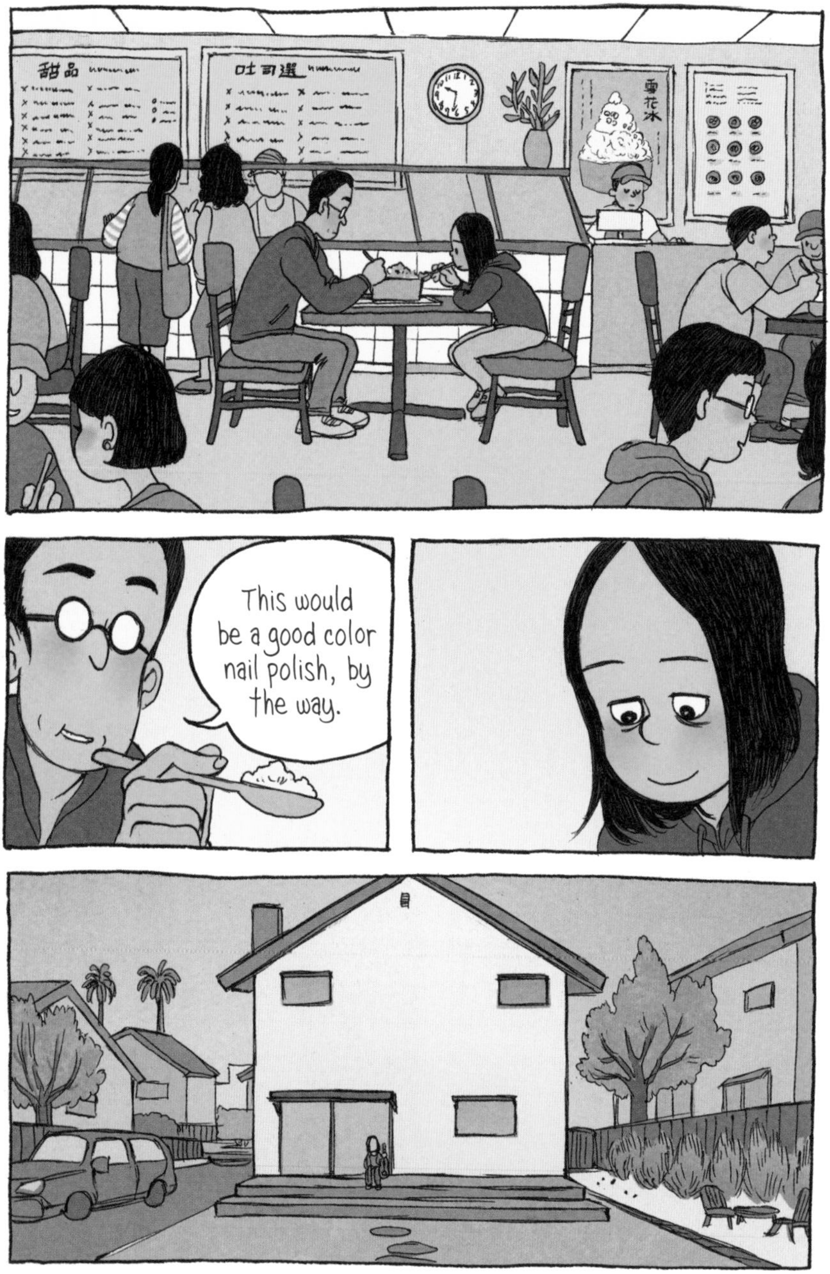
甜品
吐司選
雪花冰
This would be a good color nail polish, by the way.

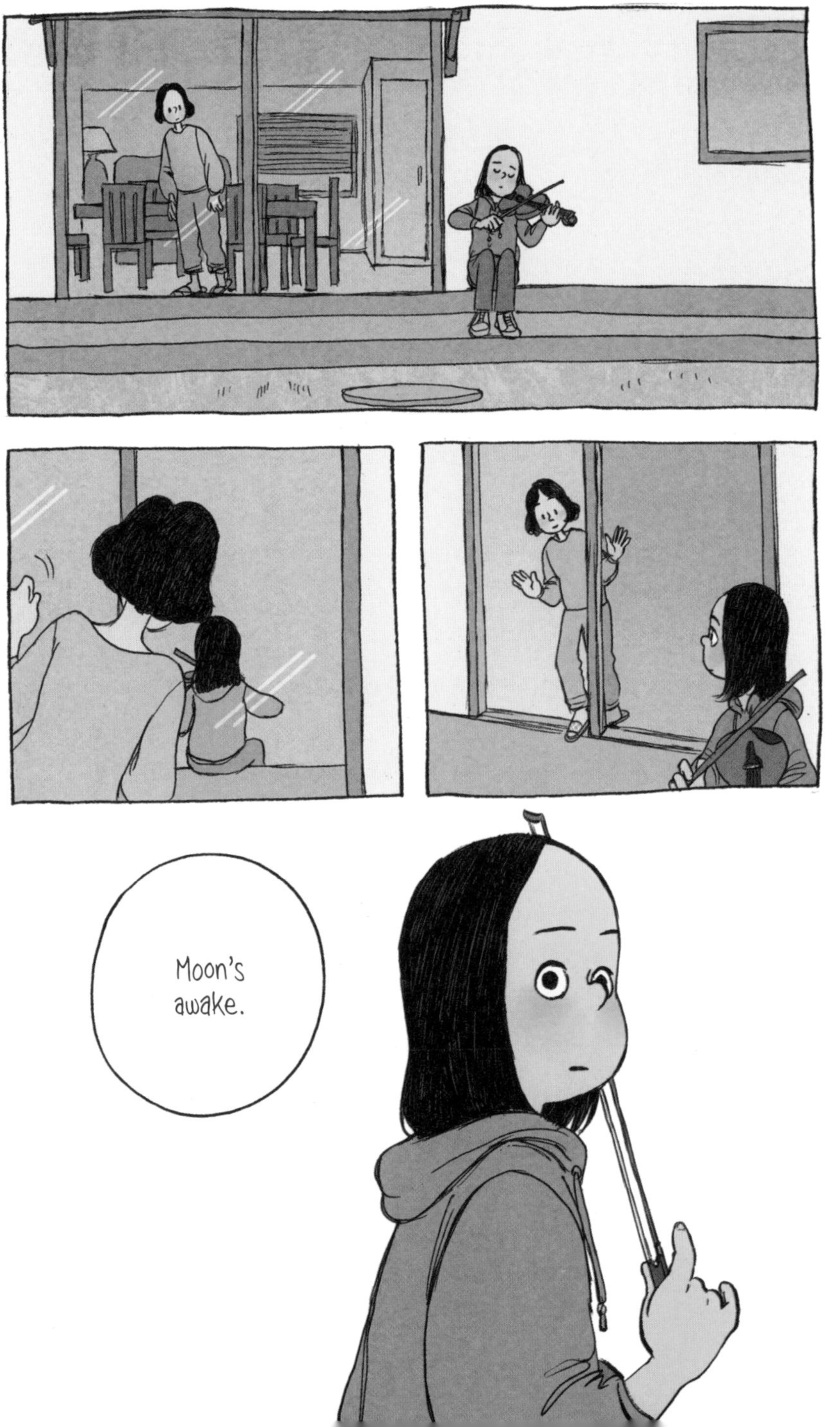
Moon's awake.

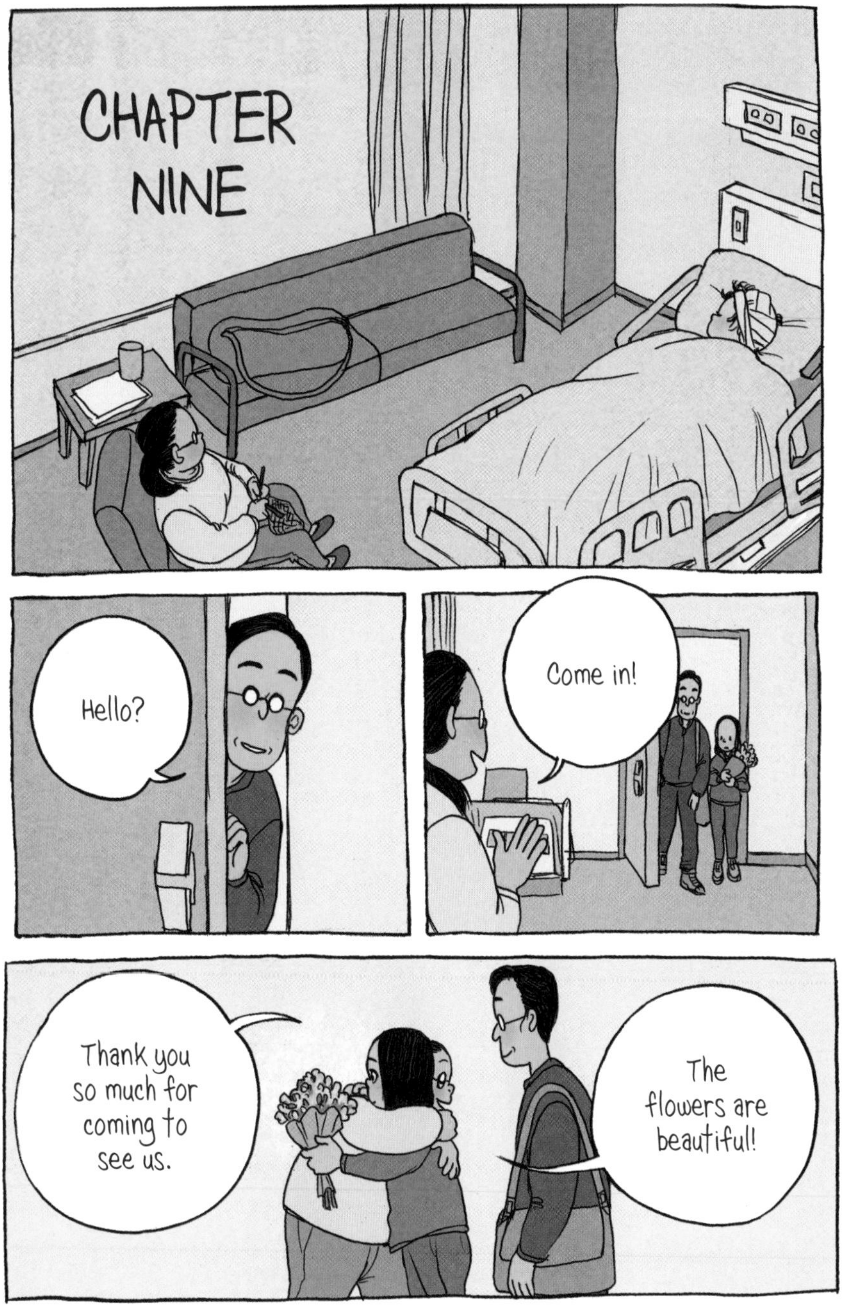
CHAPTER NINE
Hello?
Come in!
Thank you so much for coming to see us.
The flowers are beautiful!

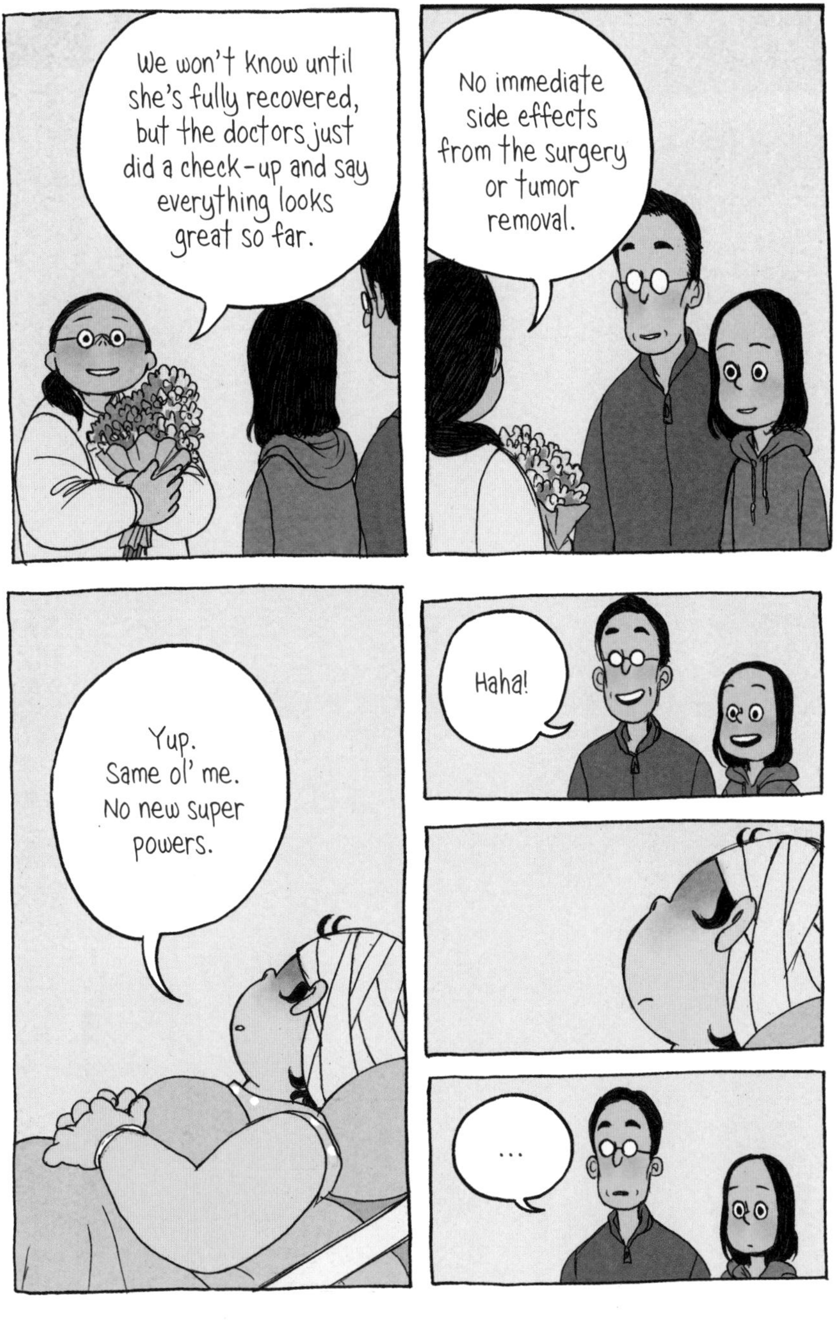
We won't know until she's fully recovered, but the doctors just did a check-up and say everything looks great so far.
No immediate side effects from the surgery or tumor removal.
Yup. Same ol' me. No new super powers.
Haha!
...

Good to see you've still got your sense of humor! Wouldn't be the same without it!

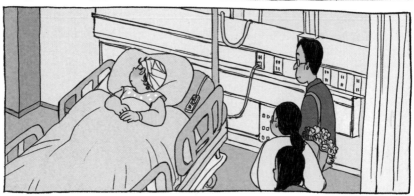

YuWen, maybe you'd like to take a break? I'll come with you to grab a snack.

Christine, you want to watch over her for a few minutes?

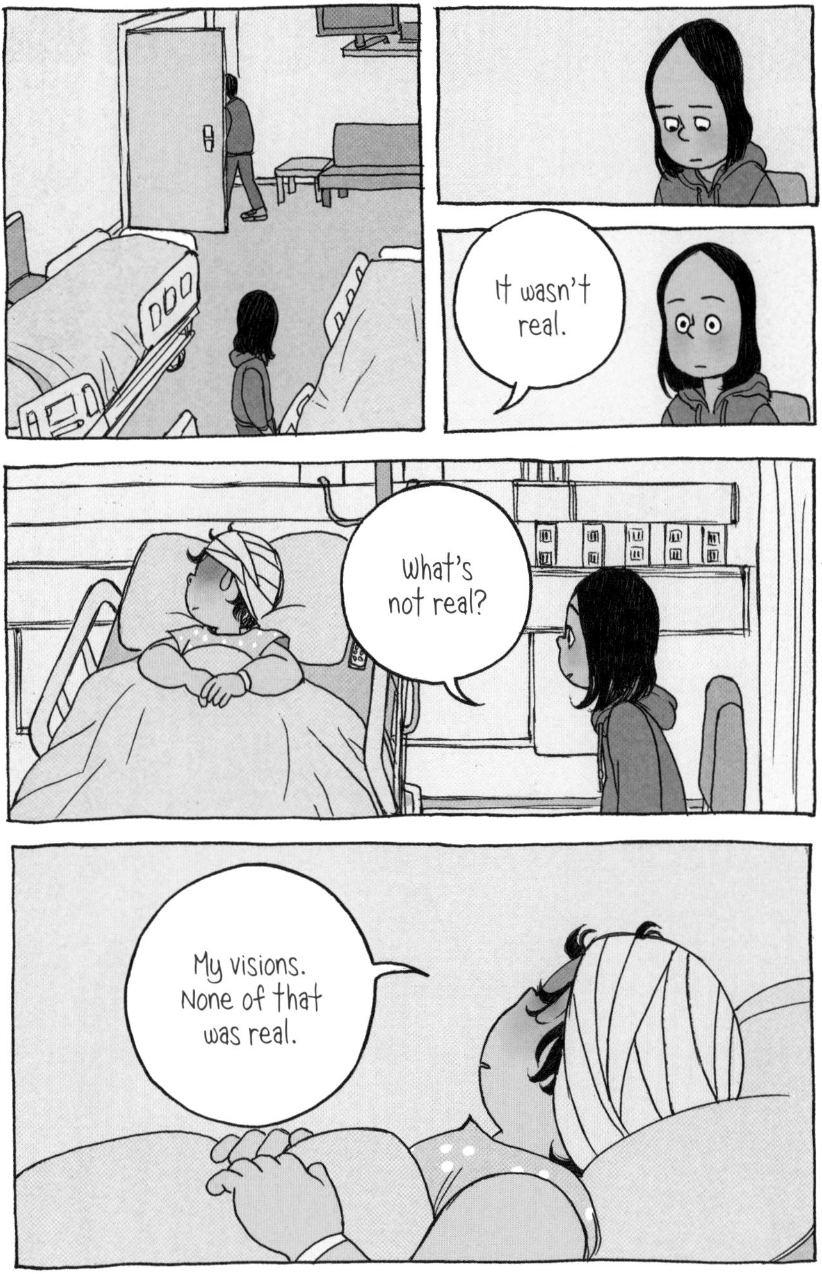
It wasn't real.
What's not real?
My visions. None of that was real.

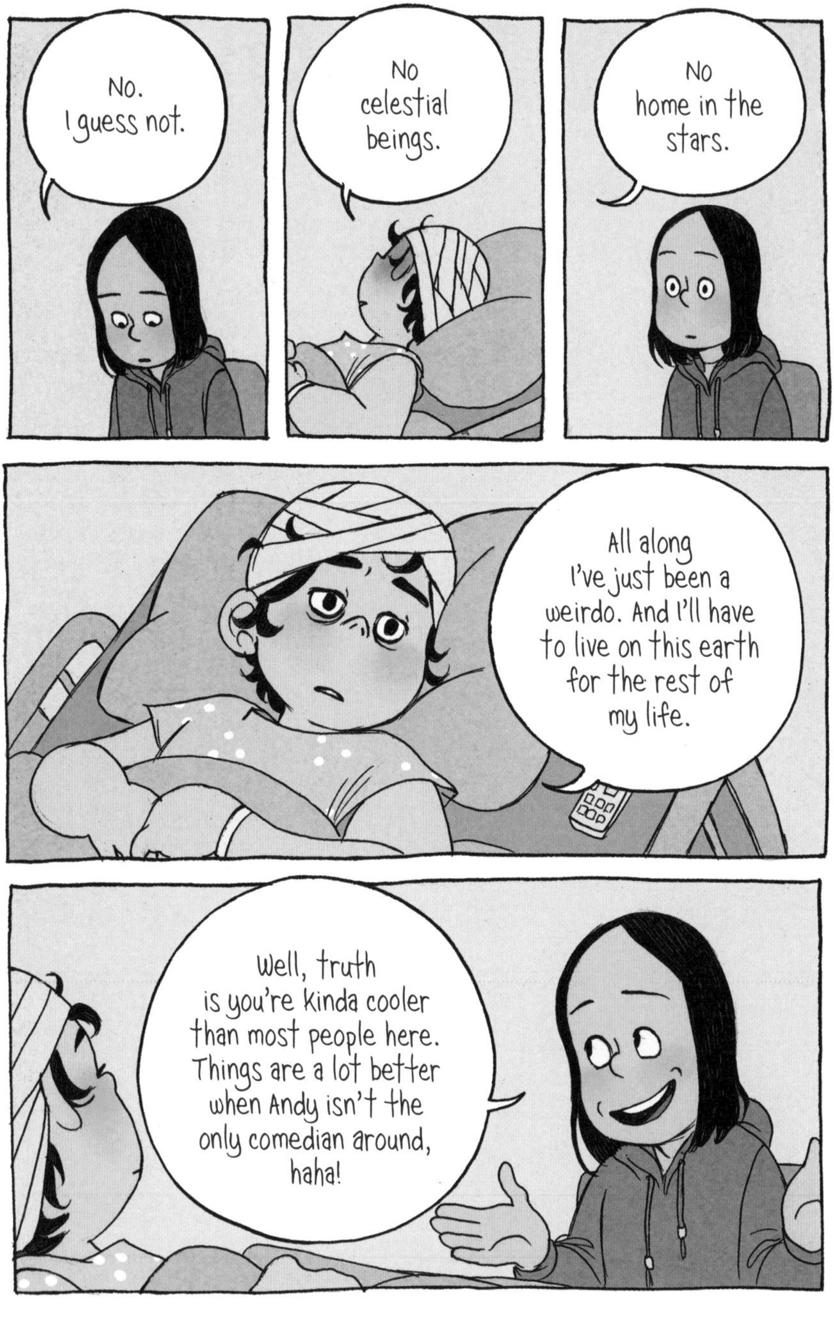
No. I guess not.
No celestial beings.
No home in the stars.
All along I've just been a weirdo. And I'll have to live on this earth for the rest of my life.
Well, truth is you're kinda cooler than most people here. Things are a lot better when Andy isn't the only comedian around, haha!

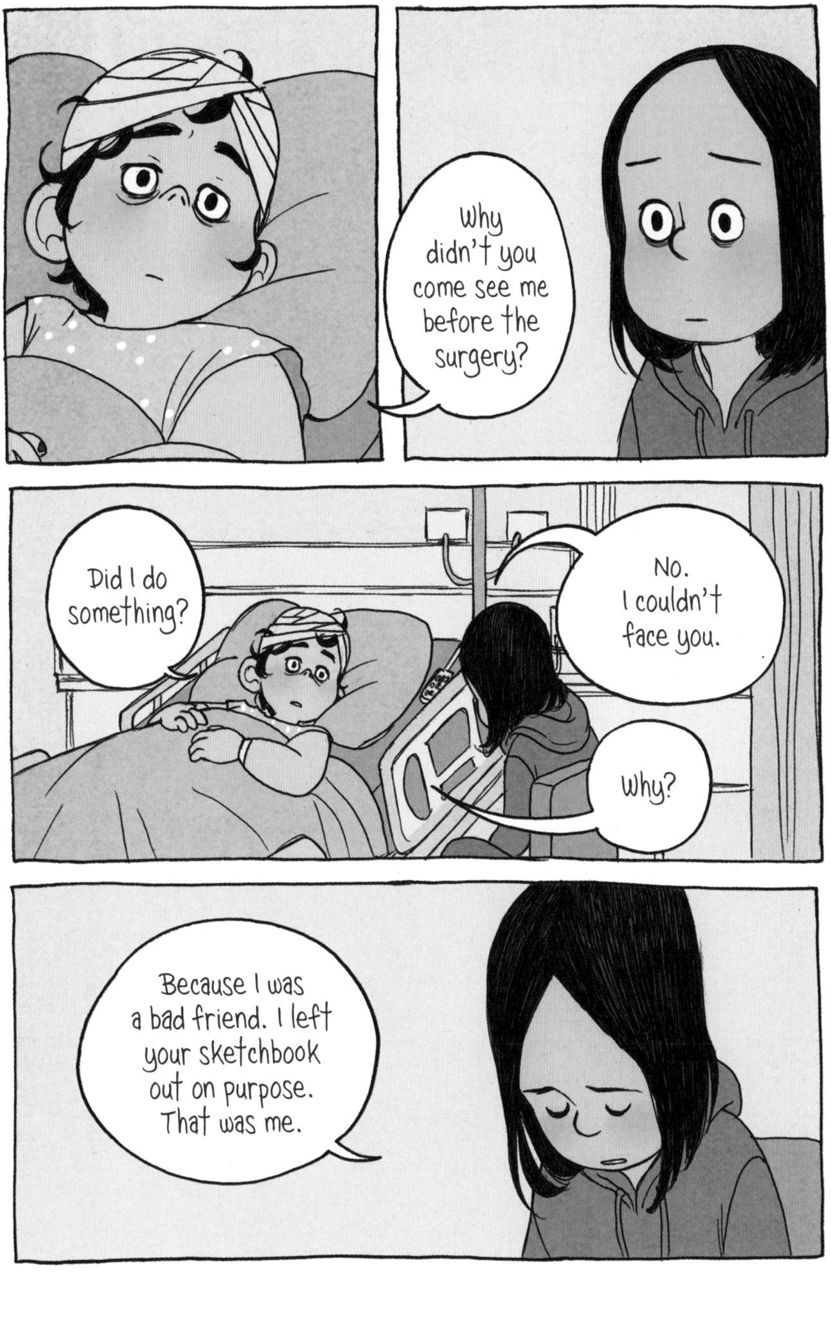
Why didn't you come see me before the surgery?
Did I do something?
No. I couldn't face you.
Why?
Because I was a bad friend. I left your sketchbook out on purpose. That was me.

Why did you do that?

You're so much cooler than me. Everybody likes you and you get to do all kinds of things I could never get away with, like be friends with your mom, or paint your nails black, or go to concerts!

I just thought, maybe if I could make people think you were less cool, we'd be more the same and you would stay friends with me.

I hurt you and I'm sorry.

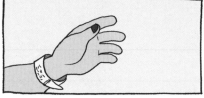

But we are the same.

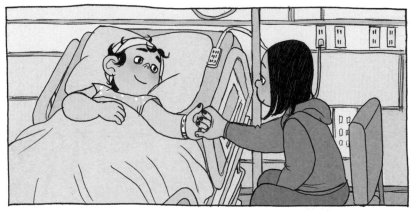

I'm glad you're here.

Me, too.

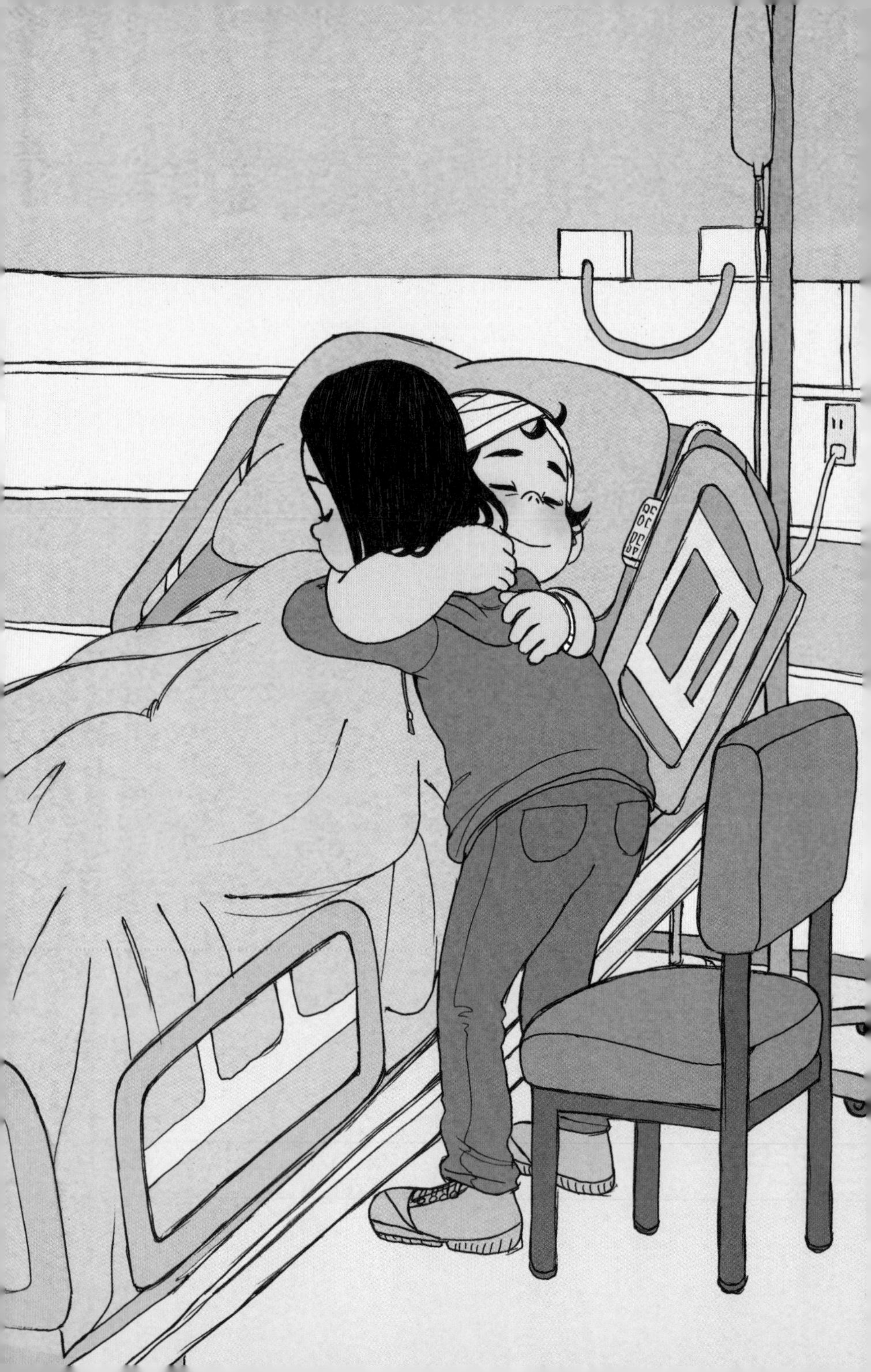

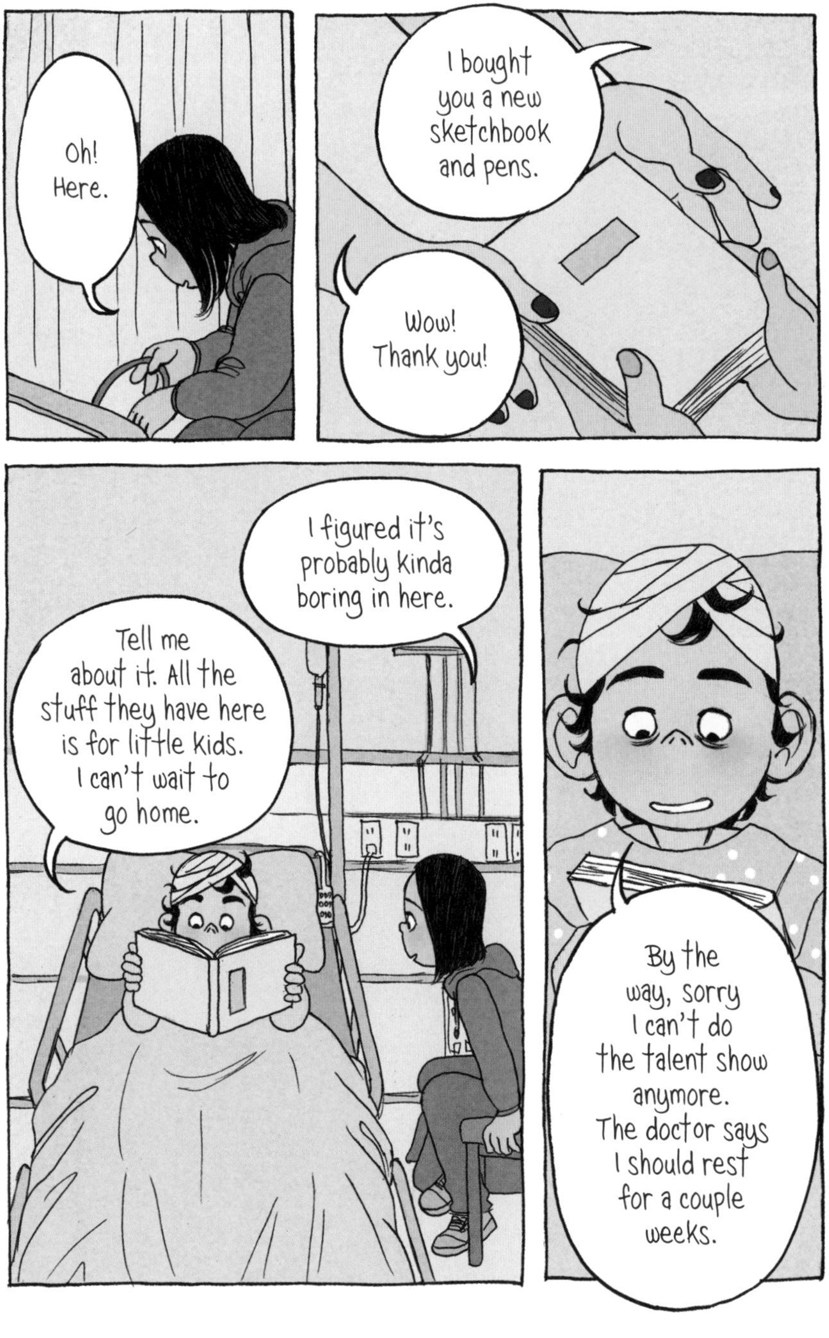
Oh! Here.
I bought you a new sketchbook and pens.
Wow! Thank you!
I figured it's probably kinda boring in here.
Tell me about it. All the stuff they have here is for little kids. I can't wait to go home.
By the way, sorry I can't do the talent show anymore. The doctor says I should rest for a couple weeks.

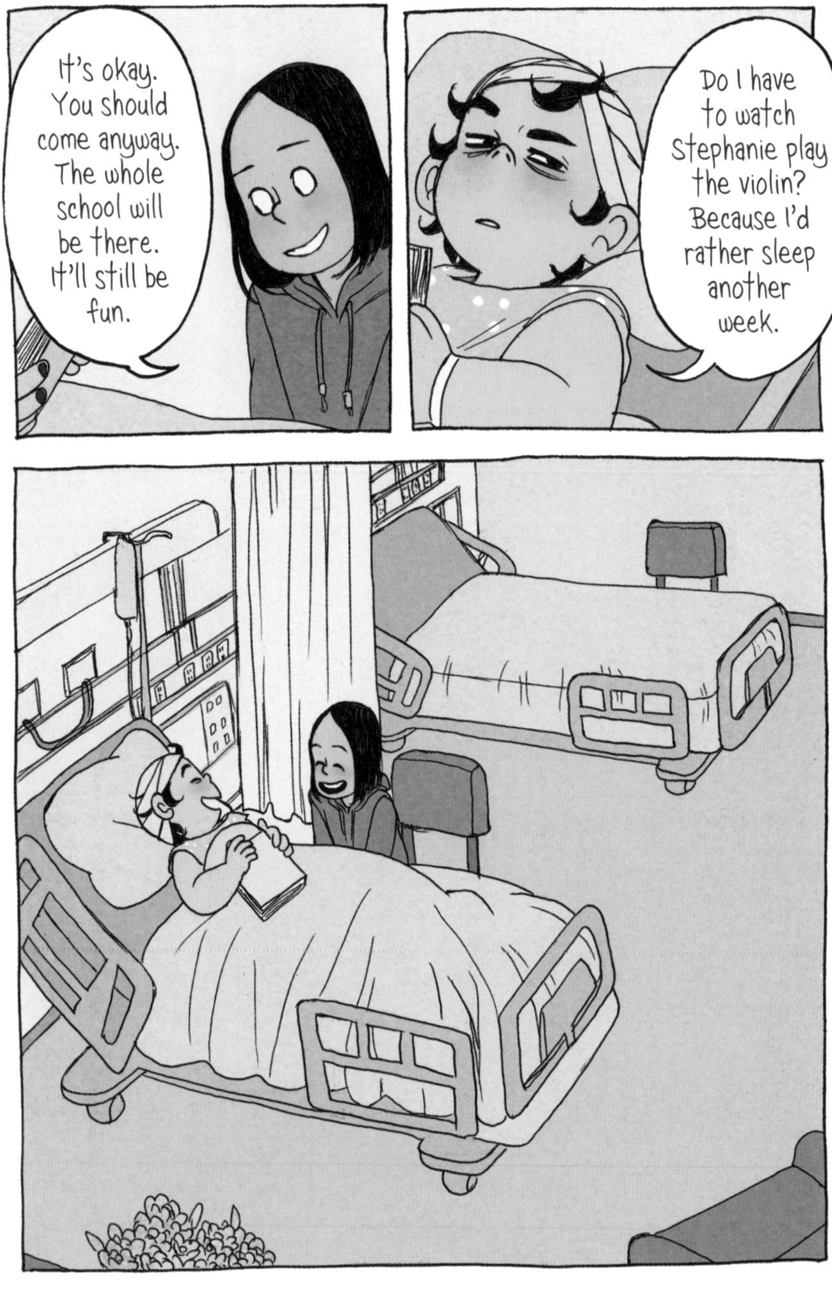
It's okay. You should come anyway. The whole school will be there. It'll still be fun.
Do I have to watch Stephanie play the violin? Because I'd rather sleep another week.

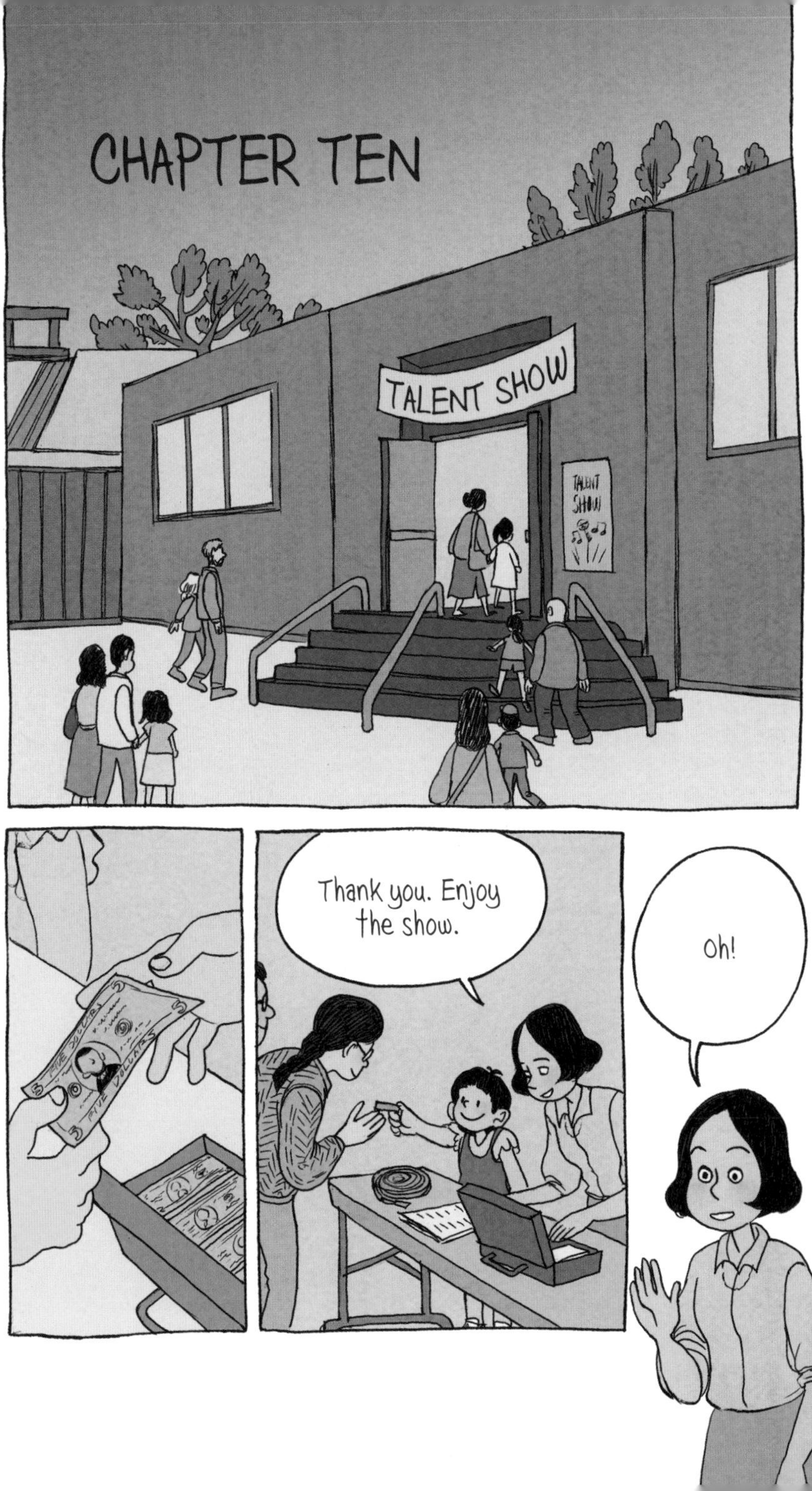
CHAPTER TEN
TALENT SHOW
TALENT SHOW
Thank you. Enjoy the show.
Oh!

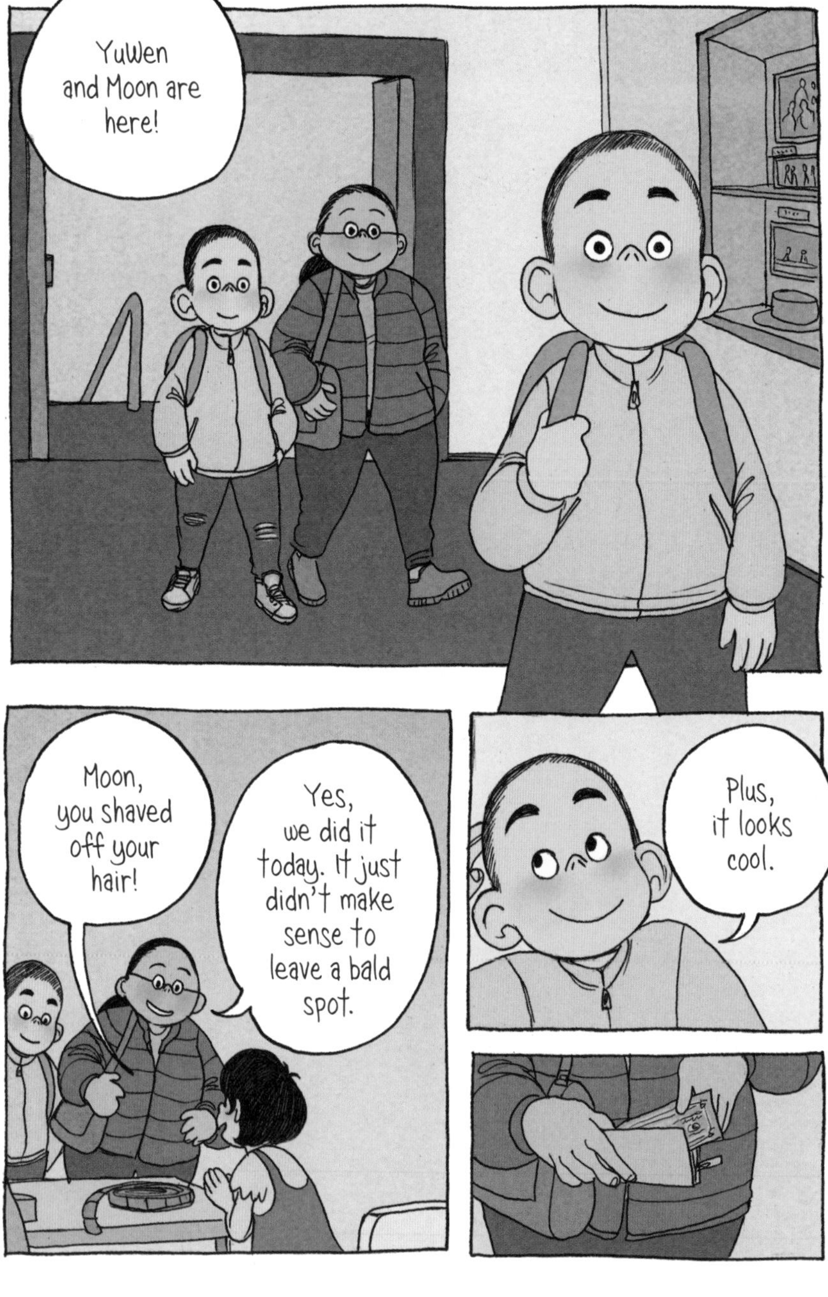
YuWen and Moon are here!
Moon, you shaved off your hair!
Yes, we did it today. It just didn't make sense to leave a bald spot.
Plus, it looks cool.

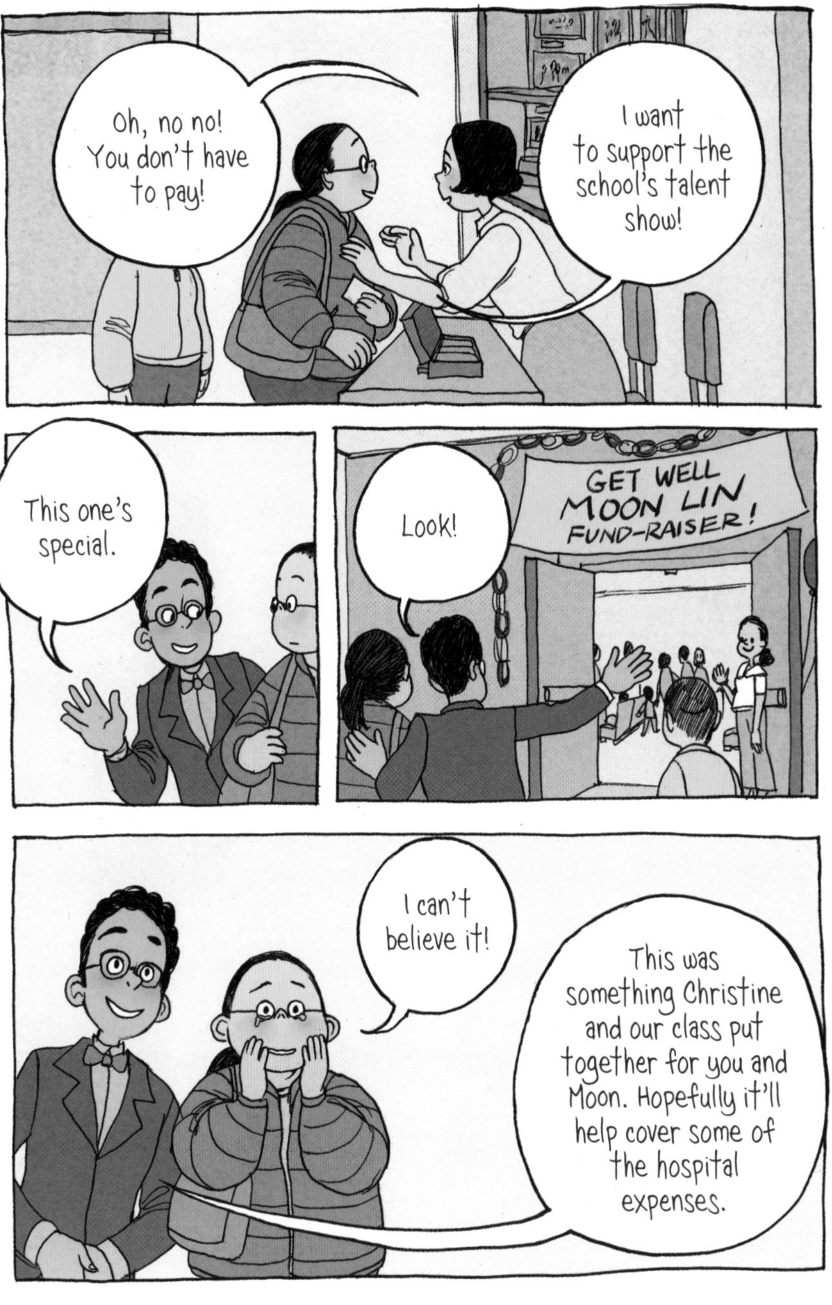
Oh, no no! You don't have to pay!
I want to support the school's talent show!
This one's special.
Look!
GET WELL MOON LIN FUND-RAISER!
I can't believe it!
This was something Christine and our class put together for you and Moon. Hopefully it'll help cover some of the hospital expenses.

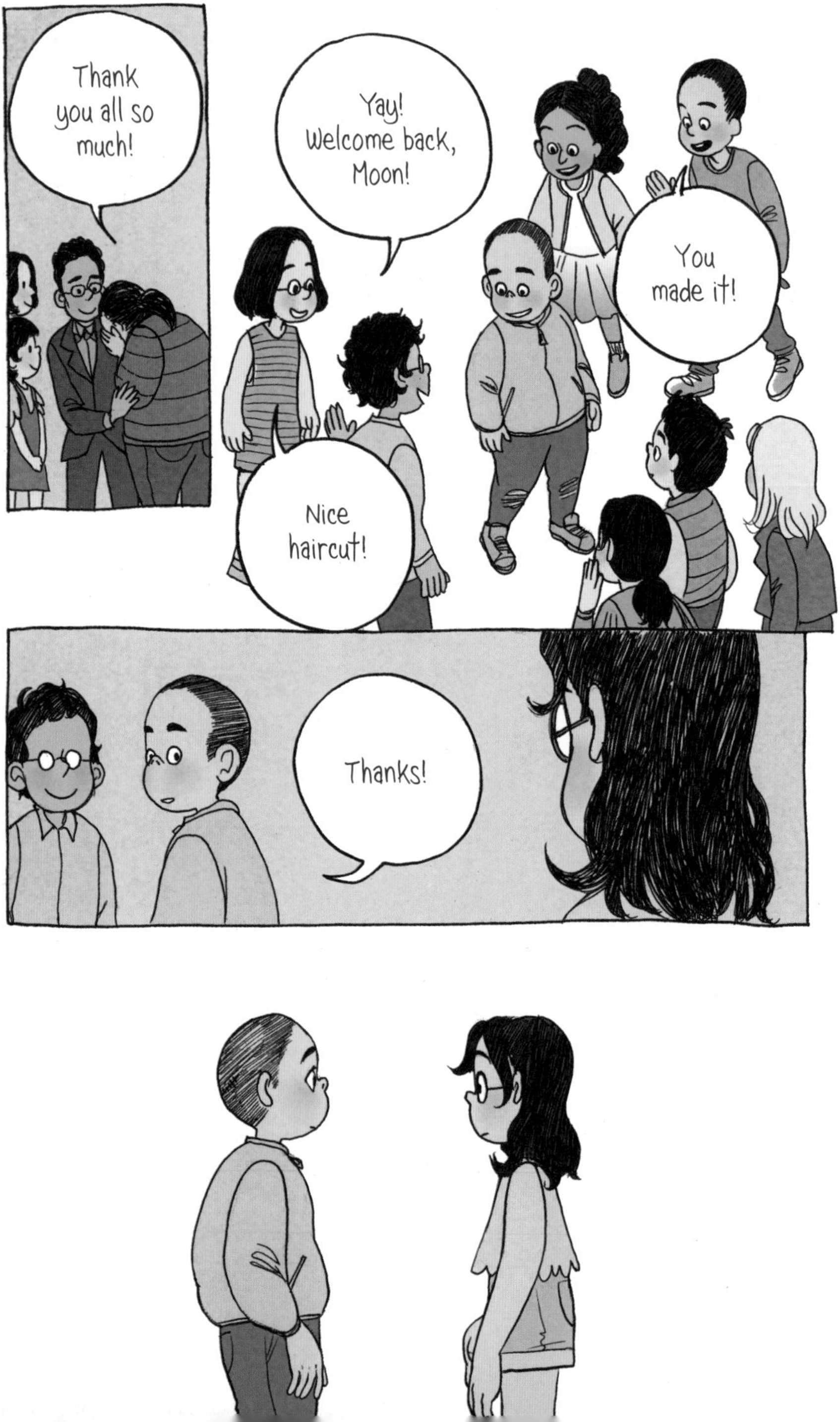
Thank you all so much!
Yay! Welcome back, Moon!
You made it!
Nice haircut!
Thanks!

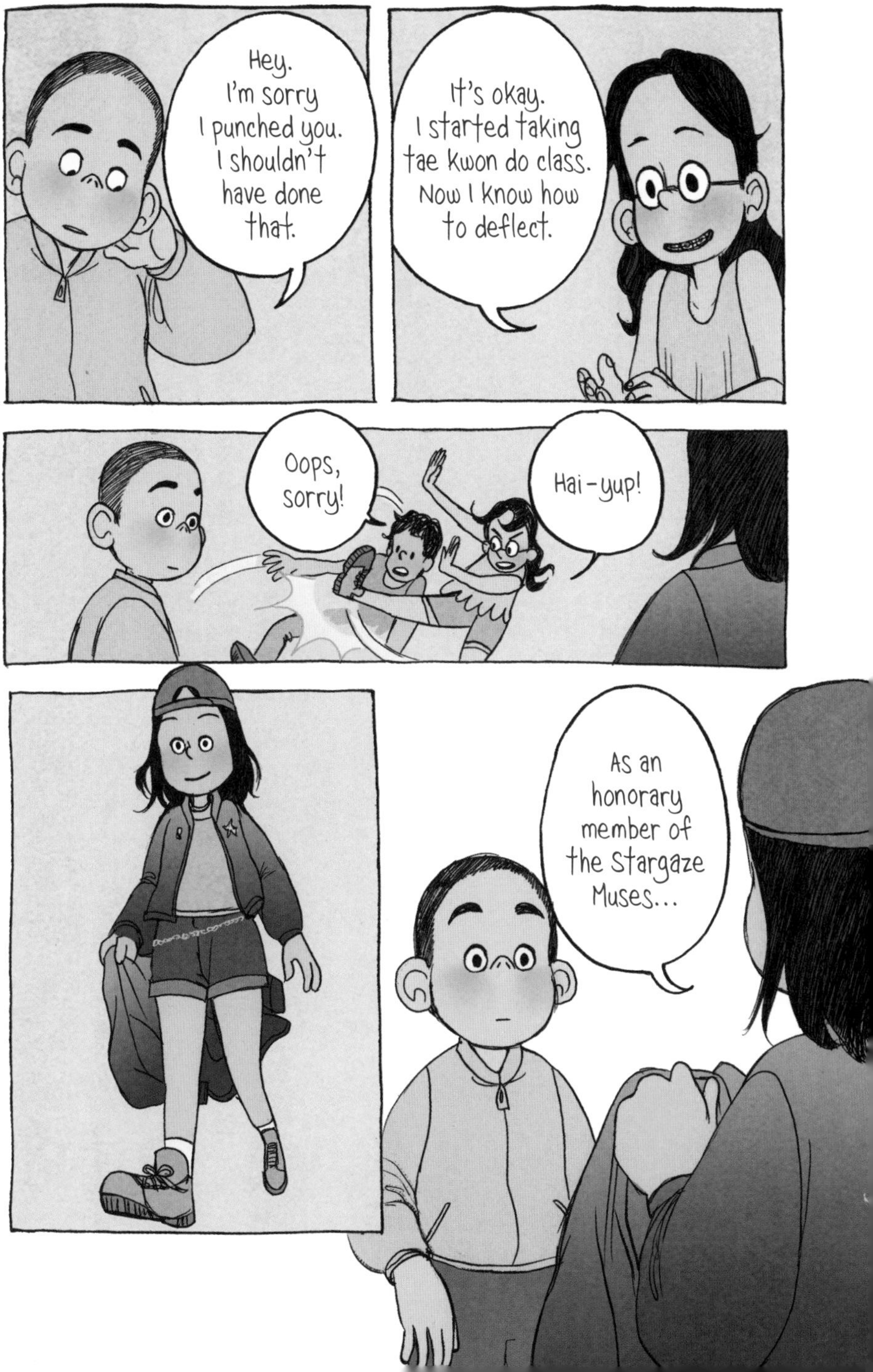
Hey. I'm sorry I punched you. I shouldn't have done that.
It's okay. I started taking tae kwon do class. Now I know how to deflect.
Oops, sorry!
Hai-yup!
As an honorary member of the Stargaze Muses...

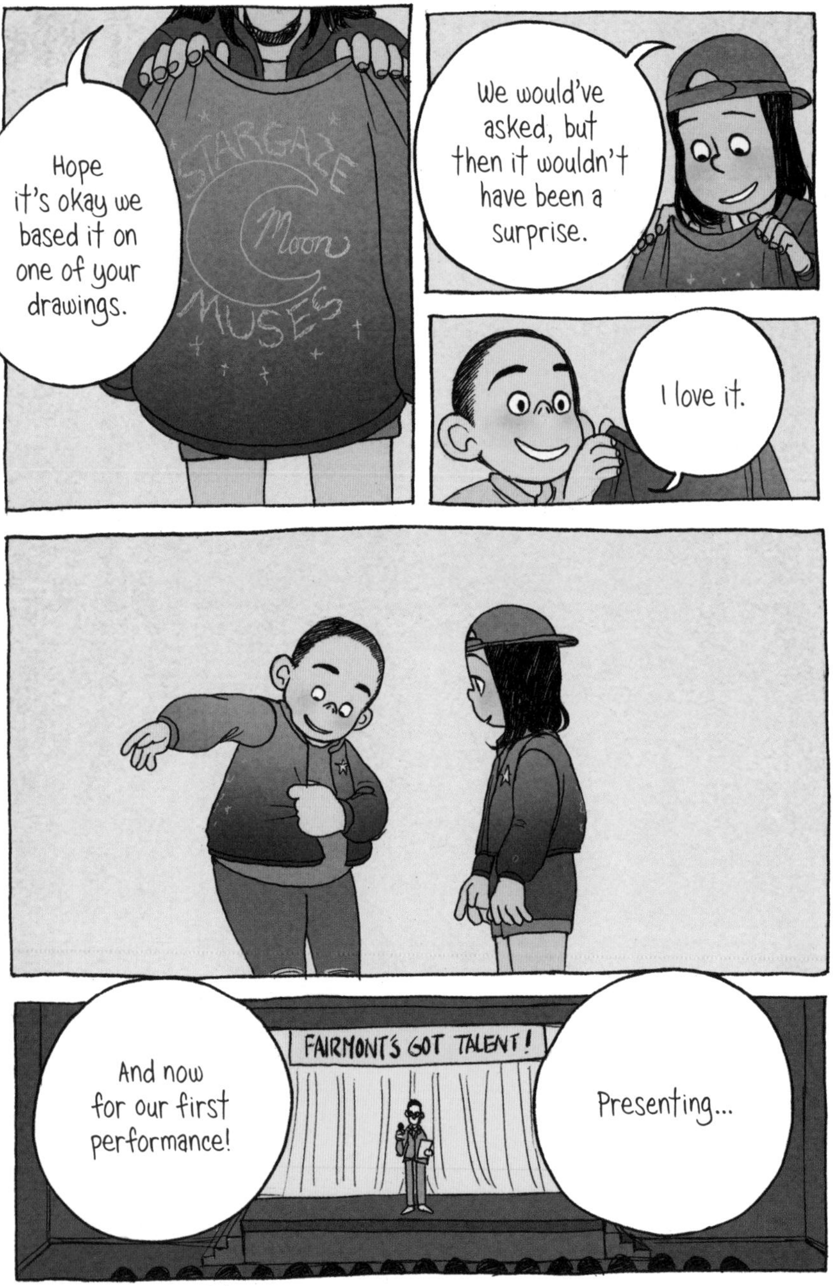
STARGAZE
Moon
MUSES
Hope it's okay we based it on one of your drawings.
We would've asked, but then it wouldn't have been a surprise.
I love it.
FAIRMONT'S GOT TALENT!
And now for our first performance!
Presenting...

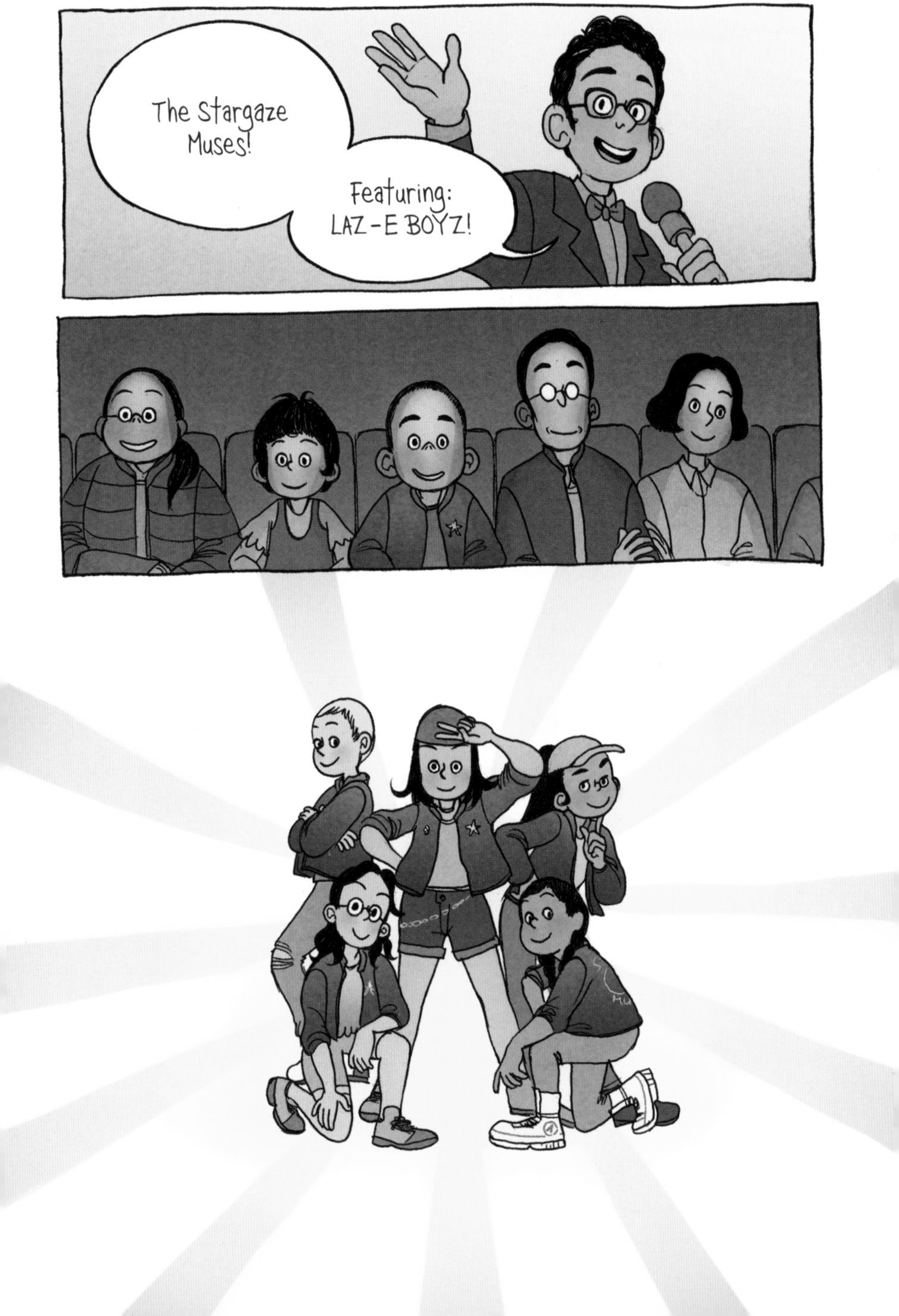
The Stargaze Muses!
Featuring: LAZ-E BOYZ!

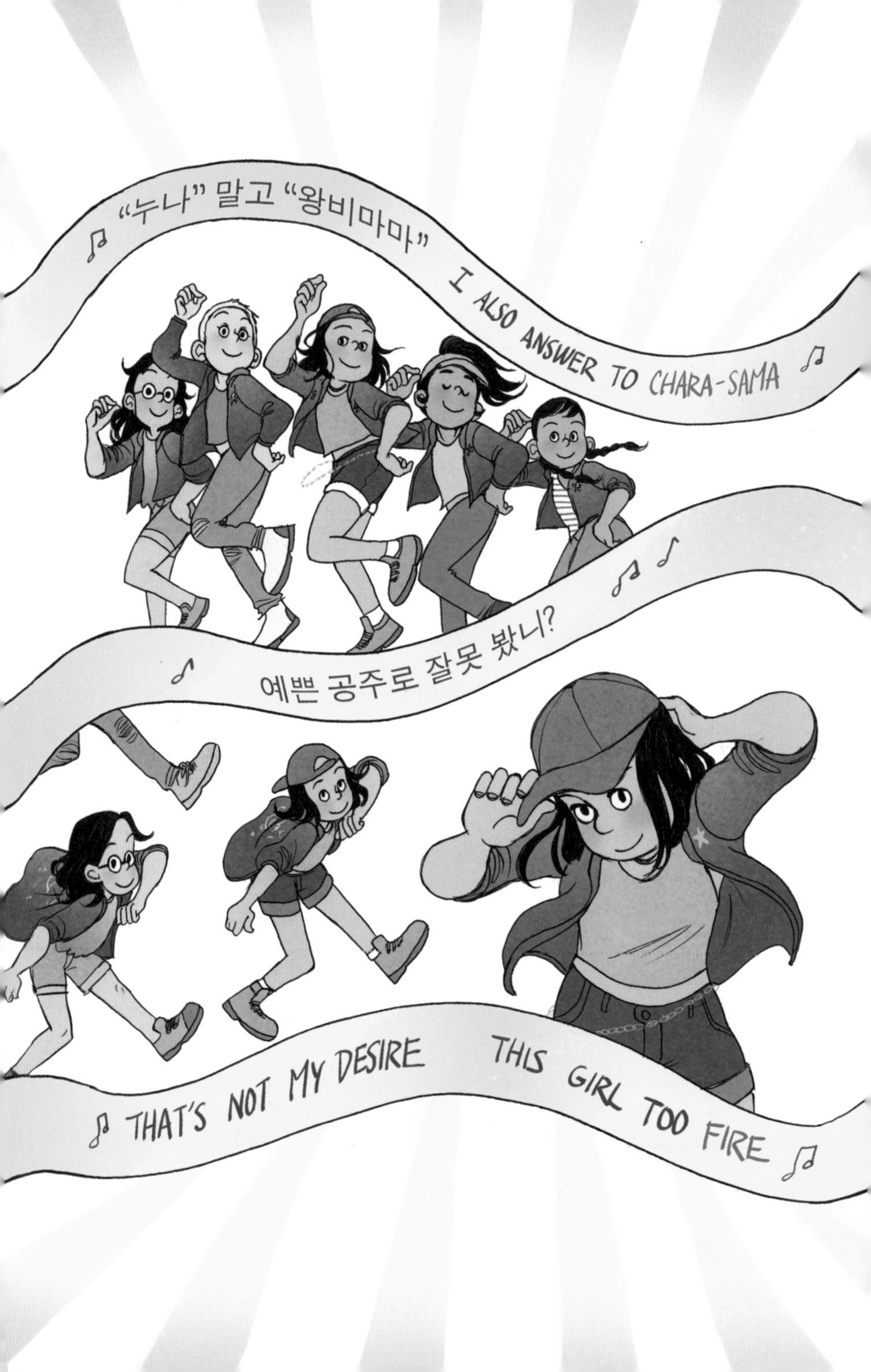

♫ "누나" 말고 "왕비마마" I ALSO ANSWER TO CHARA-SAMA ♫
♫ ♪
♪ 예쁜 공주로 잘못 봤니?
♫ THAT'S NOT MY DESIRE THIS GIRL TOO FIRE ♫

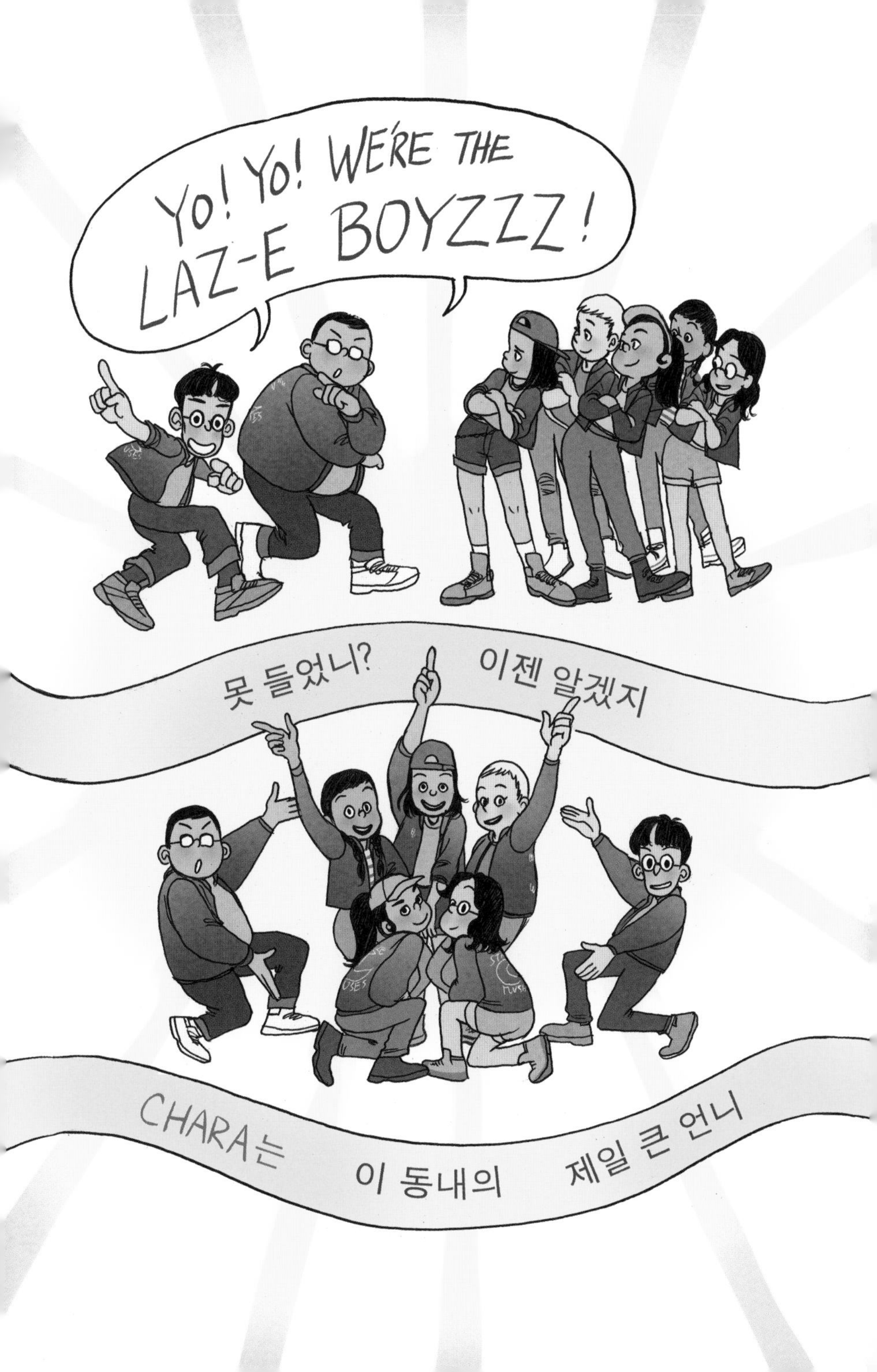
YO! YO! WE'RE THE LAZ-E BOYZZZ!
못 들었니? 이젠 알겠지
CHARA는 이 동네의 제일 큰 언니

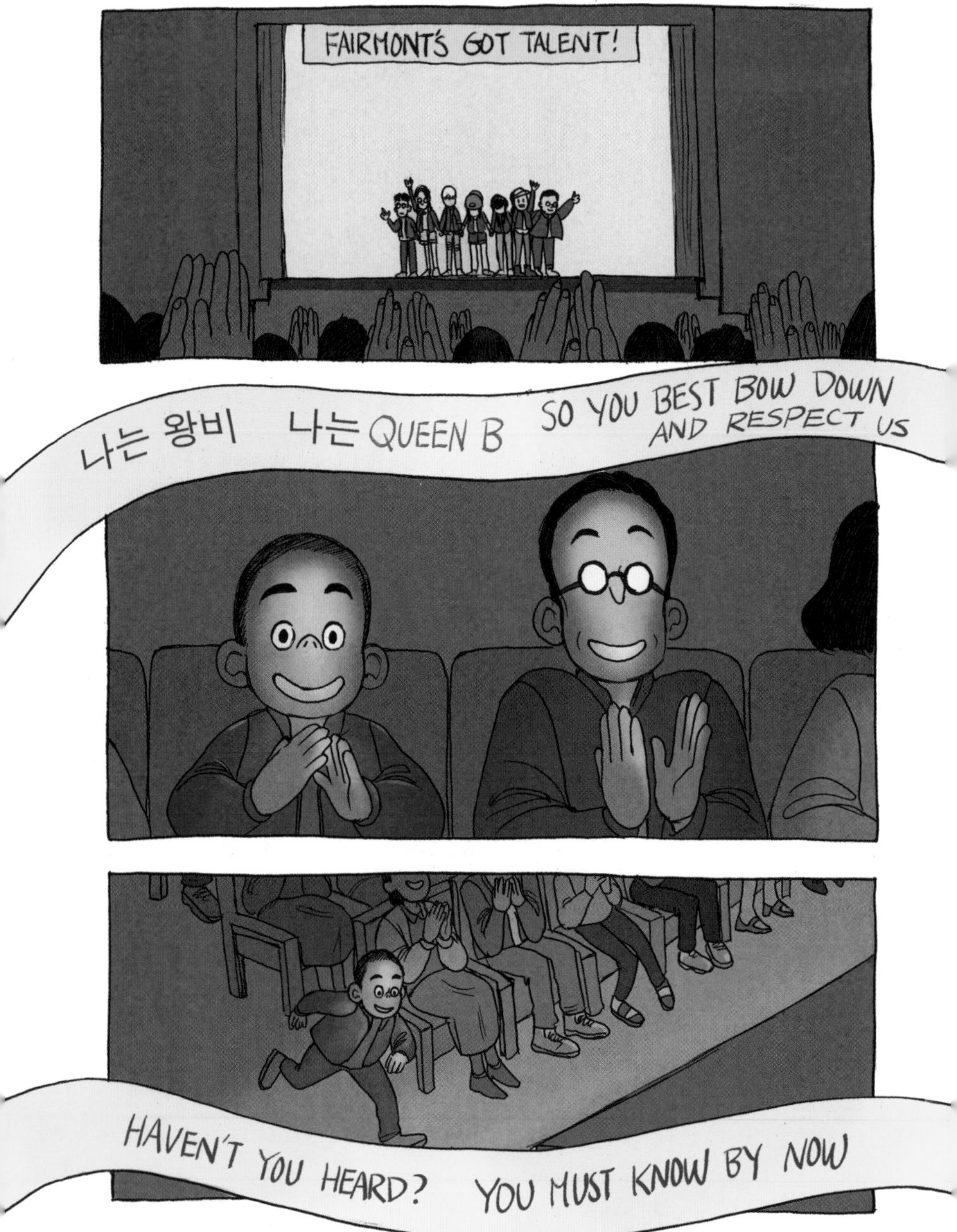
FAIRMONT'S GOT TALENT!
나는 왕비 나는 QUEEN B
SO YOU BEST BOW DOWN AND RESPECT US
HAVEN'T YOU HEARD? YOU MUST KNOW BY NOW

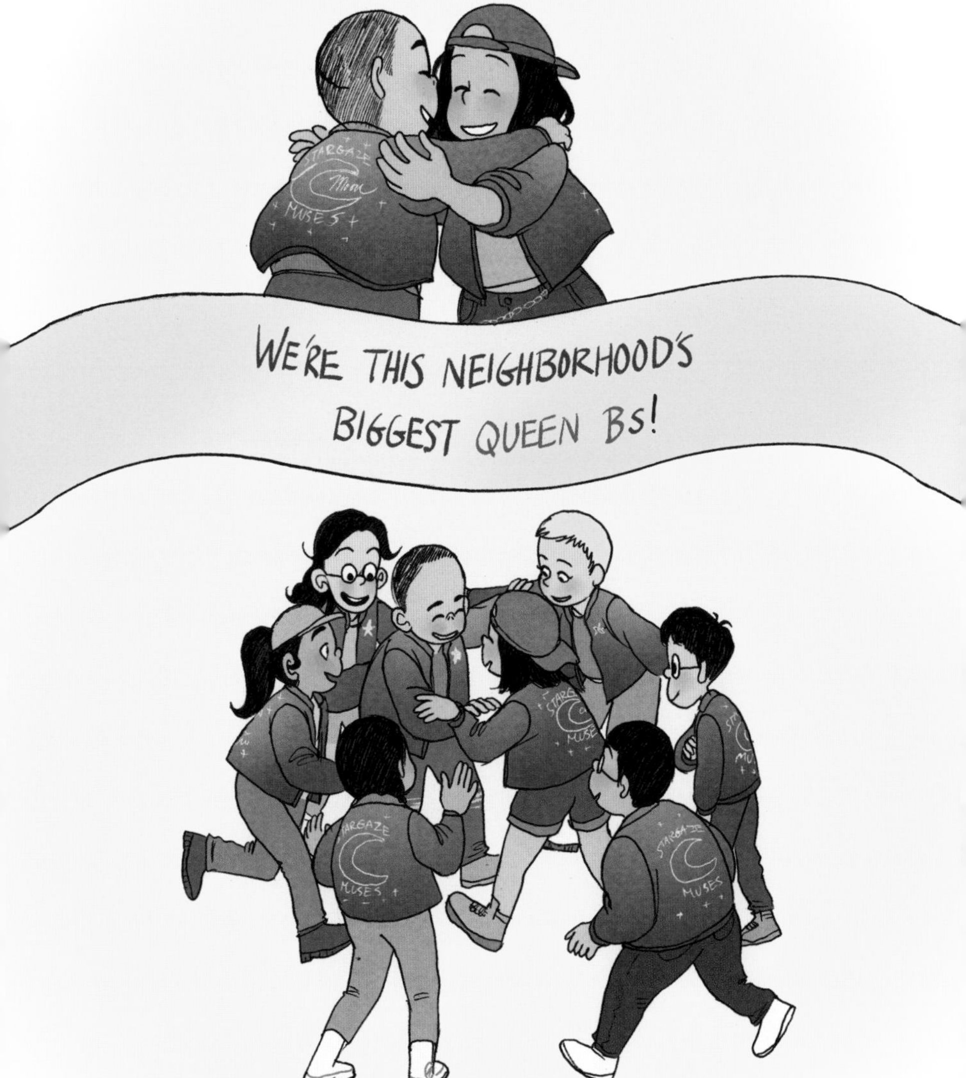
WE'RE THIS NEIGHBORHOOD'S BIGGEST QUEEN Bs!

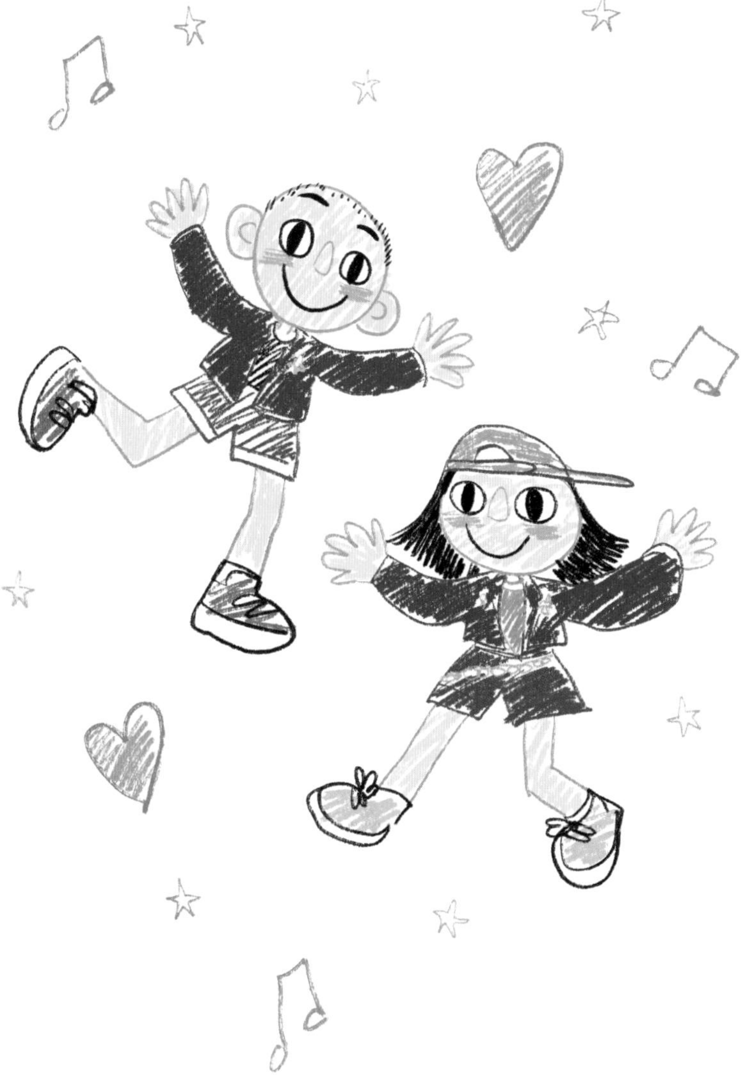

Afterword

Stargazing is an entirely fictional story, and yet so much of it is based on real events from my life. When I was six years old, I was diagnosed with a brain tumor just like Moon's. I was too young to realize what was happening, but my vision would go dark and I would see stars and shapes. At first this was fun, and I didn't tell anyone. After all, I thought, wasn't this normal? But eventually the seizures became noticeable, and a few months later I had a surgery to remove the tumor. It was sitting right on top of the visual area of my brain and it came out easily.

The whole ordeal was such a formative part of my childhood that it blends in to everything else. But sometimes I catch myself wondering what my life would be like if things had turned out differently. What if I couldn't read? Or draw? Visual art has become such an important part of my world that it's hard to imagine life without it. I owe so much to my surgeon, Dr. Roderick Smith, the nurses, and my parents for catching the seizures early and making one of the scariest decisions of their life.

Did I see celestial beings during my seizures the way Moon did? No. But I thought they'd be a good way for the book to express how lonely Moon (and I) felt. Like Christine and Moon, I grew up in a region with many other Chinese and Taiwanese immigrant families and their American-born kids. But the more you're expected to share with a group of people, the more you obsess over the ways you are different. (I was vegetarian, I was Buddhist, I didn't excel in academics, I wanted to be an artist, etc.) If I wasn't like the other Asian American kids, who was I supposed to be like?

It's taken me thirty-three years to get to a point where I can comfortably reflect on these feelings. Writing *Stargazing* was as much about healing myself as about showing the diversity of experience even within a very specific community. As our society continues to diversify (as I would hope), I imagine there will be many more Moons and Christines out there wondering which parts of them are "not Asian," and which parts are just uniquely and wonderfully them.

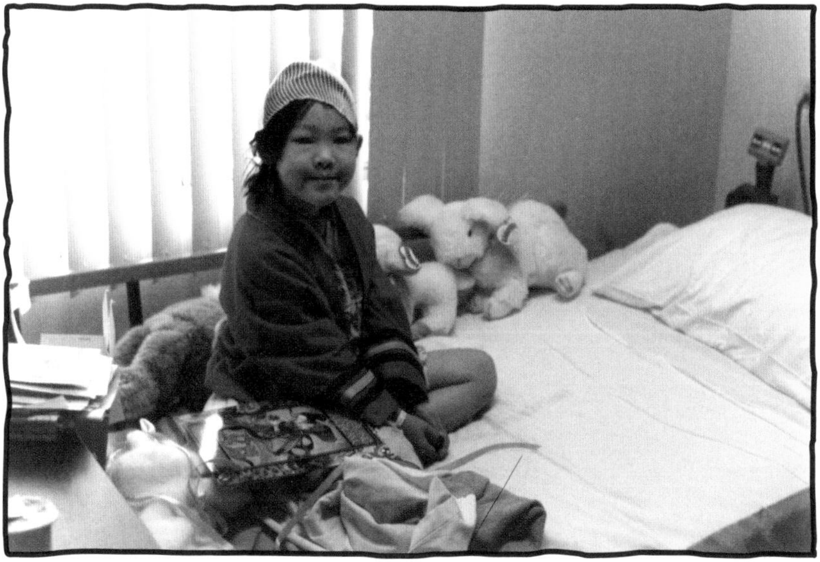

Recovering from the surgery at the hospital

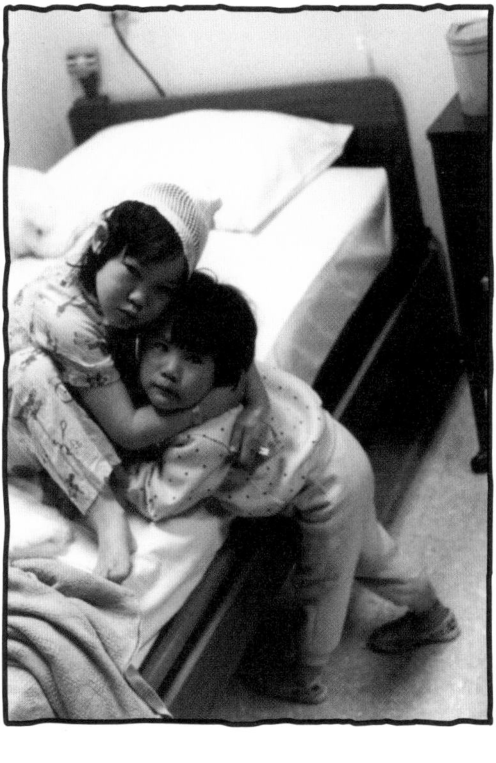

With my little sister, Lynn, visiting me for the first time after the surgery

Jen Wang is the author of *The Prince and the Dressmaker* and *Koko Be Good*, and coauthor of the *New York Times*-bestselling graphic novel *In Real Life* with Cory Doctorow. She is also the cofounder and organizer of the annual festival Comic Arts Los Angeles. **jenwang.net**

Lark Pien is a cartoonist who also colors. Her color work on *American Born Chinese* by Gene Luen Yang was nominated for an Eisner and won a Harvey award. Other graphic novels she has colored include *Boxers & Saints* (by Gene Luen Yang) and *Sunny Rolls the Dice* (by Matt and Jenni Holm). Her comics have been featured in publications by Fantagraphics, Viz Media, Illustoria, Studygroup, and Random House. She is the author and artist of three picture books, *Long Tail Kitty*, *Long Tail Kitty: Come Out and Play* (with Blue Apple Books), and *Mr. Elephanter* (with Candlewick). She likes to paint with cadmium yellow, antique white, vermillion, burnt umber, and light blue. Lark tweets sparingly **@larkpien**.

More from Jen Wang

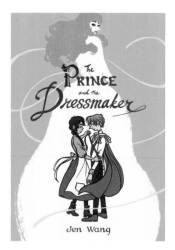

"Completely satisfying.
In modern fairy tales,
there really are happy endings."
—*The New York Times*

A *New York Times* Bestseller

"A lovely graphic novel for
gamer girls of all ages."
—**Felicia Day, star and creator of** *The Guild*